ABOUT THE AUTHOR

Sarah Barrie is a bestselling Australian author writing suspense in rural settings, with a generous splash of romance. Her debut bestselling print novel, *Secrets of Whitewater Creek*, earned her a spot as one of the Top 10 breakthrough authors of 2014, and her next three books, the Hunters Ridge series, also reached bestseller status. She has finaled in several major awards: twice in the RUBY, the Romance Writers of Australia's premier award, and three times in the Australian Romance Readers Award for favourite Romantic Suspense.

Sarah has also worked as a teacher, a vet nurse, a horse trainer and a magazine editor. When she's not writing, you'll find her ferrying children to soccer or gymnastics, or trudging through paddocks chasing cattle, sheep, chickens or the Houdini pig that never stays put very long. Occasionally, she'll attempt to ride her favourite horse, who's quite a bit smarter than she is and not always cooperative.

Her favourite place in the world is the family property, where she writes her stories overlooking mountains crisscrossed with farmland, bordered by the beauty of the Australian bush, and where, at the end of the day, she can spend time with family, friends, a good Irish whiskey and a copy of her next favourite book.

T0363185

Also by Sarah Barrie

Secrets of Whitewater Creek

The Hunters Ridge Trilogy
Legacy of Hunters Ridge
Shadows of Hunters Ridge
Promise of Hunters Ridge

BLOOD TREE RIVER

SARAH BARRIE

FICTION

First Published 2018
Second Australian Paperback Edition 2019
ISBN 9781489263520

BLOODTREE RIVER
© 2018 by Sarah Barrie
Australian Copyright 2018
New Zealand Copyright 2018

Published by
HQ Fiction
An imprint of Harlequin Enterprises (Australia) Pty Ltd.
Level 19, 201 Elizabeth St
SYDNEY NSW 2000
AUSTRALIA

® and TM (apart from those relating to FSC®) are trademarks of Harlequin Enterprises Limited or its corporate affiliates. Trademarks indicated with ® are registered in Australia, New Zealand and in other countries.

A catalogue record for this book is available from the National Library of Australia www.librariesaustralia.nla.gov.au

Printed and bound in Australia by McPherson's Printing Group

MIX
Paper | Supporting
responsible forestry
FSC® C001695

For Krista
To growing up, spreading wings and new beginnings x

CHAPTER

1

Crack! The explosion of pain radiated from her closed fist to her shoulder, reverberated down her spine. 'Damn it!' she hissed from between clenched teeth. Shooting the tattooed teen with the bad attitude would have been overkill, but it would have hurt a lot less than the punch.

'Mummy!'

Detective Indiana O'Meara swung around, pulling her gun out and settling it into its correct grip as she assessed the scene. Squeezed between a tattered lounge chair and a television cabinet at the far end of the lounge room, Matthew Davies huddled on the floor, tiny arms wrapped around knobbly knees as another perp dragged the boy's mother towards the shattered, floor-to-ceiling second-storey window.

Strung out on whatever it was that had him scratching and sweating, the guy holding onto Matthew's mother was in no rational state of mind. Desperation was pouring from him; his Metallica

T-shirt was soaked with sweat. He pulled the near-hysterical young woman more tightly against him, the four-inch-long blade of his pocket knife against her throat.

Indy flicked a glance to the door. Where the hell was her backup? She'd walked in on the scene accidentally—had stopped by to talk to Sasha Davies, a nineteen-year-old junkie with a murdered boyfriend, and had heard the commotion from the street. She'd called it in before entering the flat to find the two perps messing the place up and terrorising Sasha and her young son.

Dealers, she'd quickly surmised. Sasha must owe them money.

'Let her go,' Indy ordered, her gaze steady, 'and we'll sort this out.'

'You'll shoot me!' He dragged Sasha back another step until there was no space for more, and took a nervous glance down. 'I'll take her out with me!'

'No! Please!' Sasha's voice broke. Tears trickled down her face as she almost collapsed with fear. Indy uselessly willed her to be calm.

'I'm not going to shoot you. I'm putting my gun away. See?' She made a show of replacing it in the holster. 'I just want to talk.'

'About what? How you're gonna lock me up?'

'I'm not interested in you. Not yet. That changes if you make any bad decisions in the next few seconds. Understand?'

'What do you want?' He swiped at a trickle of perspiration on his face with his shoulder, pressing the knife against Sasha's throat. Sasha flinched. Indy noted the thin trickle of blood that ran from the blade and her heart rate kicked up another notch.

'I want us all to walk out of here in one piece. I want to know who you're working for. You let her go, you tell me that, you walk away.'

His crazed eyes were darting around as though the walls might tell him what to do. 'I just came to get the money like I was told to.'

She moved around the room, stepping carefully over the mess the two had made of Sasha's things, trying to get closer without appearing to.

'Where are you going?' He demanded, lifting his elbow outwards to make his knife appear more threatening.

'I'm getting out of the way of the door, because you can still leave. I promise you.'

'You swear?'

'I swear.'

'Okay … okay. There's a guy.'

'What guy?'

He was shaking, pallid. If he slipped, she was still too far away to help Sasha. 'Dunno.'

'Where?'

'Down near the docks—under the Botany Road overpass.'

She knew that part of Sydney, committed the information to memory. 'I need a name.'

'I dunno! We pick up the stuff from this guy, pay him cash. Cause we were friends with Chad, he sent us after Sash for what she and Chad owed.'

The name immediately registered. 'You're talking about Chad Garvin, correct? The one found dead in a garbage bag at the dump last week?'

'Yeah—yeah. He said if we mucked him around he'd send Bull after us, too.'

She inched closer, closer. 'Who's Bull?'

'The one that took out Chad.'

A little closer again. She pushed her luck, took another step. Glass crunched underfoot. 'When are you supposed to meet the one you deal with?'

A siren sounded, closed in. His eyes rounded on hers. 'You lied!'

'I didn't. I—wait!'

Panicked, he stepped back into nothing.

The knife fell from Sasha's throat as he flung out his arms to reach the wall for balance. Indy lunged, got a hand on Sasha, and twisted and threw what weight she could towards keeping her in the building. The painful, heavy landing on the tiled floor was a relief. There was a scream. When she untangled herself and looked up, he was gone.

Matthew shot up from his hiding place and threw himself into his mother's arms, wailing.

'Thank you.' Sasha's voice was trembling with emotion. She clung to her son and turned tear-filled eyes up to her. 'Thank you, thank you, thank you.'

Indy squeezed Sasha's arm in reassurance, smoothed a gentle hand over Matthew's curls. Then she stood up and moved to the broken window. Beneath her the dealer's body lay staring sightlessly back up at her.

'Damn it!' She muttered. She'd hoped he might have survived; second-storey falls weren't always fatal. But he'd landed on concrete, his blood spattering the patio.

'Look out!' Sasha's warning had her spinning as the guy she'd thought she'd knocked out launched himself at her. In the scuffle, his forehead crashed against her temple and the smack of his fist into her cheek sent her head reeling, but a well-placed elbow and a strike to the side of the knee dropped him and she got him under her, his hands behind his back, just as the pounding of feet up the stairs told her backup had arrived.

Senior Constable Patricia Langdon gave Indy a pat on the back. 'Well done,' she said, as the surviving perp was assisted from the paddy wagon towards the holding cells of the Sydney police station.

'Thanks, but I don't feel much like celebrating. I don't consider it a very good outcome when someone falls out a window.' She walked into the brightly lit station and down the corridor towards her office.

Patricia shrugged. 'A drug dealer took a two-storey dive. You'll go through the usual rigmarole, debrief. Nothing to worry about.'

The dead boy's image flashed into Indy's mind. The lifeless stare, the blood. For a moment his face blurred into another image; that of her mother and her grandmother, bodies tangled on the kitchen floor with the same, unseeing stare on both their faces. There'd been blood then, too. So much blood. She pulled herself together with difficulty, swallowed back the anger. 'He had a family. He wasn't much more than a kid. Someone's kid, Pat.'

'How's the mother and the little boy?'

She took a steadying breath, released it. 'Together and in one piece. Sasha's putting herself into rehab.'

'Then there's your good outcome—focus on that. What's on tonight?'

'A long soak in a hot bath and an early night.'

Pat snorted. 'You're such a party animal.'

'Hey—the other guy didn't exactly come quietly.' She rolled her shoulder and tried to unlock the kink in her neck.

'Indy—got a minute?' The tall, suited figure of Detective Ben Bowden stood in the doorway of his office.

'Sure, Ben,' she said, turning to her friend. 'I'll see you later, Pat.'

'Enjoy that bath,' Pat said with a smile as she walked away.

Ben stepped into the corridor and closed the door. 'I heard what happened. You okay?'

She rubbed her temples against the beginnings of a headache as a fluoro light above them flickered, on, off, on, off. 'Will be. And I've got another lead. I was out there to talk to Sasha about her murdered boyfriend, because in her initial statement to police she revealed he'd been dealing for D'Angelo. When I arrived two minor dealers had already been there awhile, messed the place up. They were there to collect the money Sasha had been too scared to pay back in person. The perp that later died told me if he didn't get the cash, a guy called Bull would come after him, just like he had Chad.'

'I'll check it out. See if that tag's come up anywhere.'

'Bull is obviously D'Angelo's standover man. And I think the skimming story is just an excuse. Chad Garvin is the sixth low-level dealer to be knocked off since the Drug Squad started on the D'Angelo drug investigation. I'm not saying D'Angelo didn't want his final payment from Sasha and Chad, but Sasha said Chad never skimmed—that he only owed for the last drop-off and would have paid up if he hadn't been killed. And I don't think Chad will be the last one to die. Every time it looks like the entire operation is close to being uncovered, we find out D'Angelo has another source, another supplier. Running an operation on that sort of scale, I've got to think D'Angelo is going to be a lot more worried about someone talking than losing a couple of grand in drugs money. I suspect he's getting nervous—ordering Bull to take out any possible leaks because of the pressure we're putting on him.'

'It's a plausible theory, but we still don't have anything solid.'

Frustration ate at her. 'We've got a shipping merchant with criminal convictions, caught on surveillance more than once associating with a known crime boss. He has contacts with two trucking companies and a freight-forwarding business, all of which are under investigation for smuggling drugs and tobacco through the Sydney docks over a thirty-year period. That's not nothing.'

'We were brought in on this to investigate several murders linked to him, remember? Let the Drug Squad pin the drug-smuggling operation on him.'

'Someone else has got to know about this "Bull". That sort of business means lots of connections. I've just got to find the one that will talk.'

He sighed and rubbed his fingers over his forehead. 'I know you're not going to like this, but unfortunately, that might have to wait.'

'What are you talking about? Why?'

'Something else has come up.'

The flare of anger wasn't helped by the headache. 'Come up? I'm in the middle of a case!'

Ben held up a hand to silence her, then continued quietly. 'You need to hear this. This request is urgent, and it's come from the top.'

They stepped aside as two officers walked past. 'Does this involve you, too?'

'If you say yes, it does. You don't have to do this, Indy.'

'Do what?'

He paused with his hand on the handle of his office door. 'We've got company.'

Interest piqued, she stepped into Ben's office. Almost immediately an amply built man with an expensive suit and a thin covering of salt-and-pepper hair got to his feet and wiped his brow with his handkerchief. His complexion was red, his expression strained.

'Indy, this is Senator Melville, from Canberra,' Ben said.

The senator held out a hand in greeting. His palm was damp, the quick shake was agitated. 'Hello, Detective O'Meara.'

'Senator.'

'Neil, please.' He sat back down in his chair, his foot jiggling as he crossed one leg over the other.

Ben moved around the desk and sat down. Indy found a third chair and sat next to the senator, waited.

'Neil is here because of his daughter's disappearance,' Ben said.

'Disappearance?'

Ben handed her a photograph of a young, attractive woman with lots of brown hair and a big smile. 'Caroline Melville went missing from a backpacking holiday three weeks ago. Despite a thorough investigation, no leads have come to light.'

'Caroline was working for Calico Mountain Lodge, in Tasmania,' Neil cut in. 'I wouldn't have allowed her to work down there if I'd known what was going on!'

She looked at Ben for some sort of clue. 'You're going to have to fill me in.'

Ben nodded. 'In December 2016, a group of trout fishermen found the body of a young woman snagged on some debris in the Tyenna River. She was identified as twenty-four-year-old Latisha Nolan.' Ben handed her a file containing paperwork and photographs. 'She'd also worked at Calico Mountain.'

'She'd been missing for almost two years before they found her,' Neil added.

Aware the senator didn't need to see the disturbing pictures, she dropped the folder below desk level and carefully checked through the images. The body was only in the first stages of decomposition. 'Two years?' She looked up at Ben in confusion. 'She hadn't been in the water more than a few days.'

'Correct. She was emaciated and had a wound to her ankle suggesting she'd been held against her will for a substantial amount of time before she entered the water.'

She frowned back down at the folder. 'I'd agree two years is substantial.'

'And there was another one—a few years before that,' Neil said. 'Tell her, Detective.' A shrill ringtone had Neil digging for his phone, a heavy sigh escaping his lips as he checked his screen. 'It's my wife—she's beside herself from all this. Excuse me a moment.'

Ben exchanged a short, telling glance with Indy as Neil let himself out of the room. 'Back in January 2014, a woman turned up on a property on the Gordon River Road, approximately three kilometres from where Latisha was found. According to the property owner, Gaylene White, she looked like she'd been in the bush a long time and was rambling about escaping "him". When Gaylene went inside to call for help, the woman ran off. Gaylene was shown photos of missing persons and identified the woman as Mandy Reeves—a backpacker who'd been missing for almost four years. Police conducted a thorough search but found nothing. She was never located. Mandy had also worked at Calico Mountain.'

'So two victims who had previously worked at this Calico Mountain, disappeared only to turn up showing evidence of having been abducted and held for a considerable amount of time. Were there any others?'

'Gretchen Bailey, who went missing shortly after Latisha's body was discovered. Same location, same circumstances. Never found.' Ben dropped another file on the desk.

'And Caroline disappeared from the same place. You're concerned we may have a serial abductor.'

'Look at the timeline. Due to the fact she was never discovered, it's fairly safe to assume Mandy was either recaptured and/or killed. If we speculate that her captor killed her, he'd need another victim, which would coincide with Latisha's disappearance just a few weeks later. Fast-forward to Latisha's discovery, and within a couple of months Gretchen has gone missing.'

'And now Caroline.' Indy chewed on her lip as she thought about that. 'Doesn't bode well for Gretchen. Any suspects?'

'Logan Atherton,' Neil spat, reappearing in the doorway. 'They all worked for him. He's some kind of hotshot horseman. My wife seems to think Caroline had a bit of a thing for him. The day before she went missing she told her he was taking her out trail riding in the wilderness. That was it.' He rubbed his fingers across his eyes. 'We haven't heard from her since.'

Indy's gaze sharpened at the vehemence of the accusation, but her voice was kind. 'Senator, what we're discussing is just one possible scenario. I assume because you're here you're aware of the details of the case. We don't know Caroline has been abducted. Have we ruled out her leaving of her own accord?'

'She couldn't leave without anyone knowing,' Neil objected. 'She had no transport. The place is out in the middle of nowhere. They shuttle their workers in and out and the shuttle driver and the guests on the shuttle all said she never got on it.'

'Could she have left with a friend?'

'I'm telling you—Atherton's taken her!' the senator erupted. 'Just like Mandy and Latisha and Gretchen.'

Indy took another look at the photos while she thought about that. 'I'm guessing from the ligature mark on Latisha's neck, that her cause of death was hanging?'

'Correct.'

'That's ... unusual. And then she was taken from wherever she'd been kept for two years, to a river frequented by fishermen to dump her? A risky move.'

'The body could have floated quite some distance—probably did. Apparently there's not a lot of depth in that part of the river but there is a decent current.'

Neil wiped his forehead again. 'Those girls ... the things they must have gone through ...' He shifted in his seat and yanked at his collar. 'The idea this man—this ... serial killer has my daughter ...'

If the senator didn't calm down, she was going to have another dead body on her hands. 'We have no proof we're dealing with a serial killer.'

His face went almost purple as he took in her statement. 'You have several missing women and one's turned up dead! Surely you—'

She held up her hand and reassured him. 'I need you to keep it together. Latisha was missing for a long time before she was discovered, and Gretchen and Mandy haven't been located. Even if Caroline has been abducted, there's a very good chance your daughter is still alive.'

'The police down there set up a tip-off line,' Ben told Indy, 'and offered a reward for information.'

'Anything?'

Ben shifted in his seat. 'An anonymous call came through almost immediately. The voice was whispered and hurried, but they think it was female. The message was: "There's more out there."'

'Damn, okay. Is our mystery woman right?'

'It's possible. About 120 people go missing in Tasmania every year—almost half are teenagers and are found within days. Of the other half, a significant number are simply overstaying visas.'

'Joining the thirty-five or so thousand others illegally working in Australia,' Indy said. But she had to admit, this case wasn't sounding that simple. 'So we're setting up a taskforce for this?' She caught the distressed look Neil aimed at Ben. Ben slowly nodded. 'There are some concerns about the possible outcomes of working the case in the traditional manner.'

'Such as?'

'The detective in charge down there, Mark Robinson, was only transferred to the station two years ago. While he was looking through some of his predecessor's cold cases he noticed some striking similarities between Mandy and Latisha's disappearances. He reopened the cases, and several people were questioned including Atherton. The day after he was questioned Atherton took off into the bushland behind his property. He was seen by hikers only a few kilometres from the spot Latisha's body was later discovered. Latisha's estimated time of death coincides with the sighting.'

'You think one of the people questioned—possibly this Atherton—panicked and disposed of her,' Indy surmised.

'He was there, wasn't he? What else could he have been doing?' the senator demanded.

'It's possible,' Ben said calmly. 'Then three months ago Gretchen's father had a rant on social media about what happened to Mandy and Latisha, demanding to know why more wasn't being done to find Gretchen. The media turned up asking questions, and Detective Robinson made noises about calling for a dedicated taskforce to take over the investigation. After a couple of weeks when nothing came of it, the media attention died down again. A couple of weeks after that, Caroline disappeared.'

'Suggesting he may have done the same thing again—panicked and disposed of Gretchen, then when he thought it was safe, grabbed another one.' She wondered what Ben had in mind—just how this was going to play out.

The senator took a deep breath and when he spoke again, his tone was pleading. 'I was told the two of you were my best hope of getting Caroline back alive. We can't risk her life by making another big fuss down there. Max was going to talk to you himself, but I wanted to see you both personally, ask for your help. Please. Please get my daughter back to me safely.' His voice cracked, his hand shaking as he removed a handkerchief from his pocket.

'Senator, I'm a homicide detective, not a missing persons specialist,' Indy said cautiously. 'Until we have proof that these cases are related—'

'She. Wouldn't. Just. Disappear.' His fist hit the table. 'That's not my Caroline! Please.'

She wasn't made of ice—would have had to have been to refuse him. So she turned it all around in her mind, and nodded slowly. 'All right. I'll review the case.'

'Thank you.' The senator rose and took her hand firmly. 'Thank you, Detective.'

'We'll be in touch,' Ben promised.

'Max?' Indy commented wryly when he closed the door behind the senator.

Ben grinned, shrugged. 'The senator and the commissioner play golf on Sundays.'

'And your opinion on Neil?'

'I'm thinking what you're thinking. He's a politician and he knows how to get what he wants. I also think, hell—if I had a daughter in that situation I wouldn't much care what I had to do to get her back or how I did it. I'd use every resource, every button I could push to make that happen.'

'Mmm,' she mumbled thoughtfully. She couldn't argue. 'So if we're not going down there guns blazing, so to speak, I'm gathering there's another strategy you're going to tell me about?'

'I spoke with the commissioner just prior to Neil's visit. He's very concerned about the possibility Caroline has been abducted and to a lesser degree about the negative media attention suggesting police incompetence over the handling of all this. Carefully worded statements have diffused the media situation, and whatever investigation we begin has to be done quietly. If Caroline has been abducted, it's obviously very important given what we know, that we allow our perp to think he's safe.'

Her brow shot up. 'You're suggesting an undercover role?' She considered that for a minute. Did she really want to involve herself in another undercover operation? In the Hunters Ridge case she'd almost gotten herself killed. She blew out a breath. 'I need to know more about Atherton. Other than the possible coincidence over the timing of his movements in relation to Latisha's discovery, why are we focusing the investigation at this point on him?'

'The circumstances all look innocent enough individually. But compare the cases together and there's a pattern. We know through witness testimony that on the day of each of the women's disappearances, they had plans to do something alone with Atherton. He'd planned a skiing visit to the local national park with Mandy, hiking with Latisha, dinner and a movie with Gretchen and a horse ride into the wilderness with Caroline. Atherton admits he'd made the plans, but that on each and every occasion, the women simply never showed up for the activity and when he went to check on them their belongings were gone, suggesting they'd simply packed up and left.'

The excuse seemed too ridiculous. 'As unlikely as that sounds, do we have any actual evidence to prove he's lying?'

'Unfortunately we can't prove anything, although on each occasion his vehicle and premises were searched. In Gretchen's case, several hair fibres were discovered between the seat and the centre console of his ute. The tissue attached suggests they'd been recently ripped out. There were also traces of her blood—which someone had attempted to clean—on the passenger seat. In Caroline's case we have a horse feedbag containing a set of her dirty clothes—also bloody—which were found tucked away behind boxes in the back of the tack room. Logan's fingerprints were on the bag and a witness claims he saw Caroline wearing the clothes on the morning of her disappearance.'

She grimaced. 'They're not going without a fight.'

Ben shook his head and handed her a picture. 'This is Atherton. His level of cooperation with police has been on a downhill slide from the beginning.'

'Any record?'

'Couple of teenage brawls, DUI on his P-plates. Nothing since. He was adopted and raised from age three by his aunt and uncle, Rosalie and Murphy Atherton, after his parents, who worked with them on their property, took off and left him behind.'

Indy grimaced. 'Ouch. That opens the door for an abandonment complex, low self-esteem, general anger against the world, dysfunctional relationship issues ... This guy just got even more interesting.' She studied her suspect in detail. Behind the hard mouth, ice-blue eyes and pissed-off expression, his features were attractive. That in itself could be a weapon. She imagined that expression softening, almost saw the transformation from commanding to charming. 'So he could play hard arse, then show a little extra kindness to a young girl, make her feel a bit special ... a guy like this would have her playing right into his hands.'

'Except that despite the arrangements he'd made to spend time with them just prior to their disappearances, no one knew of any romantic relationships he'd had with any of the girls.'

She shook her head. 'The type of person we'd be looking for wouldn't do relationships. He'd do manipulation, control. And he'd do it quietly. By the time he had them emotionally, they'd be gone. If this is our guy, he must be highly intelligent to get away with this under the noses of his family, staff and—I imagine—guests.'

'Correct. We need to have him under direct surveillance. We'll be tapping into his phone and computer, but due to the isolated location and Atherton's lifestyle, it's very difficult to keep a close enough eye on him. Which is where you come in.'

'Insert myself into his life. Study his routines, talk to friends and family, keep an eye on his every move, basically become his best friend ... Got it. Lucky me. You'd be my supervisor?'

'From here for now, with a team putting fresh eyes on the case, revising the reports, and chasing up any leads or evidence that might have been missed. Atherton's Robinson's prime suspect. Doesn't mean he'll be ours by the end of this.

'Robinson will be your contact down there. I've spoken to him—he's more than happy to cooperate and he'll be on standby at all times to get you out if necessary. That's all I can do. This has to be your decision. You sure you want to do this one?'

'No. I want to keep the pressure on D'Angelo. But … Of course I'm going to do this. The guy sounds like another Ariel Castro.'

'Sex slavery is the most common reason men abduct and keep women captive for long periods of time, but it's not the only one,' he reminded her.

'I know.' Indy compared two photos of Latisha: one of her smiling, happy, fresh-faced and healthy; in the other she was nothing more than a withered corpse. 'Whatever the reason, it doesn't look like they're having an easy time of it. Emaciated and chained … hell.' She took a deep breath and released it. 'What is this place … Calico Mountain?'

'It's a country retreat and working cattle property located in the Central Highlands. They're advertising for casual staff at the moment.'

'Handy,' she said dryly.

'We'll lodge an employment application for you.'

'No. I don't want to sit around twiddling my thumbs while I'm on a list. I'll go out there in person, see if I can beat the line. If not, there should be something I can do in one of those nearby towns to get close to them,' she suggested.

Ben nodded. 'I thought you might say that. I'll have people start working to get you set up.'

'Meanwhile, I'll go home and study the cases.'

'Detective Robinson will take you through it from his end, too,' Ben continued. 'You're to meet up with him when you land in Hobart before heading off to Calico Mountain.'

Indy held up the file. 'Is the full pathologist report on Latisha in here?'

'Yeah. I'll let you read it for yourself.'

She glanced through it. 'Then I'll see you in the morning.'

She stepped onto the pavement in a pair of army green cargos and a black T-shirt that had seen better days. Her dark brown hair was just long enough to tie back in a careless ponytail and she'd kept her face makeup-free. She'd gone shopping on the way home the day before and bought herself a decent backpack—the biggest one she could find. Big had seemed like a good idea, until she'd packed it, shouldered it, then barrelled into people in all directions trying to get onto an overloaded bus. It was a relief to stop, yet as she turned around to get her bearings, she knocked into someone else. 'Sorry,' she said, realising she'd just about taken out a businesswoman in a crisp navy suit. The woman nodded. At least the ride over had been short and, she thought with gratitude as she rearranged the pack on her shoulders, the walk to the station from her stop was only a couple of hundred metres.

Ben was waiting for her when she arrived, and he smirked at her appearance. 'You look about ten in that outfit.'

'Feel about 110.' She dropped the pack with a thud and slumped in a chair. 'Thank God,' she moaned. 'Remind me never to do this on purpose.'

Ben lifted the pack experimentally and shot her a look of disbelief. 'You'd have to learn to pack a little lighter.'

'No argument. It's huge and yet I can't fit another thing in. I almost broke the reinforced warrantied zipper trying to squeeze in an extra pair of socks I probably won't need.'

'You may need to take them out because your paperwork has to go in.' He handed her an envelope. 'Jacinda—you can still be Indy—Brown. No family—no one to miss you—and a bit of a pushover, like the others.' Indy flinched at the truth behind her cover. No, no family. Not for a long time. Ben held on when she reached for the envelope and looked her in the eye. 'That means meek and mild. No mouthing off, no showing off, no Xena-esque, Jackie Chan-meets-Miss Marple stunts. Just fit in, find out what happened to Caroline and come out in one piece.'

Indy's lips twitched. 'Got it, boss.'

'I wish I could believe that.'

Her smile widened. 'The coming-out-in-one-piece bit, anyway.' She rolled her shoulders and got back to her feet. 'Shouldn't take too long. Don't want anything else interfering with your transfer.'

'You're so full of yourself,' he teased.

'I learnt from the best.' She wasn't looking forward to Ben's transfer from Sydney to Mudgee. He was more than a colleague—he was a friend. More like family. When she'd stepped off the plane to Australia as an eighteen-year-old, sweating on dual citizenship and clutching a few small notes, she knew nothing and no one. And she'd been desperate enough to steal to survive. If it hadn't been for Ben, she would never have ended up where she was. She'd come a long way from teenage crim to homicide detective. But she was happy for him, and his fiancé, Mia, had become as much like family as Ben was.

'Here we go.' Pat came in and waved a folder. 'This needs to go in too. Your résumé to go with your ID, Jacinda.'

Indy skimmed through it. 'Thanks.'

'It's not bad. I'd hire you,' Pat said. Then she spotted the photo on the table, picked it up and studied Logan Atherton. 'This him?'

'Possibly.'

'Doesn't look like your stereotypical serial killer.'

Indy frowned. 'There isn't one. You know that. And why is everyone so sure he's killing the girls?'

Pat's expression was droll. 'The big, deadly ligature mark?'

'She might have done that herself—a way out. We don't know what's going on down there and—' Indy plucked the picture from Pat's fingers and gave it back to Ben. 'That man may be innocent.'

'Sure. But I'm going to say be careful. Because if it is him, I can see how he gets them.' Pat shook her head. 'Such a waste of gorgeous.'

The look Indy sent Pat was unimpressed. 'Assuming he is our guy he can be gorgeous for the rest of his life in prison.'

'Good luck then,' Pat said, taking one last look at her suspect over Ben's shoulder before closing the door behind her.

Ben linked his fingers together on the table. 'Indy, I need you to promise me that if you think any of them have the slightest doubt about your cover at any stage, you'll get out of there immediately. And don't take any unnecessary risks. Got it?'

She smiled. 'What is that, four warnings? Five? If I haven't got it by now I'm never going to.' Ben lifted her pack and she slipped into it, making it as comfortable as possible. 'Wish me luck.'

'I thought you were more confident than that.'

'I meant with the pack.' With a cheeky grin she waved a hand and walked out.

CHAPTER
2

Indy walked into the Hobart police station, her backpack affecting her usual long, easy stride. 'Afternoon. I'm here to see Detective Robinson.'

The neat-as-a-pin probationary constable behind the desk smiled, then stuck her head in a door behind her. 'Mark, there's a young lady here to see you.'

He appeared in the doorway. The lanky, middle-aged detective with a kind face looked her over with curiosity. 'Can I help you?'

'Would you mind if we discussed this in your office?'

'Come in,' he said, standing aside and motioning for her to pass him.

His office was just untidy enough to be relaxed. Coffee-cup rings marred the wooden desk in one corner and a half-filled 'Boss' mug sat in the same general location. He picked it up and took a sip while he gestured for her to take a seat. 'How can I help you?'

'I'm Detective O'Meara. I'm here to see you about Caroline Melville's disappearance.'

His face brightened. 'Thanks for coming. I appreciate your speed in getting down here.'

She got straight to the point. 'Senator Melville is of course very keen to get his daughter back alive.'

Mark's eyes flared briefly, but his voice remained even. 'He's been a pain in the butt. And he's got a lot of influence.'

'He's fighting for his daughter's life.'

'And making me appear incompetent. My head is on the chopping block over it. I hope for your sake you get something on Atherton fast.'

Pressure, she knew, didn't help solve cases. 'If there's anything to find, so do I. If not, I'm sure the team Ben's quietly putting together to run the bulk of the case will turn up the truth.'

Robinson's expression suggested he was unimpressed. 'Have you actually read the report, Detective?'

Indy managed a smile, but it was tight. 'I sure have. And on the surface, Atherton looks guilty as hell. But my role here is to discover undeniable evidence tying Atherton to the crime, not to read a story and jump to conclusions. I don't even have all the facts yet. On that, if you could just help me fill in a couple of blanks … There wasn't much history in the women's files. And I'm curious. Did Gretchen or Caroline have a history of taking off, fighting with family … anything that might suggest they left of their own free will without a word?'

Her tight smile became a scowl as he rolled his eyes to the ceiling. 'Of course not. Or it would have been in there. These were regular, happy young women, Detective, with jobs they enjoyed and families they kept in contact with. They weren't the sort to deliberately vanish without a trace.'

'What about any follow-up from the phone tip-off? How did you go with identifying any other possible connections?'

'Nothing of interest.' He shrugged dismissively. 'It's unlikely any of the cases we dug up are connected to this.'

Indy frowned at his attitude. *Unlikely or inconvenient?* 'What makes you say that?'

He sighed heavily, his tone impatient. 'The women in those particular cases didn't work for the Athertons. So much Tassie employment is tourism and agriculture-based and both are seasonal. We get a lot of people in and out, wanting to work their way around the country. It's hard to say how many simply move on and don't tell their families, or skip their visas and don't want to be found for one reason or another.' He took his wallet from his drawer and handed her a card. 'I wasn't sure you'd have had a chance to review the case in full and I know you're not able to carry anything on you, so I've made all the details of my investigation available through a password-protected link on this site. I realise it's not perfect. You'll have to keep a tight eye on your security, but it's the best I can do. You can log in using wi-fi at the retreat.'

'Thanks. That will be helpful,' she managed.

'It's pretty remote out there but there is mobile coverage—mostly. My number's on the back of that card. I'm available 24/7 if you need anything.'

'Appreciate that.'

Indy stood and Mark followed suit. 'The accent's going to help with that cover. If you don't mind me asking, how'd an American become an Aussie cop?'

'Both my parents were Australian citizens. I just happened to grow up in the States. Dual citizenship.'

'Right. Now it makes sense. You have everything you need?'

'Yeah, just one last thing?'

'What's that?'

'I'm having trouble believing anyone that lives and works at a tourist retreat could be keeping women alive for so many years without anyone's knowledge. Especially after multiple investigations.'

'There's a lot of land out there, Detective O'Meara,' he replied defensively. 'A lot of inaccessible areas—places you would never stumble upon by accident. But if you know the land, know how to get in and out, and have good reasons to be alone out there regularly without raising suspicion, you could hide those women with no problem whatsoever. Not a lot of people fit that bill. Logan Atherton does.'

'Lots of land perhaps, but he'd have to have somewhere to keep them,' she reasoned.

'Every building we could locate in the area has been searched. I'm not saying there's not something we've missed, the sort of wilderness out there isn't conducive to an easy aerial search. There's also more than 500 known caves in the area—some of them extensive. With the state those women were in I wouldn't be too quick to rule that possibility out. We've done all we could—had volunteers join the police, even had local businesses giving their workers time off to help out.'

Indy's gaze sharpened. 'One of those locals could be our perp. Can you really tick off an area searched by a civilian simply because they said she wasn't there?'

Agitation flickered behind his eyes as he leaned his hands on the table. 'I didn't have Logan Atherton out there, Detective.' Then before she could respond, 'Do you know that on the day Latisha was murdered, Atherton was spotted by hikers in bushland, just three kilometres upstream from where her body had been found in the river?'

'Yes, I read that.'

'When I questioned him on why he was there he told me—with a smirk—that it was "a lovely day for a swim". I'm telling you, he's been playing cat and mouse with me for years. He might panic when he thinks he'll be caught out, but he sure as hell likes the attention when he thinks he's safe.'

A chill worked its way up her spine. 'He sounds like a real character. Now, how do you suggest I get out there? I can't rock up in a police car and because I wanted to get here quickly, I haven't done my homework.'

He straightened up and gestured to the office door. 'The main bus services don't run right out there but the retreat has a shuttle bus that goes around to all the popular tourist spots and to and from the airport every couple of days. You could bunk in the motel just up on the next street for tonight, and head out there tomorrow, but I happen to know Atherton is at a campdraft out at Hamilton for the weekend. Might not be a bad idea to head up there, get a look at him, worm your way into a job.'

What the hell is a campdraft? 'That's not a bad idea.'

'I can get you on a bus out there. It's further north, but it's one of those towns the Calico Mountain shuttle runs through if you somehow miss him.'

'Sounds perfect. Let's get started.'

Indy followed Mark's instructions and got a seat on the right bus. She wished she'd been able to bring a hard copy of the case files. As the bus pulled away, she unwrapped a new roll of her favourite peppermints and popped one in her mouth, then rested her head against the window and watched the town go by.

She managed an uncomfortable nap; dropping everything to leave home so quickly hadn't allowed for any more sleep than it had preparation. When she opened her eyes it was to long, rolling paddocks, grazing sheep and the occasional pretty creek or country home. Another few minutes and the bus wound its way into Hamilton. The town was nestled between gentle green hills. There were a few small businesses and generously spaced houses. Not a big place, but, she discovered as she stepped off the bus, a busy one.

A rowdy group of kids manoeuvred around her at speed and on down the roadside, yelling and laughing. Tables outside the pub in front of her were full of patrons. She swung her pack onto her back and excusing herself, squeezed past two men with rounded middles holding beers at the entrance.

A young waitress with a short skirt and a big smile ducked past her with a tray of empty schooner glasses and rounded the bar. 'Hi, can I get you something?'

'A lemon squash would be great, thanks. Is it always this busy around here?'

The waitress shook her head as she got Indy's drink. 'Nah. This is the campdraft crowd. That why you're here?'

'Thought I'd check it out.' She accepted the drink, passed over a five-dollar note.

'That's a big pack you've got.'

'Working holiday. I heard a place called Calico Mountain is advertising for staff. I'm heading down there next.'

Something flickered behind the waitress's eyes. 'They're short-staffed all right. You sure you want to go out there though?'

'I wouldn't mind giving it a go. Could you tell me when the next shuttle bus comes through?'

'Ah ... I reckon there's one tomorrow.' Then to a weathered old man that had moved in beside Indy, 'You boys after another round, Bill?'

'Thanks Amy, whenever you're ready, love.'

'Won't be long.' Amy handed her some change. 'Gotta book though—did you book?'

'No. I didn't.'

Amy began pulling beers and loading them onto a tray. 'Shouldn't be a problem. Not with the Athertons already out here for the event. Just let one of 'em know you need a ride.'

'Would any of them be in here at the moment?'

Amy looked around briefly. 'Nope. Comp's still going on. I think Tess Atherton was entering her novice horse. When you finish your drink go up the road a bit—check it out. You can't miss the place.'

'Right.' She looked down at her pack. 'And I'd better just get a room—in case I can't get out to Calico Mountain today.'

'Just get a room?' Amy laughed and swiped the back of her wrist across her forehead. 'The place is booked out.'

A flash of worry settled in her stomach. She should have been better prepared. 'Is there anywhere else?'

'There's a bed and breakfast up the street, and a few more further afield. And the campground might have some space. Best get these out.' She picked up the tray of drinks and disappeared into the crowd.

Indy sat sipping her drink and considered her options. It was getting late. She wasn't going to have time to get to the campdraft before dark and find accommodation. But she needed to sleep somewhere. Bending to pick up her pack, she almost collided with an older woman intent on getting behind the bar. 'Sorry, love. You right?'

'Yep—sorry.'

Amy reappeared with half a dozen empty schooner glasses. 'You've been gone awhile, Marge.'

'Damn bloody Jackson ...' Marge got herself a coke and manoeuvred her ample weight onto a tall stool. 'Spewed all over the bloody bathroom. Didn't miss an inch of space. I kicked him out—took me an hour to clean up the mess.'

Amy looked amused. 'Aw come on—he's just celebrating his second place. Best he's ever done.'

'It was the maiden not the open bloody final. It's not even five o'clock! I told him to go sleep off his victory in his horse float.'

'Is the room clean?'

'Yeah—left the windows open. Needs an air.'

The young girl's face split into a grin as she eyed Indy. 'Just how desperate are you, exactly, for a room?'

'I'll take it,' she said with relief.

Marge dug the key out of her pocket and put it on the bar. 'Third on the right at the top of the stairs. You can fix me up now if you don't mind.'

'Sure.' She took out a credit card with Jacinda's name on it, handed it over.

'You might want to give the room a bit of time to breathe.'

'I'll just dump my pack and go and watch the campdraft for a while.'

'Not much left on today.' Marge handed the eftpos machine over for her pin.

'She's hoping to run into someone from Calico Mountain,' Amy said. 'She's after some work.'

A knowing look passed between the women. 'I'm Marge, this is Amy. Who might you be?'

'Jacinda—but everyone calls me Indy.'

'Well, it's good to meet you, Indy. Nice place, that Calico Mountain. Long as you ignore the rumours.'

'Rumours?'

Marge waved at a couple of patrons entering the bar. 'Hi, Stew! Barney!' Then to Indy, 'Don't go worrying about it. You better head out or the competition will be over for the day. Follow all the comings and goings up the road a bit. Can't miss it.'

Amy took off to deliver more schooners and Marge turned her attention to Stew and Barney. Over their heads, Indy could just see late afternoon creeping in through the window. She needed to get a move on.

She hoisted her pack back onto her sore shoulders and dragged herself upstairs to find her room. It was small but tidy with an over-powering smell of disinfectant. She dropped her pack and grabbed her small handbag, then on second thought grabbed her jacket from her pack. The air had held a bite when she'd stepped out of the bus.

Heading out on foot in the direction everyone else seemed to be coming from or going to, she scanned the countryside. Lots of pad-docks, some brown, green hills, a scattering of buildings. Further out were mountains, blue and distant. She walked over a bridge that spanned the width of the River Clyde and along a stretch of road with not much to break the monotony of post-and-wire-fenced paddocks.

As she turned off the road and followed the driveway into the showgrounds, she pulled her jacket more tightly around her and zipped it up. She looked around. There was a large fenced yard, and some smaller ones containing cattle. People stood about or sat in the stand; a smattering of applause broke out as a rider waved at the crowd before being let out a gate, and a small cow was herded through another.

Behind the yard were lines of cars and horse floats, and more than a few trucks. Indy found a spot on the crowded stand next to a group of men in big hats and boots who were nursing stubbies. She used her position above the general congestion to scan the crowd for any clues to who she was looking for as the announcer's voice came over the speakers. 'Last to go this afternoon is Mason Cartwright on BTR Aurora. This young mare showed a lot of promise under her breeder and trainer Gavin Perkins. Let's see how she goes with her new owner, Mason, who's just starting out in the sport.'

A young man was riding his horse through a group of smallish cows. As they parted, he zeroed in on one, moving it away from the others. It tried to run back to the group, but the horse ducked left, then right, keeping it separated. There was a shout, and the gate was opened. Horse and rider took off after the cow and she watched, breath held as they somehow steered it at speed around a post then, getting around it, turned it towards another. The horse knocked the cow, and she winced, but it seemed the cow was going to bend around the next post under the combination's guidance.

And then it didn't. The cow dug its heels in and ducked left instead of right, crashing into the horse. There was a tangle of animals then both went down, the rider over the horse's head. The crowd hushed.

The cow threw itself around and got up, leapt over the rider and ran back towards the group it had left. The horse got its feet under it and ran off in the opposite direction, reins dangling from its head. The rider didn't move for several seconds. Slowly, he pushed up onto his hands and knees. Helpers raced out and got him to his feet and he limped off, shaking his head to applause and a few shouted words of encouragement. Shaken herself, Indy noticed she was on her feet, with almost everyone else.

'Not a great end to the day's competition ladies and gentlemen but as you can see young Mason is all right.'

She let out a relieved breath for the guy hobbling away.

And that was it. As people cleared the stands and walked off in all directions, the smell of barbecuing meat had Indy heading to a food tent. It was almost dark, but there were plenty of lights going on around the trucks and floats so many of the competitors were camping in. Hoping there might be a truck or a horse float with

Calico Mountain's name on it, she grabbed a sausage sandwich and took a good look around the vehicles and makeshift horse yards as people settled in for the evening. The mood was upbeat, friendly and familiar. She paused by a yard to stroke the face of an inquisitive brown horse that poked its head through the railings to sniff at her. It snatched the last crust of her sandwich. 'Hey!' she laughed.

'How are you enjoying the campdraft?'

She turned in the direction of the vaguely familiar voice. 'Oh— Amy, right? I'm surprised you could get away from the pub. Did things slow down?'

'Change of shift. I've just come out to pick up my boyfriend. Adam's had a couple of beers so I'm driver. You want a lift back to the pub? It's pretty dark.'

'Thanks, I'd love one. I didn't manage to find anyone from Calico Mountain.'

Amy shrugged. 'Not sure where they are but don't stress, they'll still be here tomorrow. My ute's parked out the back behind the trucks—near the trees. It's white with the pub's name on it. Just give me ten, maybe fifteen minutes and we'll meet you there.'

'Thanks.' Beyond the lights of the showground and the competitor's camps, the sky was now black as pitch. A couple of spotlights shined out just enough for her to make out the ute from a small group of others, so she waited by the trees, soaking up the atmosphere.

A horse came careering backwards out of the bushes, almost knocking her off her feet. A man on the end of the lead was holding tightly, fighting for control. Something swung out, then there was a crack against the horse's side that sent it backwards again, then leaping sideways. Another crack. The horse threw its head around and copped the lead rope around the face.

'Stand still you bloody bitch. Think you can embarrass me, you piece of shit?'

The horse was in a lather of sweat and obviously petrified. The man nearly lost hold of it as it reared and spun, but somehow he held on. Welts were clearly defined on its smooth coat, exaggerated by the lights from the camps shining against its wet sides. She couldn't see very well, but she was pretty sure this was the combination that had just fallen in the competition.

The horse copped yet another blow, almost fell over in its struggle to escape the handler. 'Hey—that's enough!' Indy snapped.

'Bugger off, lady,' the young guy spat, wrestling the horse. 'This ain't none of your concern.'

'You run your horse the wrong way into a cow and the horse gets the blame?'

He took his eyes from the horse to flash her a sneer. 'This horse needs a lesson in manners. Maybe so do you.' He lashed out again. The horse reared again and crashed into a tree. When the rope tangled in a low branch, the guy ripped it off the tree and smashed it against the horse's face.

Shocked and furious, Indy got in his way. With her foot out and a hand on the back of his head, she used a lot of his own momentum to propel him forwards. Hard. He tripped over her and let go, falling head first into the tree.

Indy snatched the lead rope as the horse ran back several steps before standing, trembling, poised for flight. 'It's all right, sweetie,' she murmured, 'take it easy …'

'Fuck!' The guy's hands covered his face, came away full of blood. She saw it drip through his fingers.

'Oops,' she exclaimed dryly.

'My fucking nose is broken! You stupid bitch!'

'Did the tree attack you? Well, karma's a beautiful thing. I'll be back.'

'Back from where?'

'Finding someone to report you to.'

'Give me back my horse! You'd want to mind your own fucking business, lady, or—'

'What?' Indy challenged. 'You think I'm scared of some little thug that hides in the trees and lays into an innocent animal in the dark? Threatens women?'

'You should be,' he snarled. 'You don't know who you're—'

'How's your horse, Mason?' The voice was deep, the question casual.

Indy shot a quick glance from Mason to the stranger. All she could make out was a tall figure in a hat, leaning in a relaxed manner against a horse float. Where the hell had he come from? 'It was better before he beat the crap out of it,' she said.

'It's none of your fucking business!' Mason said with acute frustration.

'Is that any way to speak to a lady?' the stranger asked.

'I—that's no lady! That bitch broke my nose! And I wasn't beating the crap out of it, honest. I've got a dud horse, that's all.' Despite his clumsy efforts to stem the flow of blood from his nose, Mason took a quick, nervous step back as the man came closer.

'What you've got is a novice horse and an unlucky accident. It happens. Go get cleaned up, keep some pressure on that nose.' Under the commanding tone, Mason did as he was told. With a final scowl for Indy, he spun around and took off.

'I'll take her.' The stranger held out a hand and with relief Indy placed the lead rope in it. He murmured something to the shaken horse and ran a soothing hand along its neck, appearing to be checking it. 'You all right?' he asked Indy as he performed his task.

'Yeah. Is the horse?'

She heard an under-the-breath curse as his hand followed the line of the horse's side. 'She'll be fine. Why don't you go enjoy the rest of your evening—let me deal with this?'

Something about the man, the tone, had her agreeing. 'All right.'

He straightened up, tipped his hat and after she passed, returned his attention to the horse. When she reached the ute and turned around, the pair had disappeared.

CHAPTER

3

The morning was clear and cold. The sun beaming through her window was without the warmth Indy had come to expect from Australian summer days, but she stood at the window anyway and breathed in the air, shivering slightly as the breeze caught her hair. Today she *had* to find someone from Calico Mountain. She hadn't rushed down to Tassie to sit in a hotel room all weekend.

Besides, she wanted to get out to the showgrounds early to see if there was any sign of the poor horse from the previous night. She couldn't say why she'd been so quick to hand it over to the stranger—especially one that so obviously knew the owner ... Mason Cartwright, she remembered.

She wondered briefly if she'd made a mistake. But whoever he was, the stranger had had Mason backing away like he'd been ready to run for his life. It was probably sorted, but she intended to make sure whoever was in charge of the event was made aware of the incident.

She left her pack and went downstairs to join the general chaos. The air of excitement was no less than it had been the day before.

'Morning. How'd you sleep?' Marge asked when she approached the bar.

'Great actually. Could I get some coffee?'

With a nod, Marge poured the steaming liquid into a mug. 'Heard there was a bit of a kerfuffle last night. You take on young Mason?'

Indy stared in disbelief. 'You heard about that?'

'I did. Hard to keep much quiet around here.'

'Do you know what happened to the horse?'

'Story is, Logan's taking it home.'

Her stomach did a funny little twist. It couldn't be. 'Logan Atherton?'

'He's the one that stepped in last night, wasn't he?'

'*That* was Logan Atherton?' she asked again.

'Don't know who else you thought it would have been. Logan took care of the horse then went back and had a word to Mason. Told him if he hadn't already got what was coming to him from that broken nose you gave him, he would have shown him what a branch round the head felt like.'

'Oh, I see.' And she shuddered a little bit for effect, before probing. 'Do you think he really would have done that?'

Marge thought about it. 'Logan tends to get his point across without coming to blows. Most times. Besides, Mason had no right taking to an animal like that in temper. Spoilt rotten his whole life and as chauvinistic as his father. Won't hurt him to be brought down a peg or two—especially by a woman. Anyway, Logan threw some money at Jim—Mason's dad—for the horse and Mason took off to Hettie's place and got his nose reset. Hettie is the local nurse.

I don't think you'll be seeing him around any more horses for a while. Feeling pretty sorry for himself this morning.'

'Sounds like Logan's a nice guy?' Indy prompted.

'Hmm. There's a few different opinions floating round on that. Hard to tell just who a person really is sometimes, isn't it? Specially one that … Well, you can judge for yourself when you go out there. You want some breakfast?'

She wanted to dig further into Marge's comments but from the look on the woman's face the subject was closed—at least for the time being. 'No, thanks. I'll just sit on this coffee.' She took it over to a small table and stared into it as she thought about what she'd just learned.

So, the big guy in the hat had been Logan Atherton. It had been too dark to ID him from the photo.

And she was supposed to have come in being—what had Ben said?—meek and mild. Ha. She'd been here five minutes and was the talk of the town for breaking Mason's nose.

Great start, Indy. She took a sip of coffee, burnt her lips and put the mug down. There was nothing she could do about it. She'd been meek enough towards Logan anyway, had put the lead rope right into his hands without question.

She cringed at that. She'd been out of her element and happy for the stranger with the quietly powerful personality to take charge. She needed to regather her thoughts, get her head back in the right space. Because as a suspect, that made him dangerous.

She spent the morning watching the events, keeping an eye and an ear out for any of the Athertons. By lunchtime she was regretting that she'd skipped breakfast, so she headed in the direction of the food tents and ordered another sausage sandwich—there wasn't a lot of choice—and a lemonade, and found a plastic chair to sit on under a tree.

'Logan's already warming up. I'll get him a drink, too.' Attention caught, Indy looked up to see a woman approaching the van. She was wearing jeans and a green polo shirt with Calico Mountain printed on it. Could this be Tess Atherton? She was tall, with long dark hair pulled back in a simple ponytail, and was accompanied by another young woman in jeans who was almost a head shorter, her blonde hair cut in a chic city style swinging around sharp cheekbones.

A guy wielding a pair of tongs smiled with familiarity when they approached. 'Hi, Tess, how's it going?'

'Good, Drew. Logan's back on soon. Can we get a few cold drinks?'

'I've got Diet Coke and Fanta left … a few lemonades, bottled water somewhere …'

'Cokes thanks.'

'No worries. Good to see you Jules, are you back for long?' he asked, reaching for the cold bottles.

'Not sure yet. How's your mum?'

'Good. Real good.'

They took the drinks and moved away. Indy took two hurried, much-needed mouthfuls of her sandwich then abandoned the remains of her meal to follow them around the back of the showground, where a group of riders were exercising horses. Tess waved as a man on a horse the colour of gleaming gold rode past.

'And there he is,' Indy muttered in reluctant appreciation. Though there appeared to be almost a sea of long-limbed, broad-chested men in jeans and Akubras, this one stood out. The impressive combination of horse and rider were moving through some sort of routine: forwards, backwards, left, right, bending, stretching, stopping and starting.

After a few minutes, Logan pointed the horse towards the waiting women and ambled over. He took a long drink of the Coke Tess had offered and looked around, saying something to a rider as they cantered past. He was still smiling from the exchange when his gaze landed on Indy. He zeroed in on her, and he signalled his acknowledgement with a nod of his head. She couldn't help but catch her breath. Logan Atherton was ... wow. She gave herself a mental shake when she realised she was staring, admiring him.

Both women followed Logan's gaze. Indy smiled briefly, adjusting to character. She was tempted to head over, introduce herself, but he handed the drink back to Tess and moved off on the horse, and the women went in a different direction. No matter, she'd make sure she bumped into them later. At least she knew what they all looked like.

Keeping a general eye on the women's movements, she wandered around for another half hour. The hum of nerves and excitement seemed to build as the day wore on. Finals were announced, so she found a spot at the arena fence and watched a handful of riders take their turns. The cattle she'd seen the night before had looked quite small, but the ones in front of her today were larger and, she assumed, older. The combinations chasing them were faster, sharper, at times breathtaking.

Tess and Jules had found a spot in the stands and both had fresh drinks in hand. Deciding a drink wasn't a bad idea, Indy got herself another lemonade and made her way up towards them. Catching Tess's eye, she smiled politely. When she got one in return, Indy took advantage. 'Hi. Do you mind if I sit here?'

'Not at all. I'm Tess Atherton, this is Julie Miller.'

'Jules,' the other woman corrected. 'Call me Julie, no one will know who you're talking about. Including me.'

'Indy.'

'We know.' Tess's green eyes were sparkling and curious as she looked Indy over. 'We were hoping to run into you.'

'Why's that?'

'Because you broke Mason's nose,' Jules answered for them both.

Indy turned her gaze to the arena and watched another rider finish his round. 'My foot got in the way of him being an arsehole. He fell into the tree.'

'With more than a little assistance, from the way Logan relayed it,' Tess said with a grin.

Yeah, okay. Meek and mild is officially out the window. Giving up, she shrugged and took a sip of her drink. 'Apparently he isn't any better on his feet than he is on his horse.'

'We heard you were looking for a job,' Jules said.

'Of course you did. So how does it work exactly—daily news bulletin, phone chain, secret emails ...?'

'Too much mucking around. We just rely on gossip,' Tess told her. 'What kind of work are you looking for, exactly?'

Indy shrugged. 'Anything I can get.'

Tess exchanged glances with Jules. 'Calico Mountain does have a few positions going at the moment if you're interested in an interview.'

Indy looked back at them with interest. 'Definitely.'

'Here comes Logan,' Jules said just before the announcer called his name. 'He's Tess's cousin.'

'I haven't seen campdrafting before this weekend,' Indy commented. 'I'm guessing the goal is to get the cows to go around the poles, right?'

'He'll start by going into that yard over there.' Tess pointed. 'See that group of steers? He has to cut one out—which basically means he has to choose one and move it to the front of the yard. It's going to want to get back to the others so he has to block it and turn it a few times to prove to the judge he has it under control. The more control, the more points. Once he does that, he'll call for the gate to be opened.'

She watched Logan enter the yard on the big golden horse and move around, getting in among the cattle.

'Once the gate opens, he—Oh look, he's chosen that black baldy.'

Indy watched him move a big, black steer with a white head away from the others. Tess continued. 'Right, so he'll chase it out and yeah, work it around the poles in a figure of eight. So left peg, right peg, gate—which is the two pegs close together. Here he goes.'

The steer burst from the gate with Logan's horse at its rump. At spectacular speed they moved tightly around the first peg, then Logan moved the horse in a fluid motion around the steer to the other side and it turned again, around the next peg. Horse and rider were keeping close on its tail, up beside it, dropping back. The steer appeared to prop, as though it was going to dive away. Indy held her breath, heart in her throat, as Mason's accident flashed in her mind. But the horse barged in, pushed its weight against the animal and it shot back around in the right direction. Tess and Jules were on their feet, calling out and cheering as the horse stretched out to keep pace and manoeuvred the steer through the gate. It seemed so smooth and easy. But Indy's pulse was racing from the excitement and the crowd whistled and clapped and the announcer proclaimed 'Another great ride'.

Indy released a breath she hadn't realised she'd been holding. 'Did he win?' she asked.

'We'll know in a minute, he's the last rider,' Jules said. 'Wait for it ... we need to hear the points.'

'Hell yes, he won!' Tess whistled loudly as the scores were announced. Logan lifted his hat to the crowd and with a pat for his horse, walked it out of the arena. Tess took a step down then paused and turned back to Indy. 'Logan's heading off this afternoon, but Jules and I are hanging round until tomorrow. We've got a bit of a thing with some friends tonight. Come and see us tomorrow. We're'—she dug into her pocket for her wallet and handed Indy a card—'here.'

'Thanks. Ah, how do I get out there?'

'One of the staff is coming through with a fresh load of tourists around eleven. You're welcome to grab a lift. We leave from the pub.'

'Great. See you then.'

Indy hurried back into the pub just after four o'clock. 'Sorry Marge—didn't mean to be so long.'

'That's all right. Your stuff was all in your pack so I cleaned up the room around it. I wasn't looking forward to lugging it out if someone else turned up wanting the room, though. Are you collecting rocks or something?'

'You know, you'd think so, but packing light's just not a skill I ever acquired. So no one wanted the room?'

'Nope. Campdraft's over. Tess and Logan's friend, Jules, has got a bit of a welcome home thing happening cause she's just come back from Sydney, so they'll all crowd in for dinner and drinks, but I reckon the rooms will almost all be empty tonight.'

'Then can I keep my room? I'm getting a ride back to Calico Mountain in the morning.'

'So you found them all right then?' Even as she spoke people were starting to pour back into the pub for meals and drinks. 'No probs. But it looks like this dinner thing's gonna get busy. If you want to eat, it'd be an idea to get back down here round five, no later than six.'

'Thanks.' She headed upstairs feeling like the layer of dust she'd accumulated over the day was going to harden into an uncomfortable shell if she didn't hurry into the shower. Her pack was leaning against the bed. Indy dug into it for her toiletries and some fresh clothes and stopped, leant back, stared at the contents.

That wasn't how she'd packed her things. It was all just a little haphazard and her laptop was visible. She'd made sure she'd folded clothes around it to protect it. She looked around the room for any other evidence of someone poking around, opened the bathroom, looked inside. Nothing. Her gaze slid back to her pack as she chewed her bottom lip. Why would anyone rummage through her things? As far as everyone here was concerned, she was simply another backpacker looking to pick up work.

She took everything out, checked it carefully. Nothing was missing, and besides, she reassured herself, there was nothing incriminating for anyone to find. She opened her laptop and it flashed to the password screen as usual.

Perhaps she was being paranoid. Marge could have knocked the pack over—she'd mentioned she'd felt the weight of it. The contents could have shifted. Possibly. Perhaps she'd ask Marge when she went down to dinner.

She showered, then logged in to her computer. She hadn't had time to write up a report on the Sasha Davies incident before she left Sydney, so she did that and sent it to Ben with a quick update on her progress. Then she deleted all sign of it from her hard drive. She could hear the noise level increasing downstairs, and it got louder as the clock hit six.

She headed for the dining room, decided she'd be lucky to find a seat. The tables were full and people spilled out onto the verandah and the street. Beers were passed around. Men and women were talking and laughing over the noise of an old jukebox playing country music. From snatches of conversation flying across the room and the beer salutes, winks and greetings as people passed each other on their travels to and from the bar, she guessed at least most of them knew each other. She copped a few curious glances as she looked for an opening to order a meal. Amy appeared and gave her a harried look as she skimmed by, her arms loaded with trays. Marge was nowhere to be seen.

Now what?

A loud whistle caught her attention, and that of half the people in the bar. She looked around. A young man with a big beard wearing the standard collared shirt and jeans gestured for her to move across the room. She eyed him suspiciously, though there was nothing but a friendly smile on his face.

'Indy! Over here!'

Was that Tess? She craned her neck past the whistler and saw Tess and Jules signalling at her from the corner booth beside him. They were squeezed in between a small army of men and women, their tables loaded with drinks and snacks. Tess leant over and spoke to her friends and somehow they all squished together enough to make a space. She was gestured into it.

'Hi,' she greeted everyone.

'Hi. Have you ordered a drink?' Tess asked.

'I came down looking for dinner, but I don't like my chances.'

'Hey Jase,' Tess said to the guy who'd caught her attention. 'Indy needs a beer and a hamburger.'

'You serious?'

Tess batted her eyelashes and grinned cheekily.

The grin was reluctantly returned. 'Righto.'

'Oh you don't have to.'

'He doesn't mind,' Tess said in her ear as Jase pushed his way through the crowd. 'He's the chef here and his break should have ended five minutes ago. He was hiding from Marge.'

'It's busy again tonight.'

'Jules has a lot of friends.'

Jules laughed at Tess. 'Half of them are yours.'

They were an interesting pair, Indy decided. Tess was makeup-free—though with that olive skin and those big green eyes of hers, who needed any—and her long, slim out-in-the-sun hard-work figure was casually dressed in jeans and a pretty green shirt. Jules was wearing light, skilfully applied makeup, and with her petite, almost delicate frame and doe-brown eyes, she was less casually dressed, in a skirt and lacy top that Indy admired. One naturally lovely, all country, the other stylish and pretty and, if Indy was any sort of judge, citified to some degree. She remembered Marge had said something about Sydney. So what was she doing down here?

Before long the hamburger came. It was delicious and she washed it down with a beer she made last as long as she could, while she listened to the general flow of banter around her and dealt with questions as they arose.

'Your accent is gorgeous,' Tess said. 'What made you come to Australia?'

'I needed a change. Wanted to see the country.'

'Do you like it?' Jules asked.

'So far I think it's amazing.' Then to Tess, 'Tell me more about Calico Mountain?'

'It's a tourist retreat. We have a guesthouse that contains different levels of accommodation from single rooms to suites. There's a day spa and a restaurant. Jules's mum runs the restaurant. Jules is also a chef and she's come back to help because we're short-staffed.'

'Sounds nice. Relaxing.'

'It can be, but there's plenty to do. Guests can go hiking, horse riding, quad riding, mountain biking, canoeing or fishing. In winter there's decent skiing in Mt Field.' She paused and smiled. 'It's a great place to work, Indy.'

'Then I guess I'd better hope I get a job there.'

'Do you have a serious criminal record?' Jules asked.

'No.'

'How about a reasonable amount of commonsense?'

'I like to think so.'

'Then you're pretty much hired,' Tess assured her.

'Why's that?' Indy asked, taking advantage of the opening.

'It's a busy place,' Jules said with some sort of censoring look towards Tess. 'Especially at this time of year.'

'Hey, Jules!' A young man with a cute smile and a schooner of beer ambled over. 'Finally realised you can't live without me?'

'Yeah—that's it, Mal. It's weighed on me too long.'

His grin got bigger. 'How was it in the big city?'

'Busy. I didn't see you ride today.'

'Horse picked up a stone in his hoof yesterday. Bruised his heel.' His gaze shifted to Indy with interest. 'Hi.'

'And I'm forgotten,' Jules commented with amusement.

'Hi,' Indy returned.

'Town newbie or just passing through?' he asked.

'Yet to be determined.'

'When you figure it out let me know.' He winked.

'Sorry. Taken,' she lied.

He sighed dramatically. 'All the best ones are. Ladies.'

He sauntered off and Jules shot Indy a questioning look. 'You're taken?'

Indy made a pfft sound. 'No.'

Jules grinned, then her eyes slid away. Indy followed their direction and hit a set of brown eyes that shifted quickly from Indy to Jules. Tall and attractive, the man exchanged brief smiles with Jules and continued past.

'You seem to have a few admirers,' Indy commented.

'Kyle Cartwright,' Tess said. 'Mason's big brother.'

'Oh.'

'He's all right,' Jules said. 'For the most part, the Cartwrights are.'

They were still sitting there as the crowd slowly thinned and the loud enthusiasm of early evening quietened to happy, relaxed chatter. Indy was enjoying the conversation bouncing around her, though much of it was like an alien language. She must have looked lost when they started discussing Livamol, because Tess leant over and explained it was a feed supplement.

'Right. I guess I'll pick some of this stuff up if I hang around.' She fought back a yawn and slouched tiredly back against her seat.

'Where is he?' The loud gravelly growl came from the direction of the doorway, and had her jolting to attention. A block of a man with too much snow-white hair barged through a small group of patrons standing by the door, and dropped his hands onto their table, stared at Tess. Bloodshot eyes, a slight sway, pissed-off fury. Indy tensed, ready for anything.

'Where is who?' Tess asked innocently.

'That bastard—Atherton!'

'Which one?'

With a frustrated snarl, he leant in closer. The stale odour of sweat and beer had Indy's nose crinkling. 'The one that killed my daughter!'

The rowdiness of the pub dulled to a quiet chatter, then an almost eerie quiet as Tess considered the drunk. 'I'm sorry,' she said coolly, 'I don't know one of those.'

He jerked one hand from the table and Indy's automatically shot out to catch it, but he simply pointed a finger in Tess's face. 'You tell him, he's not getting away with this. Sick bastard. If my daughter ends up floating in the river like the one they've already pulled out, he'll be face down with the fish before he can spit!'

Marge shuffled across the room and put a hand on his arm. 'Right, that's enough beers for you, Warren. Come on.'

'He's taken another one—now he's going to kill my daughter!'

'Calm down, mate, let's get you home.' Marge led him outside and the noise level increased as patrons returned to their business.

Tess turned a curious look on Indy. 'Thanks for running interference. I wasn't sure he wouldn't take a pot shot that time.' Her voice was light but the colour had leached from her face. Bravado, Indy recognised, wearing off.

'What's he talking about?' she asked.

'That's Warren Bailey,' Jules told her. 'His daughter disappeared a while back. He's got this idea in his head that it's Logan's fault.'

Bailey ... she remembered the surname. It belonged to Gretchen, who'd gone missing following the discovery of Latisha's body, after allegedly not showing up for dinner with Logan. 'Disappeared?' she prompted. 'Why would it be Logan's fault?'

'She was always disappearing,' Jules said with a careless shrug. 'Warren's a mean drunk and was an abusive husband and father. Gretchen's mother got sick—had a terminal disease. She wanted to be close by but didn't want to stay at home so she did some work for us and stayed in the bunkhouse. When her mother died, I guess Gretchen had just had enough and left. You want another beer?'

'No, thanks. I don't really drink much,' she replied as she thought Jules's words over. That was a different story than she'd gotten from Mark. He'd said neither Gretchen nor Caroline had any family issues. Resentment towards an abusive father could see Gretchen take off without filling him in on her plans. But what reason would she have for not mentioning anything to her friends—the friends who had given her a job and a place to stay? The circumstances still sounded too much like Latisha's. Seeing an opportunity to press further, she asked, 'He said something about some girl in the river?'

'Some local guys found a body in the Tyenna River last year,' Tess said. 'She'd been missing a couple of years before she was discovered. It's a bit weird.'

There was concern in her face, but nothing that hinted she knew more than she was saying. 'And he's blaming Logan for that too?'

'Warren's always tended to put two and two together and get five,' Jules said. 'Especially when he's been drinking. He likes to put the blame anywhere but on his own shoulders, so of course Gretchen wouldn't take off because he drove her away. No, it's much more likely one of her closest friends dumped a woman in the local river and took Gretchen hostage.' She rolled her eyes. 'Some things never change around here.'

'So ... you're not worried something bad might have happened to Gretchen? Like what happened to that other girl?'

'I told you,' Jules said, eyeing Indy suspiciously. 'She didn't want to hang around here with her father living in town. Can't blame her for that.'

Tess still wasn't looking comfortable. 'I think we'll call it a night,' she said, pushing to her feet. 'See you tomorrow, Indy.'

Indy didn't really blame her. Having an angry drunk cause a scene like that wasn't pleasant. She'd held her ground with Warren Bailey—just—but the confrontation and discussion had left her shaken. Regardless of whether she had any further information that might be of value to the case, Tess didn't share Jules's confidence that Gretchen had left of her own accord.

CHAPTER

4

Indy checked herself out of the pub just as the Calico Mountain shuttle bus pulled up. Through the window, she saw a dozen people already seated and a few more waiting to board, carrying that air of excited expectation that followed people on holidays heading out to have a good time.

A neatly presented man with a polo shirt, name badge and a big, friendly smile stepped out of the bus. 'Morning.'

'Morning. I'm catching a ride with you. I'm not sure where Tess and Jules are.'

'Won't be far away. I'm Bob. Let me get you loaded up.' He opened a compartment on the side of the bus and slid her pack inside. A few people stepped off the bus to stretch their legs, chatting and laughing. Indy looked around, saw Tess approaching with an overnight bag slung over her shoulder.

'Hi, Tess.'

'Morning, Indy—you still coming out today?'

'Love to. Where's Jules?'

'She'll be here in a sec.' She gestured to the bus. 'Got a load this morning.'

'Does everyone come in on public transport?'

'No—though most of the people that come from the airport do.'

A man approached from behind the shuttle bus with a long, easy stride. Tall and lean, with broad shoulders, dark hair, dark eyes, he seemed to be heading for Tess. 'Latecomer?' Indy asked.

'Who? Oh, that's my brother, Connor. Hi!' Tess greeted him.

Was it the country air that did it? Indy stared into the face of another gorgeous man. Connor Atherton; the one who had been out of town during two of the abductions, she remembered. So Connor and Tess were siblings, making Logan his cousin. She wondered if there were any more Athertons floating around.

'Hi,' Connor greeted Tess. 'Congrats. I heard you nailed your comp.'

She shrugged carelessly. 'It was only the novice. I wanted to give Bramble a run. How was Hobart?'

'Long and boring, but the contracts for the cattle are sorted. I just dropped in to fuel up and see if you were still around. Did Logan go home yesterday?'

'Yeah. He took the truck and the horses back. He had to take a guest ride out this morning. Connor, this is Indy. She's after some work.'

Connor's smile was warm and friendly. 'Hi. And great. Nice to meet you.' He shook her hand and his grip was firm before he let go and turned his attention back to Tess. 'Looks like everyone's on board.'

'I'm just waiting for—And here she comes.'

Connor visibly stiffened, his expression setting itself into a cool mask. Jules's face also closed up, and the uncomfortable silence was like a heavy blanket descending on them as the two of them spent several seconds staring at one another. Connor eventually spoke first. 'Hi Jules. How are you?'

Jules's smile was forced. 'Hi, Connor. I'm fine, thanks.'

He nodded and looked at his sister. 'I'll see you at home.'

The scenery on the journey out to Calico Mountain was impressive. Around every corner, over every hill was another postcard-worthy picture. Pretty farmland, a smattering of tidy towns, then natural bushland took over. The bus turned off the main road, and after driving to what seemed like the ends of the earth, the bush gave way to green fields and the fields to rainforest, which closed in around them with cool creeks and tall tree ferns, lichen-covered boulders and ancient trees. Then another long bend and a pebble creek where forest again opened up to a clearing and Indy gasped at the majesty of the view. Stretched out in front of her was a long paddock of lush pasture. Another pebble creek cut through their path and was crossed via a low, wooden bridge. Pine trees speared towards the sky and wildflowers flirted with the tall grass in bursts of colour. In the distance, a large timber building stood proudly, framed by stunning mountains. Scattered around it were several smaller buildings and paddocks bordered by dark-stained post-and-rail fences.

'This place is beautiful,' Indy breathed.

'You should see it in autumn,' Tess told her. 'My grandparents planted 200 maples into that mountain. They turn every colour from gold through to red. They're spectacular.' The shuttle pulled up in a circular drive and Indy let the guests file off the bus before getting up.

'This is the guesthouse,' Tess told her. It was all red wood and glass and wide verandahs. 'Connor and I have apartments up the top. And that house you can see on the ridge in the distance—that's

Logan's place. Behind that hill over there is my mum and dad's house.'

Indy set that information to memory and grabbed her pack when Jules began unloading bags. 'Calico Mountain started off as a cattle property. When cattle prices fell for a few years back in the eighties, my parents opened it up for tourists and it just went from there.' She picked up the handles of two bags and started lugging. 'Come in.'

She was led through glass doors and into a vast, impressive room with high ceilings, dual staircases and windows showcasing the mountains. To her left was reception, and to her right was a large guest room complete with two fireplaces, lounges, tables and chairs. Books and magazines were scattered around, and a tourist shelf was brimming with local attractions. Enormous rugs covered the floors, the fires were glowing.

'Kaicey will handle the check-ins. This way.' Indy followed Tess and Jules through the guest room and into an area she decided must be a staff lounge. It was smaller, but had its own fireplace and inviting furniture designed for comfort. A small kitchenette held mugs, and tea- and coffee-making facilities. In the far corner by the fireplace a couple of older men in company polos played pool on a half-size table. Sharing a lounge near a window that showed off the mountains were a couple who Indy decided very quickly, by their features, could be Tess's parents.

Tess strode across the room. 'Hi, Mum, Dad.'

'Tess.' Like Tess, the woman was tall and willow slim, with large green eyes and a lovely smile. She hugged her daughter. 'I heard Bramble behaved herself?'

'Worked like a dream,' Tess confirmed, moving to embrace her father, a solid man with an easy smile Indy immediately fell for.

'And won,' Jules added, stepping in behind Indy.

'Jules!' Tess's mother wrapped her arms around the younger woman and hugged her with genuine affection. Then she held her at arm's length and studied her. 'Look at you. You're just getting lovelier. We've missed you.'

'We certainly have.' Tess's father's hug lifted Jules off her feet. 'Shouldn't stay away so long.'

'This is Indy,' Tess introduced. 'Indy, my mother, Rosalie, and my father, Murphy. Mum, Dad, Indy's here to interview for some work.'

'Well, that's good to hear.' Rosalie smiled in greeting. 'Hello, Indy.'

'Hello.' Indy's hand was engulfed in Murphy's friendly handshake. 'If you have any references on you Indy, I've got some time now,' he told her. 'Save making you wait around.'

'Thank you.' Indy dug in her pack for her résumé and handed it to him. When he sat, she followed suit.

'Well, I want to hear everything,' Rosalie told Jules, 'but I'm sure you want to unpack and freshen up—see your mum. Why don't we meet back here in half an hour or so, for some afternoon tea and a catch-up?'

'Sounds great,' Jules said, then she spoke to Tess. 'I'll just go let Mum know I'm here.'

Tess nodded and sat next to Indy, watching Murphy read over her résumé.

'You've come over from the States then,' he began. 'You like it here?'

'Very much.'

'I must admit I haven't heard of these places you worked. Then again, I've never been over there.' He closed the folder and sat back, looked Indy over. 'I'll be honest, Indy. We need to replace some staff, your references read well and it looks like you know a bit about the hospitality industry. I'll have to do a quick check of criminal records and the like, but assuming you check out and you're a hardworking, honest young lady with a half-decent head on your shoulders, you can consider yourself hired. We do a two-week trial, make sure we're happy on both sides, then we'll contract you for the rest of the season. You get standard minimum wage with meals and accommodation included. Suit you?'

'Perfectly.' Indy's face broke into a smile. 'Thank you Mr Atherton.'

'It's Murphy. Round here we're not much on formality. Tess, maybe you could show Indy round while I get on to this.' He waved the résumé in the air.

'Love to.' They walked down the hall. 'That was relatively pain-less, wouldn't you say?' Tess asked.

'Your parents are lovely.'

'I think so.' Tess stopped at the reception office. The young woman on the other side of the desk smiled in welcome.

'Indy this is Kaicey. She runs the reception and activity bookings,' Tess said. As she spoke, she quickly keyed a code into a side door. Indy memorised the numbers. 'Technically I shouldn't do this until your résumé checks out, but I'm on a tight schedule this afternoon and I have a feeling the rest is just going to be a bit of a formality so …' Indy waited while she went in, had a quick conversation with Kaicey and reappeared with a room card in a cardboard slip. 'Grab your pack and let's go.'

Instead of heading out the front doors they walked back through the common rooms and down a corridor, then out a side exit into a garden.

'There's a bunkhouse just around the corner with rooms for everyone who stays and works here. They're basic but comfortable, and there's a nice lounge and kitchen area that's communal, though you get your meals in the guesthouse,' Tess told Indy.

Across a stretch of lawn and around a bend hidden by an island of trees, Indy saw a long narrow building in the same style as the guesthouse. A verandah ran the length of the front with several steps leading up to the front door. 'This main entry generally stays unlocked.'

They walked into a space with a couple of lounges, a TV and a kitchenette, then through to a hallway that ran in two directions. Tess waved a hand to the left. 'Guys' bathroom is up that end, girls' is up this way. We're usually full at this time of year but not this season …' Tess went along the corridor and unlocked one of the rooms. 'This is one of the larger rooms.'

There was a window looking past the verandah and over a garden. 'This is nice,' Indy said.

'Then assuming all goes to plan, it's yours. There are two other women staying in here at present—Kaicey who you just met and Rachel, who helps with the food service. And four guys—Mitch, Bob, Ned and Mick. They're stockmen and maintenance staff. Nice guys—easy to get along with. Like I said, meals are in the lodge. For guests we offer a choice of buffet or fine dining. Staff get buffet meals included. We give you a couple of our shirts to wear on duty. There's a laundry next to the bathroom. If you need to go into town we run a shuttle bus every second day for the guests out to the national park sites and it stops in town, and we have a car for staff use—first-in best-dressed basis.'

'All sounds great.'

'Have a walk around, explore. When you're done, come and have afternoon tea with us in the staffroom.'

'I will. Thanks.' She left her pack in her room, then did as suggested and wandered through the lawn paths between gardens of azaleas and other flowering shrubs she couldn't name that were shadowed by golden elm trees, willows and maples. She breathed in the perfumed air and found herself smiling as she looked past the trees to the mountains.

Looking at the mountains, her smile faded. It was a beautiful spot, but women were dying out here. She needed to get this sorted. Fast.

Indy found Tess and the others in the staffroom, with antipasto platters and bottles of champagne. She hesitated at the door; she was a new member of staff, not a family friend, and they were celebrating Jules's return.

'Indy. Hi. Come in,' Jules said.

'I don't want to intrude.'

'We're in the staffroom,' Rosalie reminded her. 'If we wanted privacy we'd do this at my house. Indy, this is Nat, Jules's mum. She runs the restaurant. Come in and have a glass of champagne. Celebrate your new job here.'

'Thank you. Hello, Nat.'

Nat had a warm smile and a kind face. 'Hello, Indy. Lovely to meet you.'

'Your résumé all checked out,' Murphy told Indy. 'And Connor just got back so I'm sure he'll talk to you shortly about where to put you.'

'I'll talk to her now,' Connor said from the doorway. He strode in, eyes spitting with anger. 'But not about a job. At least, not one working for us.'

'Connor!' Tess snapped in surprise.

'You shouldn't hire anyone until I've checked them out.'

'Are you out of your mind?' Jules interrupted icily. 'This place is one step away from closing the doors. Everyone's working double and triple shifts to keep it going and you're playing the usual "Connor controls the world" bullshit?'

The silent standoff spoke volumes. And Mr Volatility had Indy wondering if she should move the investigation from Logan to Connor, regardless of Mark's report having ruled him out.

Connor lifted his brow at Indy. 'You want to tell everyone who you really are, or will I do it?'

He *knew*? How the hell had he found out? She felt the colour drain from her face. She couldn't admit anything. Wouldn't. 'I don't understand. What are you talking about?'

'Connor, what's going on?' Murphy asked him.

Connor's eyes never left Indy's. 'She's lying to you. She's come here to get information on us.'

Ben's words echoed in her head. *If you think any of them have the slightest doubt about your cover at any stage, you'll get out of there immediately.*

She needed to leave without the situation escalating. But how? She scrambled for something to say. 'I told you,' she began more forcefully, 'I don't know what you're talking about. Tess, Jules, I thought I'd give this a go, even though everyone warned me not to—because I had a great time with you both over the weekend. But I'm not going to stand here being threatened. I don't know what happened to all those women the people back in Hamilton were talking about, but that on top of this—him—I think I've made a mistake.'

'Not bad,' Connor muttered, 'Are you an actress, too?'

'Sorry for wasting your time Murphy and Rosalie.' With one last glance around she headed for the door.

'Great,' Jules exclaimed to the room in general. 'If it's not the gossips in town scaring them off, it's bloody Connor!'

She headed straight for the bunkhouse, bitter disappointment churning in her gut. She'd achieved nothing. This whole thing had been a waste of time.

She hefted her pack onto her shoulders, and left the keycard in the door. As soon as she was out of sight she'd call Mark, have him collect her. Aware of the lengthening shadows, she picked up her pace.

'Wait!' Connor called out from the guesthouse as she made her way past. He jogged down the stairs. 'I said wait, damn it! I want to talk to you. I want to talk to your damn boss!'

She turned and glared. She was holding onto her temper by a thin thread and managed to keep her voice low and even. 'I'm not sure what you think you know about me, but I wouldn't suggest you try to stop me leaving.' She kept that glare pinned on him for several seconds, then spun back around, almost collided with a rider on a big black horse that seemed to have appeared out of nowhere. She looked up into the face under the hat, and Logan Atherton's ice-blue eyes stared back with a cool intensity that just about halted the breath in her lungs.

'Hello again.' His voice was as deep as she remembered and those eyes were just as piercing. Hypnotic, she thought, then gave herself a mental shake and noted several more horses and riders appearing from the edge of the trees to gather around. When she turned back, Logan's glance was bouncing between her and Connor. He shifted around in his saddle. 'Mel—take the group back. I'll catch up,' he said.

A slim young woman with a crop of short brown hair moved past them on a pretty grey horse. 'No worries, Logan.'

Indy ignored the woman's curious stare, and once the string of riders were out of the way, she made to step around Logan's horse. As she moved left, the horse swung sideways in one smooth, economical movement, blocking her path.

How was she going to get out of here if they were all intent on preventing her from leaving? Her initial anger at the situation was suddenly tinged with nerves. 'What do you think you're doing?' she demanded.

'Just hold on.' Then to Connor, 'Problem?'

'I'll tell you about it when I get her back inside.'

'I'm not coming back inside,' she told Connor. 'Excuse me,' she said to Logan. This time she got around the horse and moved quickly to put some space between them.

There was a frustrated breath and Connor's footsteps crunched on the gravel behind her. 'I'm not letting her walk out of here. Can you do something?' he asked Logan.

'Like what, exactly … get a rope on her?'

Indy's step faltered. He couldn't be serious. Hell, she didn't need this. She needed to figure out what had happened. Had the senator opened his mouth? Had someone in the station overheard her talking to Mark? Whatever had happened it'd ruined the chance to keep a closer eye on Logan. She could only hope Caroline didn't pay the price.

Approaching hoof beats warned her he was coming, and the horse caught up and ambled along beside her. A minute passed, then another.

It occurred to her she was distancing herself from the guesthouse, from the people there, and heading off on an isolated strip of road in the middle of nowhere with her prime suspect. The danger didn't escape her, but nor did the opportunity. Logan didn't—yet— know who she was. This could be her only chance to get a gauge on him before he found out.

She took a quick glance over her shoulder. He was sitting relaxed in the saddle, taking in the scenery as though he didn't have a care, or a schedule, in the world. 'You're planning on following me … how far exactly?'

'It's a long way to town. When you've walked off the mad, I'd like to talk to you.'

She wondered why, wondered how he would react if she refused to cooperate. 'I'll hitch.'

'You damn well won't,' he growled. 'Hold up.'

She stopped, then cursed as she realised she'd done what she was told. Again. The guy radiated an absolute authority that was extraordinary.

A good trait for a serial killer.

'Look, I don't know what happened with Connor, but it can't have been that bad.' His expression held amusement. 'His face is still intact.' And oh yeah, as expected, the guy's eyes softened like a summer's day when he turned on the warmth. 'But whatever he said,' Logan continued easily, 'I reckon he could be forgiven because Jules just got back and he's going to be feeling between a rock and a hard place for a while. She doesn't like him much.'

'And if I was hanging around, we could start a club. But I'm not,' she shot at him, and resumed walking.

He sighed, but let her get far enough away to have her wonder if he was giving up, before calling out, 'You don't really want me to rope you, do you?'

'What?' She turned as the horse again caught up, another witty comment on the tip of her tongue. It died there. She wasn't sure from his expression if he was kidding. A tingle of apprehension put her on alert as she realised she could be about to get a very good idea of who this man really was. 'Back off! Just back the hell off!'

Instead, he slid from the saddle and towered over her. 'You can't walk right back to town and I'm not letting you hitch. So … you want to walk back, or am I putting you on this horse?'

It didn't matter that he was standing by casually, she had no doubt that underneath he had the reflexes of a panther. And the tone didn't leave room for argument. What exactly would he do if she refused? She wanted to find out, but this situation wasn't safe. He was large and agile, and even with her self-defence skills, she wasn't convinced he couldn't overpower her. And there'd be no outrunning him with that horse. She considered her options, couldn't find one she liked.

'Well?' He shifted his weight and instinctively she took several quick steps backwards. She caught the smirk, a second before he hid it under his hat by dropping his gaze down to study the ground.

Funny, yeah, absolutely freaking hilarious.

He looked up again and his eyes, amused but kind, had her questioning the intensity of the last few seconds. 'It's Indy, right?'

'Yeah. So?'

'So let's go sort this out, Indy.' He made a sweeping gesture with his arm in the direction of the guesthouse.

She started back to give herself more time to think. She'd have to keep denying she was anyone but Jacinda Brown, and call Mark—get him to get her out of there by nightfall.

Connor was standing with Tess and Jules on the front steps and she headed for them. The expression on Tess's face was as cool as Connor's. Jules just looked pissed off. 'I'm not going back inside,' she told Connor. 'I'm going to call someone to pick me up. Until they get here, you can—'

'Are you really from a newspaper?' Tess cut in sharply.

Indy didn't need to fake the blank look. 'What?'

'She has no idea what you're talking about,' Jules snapped at Connor. 'Just like she said.'

Tess's stare was assessing. 'If you're telling the truth, come back inside. I'm hoping this is just a misunderstanding.'

'I'll put the horse away, catch up,' Logan promised. With a long, considering look at Indy, he led his horse away.

Logan headed back towards the stables, hurried the horse along just a bit more than the gelding's normal ambling walk allowed for.

When he tossed his head in objection and gave a half-hearted tug at the reins, Logan chuckled. 'Come on Brodie, your feed's waiting.' He didn't want to miss too much of what was going on back at the guesthouse, found himself needing to know the outcome of that discussion. But he slowed his pace a touch, told himself she'd still be there when he got back.

Or she wouldn't. It'd be a damn shame if she was working for a newspaper. He'd enjoyed watching her take on Mason the night before, been pleased to hear from Tess that she was coming out here in search of some work. But a reporter? He scowled down at his boots. That would end badly. He couldn't afford to have one of those sticking their nose in. Not again. Especially with Caroline still fresh in people's minds.

He rounded the bend that brought the stables into view and saw Mel in the mounting yard helping guests unsaddle horses. As he got closer he called out and met her at the gate. 'Take Brodie for me, would you?'

'What's going on?'

'Not sure yet. Thanks.' He closed the gate behind Mel and Brodie and headed for the ute. He reckoned there was a good chance from the look he'd seen on Indy's face that she wasn't a reporter. But it had occurred to him to wonder why she'd chosen to come out here for work when she had to have heard the stories in town. If there'd been any doubt of that it would have been erased when he'd caught the suspicion in her cool blue eyes back out on the road, and she'd been so keen to keep some distance from him. Couldn't blame her for that—thanks to Robinson and his damn investigation. He had found her quick retreat at least a little amusing, though, if for no other reason than she seemed so damn determined to be brave. He enjoyed women who challenged him. So he started the ute and pointed it towards the guesthouse, hoping she was who she said she was. It'd be a nice distraction to hold on to her for a while. Or maybe more than a while, if he had his way.

Indy followed Tess back into the staffroom, followed by Connor and Jules. Her mind was racing. Working for a newspaper? Where the hell did Connor get that from? And even as she wondered, relief—and hope that this might not be over—had her calming down, getting back into the persona of Jacinda. Because regardless of where he'd gotten the idea, her cover wasn't blown.

Rosalie and Murphy were still there, and Rosalie gestured for her to sit.

'Don't get too comfortable,' Connor warned. 'I know what you're up to.'

'What's that exactly?' Rosalie asked.

'I ran into Mason at the campdraft.'

Jules folded her arms and sniggered. 'How did he look?'

'Not pretty. Apparently someone broke his nose,' he said with a steely look at Indy.

'You broke his nose?' Murphy asked Indy with a frown.

'He was beating up his horse,' Tess told him.

Murphy's face settled into a comfortable smile. 'Well then, that's reasonable.'

'If we can all focus on the real issue here?' Connor snapped. 'While I was getting that story, Eddie Smith turned up, came over to say hello.'

'Your mate from the paper?' Tess asked.

'He was there covering a story related to the campdraft, said it was lucky he ran into me. Apparently one of his junior reporters back at the office had copped a phone call a couple of days before from some woman from a mainland publication. She was asking questions about missing women and who it would be best to talk to out here. When he finally convinced her we wouldn't talk to her, she made some joke that perhaps she might have to come down here looking for some work.'

'Oh dear,' Rosalie said. 'We knew the story would hit the mainland once a senator's daughter was involved.' Rosalie lifted her gaze from the floor and turned soft, kind eyes on Indy. 'Indy, we could never do anything to those girls. People that work here become like family to us. They live here, work with us, share meals with us—'

'Don't panic yet, Mum,' Tess interrupted gently. But when her gaze hit Indy's it was hard. It didn't need to be. Indy genuinely felt sorry for Rosalie. The woman didn't appear to have a nasty bone in her body.

'No, don't,' Jules said to Rosalie, echoing Tess. 'Because this is ridiculous. That woman could have been anyone and you've already decided it's Indy?' Jules scoffed.

'Oh come on Jules, what are the chances? The paper gets that call, and within a couple of days this one walks into town when we're all there, hears all the rumours and still wants to work for us? And I won't have her here spying on us—whether you've all decided she's your new best friend or not!' There was a thoughtful silence, and a muscle worked in Connor's jaw as he considered them. 'Do I need to remind anyone what happened two weeks ago?'

'No,' Tess said. 'And you're right to be cautious. We don't need any more trouble. But to me it seems like a pretty dumb thing for a reporter to announce she was going to sneak in here if she actually meant it. I think you should hear Indy out.'

'Under the circumstances, I'm not risking it. We'll find someone else. We've had a few responses to our latest set of ads.'

Indy wasn't sure what had happened two weeks earlier, but it didn't slip her attention that Connor was very quick to believe someone was poking around—and was very on edge about it.

'I'm not a reporter,' Indy said calmly. 'Why don't you have your friend Eddie call back the number she called through on, find out if you can talk to her? After all, that's what she wanted, right—a conversation?'

'Yeah—do that,' Jules said. 'Meanwhile, Indy, please stay. We need help.'

Connor's furious gaze turned on Jules. 'You think you can just walk back in here and—'

'Damn straight,' Jules snapped. 'We need staff badly enough that despite the fact I'd rather visit the depths of hell than spend time with you—here I am. And Indy's here, wanting to work!'

'Connor, why don't you call Eddie,' Rosalie suggested. 'You'll feel better if you check.'

'Fine.' He did. Right in front of them. And got the number. 'Where's your phone?' he asked Indy.

There was no way in hell she was giving him her phone but she pulled it from her pocket, watched him dial the number and frown as the seconds ticked on. Eventually he hung up. 'No answer, no voicemail. That's not right.'

'Well whoever it is, it's not Indy,' Jules said. 'So can we move on?'

Connor's scowl moved. 'I'm not convinced. And I'm going over your résumé with a fine-tooth comb. If you're not who you say you are, I'm calling the police.'

'Murphy's already checked her résumé,' Rosalie said. Then to Indy, 'We understand if you don't want to work for us now. We're very sorry for the upset.'

The résumé would check out, she knew it would. Because Ben had arranged it that way. But after this, there would be a cloud of suspicion following her around that would make it very difficult to investigate the case without raising more doubt. Still, she wondered if perhaps this could work in her favour. If whoever was taking these women was here, the idea a reporter might be poking around could stir him into making a mistake.

It was a risk. Just the possibility she was a threat could be enough to see her disappear like the others. But under the circumstances, she wasn't ready to concede defeat.

She took a steadying breath before answering. She couldn't do a complete backflip. 'I'm not sure about this.' She looked at Tess. 'But I need the work, so I suppose I could start the trial. If I'm not comfortable, I'll leave.'

'Sounds fair,' Tess said.

Connor lifted and dropped his hands in a frustrated gesture.

Murphy cleared his throat. 'It looks like you've worked in a few different basic hospitality positions in the past. What are you good at?'

Indy dragged her gaze away from Connor's hard stare. 'I can do office work, clean ... I like working outdoors and I'm not bad in the garden. Anything else, I can learn.'

'Logan's rushed off his feet,' Jules said.

'And we need a cleaner, and someone else on reception for a few hours a day wouldn't hurt,' Tess reminded them. 'Besides, we'd have to check with Logan—'

'Sold.' Everyone glanced behind them. Logan had appeared in the doorway, his expression unreadable. 'Another set of hands around the stables will mean I can lead out some of the activities we've had to cancel recently.'

Perfect. 'I don't know the first thing about that sort of work, but I wouldn't mind giving it a go.' She worked a cautious smile onto her face and aimed it at Logan.

'And that's good,' Jules quickly added. 'Logan really hates retraining people that think they know their stuff.'

'That's settled then,' Rosalie said. 'The more Logan can stretch himself out, the better. There are forms to fill out, will you take care of it Connor?'

Connor's glare didn't inspire confidence. 'Follow me.'

Indy's gaze again brushed Logan's as she moved across the room. A considering smile touched the corners of his mouth, his eyes probing hers just enough to make her uncomfortable. She managed to keep her smile in place, but it cooled dramatically under the direct challenge of that stare. *Just try and intimidate me,* she told him silently. *See how that works out.*

She headed through the guesthouse and up the stairs after Connor, followed him to his office and looked around. It was neatly ordered: books, folders, rows of external drives in containers marked 'tax', 'shifts', 'schedules' and 'misc'. Her résumé dropped on Connor's desk and he fished out some paperwork, bringing her eyes back to him. 'You need to fill these forms in. I'll be checking them carefully. You'd better be who you say you are.' There was threat in the tone that he didn't make any effort to temper.

She opened her mouth to tell him again that she wasn't a reporter, but she bit down on the words and kept them to herself. It would be better to keep him guessing. She was here to investigate Logan, but she was going to be keeping a very close eye on Connor, too.

Because Connor Atherton was either very anti-media or hiding something.

Maybe he was both.

CHAPTER

5

'How'd you go?' Jules asked, appearing from the office as Indy came downstairs. 'Employment forms done?'

'Yes. Connor was ...' Indy smiled wryly, '... straight to the point.'

'What are you up to now?'

'I'm not entirely sure.'

'Let's go see Tess, get you set up.'

She followed Jules to reception, where Tess was checking out a couple of guests. 'Are you staying here?' she asked Jules as they waited.

'No. Mum's got a place in town. I only get down here once or twice a year so she wants to make the most of my visit.'

'Hi,' Tess said, joining them. 'What are you two up to?'

'How are you going for time?' Jules asked Tess. 'Indy needs her staff uniform and I can't remember the code.'

'The code is Dad's birthday, but I'll come down with you. I'll just have to be quick. I'm meant to be minding the office while Kaicey is on her break.'

The phone rang and Tess did a one-eighty, answered it and took a booking.

'Sorry,' Tess said, locking the reception office door behind them and leading them down the corridor. 'The supply room's over near the staffroom,' she said for Indy's benefit. 'Shouldn't take long.'

'Another booking?' Jules inquired.

'We're still down by eight guests from where we were last week.'

'Yet you all seem so busy,' Indy noted. 'Still hiring more staff.'

'Dad says if we start cutting back on services and activities because we have less guests, that it's the beginning of the end. But we lost a few staff with all the negative media attention, so in order to keep everything running smoothly, we're taking on extra shifts. We just have to ride it through,' Tess explained with a shrug. 'We're cutting prices and doing lots of deals to draw more guests in. Here we are.'

The storage room was stacked with shelves of plastic containers. Tess brushed her gaze over Indy, reached for one and opened it up. 'I think you'd be about the same size as me. These should fit.' She pulled a shirt from its plastic bag, held it up, nodded and handed it to her, then grabbed her another. Then she put the container back, reached for another one. 'I'll give you two hats as well. You'll need more than one. You can replace this at any stage but the rest come out of your pay.'

'Sounds reasonable.'

'I'd be inclined to run them through the wash before you wear them. And don't forget dinner's buffet between five and nine. You can eat in the casual dining room or in the staffroom, you just need to make sure you're neatly dressed for the dining room. I'll be down there around seven if you want some company.'

'Along with everyone else,' Jules said. 'It'd be a good chance for Tess to introduce you to a few more of the staff.'

'That'd be great, actually.'

'Good. I'd better get back. And Indy? Thanks for giving this a go. Despite the rumours this is actually a great place to work. You'll get to know Logan when you're working for him—realise how silly the accusations are.'

Would she? She wasn't so sure.

Indy took Tess's advice and used the laundry, then got on her laptop to do some work. She sent Ben an email outlining the situation at Calico Mountain, then erased all sign of it from her computer before looking up everything she could find on Connor Atherton. He did appear to have strong alibis for the time of both Gretchen's and Caroline's disappearances. So what was he hiding? Or was he simply sick of the media interfering with their business?

Restless, and with plenty of time until dinner, she found herself wandering the gardens. Around the front of the guesthouse and along another drive, she wound her way through heavier stands of trees to the stables. One long stable building with a breezeway stood surrounded by a couple of large sheds, a small and a large round yard, several turnout yards and beyond them, a few larger paddocks.

She wandered through the breezeway, past an office, a large tack room and a feed room, then stroked the heads of a couple of curious horses in clean stables. At the other end the breeze was stronger and briskly cool, and carried the perfume of pine and eucalyptus. The landscape gradually dropped away and paddocks ran down green grassy slopes where horses grazed peacefully.

The view that stretched to the mountains beyond was spectacular. It was so lovely she climbed onto the post-and-rail fence and sat staring at it while she thought about what she knew so far, bouncing ideas and impressions around in her mind. The Athertons were a cohesive unit with what appeared to be a well-run business, though

Jules coming back was an obvious upset to the norm. Rosalie and Murphy seemed lovely at first glance, and Tess was smart and genuine. Jules had surprised Indy with her bravado towards Connor, mostly due to her size and generally bubbly personality. Jules's mum Nat had made an effort to be nice, and she'd caught a welcoming smile from one of the two older men playing pool earlier in the staffroom. She'd have to make an effort to get to know each of the staff, fit in as many casually probing conversations as possible. There certainly didn't seem to be any tension between the staff and family, except for what she had witnessed between Jules and Connor, and despite what was going on everyone seemed relaxed and at home here. But initial impressions weren't always correct. Time would tell. She'd make more accurate profiles on everyone as she got to know them.

She was a million miles away with her thoughts when footsteps jolted her back.

'Easy,' Logan murmured. He was carrying a saddle on one lean, muscled arm and a bridle was draped over the other. 'Everything okay?'

'Yep. I was just taking a look around. Did you want something?'

'I'm not exactly sure I've figured that out yet.' The comment had her sending him a sideways look as he dropped the saddle on the fence rail, and placed the bridle over it. 'You chose a good place to end up.'

'It's a gorgeous view.'

He leant on the fence and she watched him in her peripheral vision as she pretended to stare at the countryside, every sense heightened by his presence. He exuded more than charisma or confidence, but she couldn't put her finger on exactly what it was.

'You think you'll hang around?' he asked.

She met his gaze, unsettled to feel a thousand tiny sparks run through her. Whatever it was had a lot to do with those eyes. They hinted at strength, and at … gentleness. She pulled her thoughts up with a jolt. Was that how he lured his victims?

She shrugged. 'I'll see how it goes.' A horse in the paddock in front of them lifted its head and walked up the hill towards them. The big white blaze on her face was familiar. 'Is that the horse from the campdraft? Marge told me you bought her from that abusive little turd that laid into her.'

'Her name's Aurora,' Logan said. 'And yeah, I did.'

'Why?'

He shrugged. 'Couldn't leave her where she was.'

'What are you going to do with her?'

'Nothing yet. She's just got to learn the routine—get used to the sights and smells and have a bit of TLC.' The horse stepped forward and Logan patted her. 'She's a good girl. She'll be a good riding horse.'

Indy wondered if a man who showed such compassion for an abused animal could be capable of abducting and killing women.

His name was called and he sighed. 'Looks like I'm needed.'

When Indy also moved, he held out his hand to help her down.

'I can manage on my own—thanks.' She dropped to the ground and dusted herself off.

His brow rose, and he dropped his hand. 'Still bristling from Connor?'

'Connor's not the one who threatened to rope me,' she said with a touch of sarcasm.

A grin spread across his face. 'I was having a go at Connor. And I thought I might have made you laugh. But you didn't laugh. And your outraged reaction was just so perfect …' She narrowed her gaze and a laugh rumbled in his throat. 'Okay, I'm sorry.'

The apology was unexpected, his humour contagious. It wasn't as difficult as it should have been to reluctantly smile back.

'And you should know,' he continued more seriously, 'two weeks ago a reporter from one of those current affairs shows turned up wanting an inside story on Caroline. She cornered Murph—hassled him. His heart isn't great, and the things she accused us of—Murphy of—had him upset enough that he had an angina attack. Connor was with him and for a few terrifying minutes, he thought he was going to lose his father. We have to make sure the wrong people don't turn up here causing trouble. It could kill him.'

Connor's furious reaction was suddenly much more understandable. 'Caroline?' she asked, playing the part.

He watched her closely. 'A woman that went missing from around here not long ago. You didn't hear?'

'I thought her name was Gretchen.'

'That's another one.'

'Seriously?' she asked in feigned surprise. 'Besides, I thought it was you, not Murphy, who was copping most of the accusations.'

He studied her deliberately wary expression and nodded slowly. 'I don't want to scare you off, but you need to be aware of it, because you'll hear plenty of stories. On that, I'd appreciate it if any questions you have could be aimed at me, rather than garnered through the grapevine.'

'Of course.'

'Thanks. And if anyone does act suspiciously nosey, let me know.' She felt a definite shiver as his mood went from friendly warmth to chilling in the blink of an eye. 'We don't have anything to hide and we're cooperating with the police. The last thing we need is another reporter in here putting things together the wrong way.' His name was called a second time, and he picked up the saddle and bridle. 'I'll see you later.'

She watched him collect his things and head back into the stables. So his story was the anti-media sentiment was based purely around protecting Murphy's health and ensuring no more negative publicity than necessary fell on the business. It sounded reasonable.

But cooperating with police? Mark had painted a very different picture.

The dining area was split into two adjoining rooms, decorated throughout in inviting tones with soft furnishings and dark polished wood. Fireplaces blazed, creating warmth and a feeling of comfort. Two long buffet tables were at one end of the larger room, one filled with steaming hot food, the other with salads and seafood. Yet another table offered an assortment of hot and cold beverages. Booths hugged walls, tables were scattered at comfortable distances. The buffet room, from the looks of the crowd, was most popular with families, while the more intimate atmosphere of the smaller room beyond, where the tables were all draped in white linen, set with flowers and candles and gleaming cutlery, contained a sprinkling of couples.

'Indy.' Jules was seated with Rosalie at a table by one of the large windows in the buffet room. 'Grab a plate and come over here.'

Indy smiled and nodded, and moved to the buffet where she ladled thick, fragrant pumpkin soup into a bowl and paired it with a small, warm sourdough roll. The scent alone had her salivating.

'You're going to eat more than that, aren't you?' Jules scoffed when she joined them.

Indy looked down at her bowl then back to Jules curiously. 'I love pumpkin soup.'

'It'll do for starters.'

'There's so much to choose from,' Indy said. 'I'd never eat this well at home. I'll explode.'

'Ha! You're working for Logan,' Jules objected.

Rosalie's grin was wicked. 'Jules is right—you need to make sure you eat up.'

'Aren't you supposed to be working?' Tess asked Jules, taking the seat next to Indy.

'Even the chef gets a break. I was starving.'

A twig of a man with slicked-back greying hair and a wide smile in a crinkly face appeared behind Tess and sat himself at the table next to theirs. 'Evening.'

'Mick,' Rosalie said in greeting. 'This is Indy. She's working here at the stables.'

'New girl, eh? Aren't you the brave one.'

'Don't go scaring her off! Connor's already had a decent go at it,' Jules warned.

'You staying in the bunkhouse?' he asked Indy.

'Yep.'

'I'll tell you all the evil Atherton stories later then—when they're not around.' He winked at her with a grin for the others. His whole demeanour was friendly and affable, and Indy instantly liked him.

'You freak her out—you're doing her work,' Tess threatened.

'I'm already picking up the slack,' he argued without complaint.

Another man walked slowly past in a Calico Mountain shirt, looked at Indy with interest. Around forty, weathered skin, hollow-cheeked with small, sharp eyes and a mat of untidy dark hair. She met his stare, got a smile, a nod. He moved on.

'Not enough for the last couple of shuttle runs.' Mick shovelled a mouthful of roast potato into his mouth and swallowed it. 'You put farting Steven on the bus again and I'm leaving.'

Tess's fork paused halfway to her mouth. 'Farting Steven?'

'The guy's been on two trips in four days and insists on sitting up the front feeling sick. By the end of it I'm greener than he is. If he thinks he's going to Queenstown on Tuesday, he's dreaming.'

Tess's face was thoughtful. 'He's with that small group that came out here for the hiking, isn't he? They're leaving tomorrow.'

Mick breathed a sigh of relief and dropped back against his chair to take a swig of water. 'Excellent.'

Indy listened to the conversations as they floated around her, learned what she could about the staff members, the routines, and helped herself to some more food. Murphy came in and out, while Connor appeared, eyed her suspiciously and sat elsewhere. She was just about to leave when Logan walked in and approached their table. 'Evening.' Then to Indy, 'You all set for tomorrow?'

'Ready to give it a go,' she said brightly.

'Be prepared for a challenge,' Jules said.

Indy's brow lifted, then dropped into a frown. 'Hopefully I won't make too much of a mess of it.'

'You'll be fine,' Tess said. 'And if not, we'll find you something else to do.'

'No, you won't,' Logan said. Then to Indy, 'Meet me at the stables at six-thirty.' He sent her another one of his penetrating stares. 'I'll make sure you don't make a mess of it.'

When her heart thumped in her chest she gave herself a mental slap. *Potentially abducting women*, she reminded herself. But that *look* ... Did he simply persuade women to disappear? Is that why there was never any evidence?

No, that wasn't true. There was evidence. There was evidence Gretchen had gotten into his ute the day she'd disappeared, and that she'd been injured. There was evidence that Caroline was supposed to have been heading out on the trails with him, and somehow her bloodied clothes had ended up hidden in the back corner of his tack room. There was evidence, all right, just not quite enough. Not yet.

When he walked away she managed to take her eyes off him and noticed all three women at the table were exchanging raised eyebrows and amused expressions. *Good, let them think I'm falling under his spell, just like Gretchen and Caroline.*

She smiled, made it a little shy. 'Is he always this ...' she gestured with her hands as though her mind had gone blank and she couldn't think of a suitable word.

'Friendly?' Jules suggested with a mocking grin. 'Intense?'

Tess shook her head. 'No,' she said to Indy, her tone full of interest. 'No, he's not.'

'I have to get back to work,' Jules said, slipping from her seat. 'Let me know how you go tomorrow, Indy.' With a wink, she disappeared into the kitchen.

She smiled at Jules, and when she turned her attention back to Tess she was deep in conversation about invoices with Rosalie. Damn. She'd wanted to play that out a little longer. Wanted to ask if he'd been 'friendly' with any other new staff, particularly Caroline. But now that conversation had moved on, she couldn't find a way to bring it back up. There'd be another opportunity. That look he'd pinned on her and the reaction from his family had pretty much guaranteed it.

CHAPTER

6

The alarm slowly penetrated her consciousness, though even once the insistent buzz had pulled her from the thick haze of sleep, it took her a moment to orient herself. Disentangling one arm from her blankets she groggily felt around on the little side table for the button. She found the alarm, but her awkward swatting sent it clattering to the ground. It kept buzzing.

'Shit.' She leant over the side of the bed, floundered in the dark and felt the cord, tugged on it, and the noise finally stopped. Whoever was in the room next door was going to be pissed off.

Though she no longer had the clock to go by, the alarm had been set for five-thirty. Freezing, because she'd left the window open all night, she kicked off the twisted blankets and sat on the edge of the bed shivering as she concentrated on getting her bearings in the darkness. After a moment's thought she stood. And walked into the wardrobe. She paused a moment until everything stopped hurting, then lifted her arms out in front and felt for the wall, the light switch. Flicking it on, she screwed her eyes closed against the shock of bright light that flooded the room. Headache? Where'd that come from—last night's long session on the laptop or her run-in with the wardrobe? Who knew? And at this time of the morning—who cared?

Teeth chattering, she pulled her jumper over the large T-shirt she slept in. It was three weeks until Christmas. This should be beach and bikini time, but she'd have felt more comfortable in a Santa suit. Grabbing what she needed, she headed for the showers.

As soon as she opened her door the warmth welcomed her and the shower cut through the last of the chill. Feeling more human, she headed back to her room to dump her things and put on her well-used boots. She'd have to invest in more clothes. What she had just wasn't going to cut it.

The guesthouse was filled with the aroma of cooking breakfast and wood smoke, and she couldn't resist taking a peek at the dining room. She found Jules setting up the buffet. 'Indy, good morning. How'd you sleep?'

'Wonderful.'

'Probably a good thing, you've got a big day today.'

'I didn't think anyone would be up yet.'

'Are you kidding? First horse ride's heading out to catch the sunrise, and we've got a group of hikers to feed in half an hour or so. You want a coffee?'

She almost groaned. 'No—I don't want to be late.'

'Okay. But follow me—two seconds.' Curious, Indy followed Jules to the back of the guesthouse and into a cloakroom. 'We keep all this stuff for the guests,' she explained, and lifted out a moleskin coat. 'This should fit. What size shoe? You should wear gumboots in the stalls ...'

Much more suitably dressed, Indy stepped outside. The cold air took her breath away. She hugged the coat more tightly around her and looked around. Dawn was breaking over the mountains in brilliant red and orange hues. Somewhere nearby a bird sang a lone chorus; further off, cattle bawled. The world was waking up.

She headed briskly towards the stables, mentally preparing herself for the day ahead. As she got closer the quiet was broken by the sound of animated chatter. About a dozen people stood in a yard by patient, saddled horses. The woman she'd seen the day before—Mel—demonstrated how to get on and the guests began attempting it with various degrees of success. There was laughter, excitement. As the last rider scrambled into the saddle, there were instructions to listen to, then they began filing out. She found herself envying them their ride. She'd have to make sure she tried it. Maybe on a day off.

She continued into the breezeway of the stable block, where a few horses still occupied stalls. They turned liquid brown eyes towards her and pricked their ears. One nickered in greeting.

'Careful!'

A bale of hay landed with a thud at her feet. After an initial scramble backwards, she looked up to see Logan hefting yet another from the loft. Two more followed before he jumped lightly down in front of her. 'You're early. Good start.'

Despite the cold, Logan was bordering on hot and sweaty; his heavy drill shirt was rolled up at the sleeves and undone, revealing a T-shirt tight over his broad chest. His jeans clung to long, muscular thighs, and his dark hair was untidy, as though he'd been running his hands through it. The surge of awareness that hit her was as powerful as it was unwelcome.

'Second thoughts?' he asked.

'No. Of course not,' she snapped, annoyed at herself.

There seemed to be a quick flash of humour in his eyes before he continued.

'Good. Then we should get started. Yesterday you said you know nothing about horses.'

'I have some friends who have horses, but I haven't had much to do with taking care of them.' She cautiously lifted a hand to stroke the face of an inquisitive small white pony. When it sneezed, she jolted, pulling her hand back.

He grinned. 'Then we'll start from scratch. We have a rotation system working. We offer a group ride each morning, and private lessons through the day. If there's enough demand we put on an extra group trail ride in the afternoon. No rides on Fridays—horses and people get a day off. Horses on the early ride come in at night, go out for the day after their ride. Horses for the afternoon lessons come in for the day, then go out at night. When we're busy some horses do both. I write up who needs to be where on the board each day so when you get to know them you can make sure everyone's in the right place. This morning, Mel's taken the trail ride—she's my assistant, so we're cleaning out the stables and feeding up.'

'Sure. What would you like me to do?'

'I'll show you.' He unlatched the stable door of the little white pony and indicated she go in. She stepped through, and when Logan came in behind her, moved again to give him some room.

Two hands immediately descended firmly onto her shoulders, pulling her back. Working on instinct and a sudden shot of adrenaline, she ducked and spun, ready for anything.

He didn't immediately speak, just watched her with what she considered to be a dangerous level of suspicion. 'Skittish little thing, aren't you?'

'I'm not a horse,' she snapped, still wary.

His expression lightened and he looked her up and down. 'No, you're definitely not. But you'll end up kicked by one if you charge around behind some of them the way you just did this one.'

'Right.' She swore silently. Because he'd only been keeping her safe and she'd been ready to take him out, in the process very nearly giving him another demonstration of her hand-to-hand combat expertise. 'Sorry.'

'This is Annie.' His voice hinted at amusement, but he was watching her closely. 'She's a real sweetheart. We had a party of three cancel last night so she and her friends here missed out this morning. We'll let them out now.'

He slipped a halter onto Annie's head and led her out. 'For the time being I'll halter them and you can help me lead out. In a few days, you'll do it yourself. Think you can hold her?'

'Sure.' She stroked the pony's soft cheek, laughed when she put her nose up and blew warm breath on her face. 'You are so cute.'

'You just about ready?' Logan asked. He had the other two horses haltered and waiting.

'Yep.'

'Follow me.'

She gave the lead a small tug and the pony followed. Not so hard. Until she walked Annie past the bales of hay. The pony stopped, dropped her head to eat. And refused to budge. Logan was getting further away. 'Ah ... come on, Annie.' She pulled on the lead. The pony just dug her heels in. She pulled again, but the pony simply looked at her for a couple of seconds then returned to eating. What now? She could wrestle a drug dealer, take down a career criminal, but she couldn't move one docile little pony?

Logan, already at the paddock gate, released his horses and turned around.

'Problem?' he called back.

'Ah ... No ...' She tried again, speaking low and conspiratorially. 'Come on, Annie. For the sake of all womankind don't make me look like an idiot. Move.' She yanked hard on the lead and, giving in, Annie quickly stepped forward. Feeling awkward under Logan's gaze, she moved out of the pony's way, tripped over the edge of another hay bale and felt the world tilt. Before she knew what had happened she was sitting on her butt. Annie stood quietly beside her, chewing happily in Indy's ear.

Despite her long coat, the ground was cold and damp. One hand stung slightly where it had grazed the concrete. Nothing was more acutely uncomfortable than her utter humiliation. Two hands under her arm easily lifted her to her feet. 'Are you all right?'

She stepped quickly away and pretended she hadn't noticed the iron-like strength of his arms, or smelled the very male, woodsy scent he wore. 'I'm fine.' She brushed herself off, and eyes pinned solidly on Annie, she recovered the lead rope. Tugged. 'Let's go!' Indy's tone was deadly. Without so much as a hint of an argument, the pony followed her down to the gate. Logan jogged ahead and opened it.

Fully prepared to dislike horses for the rest of her life, she figured out the buckle on the headstall and took it off. 'Off you go.' But instead of moving off, Annie pressed her face into Indy's chest and gently rubbed her head up and down. Indy melted instantly. 'Oh ... all right.' She stroked the pony's neck before with one last pat she turned for the gate.

Logan had a considering expression on his face that turned to a friendly smile when she caught it. Playing the part, she sent him one back, then not sure what to do, she stood there until he inclined his head. 'Come on.' In the stables, Logan handed her a stable rake and steered a wheelbarrow to the door of one of the stalls. 'Watch.' He began cleaning it, talking her through the simple process. 'Then we clean the water and refill the hay nets for the evening. I'll show you how to mix feeds later. Think you can finish off this stable?'

'Sure.' She took the rake, and did as he asked.

'Pretty good,' he commented. 'Eleven more to go.'

Oh shit. 'Okay.'

She put her back into it, grateful for the physical labour.

She worked hard—knew she was going to ache the next day, but she'd worry about that later. To challenge herself she timed how long it took her to clean each stable, averaged at ten minutes. That's how she knew she'd done around two hours straight manual labour when she straightened from dumping the last load of manure on the pile.

Logan entered the stables and walked through the breezeway assessing her work, before aiming a look of disbelief straight at her. 'You're done?'

'What's next?' she asked with oh, so much more enthusiasm than she felt.

'Mel's coming back in from the morning ride. We need to unsaddle the horses. Come and I'll show you what to do.'

The horses were walking into the yard as she followed Logan outside. He showed her how to unsaddle, how to remove dirt and sweat from the horses' coats. When they were done, she helped feed the horses that had just returned.

Finished, she stretched out her already aching muscles, pleased with herself. She was looking forward to a hot shower. Then it hit her: it was only just after nine o'clock. She still had a full day's work ahead.

'You ready?' Logan said from behind her.

She groaned inwardly—she really wasn't sure. 'For what?'

'Breakfast.'

Thank God. 'Absolutely.'

'You know, you probably shouldn't go too hard at it your first day,' he said as they began to walk towards the guesthouse.

'How long is it supposed to take?'

He hesitated. 'Probably about that long but …'

'About how long?'

He grinned down at her. 'If you can do what you did this morning with a little less help and still hit breakfast by nine or so, that's plenty fast enough. And we don't always have that number of horses to go out on the morning ride so there's not always so many stables to clean. Assuming you're planning on coming back?'

'You don't think I should?'

'Sure. You're doing well. You like horses?'

'Yes. Why?'

'I wasn't sure you'd say that after being sat on your behind by the pony. And yesterday you looked at Brodie more like he was a man-eating lion than a placid old stock horse.'

'It wasn't the horse I was glaring at,' she said pointedly.

His grin was wide and amused. 'You really believed I'd rope you?'

They reached the guesthouse and following Logan's lead, Indy took her boots off. 'That was never going to happen.'

'It wouldn't have been easy. You move pretty quick in reverse,' he laughed.

Amusement tugged at the corners of her mouth. The guy was disarming, she'd give him that. For one brief moment she allowed herself to hope he wasn't guilty. Then she quickly reeled the thought in and led through to the dining area.

'Make sure you fill yourself up. It'll be hours before lunch.'

Mel strolled over. 'Logan, Pepper's arthritis is playing up. I think we should swap her with Bandit for a couple of days.'

'Sure,' he replied easily. 'Mel, I didn't introduce you before. This is Indy, she's going to be working with us from now on.'

Mel smiled but the welcome didn't quite reach her eyes. 'Figured as much. Hi, Indy. Hope you're a harder worker than the last one.'

'I'll do what I can,' Indy replied with about as much sincerity.

'Indy. Come have coffee with me.' Indy turned to see Tess dropping into a chair. She was bleary-eyed and yawned widely.

'Okay.' Relieved to have an excuse to get away from Logan and Mel, she made herself a coffee and sat down opposite Tess. 'Are you all right?'

'Sort of. I had to clean some rooms this morning for a hen's group. They're already up there with champagne and fruit platters. How was your morning?'

'Honestly? I can't believe it's only nine o'clock.'

Tess nodded in understanding. 'Want me to have a quiet word to the slave driver?'

'No,' Indy said quickly. 'No, of course not.'

Jules wandered over and sat next to Indy, while Logan dumped a plate laden with food down next to Tess. 'Looking good, Tess. Heavy night?' Jules asked.

'Busy morning. And many more to come in the foreseeable future if we're going to keep running. I did get another employment inquiry through this morning though.'

'Good. Hire them,' Logan said.

'I think I'd better find out who they are first,' Tess teased. 'On that, go a bit easy on the new girl. I like her.'

Logan's gaze moved over Indy's face. 'So do I,' he said evenly.

Surprise had her gaze bouncing off his.

Tess's smile was immediately brilliant and Jules cleared her throat. 'Did you ask Logan about the quads?' she asked Tess.

Playing the part, Indy flicked a mock-relieved glance at Jules for changing the subject, and got a wink in understanding.

'No, I forgot,' Tess said. Then to Logan, 'Because Tina left, Jake went with her. And as I no longer have anyone to help with the cleaning *or* to take the quad rides and canoes out. And

I'm drawing the line on fitting that into my schedule too—you up for it?'

Logan took his eyes off Indy to answer. 'Yeah. When you've got a proper, Logan-approved timetable.'

Tess pulled a face. 'Got any time now?'

'Of course he does,' Jules said, sitting down. 'And then he can have a go at fixing my deep fryer.'

Logan chuckled. 'And she's back.'

'Shut up. You missed me.'

'It's been quiet.' He tucked into his breakfast. After a few mouthfuls, he leant back and caught Mel's attention as she walked past. 'Mel, think you can keep an eye on Indy for the rest of the day?'

To Indy's mind, the woman looked entirely too smug. 'Yep.'

'Oh hell,' Tess said quietly when Mel was out of earshot. 'There's an initiation by fire.'

Logan frowned. 'What do you mean?'

'She's already scared off Isabelle, now you're setting her loose on Indy.'

'Who's Isabelle?' Indy asked.

'A new girl we managed to keep for all of two weeks,' Tess said.

'Was she scared off by the rumours as well?' Indy asked casually.

Logan shook his head and swallowed a mouthful of coffee. 'According to Mel, the girl had illusions of playing with horses all day and left because she actually had to work.'

'I'll bet she had to work,' Tess agreed. 'You know she's over at Blackhills Riding Ranch now, right?'

'No, but if she's working for Steve, she'll be wishing she hadn't walked out of here.'

'Actually, I ran into her in town just before I headed off to pick up Jules. She said that working for Steve's a bit challenging at times, but she's enjoying herself. Want to know what she called Mel?'

'I do,' Jules said over a sip of her coffee.

'Her exact words were "a sadistic, slave-driving bitch."'

Jules snorted, muffling the laugh. 'Good luck, Indy.'

Indy released a long, slow breath. 'Well, I guess at least I've been warned.'

'You'll be fine,' Logan argued with a slight frown. 'You get on with Jules,' he added with a grin.

'Watch it,' Jules warned.

Indy frowned in genuine confusion. 'What's Jules got to do with Mel?'

Tess blew on her coffee to cool it, her eyes sparkling with mischief. 'When Jules plays bitch, people lose the will to live.'

Jules leant in and stared threateningly at Tess. 'Remember that, smart-arse.'

Logan laughed at them. 'Eat up ladies. We've all got work to do.'

Indy followed Mel down to the stables. 'We need to pull the stable bedding down and get the horses in that Logan's going to need for lessons today. We'll do that, give them some hay,' Mel said. 'It's not good for them to stand around without something to chew on for too long, then I'll get you started on cleaning out the horse troughs.'

'Okay.'

As Indy began to level out the stable bedding, Mel hung at the stable door. 'So did you ask to work down here or were you just put here?'

'Logan suggested he needed extra help.'

Mel's expression cooled. 'Do you know anything about working with horses?'

'Not much.'

'Then you'll have to make sure you listen and do things exactly as I tell you to.'

'No problem.'

'For the time being I'll watch you, make sure you do it properly.'

A little annoyed that Mel was following her around while she was doing all the work, Indy kept her mouth shut and went from one task to the next. Eventually Mel left her to fill hay nets, only to return before she'd had a chance to get them all done.

'You've put too much in that one,' Mel chided.

Indy straightened and compared it to the rest. There didn't really seem to be much difference in size. 'I put one biscuit in, just like the others.'

'Some bales are cut bigger than others. Take it out and pull some off. And you've made a mess on the floor. It's lunchtime but you'll have to finish the nets and sweep it up before you take your break.'

'Okay.'

'Clock's ticking. You're going to have to work on picking up the pace or you're going to end up missing meals.'

'Got it.'

Mel strolled out, and Indy quickly adjusted the hay net. Then checking Mel had left, she snuck into the office and sat at the computer. It was open on an Excel chart—it looked like a schedule of riding lessons. She minimised it, pulled up the employment records and schedules for the last year, and emailed them to herself. Then she removed the evidence of the sent email from the program and brought the Excel file back up.

Hopefully the files would give her a better idea of Caroline's movements in the lead-up to her disappearance. Because she might not have much time.

CHAPTER

7

Mel wasn't quite the slave-driving bitch Tess and Jules had made out, but she had an aversion to being friendly that made it difficult to talk to her, and a habit of disappearing into the office when Logan wasn't around while Indy did what she thought was probably Mel's work.

But in spite of the extra work, or possibly because of it, Indy was feeling pretty comfortable with the routine by the end of the week. For the most part Logan came across as a friendly, easygoing boss. But she'd caught him watching her with that thoughtful expression on his face on several occasions, and it kept her on edge, kept the nerves at just the right level to ensure she was focused at all times on the role she was playing. And she liked working out in the open, around the horses. It wasn't a bad job to have while learning as much as she could about Logan. Which so far wasn't much, she admitted as she added chaff to the feed buckets on Sunday afternoon.

Logan spent most of his time taking tourists on various activities or training horses. She noted that no matter how busy it got, he was out on the trails alone for at least a small amount of time every day to exercise horses, and that day he'd gone out to get some loose cattle or something. She wondered where he went, and if there was an ulterior motive, but she couldn't follow him—couldn't make sure he wasn't checking up on Caroline out there. Somewhere.

But after looking at Logan's computer records for the day of Caroline's disappearance, she couldn't make the timeline for an abduction work. Caroline had been rostered on to work with him from six. There'd been no guest ride scheduled but there were riding lessons on from nine. She knew from Mark's report that a guest witness claimed to have seen Caroline that morning at approximately seven-thirty. That didn't give Logan enough time to take Caroline beyond the searched area on horseback while getting back in time to put away two horses and saddle others, ready to teach lessons.

It just wasn't possible.

'Are the feeds finished?' Mel asked, appearing with a halter and lead rope in hand.

'Almost. I just wanted to ask Logan about the joint supplement— I wasn't sure whether Pepper still needed any.'

'She lives on the stuff. It always goes in.'

'Got it,' Indy said. She decided to try talking to Mel. 'Is he up on the trails again? He seems to go out on his own every day.'

Mel eyed her suspiciously. 'I don't keep tabs, but there's always something needing doing—even if it's just to exercise his horses. Why?'

'It must be nice,' she improvised. 'You know—out there in all that wilderness alone. Tranquil.'

'Whatever you say.' Mel folded her arms and leant against the wall, while Indy added chaff to buckets.

Blood out of a stone, Indy thought. She tried again. 'Do you ever go out there?'

'Sometimes. Cattle need to have an eye kept on them, horses need to be worked, fences need to be checked. Logan's not always here.'

'Where does he go?'

'Away for comps and stuff.'

'So ... you must know all the trails pretty well then, if you go out on your own. Aren't you worried about what's happened to those other women?' She looked up to see annoyance flash across Mel's face.

'Yes, I know all the trails. No, I'm not worried. I grew up around here. I'm not going to go getting myself lost or drowned or hypothermic.'

'Is that what you think happened to Caroline?' she pushed.

'Probably.'

'But Logan said she never showed for the ride they were supposed to go on that day.'

Mel hesitated, shrugged. 'Doesn't mean she didn't go on her own.'

'Did a horse come back without a rider? Is one missing?'

Mel fiddled nervously with a locket that sat around her neck. 'No. Maybe she walked. I don't know. I wasn't here. It was my turn to do the supply run.'

'It just seems odd. Especially because they found her clothes here right? I heard they had blood on them!' She made herself shiver.

'I don't know what happened to Caroline, so just drop it!'

It was time to back off, so Indy smiled a little, nodded. 'Sorry. I didn't mean to upset you. Was just thinking about it.'

'Then you've got too much time on your hands. Are you going to get that finished or talk all day?'

Indy bent down to get another scoop of chaff. 'Almost done. Then you need a hand cleaning the saddles, right?'

'Change of plans. You need to clean the horse troughs.'

Mel was obviously upset by her questioning. 'I did them yesterday.'

'Not well enough,' Mel snapped.

'They were spotless.'

'And now they're not. Just do it.'

When Mel was about to stalk away, Indy asked, 'You seem a bit stressed out, is something bothering you?'

Mel turned back around, eyes spitting anger. 'You are. You're bothering me, Indy. You talk too much, you ask too many questions. I'm not your friend, I'm your boss. So go and get the bloody troughs clean.'

'Okay …' Indy went outside and got to work. At least it wasn't difficult; the troughs were as clean as she knew they'd been. But the water was cold, so it wasn't exactly comfortable work either. She'd hit a nerve of some sort with Mel, and was far from convinced she was telling the truth. She scrubbed another trough, shook the water from her hands and rubbed them together to warm them up. But if Mel knew what had happened to Caroline, what possible motivation could she have for keeping it quiet?

She was just beginning to wonder how long she should continue to pretend to be doing useful work when she heard voices. Two riders were at the far end of the paddock in front of her, moving the cattle and calves that had been in there since she arrived. One rider spotted her and waved. It was Tess, riding a stunning horse with a coat of rich orange with large splashes of white on its face, legs and body. Indy hadn't seen it before—she guessed it must be one of the horses kept at Logan's. He'd mentioned he had separate stables near his house. Jules was on another horse she didn't recognise. One of Logan's stockhorses perhaps. She waved back as Jules cantered up to a nearby gate and opened it. 'Hi, Indy, you mind getting the other gate for me? We're bringing the cattle across the drive and into the back paddock.' Jules opened the gate out from her side of the road and Indy opened the one closest to her, forming a wide channel across the drive for the cattle to go through.

'Why do they have to move? There's still loads of grass isn't there?'

'We bring them down here where we can keep a close eye on them to calve, then they go back out into the big paddocks where there's more feed. We've got a different lot to bring down here this arvo. They're due to drop in the next couple of weeks. Why?'

'I just like seeing them.'

'They are pretty. Here they come.'

From behind the herd, Tess pushed them forward, the cows calmly ambling towards the gates. The calves trotted and bounced along beside their mothers as they came through in a sea of black and brown bodies, picking up pace as they spotted the fresh pasture. They were just about all through when Indy noticed one calf still on the inside of the fence. Unable to get through the squeeze of bodies, it ran along the fence line in the wrong direction, calling to whichever cow was its mother.

Indy left the gate and jogged along the road ahead of it, climbing through the fence to chase it back the other way. The startled calf ran around her, kept going in the wrong direction, bleating even more madly.

'Wrong way, baby! Come back here,' she called after it.

A bawling sound like a trumpet had her spinning around. An enormous black cow had turned against the push of the herd and was barrelling back into the paddock.

Straight towards her.

She stared, heart in her mouth as the enormous, angry animal approached, bearing down on her like a truck. The sheer size and power of it had her faltering, not sure whether to stand still or run.

In a blur of horse and dust, Tess cut between them, the horse skidding to a stop and spinning, sending the cow around Indy to where it reunited with its calf.

'Not a good idea to put yourself between a cow and her calf,' Tess called out. 'You okay?'

'Yeah.'

'Out you get.'

Indy climbed back through the fence while Tess got around behind the pair and pushed them up to the gate with the last of the stragglers.

'Thanks,' Indy said as she closed one gate and Jules shut the other.

'Can you ride?' Tess asked.

'No.'

'Get Logan to teach you. It's a handy skill to have around here. See you at dinner.'

Tess might have made light of that lesson, but Indy wasn't sure she hadn't just saved her life. She stared back over the paddock. She had no idea how Tess had got that horse from the other side of the herd to between her and that cow so fast, but she wouldn't mind learning.

She cleaned the last trough then headed back towards the stables. If she didn't give Mel a hand cleaning the gear, she'd be late for another meal. She caught a faint, sweet scent as she entered the stables and hesitated. What was that? She knew she'd smelled it before but she couldn't quite place it. 'Mel?'

'What's up?' Mel came out of the office, closing the door tightly behind her.

'I was just wondering if you were ready for a hand with the saddles?'

'Oh, the saddles, yeah … I'm still pretty busy. How about you get started on that?' With a pleasant smile she let herself back into the office. And closed the door.

With a roll of her eyes, Indy walked into the tack room. If she didn't miss lunch it would be a miracle.

Logan led a hot, sweaty Brodie into the breezeway and noticed Indy was putting the horses in for the evening. Damn if she wasn't easy on the eyes. The habitual ponytail was somehow flattering to the slash of her high cheekbones and those big blue eyes, the snug jeans hugged every toned curve; even that light, purposeful stride of hers was hot, he decided as she led Gizmo, a little black and white pony he reserved for the most nervous riders, into one of the stables. She already looked more confident around the horses, and she wore a smile on her lips that by nature seemed to perpetually tip up at the edges. Except when she was glaring at him. And for all her easy friendliness he hadn't missed the odd quiet study and thoughtful frown. She'd heard the stories about him, and had to be wondering. He would have thought less of her if she wasn't. 'You almost done?' he asked, and noted she tensed, just the smallest amount, when he came in behind her.

'Last one.' She took off the halter, patted the pony and slipped out of the stable. And though there was that friendly, easy smile, she was, as always, watchful. Cautious. 'Have you been up on the trails?'

And curious. 'Yeah. I was moving cattle down the mountain with the guys and noticed a few head from the steers' paddock wandering on the wrong side of the fence. Their gate was open. I'm guessing it was careless hikers.'

She stepped out of the stable and took his horse, removing the bridle and replacing it with a halter. 'Lucky you were out there.'

'Yeah but it ate into my time. Do you happen to know if Tess and Jules got that group of cows and calves moved this afternoon? The next lot should be turning up any minute.' He took the gear she'd just removed from Brodie into the tack room.

'Yep. I helped.'

That surprised him. 'Good for you.'

'I nearly died. I think.' She untied Brodie but he took the lead rope from her to wash down himself.

'You what?'

'I got between a cow and a calf. Apparently that's akin to suicide.'

A cold chill ran through him. 'What happened?'

'Tess happened. One second she was wandering around behind the herd over the other side of the paddock, the next she and her horse were sliding between me and death.'

He smiled at her animated recount, at the way her eyes lit up, and was pleased they seemed to be having a conversation without too much tension for a change. 'Tess is pretty damn handy on a horse.' He put Brodie in the wash bay, and turned on the hose.

'Thank God,' Indy said, leaning on the door. 'She didn't seem to think it was a big deal. I did,' she admitted.

'She does that sort of thing every day. You don't. Was she on Flash?' At her blank look he continued. 'The sabino.'

'Still not making sense to me.'

'The chestnut with all the white markings.'

'Is that what you call that orange colour? Then yes, she was.'

'Don't worry, you'll pick all this up.'

'She said I should ask if you would teach me to ride.'

He stepped towards her to pull a cotton rug off the door. 'I'll get you up on a horse. Can't work here and not know how.' He tossed the rug over Brodie's back and because she was still standing there, watching him, he winked at her over his shoulder. 'I'm glad you're not dead.'

He caught the flicker of something he couldn't quite read, then she smiled back at him. 'Me too.' She looked past him to the paddock.

He turned around and saw the new group of cattle coming down from the mountain. Mick and Ned pushed them along, wide-brimmed hats covering their faces, stockwhips dangling lazily from the horse sides. The cows' bellies were huge with calves and good grazing. 'Let's go open the gate.'

Indy made a pained noise but nodded. 'Yeah, I'll just stay on the outside of the fence this time.'

For the next few minutes the noise of bawling livestock didn't allow for conversation. Logan watched Indy carefully to gauge her reaction to the cattle after her recent fright. She had a smile on her face. Good. So far, she hadn't shied away from any task he'd put in front of her. He had a feeling that was how she attacked life in general. It was a damn attractive trait. As the last of the cows moved through, Mick pulled up his horse and acknowledged him. 'You beat us back.'

'Only just.'

'Hi, Indy.'

'Hi, Mick.'

'You met Ned yet?' he asked as Ned pulled his horse up close by.

'Hi, no. But I saw you at dinner the night I arrived.' Almost imperceptibly cooler, and a step away, Logan noted. The way Ned was looking at her, he wasn't surprised. He moved closer to Indy and stared up at Ned with a proprietorial warning he had no right to make.

'Nice afternoon up there?' Indy asked Mick.

'Bloody gorgeous. You should get out there, take a look.'

'I will—when I can ride,' she said.

'One way to learn,' Ned said. 'I'll take you out if you want.'

Mick dismounted from his horse and pulled a bottle of water from his saddlebag. 'I'm sure Logan would take you on one of the trail rides if you asked. You don't need to ride too well to sit on a plodder.'

'We were just talking about doing some riding,' Logan agreed.

Ned got off his horse, led it over to the gate to close it. His horse suddenly dropped onto its hindquarters, bunched and sprang, knocking him hard into the gate as he was latching it. 'What the bloody hell—get off!'

'Snake!' Mick called out in warning, and Logan saw it—about five foot long, almost black in colour and completely still, head up.

Indy was too close. Without thinking too much about it, he lifted her off her feet and put her behind him, copped an elbow in the ribs for his trouble that was hard enough to make him cough. 'I see it,' he gasped with a quick, unappreciative glare in Indy's direction. She was standing there, primed for battle, eyeing him back like *he* was the snake. So much for less tension, he thought, and felt a distinct stab of disappointment.

Mick backed his horse up closer to Ned's while Logan picked up a long stick. 'Must have been stirred up by the cattle.' As he took a step towards it, the snake dropped its head and shot off into the undergrowth.

He tossed the stick, shook his head. 'I don't mind seeing them out in the bush, but that's a big tiger, too close to the stables. Everyone will need to keep an eye out in case it comes back.'

'You think it will hang around?' Indy said.

'Could just be passing through—probably is,' he said, deliberately rubbing his ribs. 'You're welcome, by the way.' She smiled sweetly in response, dragged a smile of his own out of him. 'You all right Ned?'

'Yeah, yeah.' But his hand had gotten stuck in the gate; blood dripped from a small gash and two of his fingers already looked swollen.

'You should get that seen to,' Indy said.

Ned made a dismissive noise. 'Got work to do, the horse to take care of.' But Logan noticed his hand was shaking and he looked ill.

'Sit yourself down in the stables a minute,' Logan ordered. 'Indy, would you run up and get Nat? She's best with this sort of thing.'

'Yes, of course,' Indy said.

'Don't need a bloody nursemaid.'

'That hand swells up, you're out of action,' Logan told him. 'You want Rosalie on your back for being stupid?'

'Nah. Nah—righto. But a cold beer sitting in my hand would do just as well.'

'I'll be right back,' Indy promised, and hurried off.

He'd picked her up. Indy couldn't quite get past it. Like she'd weighed nothing more than a bale of hay. There was something ... unsettling about that sort of easy strength. And about the fact that with everything going on at that moment, his first thought had been her safety. But she couldn't trust his motives, couldn't afford to let one action sway her judgement.

She jogged up to the guesthouse steps and walked down the corridor into the kitchen. The mix of sweet and spicy scents coming from large ovens and simmering pots hit her, smelled like heaven. At one stainless steel bench Nat, in a well-worn white apron, was sprinkling seasoning over a large roasting pan of vegetables.

'Hi, Indy. How's it going?'

'Hi Nat, good. But a snake frightened Ned's horse and it shoved him into the gate, hurt his hand.'

'And Ned admitted he's hurt?' Jules said, emerging from the cool room. 'Must need an ambulance.'

Indy grinned. 'Logan threatened him with Rosalie.'

'That'll do it,' Jules said.

Nat wiped her hands on a towel. 'I'll get an ice pack. Where is he?'

'Stables.'

'Deal with that then have a break,' Jules urged.

'I wouldn't mind putting my feet up for five minutes. Thanks, love,' Nat said, and hurried off.

Jules put the lid back on her soup and asked Indy, 'How are you going with Mel?'

'Believe it or not, I've had worse bosses.'

'Logan's your boss, not Mel. Don't let her tell you otherwise,' Jules warned. 'I've had a few crazies too. One particularly memorable chef used to like to throw knives.'

'Where did you work in Sydney?' Indy asked.

'At Le Meilleur.' Jules began moving pots and pans around—to Indy's eye, she seemed to be reorganising the kitchen. 'Despite his habit of throwing sharp objects, I did like that chef. I guess he rubbed off on me because I went from there to another French restaurant.'

'Is that what you've always wanted to do?'

'Mum's had a position here since I was five years old. I used to hang around the kitchen a lot and help out, then I started cooking too. People liked my food, I got a buzz out of it, studied formally. I always wanted to travel and so I did that and apprenticed in a heap of different restaurants. I came back here to work for a while but when Connor and I split I took a position in Sydney.'

'It can't be easy, coming back.'

She shrugged. 'Connor's here but so is Mum. The Athertons are like extended family and they needed me. It's as simple as that. Hopefully before too much longer Caroline will turn up and Latisha's killer will be found. Once everything simmers down I'll go back to Sydney.'

'What about Mandy? I know you said Gretchen probably left by choice, but there was talk in the pub about a Mandy, and that the police thought there could be more missing women out there, being held somewhere.' She took a chance with the lie. She needed to make some progress.

Jules shuddered. 'God, I hope not. I did hear there were more though—three or four I think. But that's over decades. The police told us a lot more people than that go missing each year.'

Jules had heard there were more. Had Mark been discussing elements of the case with her? Could he really be that incompetent? She needed to follow this up. 'Have ... the other ones you heard about all vanished from here?'

Jules looked surprised. 'No, not at all. I couldn't even tell you who they were.'

'I guess the police have been keeping you all up to date with their investigation then.'

Jules hesitated for a fraction of a second. 'Yeah. Yeah, the detective in charge has been looking into it all for a long time. Because he keeps coming out here to hassle Logan, he occasionally lets things drop. It doesn't hurt to take note of what he's up to. You never know who he's going to point a finger at next.'

'Doesn't sound like you think very highly of him.'

'I don't agree with the whole stalker in the bush theory if that's what you mean. Why?'

Indy pulled off a nervous laugh. 'It's just that I keep hearing bits and pieces. It is a little creepy. And I was thinking it would be nice to explore the trails. I didn't want to head out there alone without an opinion or two on whether it's safe.'

'The most you have to worry about is getting lost. And you won't because there's signposts everywhere. But to be safe, talk to Logan about going out with a group first—get an idea of where everything is.'

Jules looked over a menu Nat had out on the counter. Angling her head in thought, she slowly nodded to herself. 'I think we need something chocolate. I'll make something ridiculously decadent for the fine dining dessert tomorrow night. Then I'll put a bit aside for us.' Decision made, she busied herself pulling ingredients out of a refrigerator. She smiled wickedly and dropped several blocks of chocolate onto the bench. 'Decadent.'

Indy watched as butter and cream were placed next to the chocolate. 'I look forward to it. I'll see you later.'

She went back to the bunkhouse, and found Mick in his usual spot on the verandah nursing his usual stubby of beer. 'Thanks for your help earlier. Ned's a stubborn bugger.'

'How did you get here so fast?' she asked.

'Nat turned up so I left 'em arguing over the ins and outs of infection. Noticed Logan got back all right.'

'Yeah, he said something about steers being out, right?'

'That explains it then. Wondered where he'd disappeared to. Didn't like to ask,' Mick said.

Interesting statement, Indy thought. *Didn't like to ask?* 'Why's that?'

He tipped the last of his beer into his mouth, draining the bottle. 'Bit mysterious at times, that one. Likes to take off on his own.

Or with company—of the female sort.' A grin spread over his weathered face.

'Really?' Indy kept her tone dryly amused and rolled her eyes. 'I suppose that's why Caroline wanted to go riding with him then? Everyone said she had a thing for him.'

His smile dropped into a thoughtful frown. 'Bit weird that, eh? Seemed all keen as mustard to go up on the trails—when she was bragging about it to anyone that'd listen at dinner the night before, then there she was the next morning at the stables dressed like she was going inta town.'

What? She focused on trying to keep her tone casual. 'You saw her that morning?'

'Yeah—she nearly had a stroke when I just about walked in on her getting changed in the tack room,' he chuckled. 'Reckoned she'd slipped in the mud catching a horse—it was wet that morning. When I saw what she'd changed into I didn't think too much of it other than they must have changed their plans for the ride cause of the weather.'

How had this been missed? She had to risk asking more questions. 'So where was Logan?'

'Logan went out early on his stallion. He rides in any weather. Besides, he reckoned he didn't know anything about changed plans. There was just no sign of her when he came back in to saddle up another couple of horses for their ride. She'd just gone.'

'But ... when you saw her ... was she hurt? Bleeding?'

'Don't think she hurt herself, just slipped over is all I remember.'

'Why didn't you tell the police? I heard her clothes were found with bloodstains on them. They think Logan hurt her, don't they?'

'I told that Robinson. First off when he came poking round, I wouldn't talk to him. Said I didn't know nothin' because that cop's good at twisting your words round and he's got it in for Logan. Logan's as good a boss as they come. He's not goin' round murdering women.' Mick wiped his arm across his forehead. 'But then Logan said I should tell Robinson what I saw. That it might help. So I did. The bastard all but called me a liar. Wanted to know why I'd changed me story after chatting with Logan.'

'I see.'

'That Robinson comes back and starts asking questions again, you're best to steer clear.' He got to his feet with a groan. 'I'm off to have a shower. Old bones are a bit stiff from the long afternoon in the saddle.'

Turning the implications of Mick's statement over in her mind, she headed out into one of the large paddocks instead of back to her room, and when she was sure no one could get close enough to overhear her, called Ben.

'Mark Robinson doesn't deserve to be a detective.'

'Hi, Indy, I'm great, thanks. How are you going?' Ben teased.

'Sorry. Just had to get that out.'

'Want to tell me why?'

She told him what she'd learned, adding a few choice sentences about the lack of vital details in the reports.

'So Caroline had been uninjured and in the process of getting changed—for what?' he asked when she'd finished.

'Mick didn't know. But other than the blood later found on her clothes, I would have said there was a good chance she was taking off without telling anyone.'

'Maybe she was. What if Atherton came back, caught her out? The confrontation could have triggered him to act, perhaps injure her in an attempt to subdue her ...'

'Like Gretchen.'

'And he cleaned up the mess he'd made with what was on hand: her dirty clothing. He'd have been in a hurry, so he might have stashed them away to dispose of later.'

'He or another perp.'

'Can we account for his whereabouts?'

'Mick said he was out riding.'

'Unless someone saw him, there's no way to verify that. What do you think of him?'

'I'm not sure. He's got a way of drawing you in, he has a charm about him, but he's also a bit intimidating. He's friendly, but there's something under the surface that would make anyone hesitant to cross him. I just don't know yet.'

'So what's next?'

'More digging into Caroline, now that it's more likely she left by car, that changes things.'

'Just remember no one saw Atherton leave the property with any of the women, and Gretchen's blood and hair were found in his ute. I can tell you that's not road registered. He's unlikely to risk exposing himself by being pulled over.'

She stared out over the mountains as Mark's words echoed in her mind. *If you know the land, know how to get in and out … you could hide those women with no problem whatsoever.*

'If Caroline was taken in a vehicle, it makes the whole scenario of them being out there somewhere much more plausible. He could get further, faster. And there are plenty of accessible trails. I'll take another look at the maps, widen the possible search radius.'

'Be careful.'

'Will do,' she promised.

'And keep in touch.'

'Yes boss,' she said playfully, and rang off. As she walked back towards the bunkhouse, Logan and Jules were at the fence to the next paddock. From the direction of their bodies and the occasional point or wave of the hand, Indy gathered they were discussing the cattle.

'Hi, where've you been?' Jules called out.

'Walking. It's so nice out here.'

Logan's gaze was on her. It travelled down to her feet, slowly back up. When she met it he had a touch of a smile on his face. 'Who was on the phone?'

He hadn't actually touched her, but her skin was tingling. How was it possible she could have that sort of physical reaction to a potential serial abductor? A possible murderer? She mentally chastised herself. Doubts might be creeping in as to the accuracy of the information the case was built on, but she was a long way from concluding he was innocent. There was so much circumstantial evidence in this case, so much speculation. She needed to be on top of her game.

'Indy?' Jules asked, with a puzzled expression.

She blinked and shook her head. 'Sorry—just a friend I haven't seen for a while.' She climbed through the fence and stood beside Jules. 'What are you up to?'

'Debating the best cattle breeds. I prefer the Angus, Logan's a Simmental man.'

'Why the preference—looks?' Indy asked naively.

'Steaks,' Jules said with a grin. 'And as I'm the chef ...'

'I'm not getting rid of my Simmentals just because Angus are the "in" thing,' Logan replied calmly. 'We have a hundred head of Angus about to drop calves and statistically around half of those will become steers. How many do you need to cook?'

'I feel ill,' Indy muttered. 'I think I'll leave you to it.' She headed back towards the stables, heard the spirited conversation between Logan and Jules continue.

CHAPTER

8

Logan signalled to the nervous young stockhorse to move on and she scuttled forward into a trot around him in the round yard. He spoke again, his voice low and calm, and the filly's head dropped into a more relaxed position. Indy almost felt her take a deep breath. The man seemed to be able to magically convince the most nervous or stubborn horses to work with him. He had them following him like lambs and working off cues she couldn't even see. And he never raised his voice, never seemed to get angry or frustrated or impatient. This might not be a man who let emotion get the better of him, but he wasn't emotionless either. As a homicide detective, she'd learned enough about people to know empathy when she saw it, and he had it for the horses. Empathy wasn't a trait most convicted serial abductors or serial killers possessed. Logan was no psychopath. She knew that didn't mean he wasn't her perpetrator, but in her experience it greatly lessened the chances. 'What are you doing?' Mel asked from behind her.

'Watching Logan work this horse. Why?'

'Because you're not being paid to sit around watching Logan.'

'It's my lunch break,' she said, then, seeing the scowl on Mel's face, 'Oh, get over it.'

The scowl just got worse. 'Watch how you speak to me.'

'I do. Trust me.' Indy hopped down from her spot on the fence and landed lightly in front of Mel but snagged a splinter in her thumb as she let go of the rail. She gritted her teeth and counted to ten as it stung sharply. 'Because I feel sorry for you.'

'Sorry for me?'

'Wouldn't it be nice to have a friend or two around here—rather than hating everyone?'

In answer, Mel stormed off towards the guesthouse. Indy was sure the woman had to have some sort of disorder. She wondered why Logan kept her on, then remembered how much nicer Mel was to her when Logan was around—and how short-staffed they were. She checked her thumb, grimaced. 'Ouch. Damn it.' She shook it, blew on it—she'd get the splinter out later. Because she couldn't miss the opportunity, while Logan was busy and Mel was gone, to check Logan's saddlebags. With everything that had gone on that day, she knew he hadn't had a chance to unpack them.

She went into the tack room and took another quick look around before unzipping the first bag. A snake bandage, matches, a Leatherman and some spare sunglasses. An unopened bottle of water. She zipped it back up, reached for the other side—had her hand on it when the clip-clop of hooves in the breezeway had her scrambling to find something else to be doing.

Logan's voice floated in. 'You there, Indy?'

'Right here.' She walked out of the tack room with a grooming kit in hand.

'What are you going to do with that?'

'I thought I'd get Pepper out. She hasn't had a groom recently and her tail's filling up with grass and knotting.'

'Nice of you. But it's lunch time. Go grab something to eat.'

Because her thumb was still throbbing she sucked on it. 'I'm not really hun—what?'

'What have you done?' His tone was too gentle for a splinter—she felt like a sook.

Embarrassed, her hand went behind her back. 'It's nothing, I just—'

'Show me.' He stepped in to her space and ran his hand lightly down her arm, retrieved her hand to inspect it. That familiar, unwanted awareness threatened to form goosebumps on her skin and she wanted to snatch her hand away, retreat. But she kept still, wondering where the line was between keeping her sanity and the part she was meant to be playing. 'Ouch. That's got to hurt,' he murmured.

Hurt? He was possibly three inches away from her. Her body was way too involved with his proximity to remember to send pain messages to her brain. 'Ah … that's what I said, initially,' she told him, keeping her voice light, 'But it's fine. Really.' She gently tried to remove her hand. Failed. But the move brought his eyes back to hers. And the look outdid the proximity issue. 'It's just a splinter. A tiny piece of—where are we going?'

He was towing her by the wrist to the office. 'Sit. I'll get it out.'

She sat but shook her head. 'I'll do it myself, thanks.'

'Don't be a wuss.'

She couldn't care less about the splinter. She just needed a moment to pull herself back together. 'Honestly, it's nothing.' He opened a first-aid kit and removed some of the contents. 'Looks like you're prepping for major surgery,' she said in an attempt to switch the mood.

'It's not just a splinter. It's half a fencepost. Soak it in there for a minute.'

'Logan …'

He stopped what he was doing to look up into her eyes. 'Shhh. You're fine. I'll be gentle.'

'I know I …' Flushed and embarrassed, she decided it would be quicker just to let him remove it, so she rested her thumb in the diluted antiseptic. 'You're missing your lunch.'

He bent and opened a cupboard containing a small bar fridge. Indy caught sight of bottled water, tubes and bottles of medicines she assumed were for horses, and a few containers of various sizes. Logan pulled out a packet of Monte chocolate biscuits and opened it, put them near her on the desk. 'Emergency stash. Do you want me to make you a coffee?'

'No, I want you to give me the tweezers so I can pull this tiny bit of wood out of my thumb and we can go get a proper lunch.'

'You're cranky when you're being a wuss.'

She opened her mouth to protest, realised she was going to snap and prove his point. Instead she laughed with a sigh. 'Right, consider it soaked. Go for it.'

He picked up the tweezers and studied her thumb with an endearing amount of concentration. 'On three, okay? One …'

'Ow!' she complained as he pulled it out. 'How is that three?'

'I guess maths isn't my strong point.' But his eyes were dancing and she found herself smiling back. The moment held a beat, then two. Hypnotic, that's what she'd thought of that stare once before. It was what she was thinking again. Hypnotic and, as his eyes flicked to her mouth and back, tempting.

No, she didn't want to feel this. Wouldn't. She tugged her hand free. 'Thanks.'

'Hold up.' He was all business as he covered her thumb with a small dressing. 'Done, and you still have enough time to go eat one of those salads you seem to like so much.' He took a biscuit and tossed the rest back in the fridge. 'After lunch, I need you to bring Aurora in, okay? It's about time we started doing something with her.'

'Okay. Great.'

'And I'm more than happy for you to watch me work the horses—as long as the work's done. I'll mention that to Mel.'

He'd overheard. She smiled because that was exactly what she needed—it would give her more time with him. Time to try and coax him into making a mistake, an error that might give away that one piece of the puzzle needed to trap him, or, just as importantly, rule him out once and for all and turn the investigation inside out. 'I'd like to see how Aurora goes. So thanks.'

Indy pushed through the door to her room and yawned. Afternoons with Mel were getting more intense as Mel realised Indy could handle more tasks, and Aurora hadn't wanted to be caught for her lesson with Logan. Indy had chased, coaxed and begged for half an hour before she discovered the mare liked peppermints. From the first treat the horse's nose had been glued to her pocket and the crisis had resolved, but not before she'd given Indy a decent workout running up and down the entirely-too-steep hill that was the paddock.

Logan had worked her and Indy had watched on as the mare had moved calmly around the yard. Indy forgave the drama—she had a soft spot for the mare, and was pleased she was doing well. Then Logan had taken off and Mel had taken over. And Mel hadn't forgiven Indy for her earlier comments. Following that couple of hours from hell, she badly needed a shower, then she intended to go over her files, making some plans for how to move forward.

She put her phone on the charger and grabbed some clean clothes and a towel. Then she almost crashed into Kaicey as she stepped into the hallway.

'Hi. Guess what? We're getting company,' Kaicey said.

'Which is great,' Jules added, coming up the hall behind Kaicey dragging an industrial-sized vacuum cleaner. 'Except I had to leave my vol-au-vents to come down and prepare the rooms because Tess and Rosalie are flat out getting guest rooms done.' She dipped a hand in her pocket, pulled out a key card and tossed it at Kaicey. 'Unlock three and four, would you?'

'Does everyone walk in here without notice?' Indy had to ask.

'One was expected, the other one's a backpacker—turned up in town much the same way as you did. Only she saw our ad, called first, emailed her résumé across. They've both worked in a couple of other places and their references are okay. Don't take this the wrong way but we're not too fussy who we take on trial at present.'

Indy laughed. 'I need to shower, because if I offer to help you in these clothes I'll do more harm than good, but I'll be back to give you a hand.'

'Don't stress—won't take long.'

The water on her tired muscles was heaven, so she let the spray do its work. By the time she emerged from the bathroom, the women were gone. She dumped her dirty clothes in her basket and turned to check her phone. Where was it? She'd left it on the charger but the cord sat in place, the phone nowhere to be seen. She checked the entire room though she knew she wasn't going to find it. Her stomach began to churn. Someone had to have been in there, taken it. She moved silently back out into the hallway, listening and watching for any sign of anyone in the dorm. When she reached the common room she stopped in her tracks. 'Is that my phone?'

Ned jolted, looked up sheepishly and put it on the coffee table. 'Dunno, is it?' Indy picked it up and checked the screen. It was locked. 'I wasn't prying or nothing—was just looking to see if I could find who it belonged to, but I couldn't get into it.'

'How could you not know it was mine? It was in my room, wasn't it?'

'What?' he asked with a convincing look of surprise. 'Never went anywhere near your room.'

That didn't make sense. 'Then where did you get it?'

'Eh? Oh, ah … just here, on the table.'

'That's not possible.'

Ned shrugged, still eyeing her warily. 'Musta dropped it. Someone's left it or somethin'.'

She watched him closely but his face wasn't giving anything way. He wasn't going to budge, so she'd find out what else she could and think about it later. 'Must have,' she finally replied. 'Ned, how many people have access to our rooms?'

'Ah, obviously the Athertons, the cleaners maybe. Why?'

'Because my room was locked and that phone was in my room. Who else has been in here in the last few minutes?'

'Dunno. Only came in just a moment ago. Glad you found your phone.' And then he got up and hurried away. She stared after him. There was something not quite right about that man. Something she didn't trust.

She headed up to the guesthouse for dinner, mulling over whether or not to mention the phone incident to anyone.

'Did someone die?' Tess had reached the dining room just ahead of Indy and was standing in the doorway, waiting.

'Huh? Tess, sorry, was miles away.'

'I can see that. Grab some food and tell me about it.'

She considered that, decided it could work to bring it up quietly with Tess. She wasn't as suspicious as Connor. They loaded their plates, found a table. 'So?' Tess asked.

Back in character, she shrugged carelessly. 'It's probably nothing. Ned's just um …'

Tess grinned and nodded her head. 'Got a bit of a crush on you. Don't worry about it. Dad'll tell you he's a few sandwiches short of a picnic and still the best stockhand he's ever had. He's been here for twenty or more years. Every now and again he gets sweet on someone. It'll pass.'

A few sandwiches short… 'Has he ever been diagnosed with any mental or psychological disorders?'

Tess's face went blank before she frowned. 'Ned? Nah. Ned's just Ned. Why?'

'I was wondering if somehow getting into my room and taking my phone might be him getting carried away with his latest possible infatuation,' she said and wondered if she might be able to find any possible patterns of behaviour linking these actions to occurrences with the other victims.

Tess's fork clattered on her plate. 'He what?'

'I put it on the charger in my room, locked my door while I showered. When I came out he was playing with it in the common room.'

'He got into your room? What did he have to say?'

'I don't know if he did, but I don't know how else it got out there. He swears blind he found it on the table. The thing is, no one else was around.'

Tess's expression was stunned. 'I'm … beyond shocked. I'll have Dad talk to him. He gets through to him best. If it was Ned, he'll find out. And we'll reset your entry key card.'

'You said he's been interested in other women working here,' Indy continued, needing more information. 'Has he had any other ah ... interests recently?'

'He loved Caroline. She was so nice to him. Used to have a beer with him and Mick at the end of each day.' Her brow creased sadly. 'Used to.'

'It must be upsetting for you, sorry. Did you know all of them? Jules said there were others—women that didn't work at Calico Mountain.'

Tess's expression went blank. 'Others? Connected to all this? I didn't know about that.'

'Jules said the detective told her.'

'Really?' she asked sceptically. 'I wonder when...' She shrugged. 'I'm surprised because Detective Robinson's been nothing but a complete arsehole whenever I've been anywhere near him. It's got to the point where Mum and Dad won't come out of the house when they see him coming. I know he has a job to do, but I wish he could leave them alone. Dad's heart's not good and Mum's really struggling with the girls going missing. After Caroline, they talked about closing the bookings until it was sorted out. But Connor talked them out of it. We can't afford to do that. It's already been going on for years. Who knows when we'll have answers?' Tess shook it off and smiled. 'Just gotta hope they turn up okay, right?' Then, 'Have you met the two new girls yet?'

'No.'

'Carly is going to be on activities and Gina is helping with the cleaning. And we have more applications coming in, so hopefully we might even get back up to full staff soon.'

'That must be a relief.'

Tess sighed. 'Assuming we can keep them once they walk in on this mess.'

'It doesn't come across as too much of a mess. I like it here.'

'Do us a favour and tell them that, would you? If I have to work too many more fifteen-hour days, I might just make myself disappear.'

Logan cantered Aurora around the yard, changed leads a couple of times, felt her hindquarters bunch perfectly under her as she stopped, spun around his leg and halted. He leant down and gave her neck a pat. 'You're a good girl.' And she was going to make a great stock-horse. He briefly considered taking her out to a couple of campdrafts, selling her on as a serious competition horse. The mare had talent. But his gaze flicked to Indy, sitting on the fence rail with a relaxed smile on her face as she watched the mare work, and he remembered the scene when he'd first laid eyes on her.

He'd thought a lot about that evening, about the fierce way she'd protected the mare from Mason's nasty temper. She had a temper of her own—and the skills to back it up. She was impressive: an intoxicating mix he had yet to fully figure out. He intended on finding out everything he could. Indy really liked the mare, so he'd encourage that relationship. Having a pet project was a good way to keep her interested in the work, made it more likely she'd hang around.

Mel walked past. He caught the glare at Indy, but she didn't comment. He'd told Mel Indy could watch and Mel had seemed fine with that. Until just now. He only hoped whatever animosity was there wouldn't come to a head. He dismounted, led her towards the gate. 'She looks good,' Indy said.

'She's doing well.' He took her back to the stables and tied her up. Indy followed and the mare lifted her head to watch her expectantly. Curious, he saw Indy slip her hand into her pocket and retrieve what looked like a peppermint.

She fed it to the mare and stroked Aurora's face. 'There you go.'

'You spoiling her?' he asked.

'Every chance I get. She's so pretty. What do you call this colour?'

He couldn't help the twitch of his lips. 'Brown.'

'Of course it is,' Indy said dryly. 'Because if I'd called Tess's horse orange you would have laughed and said chestnut or sabino or whatever it was. So I expect some weird alternative term and there isn't one. And I still end up looking stupid.'

He pulled back the grin. 'I've never thought you were stupid.'

'I must be imagining the constant smirk you have on your face then.' When it reappeared, she pointed a finger at him. 'And there it is.'

'If you want a compliment, I'll tell you how I think you look.' He deliberately warmed his tone, interested to see how she'd respond. 'You want to know?'

Her expression went blank, then she eyed him suspiciously. 'What … girl doesn't want a compliment?' she asked slowly, 'But …'

When she trailed off, he decided he didn't want to let it go. 'But?' Aurora nudged him impatiently and he dragged his eyes from Indy to stroke her neck. 'All right. Just a minute,' he told the horse.

'But … you don't pay me to stand around getting compliments,' she finished quickly before dropping her gaze to the horse. 'Aurora has spots.' It was a very obvious and deliberate attempt to change the subject. And regardless of her brush-off, she was definitely flustered. 'I hadn't noticed them before.'

He struggled with the laugh as she turned those gorgeous blue eyes back on him. 'They're dapples.'

Her gaze hit the ceiling and she sighed in defeat. 'Fine. The orange horse is a chestnut—sabino with all that flashy white, the brown horse is brown and the spots are dapples. Am I getting it?'

'Almost,' he said solemnly. 'Except not all horses with brown coats are brown. It depends on—'

'Okay stop—just stop. Was the rest right?'

'Yeah,' he said on a laugh. 'You're getting it.'

'Hurray. Personal victory. One step at a time, okay?' She smoothed a hand over Aurora's coat. 'Did she always have dapples?'

Still grinning, he nodded. 'With some good grooming, feed and exercise, a rug or two, they become more pronounced.'

'What's feed and exercise got to do with it?'

And she wanted to learn—to know everything. Sharp mind, inquisitive nature. She didn't like making mistakes, but she knew how to laugh at herself. No wonder he was so damn attracted to her. 'Doesn't matter how much you brush it,' he told her, 'if you've got an unhealthy horse, the coat's not going to glow. Sure you can clean it up and spray stuff on it, but a healthy coat—one that really shines—shows up the dapples, that comes from the inside.'

'And she loves the attention. She's happier than she was when she got here. She wouldn't come near me at first, hence the bribery with the lollies.' Indy stroked her neck and Aurora nuzzled around at her pockets for another treat.

'Looks pretty happy to me. Could you grab me a clean sheet for her? One of the combos.'

'Sure.' Indy found one, came back. 'I was going to ask about exploring the trails a bit. Maybe take one of the quads out tomorrow on my day off.'

'That'd be fine.'

'Any suggestions which way to go?'

'We have a map of the main trails at the desk—and they're clearly marked once you get out there.'

'Thanks.'

'You have to sign the book at reception though—so we know where you are,' he told her. 'Then you sign it again when you get back.'

'Does that go for taking horses out too?'

'Of course. But I'm not letting you take out a horse until I've taught you to ride one.'

'Fair enough,' she said.

'And stay on the wide, marked tracks—don't go off on any of the smaller trails. You'll get yourself lost. A horse will find its own way home, a quad won't.'

'No smaller ones. Got it.'

He dropped the curry comb into the tack box and picked up a body brush, had an idea. 'If you like exploring trails, I should take you into Mt Field National Park.'

He caught the quick shadow of suspicion before she hid it behind a light smile. He almost grimaced and again silently cursed the investigation that had zeroed in on him, making everything more difficult.

'Sounds ... nice. Why Mt Field?'

'It's right behind us. And it's one of Tassie's most diverse national parks.'

'You sound like a tour guide,' she joked.

'Part of the job description.'

'Okay ... so.' She leant back against the stable door and folded her arms. 'What do you suggest?'

'The walk to Russell Falls is pretty popular. It's a three-tier waterfall—some reckon it's the prettiest in Tasmania. And you should see the tree ferns, they're incredible. Huge. If you want to go higher there are alpine plants at the summit that are unique. You can get up there on the Pandani Grove Walk around Lake Dobson. There's platypus in the lake.'

'Sounds like a nice hike.'

'And it's a pretty good skiing venue in winter.'

'You ski?'

'A bit. I like snowboarding better. And there's a track to Tarn Shelf from the ski huts you'll probably want to check out.'

'What's Tarn Shelf?'

'It's a lake on a shelf that was carved out by glaciers during the last Ice Age. Pretty spectacular. Unless you prefer caves?'

Something flickered behind her eyes, and he wondered what thought he'd triggered. 'I could be interested in caves. Are there many close by?'

'Hundreds. Some are supposedly pretty long and deep, but unless you're an experienced caver Junee Cave's your best bet. If we get a quiet day next week, I'll take you out for a look around. I'm running a campdrafting clinic in Powranna this weekend.'

She pushed away from the door, stroked Aurora's face. 'What will I do while you're gone? Will you leave instructions?'

'Mel will still be here. She'll let you know what to do.'

'Oh, that will be fun.'

The sarcasm was there. 'Problem?'

'I guess we'll see.'

He checked his watch and picked up the rug to throw on the horse, then changed his mind. 'You know what? She's still looking a bit rough. Could you finish grooming her for me? I've got a few things to do before one of my clients turns up at three.'

'Love to.' Indy took the brush and began running it over Aurora's back, while Logan haltered Brodie in a nearby stable, brought him out and tied him next to Aurora. He watched her work, the way the muscles in her toned arm moved as she stroked the brush over Aurora's coat. The woman had a body on her, that was for sure. He appreciated that because he was male, and what male wouldn't, and he appreciated the real affection she had for Aurora because he was also a horseman, and being physically attractive on its own didn't hold as much weight with him. As for that personality of hers ... it continued to intrigue him. She was so much more than the other women he had always gone for. She had a confidence about her he found appealing. She was strong, without needing to prove it, to the point where he'd wondered on a couple of occasions if she was going out of her way to hide it. And it came with a hot streak he just knew would make her challenging as an opponent. A smart one. There was always some thought or other just behind her eyes that he couldn't quite read. He found himself wanting—needing—to get closer to her.

Aurora relaxed under her attention, dropping her head and closing her eyes on a contented sigh. 'You want me to show you something?'

She looked over her shoulder. 'Okay.'

'This is a bit different to the quick rub over when the horses come back from the trails.' He stepped in behind her, put his hand over the one she was holding the brush with. There was tension in it as her eyes moved to his. He held the gaze for two beats, then moved her hand under his in a sweeping motion. 'Don't be scared to brush firmly over the body when you use this soft brush. It will massage her muscles as you work. And remember to follow the lay of the coat. Look at the lines, the patterns.'

'Okay. Got it.' He took his hand away, pleased Indy's voice was unsteady. She brushed the horse like he'd shown her.

'Thanks,' she said.

'You're welcome.' When Aurora turned her head to nuzzle Indy's side, Logan chuckled. 'She really likes you. Do you think you could fit a daily groom into your schedule?'

Indy's face brightened. 'Yes—of course. I'd like that.'

'Then I'll take you through the whole process, the different brushes, before I go away. You know how to put her rug on?'

'Yep.'

He saddled Brodie, threw on the saddlebags, retrieved one of the containers he needed from the fridge, and packed it in. It was time to go up on the trails.

CHAPTER

9

The morning was perfect for exploring, so Indy signed herself out on one of the quads and took off early. She stayed on the marked tracks, enjoying the coolness from the tall trees canopied high above her and the damp, lush undergrowth surrounding the trails. There was so much wildlife, so many birds and wallabies and lovely spots to stop and absorb.

She spent most of the day getting around and marking off any smaller trails she came across. Gates led out beyond the property's massive reach onto fire trails leading into the national park. But where did they go and how far? She made notes. There were so many little twists and turns, and she was suspicious that many of the smaller trails were made by animals. It would be impossible to search them all. If there was a structure of some sort at the end of one of these trails, the only way to find it would be by following the perp straight to it.

On her way back in, she slowed to cross a muddy depression on the track. Hoofprints, she noted, and they led off into what looked like no more than an odd interruption of low foliage—no trail to speak of. She pulled off to the side of the track and took a closer look. She'd seen the odd hoofprint here and there—no surprise, but these were fresh. The ground they had moved off into was soft and water trickled along in a thin stream. She could hear what might have been more water falling from somewhere close by.

Deciding to follow it, she fought with the mud that sucked at her boots and kept an eye on the deep impressions made by the horse's hooves for several metres before there was an opportunity to find dry ground. The undergrowth was thickest around the waterway, but the foliage thinned just beyond. She lost the trail, looked around for any more signs of hoofprints. The water she'd heard was louder here so she assumed she was close to a waterfall. Working on instinct, she headed in that direction.

That's when she heard murmuring and stopped, listened.

She spotted the horse first—the one from the campdraft. Below her, down the slope, he shone like a golden statue, standing on a sandy bank at the base of a series of small falls. Logan was sitting propped against a tree nearby, loosely holding the reins. He was talking to the horse, fiddling with a stem of grass and flicking idly at the seeds. The horse stretched down to sniff at the grass, sneezed. Logan jolted as he got sprayed, then chuckled and wiped his face, offered the stem to the horse.

Indy smiled at the pair. But what were they doing out here? They looked like they'd been there awhile—or were happy to be. But the horse jerked its head up, his attention caught by something beyond them. Logan got to his feet, seemed to be scanning or listening. After a moment he went to one of his saddlebags and pulled out a container, left the horse tied to the tree and walked out of sight.

Indy desperately wanted to follow, but the ground was noisy underfoot, the undergrowth not thick enough to hide her. She chanced a few steps, but not knowing where he was or how far he'd gone, she resigned herself to staying put.

It took him fifteen minutes to reappear, and when he did, he placed the container back in his bag and threw the reins over the horse's head. He was leaving. And she'd left the quad back on the main trail. Could she get there ahead of him? She moved as quickly and quietly as she could, cringed at every snap of a branch or swish of a shrub. If he was looking, he'd notice the footprints in the mud, was bound to hear the quad start up. And he knew she was out here this morning.

Nothing she could do about it.

She made it back and had a nervous hand on the key to start the quad up when a small group of hikers came around the bend. She recognised them as a group that had only arrived at the guesthouse the day before.

'Hi,' one of the young women greeted her. 'We're trying to find our way to a gate out to the national park.'

'Ah … sure, I have a map.'

'We do too, and it's great, but it doesn't tell us anything past the property border.'

'Then you've got the wrong map. Look.' She opened hers up, and pointed out a couple of options. They were all gathered around the quad when Logan emerged.

He pulled up the horse. 'Everything okay?'

'Logan—hi!' She did her best to infuse her greeting with surprise. 'Where did you come from?'

His narrow stare said he wasn't convinced. 'Around. What's happening?'

'We want to get out to Mt Field,' one of the group said.

'It's getting a bit late for that. You should probably head back, come back in the morning. Better yet, take the shuttle to the main part of the park. You'll see more highlights that way.'

They exchanged looks, hesitated. Then one of them said, 'Sounds like a plan. We might just go a little further along, then head back.'

Logan nodded and when they wandered off he turned his attention to Indy. 'What are you up to?'

She knew suspicion when she heard it. 'I was exploring, like I told you I was going to. I came across that lot, stopped to help.'

'Right here.'

'What's wrong with here?'

'Nothing,' he said eventually. 'You should probably head back too.'

'Yeah, will do. See you tomorrow.' She turned away, started to leave.

'Indy. Everything okay?'

She turned back, saw the cool expression. 'Yeah, it's fine.' She forced a lightness into her tone she didn't feel. Now she knew he was hiding something.

Back in her room, she opened her computer and looked on her own maps for the spot she'd seen Logan. She'd been almost certain there was nothing out there to find. She followed the line of the waterway from the track, searched the nearby area. Nothing showed. It was just trees; a thin line of them snaking through the terrain following what she discovered was a creek. It didn't make sense.

A knock on her door had her quickly closing her laptop. Ned was on the other side. 'Just thought I'd make sure everything was all right.'

'It's fine, why?'

'Because the quad's outside the bunkhouse. You're supposed to return it, sign it back in.'

'Yes, of course. I'm on it.' She saw him crane his neck to look past her into her room. 'Is there anything else?'

'Nope. Except to say Murphy came to see me about your phone. I told him what I told you, because it's the truth. It was sitting on that table when I found it.'

'Okay,' she said. 'No problem.'

'I thought maybe Jules and Kaciey might'a seen something. They were cleaning out the rooms that arvo, right?'

'I'll be sure to ask.'

He nodded. 'What are you up to? Must have been pretty important the way you came flying back here.'

'Not really. Goodbye, Ned.'

'Huh? Oh right. See you later then.' He strolled away and Indy made sure her door was locked before heading out after him to return the quad. Strange, strange man.

She put the quad away, and went up to the guesthouse to sign herself back from the trails.

She was about to leave when there was an enormous crash from upstairs. Concerned, she took the stairs two at a time and raced down the hall. Tess stood in the office surrounded by papers and books and computer equipment.

'Ah—are you okay? Indy asked.

Tess threw up her hands in a fluster. 'I tried to put something on the top shelf and it collapsed—onto the next shelf, which then collapsed onto the next one and then it all fell onto the floor. Now I have this mess from hell.'

Indy grinned at her pained expression. 'Want some help?'

'I think so. Yes, please.'

'Where should I start?'

'Anywhere. I'll find some boxes to put everything in.'

When she left, Indy began picking things up, sorting them into piles. The plastic boxes of hard drives she'd noticed the first time she was in the office were scattered around on the floor: old wage records, taxes, employee files, schedules. She wondered whether they'd line up with the information provided during the investigations of the missing girls.

'I found some—probably not enough.' Tess reappeared with Kaicey and they dumped half a dozen plastic crates on the floor and unstacked them. 'Thanks Kaicey, you'd better get back downstairs.'

Tess's phone rang. Indy waited. When she was done, she swore under her breath and clutched her hand in her hair. 'Now I have to go out on the south trail and collect a few hikers that have left it too late to get back before dark.'

'Oh that lot? Yeah. Logan warned them to head back but they wanted to keep going.'

Tess's look was startled. 'Were you out there with Logan this afternoon?'

'No, I borrowed one of the quads and went out alone, but I ran into him when I was talking to that group you have to rescue. Why?'

'Oh, it's just that he said he wasn't going ... doesn't matter. I have to get these visitors.'

Indy wondered what Tess was going to say, but was more intent on getting her hands on those files. 'You want me to keep going at this?'

'Do you really not mind?'

'Of course not. Just a general sort into the containers?'

'Thanks. I'm going to be at least half an hour, so can you make sure the office is locked when you're done?' She grimaced. 'If you're done?'

'No problem.'

Tess left and Indy closed the door and got to work. She checked the computer—a document was open. She had to assume Connor hadn't finished working for the day and intended to come back.

Working quickly she found a container of spare drives and inserted one into the computer, before pulling up files and copying the ones she wanted to review. She began with the employment records. If she was going to look for reasons why those women were taken she needed to know the details of everyone else who had worked with Logan. Look for differences as much as similarities. What else? Schedules. She could crosscheck these records against their own. She kept going, copying any piece of information that might be relevant. And she pushed back the guilt—this was her job. This was why she was here. A key in the door had her ripping the drive from the computer and turning off the screen. She barely had time to drop to the floor when Connor came in.

'What the hell are you doing?' he said, looking around in shock.

On her hands and knees on the floor, Indy glanced up. 'Yes, I know what it looks like.' She went for a big smile. 'But I'm not ransacking your office. Tess had an argument with your shelves and everything collapsed. We were about to clean it all up when she got a call to pick a group up off a trail so she left me to it. I'm just collecting everything.' She held up the drive she was copying to as though finding it on the floor. 'I said I'd get it all into the crates she left over there.'

He didn't immediately look convinced, so she added, 'Kaicey can verify it.'

When he called down to do just that, she got up—*please God don't let him turn on the computer monitor*—and made a show of moving to another area of the room to continue picking everything up.

He stepped over some mess towards his desk and she started to sweat, but he simply picked up part of a shelf and studied it, then studied the wall. 'I think I can fix this. I'll be back in one minute.' To Indy it sounded more like a threat than a statement of fact. He strode out and she turned on the monitor, quickly closed the program. Relieved, she moved back away from the desk and stashed the external drive into her sock and covered it with her jeans, straightened as Connor appeared with a toolbox in hand. 'Don't bother packing everything into the crates. You can leave this to me.'

'Right,' she said, and left.

Immediately, she went back to her room to look at the files she copied. 'This is going to take a while,' she murmured with a yawn. And because it was late, she went back into the common room and made herself a coffee. Then she sat on her bed and got to work.

Two hours later she closed her laptop and got up to stretch. The only interesting discovery she'd made was Caroline had requested shift changes twice due to 'family visiting'. She flagged it, because it seemed off that the senator hadn't mentioned two visits in the three weeks leading up to her disappearance, then with another yawn and a stretch Indy moved on to taking a good hard look at Ned.

But as Ned was a permanent, full-time member of staff, there was very little information on where he was, when. He did stock work when it was needed, farm maintenance when it wasn't. His days off were set around what needed to be done when, and so were his hours. He had more freedom to come and go than Logan or Connor. When it became clear that nothing in the records was going to help her learn too much more about him, she closed her laptop. And was almost instantly asleep.

CHAPTER
10

Logan had gone for the weekend, so Indy made sure she got to the stables just a little bit early. She didn't need to give Mel a reason to be on her back. She yawned heavily, couldn't seem to stop. When the alarm had gone off, Indy thought it must be some kind of horrible mistake. 'Mel?'

'I'm in the office.'

Indy walked to the doorway in time to see her flicking lazily through screens on the computer.

'Morning.'

'Hi. You should get the horses saddled. We've got six for a ride this morning.'

'Me personally? Aren't you helping?'

'Oh, what do you expect—another grooming lesson?' she asked with a hint of snap. 'Surely you can handle half a dozen horses on your own.'

Had Mel witnessed that? 'Are you annoyed because Logan showed me how to groom Aurora?'

Mel got to her feet and looked Indy in the eye. 'You keep your hands off Logan. You know what I'm talking about.'

'I've never actually had them on him. What's wrong with you this morning?'

'Nothing yet. But keep talking …' Mel grabbed her jacket from the back of her chair and threw it over her shoulders. 'Better yet. Don't.'

Indy shook her head in disbelief. 'Do you have any idea how difficult you are to get along with?'

'It's only going to get harder,' Mel said over her shoulder as she wandered past. 'You should think about that. There's more than one business hiring around here.'

Interesting comment. 'Such as?' she called after her.

Mel turned, walked a few steps back and considered Indy carefully. 'Talk to Marge at the pub. She always knows who's hiring.'

'Is that what Caroline did?'

Mel's face went blank. 'What?'

'You didn't like Caroline, either. Did you suggest she go ask Marge about a different job when she left here?'

The blank look turned into a scowl. 'What is it with this fascination about Caroline? I didn't talk to her before she left. She just took off. I told you that! I've got work to do. So do you.' Then with one more nasty look, 'Talk to Marge.'

At the end of the day, Indy sat on the bed to email Ben, and after a few minutes, heard unfamiliar voices outside her door. Jules was talking to two women standing by the open door to one of the spare rooms. 'And this is Indy,' Jules said with a smile for Indy.

Hi,' Indy said. 'You must be the new staff?'

'I'm Carly,' the tall redhead said, 'and this is Gina.'

'Hi.' Gina smiled and flicked her dark hair behind her shoulders.

'So you're all set,' Jules told them. 'Any questions, ask Kaicey at reception or come and find me.' Then to Indy, 'Are you coming to dinner?'

'Yeah.' She yawned.

'Let's go.'

'What are the new girls like?' Indy asked as they went.

'I think Carly's going to work out fine. Seems pretty sensible. Not sure about Gina—comes across as a bit of an airhead.'

'What's she supposed to do?'

'Clean. What could go wrong, right?'

'Absolutely,' she agreed, then sensing a problem, 'Is something else bothering you?'

Jules looked slightly sheepish. 'Yeah, actually. Tess told me Ned pinched your phone. I feel like maybe I need to apologise because I think it could be my fault.'

'How's that?'

'When you were in the shower, I had Logan bring over a new mattress for room five. The thing is, after we cleaned the rooms, Kaicey and I had to get back and there was a couple of minutes' delay in Logan getting over there, so I left the master key in the lock of room five for him.'

'Oh, I see.'

'I know I shouldn't have,' she rushed on, 'I just didn't think. We've never had anyone steal anything or break into anyone else's room before. I guess Ned must have just seen it as too big a temptation. I mean, the only other person there was Logan. He's not going to go in and take your phone and leave it on the table.'

'No. No of course not.'

But would he? Could Logan be stalking her movements? Why? Because he was considering her as his next victim or because he was suspicious as to her identity? If he thought she could be here to investigate him, he'd want to know, to be more careful—or worse, eliminate her as a problem. And it followed logically that if he'd been concerned she'd come back before he could replace it in her room, the best thing to do would be to leave it around. She didn't like the idea, but Logan's actions on the trail had been suspicious to say the least. 'It doesn't matter. I got the phone back and nothing else is missing. Don't worry about it.'

'Thanks, Indy. It won't happen again.'

Indy wasn't so sure. Regardless of who had wanted to check her phone, someone was actively prying. As cautious as she was already being, she'd have to work even harder to make sure she had nothing incriminating on any of her devices.

By lunchtime on Monday morning Indy was proud of the fact she'd kept up with Mel's punishing schedule, but she was ready to collapse. Too tired to care about food, Indy bypassed the buffet and gratefully sat at a booth with Jules. Dropping her head into her hands, she yawned.

Jules's gaze travelled over her. 'Another fun morning with Mel?'

'Hmmm. She's a Jekyll and Hyde. Jekyll's not a lot of fun, but Hyde's pure evil. I don't know what's wrong with her.'

'Logan's back now, so at least things should return to normal today. Oh, and look, here they come.'

As Logan and Mel strode through the door, Mel's voice carried clearly. 'I'm telling you Logan, she's hopeless. I hardly get any of my own work done ...'

'What work?' Indy rolled her eyes, earning a look of sympathy from Jules.

At the disgust on Indy's face, Jules got to her feet. 'Just stay put. I'll make us both a coffee.'

Jules came back a few moments later and put a steaming mug of coffee in front of Indy. Tess was right behind her and slid in beside Indy, a sympathetic smile on her face. 'Wow you look even worse than Jules said. I feel like I should apologise—offer you an office job or something.'

Indy shook her head. 'Nope. Mel from hell is Logan's fault, and I'm holding it against him.'

'Indy, you should probably know, the reason Logan tolerates Mel—' Tess began.

Jules cleared her throat. 'Speaking of,' she warned.

'Ladies.' Logan sat across from Indy, shoving Jules over in the process. Mel sat herself at the table closest to their booth, with Kaicey in tow, and glared at Indy.

Indy felt Logan's eyes on her, ignored him and sipped on her coffee. 'Hi.'

She flicked him a glance. 'Hi.'

'How've you been getting on with Aurora?' he asked.

'I haven't had a lot of time to spend with her, but she's fine.'

Frowning a little when she said nothing else, he continued. 'What have you been doing?'

'Not much,' Mel muttered. Kaicey sniggered, then sent Indy a wide-eyed apologetic look. Indy eyed them both, thought about it, and decided to let it go. Logan's gaze travelled over her face and his smile softened. 'What's up?'

In an attempt to look anywhere but at Logan, she glanced at Jules, caught her staring hard at Mel. Mel cleared her throat noisily. 'So, Indy.' The tone was only outdone by the frigid look she levelled at her. 'I realise you came here knowing nothing about horses, but surely you know how to work a washing machine?'

As everyone within earshot went silent, Indy considered the question, considered Mel. 'Yes, that's right.'

'The horse rugs I had to unload, when you forgot to, came out still filthy.'

She took a calm sip of her coffee. 'That would be because there's barely any detergent left. I believe stock inventory is your department?'

'And the tack wasn't wiped clean after the ride this morning,' Mel added.

She somehow managed to smile at her. Briefly. 'I'm sorry, I thought you worked here too.'

Mel's eye's flared. 'What I'm doing is picking up all your slack. You don't seem to be taking your work very seriously. You like to cause trouble though, don't you? I've been talking to poor Mason.'

Indy lifted her brow in surprise. 'Wow. It's kind of flattering to know you've been spending all your spare time gossiping about me.'

'His eyes are still black from the broken nose you gave him.'

One shoulder lifted in a careless shrug. 'What was he hoping for—a pretty shade of purple? And would talking to all these people be the reason why you're never at the stables? I wondered where you were.'

'If you'd do that to a person, just for disciplining their horse—'

'It was an uncalled-for beating,' Logan corrected her.

'Still, are you really sure it's a good idea to keep someone like her on?' Mel asked Logan, then turned to Indy. 'After all, if you'd go and do something like that, I have to wonder what else you're capable of.'

Indy put down her coffee, folded her arms on the table and smiled slowly and menacingly. 'I should probably warn you you're pretty close to finding out.'

Looks were exchanged, chuckles smothered. Mel turned imploring eyes on Logan. 'Are you going to let her speak to me like that?'

'Seems to me,' Logan began in his lazy tone, 'the two of you are big girls. I don't care if you carry on, as long as you do it on your time and not mine.'

Indy needed to leave before she physically removed the superior look from Mel's face. 'Well. As much fun as this has been ...' But as she tried to get up, Logan flinched, and from the look on Tess's face Indy could only assume she'd just kicked him, hard.

'Ah, right.' He frowned thoughtfully and rubbed his fingers over his forehead. 'Mel, I've got a private riding lesson booked in a while, and I'd like you to lead the quad bikes out. Take Carly so she learns the ropes. She hasn't done that tour yet.'

'Really? Cool. I'll get Indy going and—'

'I'll do that, you get the quads out.' When an awkward silence continued, he raised his brow. 'Now would be good.'

She looked down at her plate. 'But I haven't ... Sure.'

'Why didn't you defend Indy?' Tess hissed at her cousin when Mel was out of earshot.

'Tess, I don't want—' Indy began.

'You think I needed to?' Logan cut in with disbelief. He looked at Indy with a lopsided grin. '*I* was scared.'

Indy rolled her eyes, 'I think I might get started too.' She stepped over Tess and with a brief smile, walked back to the stables to attack the feeds. What the hell was it about Mel? The woman was hard to get along with at the best of times, but up until now she'd kept a façade of reasonable friendliness in front of Logan. To sit there in front of her and tell Logan he should fire her? What was that about—that damn moment over grooming Aurora? Did she think, that after her earlier comments about other work, she might push Indy just far enough to go find it? She was worried, because Tess had hinted there was a reason Logan kept Mel on. She had to hope it wasn't a strong enough one that if it came to an ultimatum, Indy was out. It could jeopardise the entire investigation. As much as the idea grated on her, she was going to have to suck it up and continue to bow to Mel. She didn't have to like it, but there was more at stake than her ego and a few blisters.

Logan went looking for Indy, found her in the feed room. She tossed a scoop of lucerne chaff into a bucket of grain, then another. The third she slapped in hard enough to topple the bucket. 'Damn it!' She bent to clean it up.

'Did something happen between you and Mel while I was away?' he asked, stepping in.

'Nope.'

'So you're okay?'

'Fine,' she muttered.

He pressed a bit more. 'Look, I've heard from other workers that Mel can be difficult at times to get along with. If something happened, you should say so. Mel has high expectations and she's not great at talking to people.'

'Tell me about it.' She put the feed scoop down and turned her back to him to open another bag of chaff.

He turned her back around and let go when she jerked at his hold. 'She won't say anything like that again. If she does, there'll be consequences. All right?'

'There'll be consequences, *all right*,' she echoed.

His lips twitched, and he nodded. She was fine, just pissed off. 'What are you up to with the work?'

'I'm up to date. With all of it.'

He thought he caught the slightest inflection on the 'I'm', so he clarified. 'You mean, you and Mel.'

'No, I mean me.'

What the hell had Mel been doing? 'Are you joking?'

'Why would I joke?' She picked up the scoop, wincing as the dressing on her finger ripped away.

He took her hand and checked the wound. It had almost healed, but there were two open blisters on her fingers. 'I'm sorry about Mel. I'll talk to her.' His thumb skimmed over her wrist of its own accord. He felt the tiny tremble of her hand as she pulled it away.

'Forget it. You'll only make the situation worse.'

'How's that?'

Indy spared him an unimpressed glance. 'Jules said she's chased off every female you've tried to employ.'

'Jules shouldn't have said that. That's not true.'

'Fine, but defending me won't help the situation. If you don't know why, work it out.'

Was she suggesting Mel had a thing for him? Hell, he hadn't thought of that. 'You think she ... that she's ...?'

'In love with you? It crossed my mind. Either that or she really is a sadistic slave-driving bitch.' Indy closed her eyes and her features settled. When she opened them, she continued calmly. 'It would be great if instead of having a go at her you could just give me a list of responsibilities that are mine, so I can tell her to go to hell and still keep my job.'

He sighed heavily, nodded. 'I can do that. Why don't you go on the supply run with Jules this afternoon while I sort something out?'

'Okay.'

'She leaves in about half an hour. I'll let her know you're going.' He watched her walk away, then took himself up to see Connor.

Connor looked up from the paperwork on his desk with a curious expression. 'Come on in.'

Logan sat on the chair opposite and ran a hand over his head. 'Mel's being difficult.'

'Well, duh.' Connor sat back in his chair, looking more amused than Logan thought he should.

He frowned. 'Why is that everyone's attitude? Mel's all right.'

'In front of you she is,' Connor shot back. 'But if you believe what some of the other staff have said—'

'What am I supposed to do? She's got nowhere else to go.'

'I think she's got enough value out of that excuse over the last couple of years.'

'And she's a good worker,' he defended.

'That's lucky—it's not like you can keep anyone else on long enough to train up.'

'You're not being helpful.'

Connor shrugged. 'You know, I don't think you've bent over backwards quite enough. Maybe you should just marry the woman. Then she could stay at your place and play house. Keep out of everyone's way.'

'Really not helpful.'

Connor's grin faded and he shook his head. 'Mate, you know it wasn't your fault. You can't carry this around forever, and honestly? Mel's taking advantage of the situation.'

Logan rubbed the back of his neck and nodded slowly. 'Apparently, she had Indy doing a lot of her own work while I was away.'

'Indy quit?' Connor asked sharply.

'No … Mel took her on in the lunchroom and …' a grin split his face, 'lost.'

From the doorway, Jules laughed. 'Fully. Seriously Logan, you're a softie through and through, and that's great, but Mel? Not a team player.'

'I'll figure something out.'

'Of course you will. In the meantime, I'm going out to Hilltop Farm.' She looked at Connor and her smile dropped. 'I need a spare set of keys for the truck.'

Connor took a bunch from a drawer and handed them to her. 'You still right to drive it?'

'You're worried I'll get hurt?' Jules asked sarcastically. 'What have I got to lose? Oh that's right—nothing.'

Logan looked from one to the other—wondered just what the hell they were on about. It made no sense to him, but Connor had lost some colour.

Jules headed for the door. 'See you later, Logan.'

'Yeah—bye. Oh, I told Indy to go with you.'

'Okay. I'll find her,' she threw over her shoulder.

'She really hasn't forgiven you,' Logan said when Jules had left.

'She probably never will. Not sure I blame her.'

'Mate—what exactly did you do?'

Connor's face closed up and he returned to his desk. 'It's over with. So,' he began, changing the subject, 'Indy.'

'What about her?'

'If she can't work at the stables—'

'Of course she can work at the stables.'

'With Mel?'

'With me.'

'But that's not logical. You're only there half the time.'

'Carly's going to free up some of my time by taking over the majority of the activities,' he pointed out.

'True. But I have applications coming in since we readvertised. I should be able to get you someone else. Someone we can be more certain is legit and that Mel might get on with a little better.'

'You just finished telling me Mel doesn't get on with anyone. Besides, Indy's a great employee. She works hard and fast and likes the horses, knows how to follow instructions. I like to think my radar's pretty good at picking people and I like her. So I'm going to say she's not some sneaky reporter that's here to destroy us, and I'm asking you to drop it once and for all.' He didn't mention her following him out on the trail. That would lead to too many difficult questions. He'd figure that one out himself.

Connor nodded slowly. 'All right. But we have three possible new staff coming out for interviews in the next couple of days. If that changes, I might be able to get you a replacement. One of them—Larissa something or other—has experience with horses.'

'Good to know. But that won't be necessary.' His voice was firm, final, as he got to his feet.

'Where are you off to?'

'To figure out how this is going to work,' he said.

CHAPTER

11

'Hey, Indy!' Jules called out, coming downstairs as Indy was looking for her. 'Logan said you're coming with me?'

'Yep. Supply run, right? Where are we going?'

'A place called Hilltop Farm. Is everything all right?'

'Sure,' Indy feigned surprise. 'Why?'

'When you charged up the hallway just then you looked like you wanted to hit someone.'

'Honestly, I'm not sure I don't. Let's leave it there.'

Jules pressed her lips down against a grin. 'Okay ... Thanks for coming—I prefer to have someone with me. It's a bit of a hike and there's no phone reception for the last part of the drive.'

'What sort of supplies are we picking up?'

'Food. You wait until you see the place. The farm is huge. They have the best, freshest produce in Tassie, so I source whatever I can for Calico Mountain from there.' They walked out to the truck and climbed in. Jules hesitated before turning it on. 'You don't get carsick do you? It's a bit of a long, winding road and the truck isn't the most comfortable mode of transportation—especially on the bumpy bits.'

'I'll be fine,' Indy assured her.

The road really did seem to go on forever. 'Do these people sell off-farm?'

'Yep—in a big way. We import their produce up to the mainland to use in my restaurant—and there's plenty of others use their goods, too. Why?'

'Because I can't imagine transport trucks getting in and out of here.'

'We're coming in from the wrong end, that's all. There's a lot of wilderness to cut through coming this way but if you come in from the other side it's not too far from Hamilton and the roads are much better.'

'That makes more sense.' They continued through a piece of road barely wide enough for the truck to fit through, with a drop of several metres on one side and towering trees so thick they blocked out much of the sunlight. 'No wonder you like company.'

Jules shot her a grin. Indy wished she'd just keep her eyes on the road. 'This is the worst bit.'

'There's so much land out here—and so much dense forest.'

'Geographically Tassie isn't huge but there's still plenty of it. And a heck of a lot of it isn't populated and isn't easily accessible. It all adds to the feeling of size. Look, here we are.'

They drove around a bend and out of the trees. Ahead of them were large brown fields with warning signs posted on all the fences. 'Why the signs?'

'They're growing opium poppies.'

Opium. It clicked right away—the scent she'd picked up at the stables on a couple of occasions was opium. Mel had to be smoking it. And that explained the mood swings. 'Oh—right. That's big down here, isn't it?'

'There're growers all over Tasmania licensed to supply poppies to the big drug companies. Half the world's medicinal opiates come from here. It's very tightly regulated.'

'So poppies and produce?'

'Right. They grow veggies as well. Poppy growing is best suited to the rotation used by mixed-cropping farmers. You shouldn't grow them in the same field in consecutive seasons.'

'Oh—look at the pigs.' Rows of paddocks with rounded shelters housed black and white pigs.

'Best bacon in Tasmania.'

Indy shuddered. 'Ew.'

Jules sent her a sideways look. 'Where did you think it comes from?'

'I don't think. I don't have to think. By the time I see bacon it's packaged and bears no resemblance to the real thing.'

A smile slid slowly over Jules's face. 'You'd better close your eyes.'

'Why?'

'Because we're coming to the deer.'

'They kill Bambi here? I don't like this place.'

'You will when you taste my venison,' Jules said with confidence.

'They sell meat directly out of here, too? Is that legal?'

'They're licensed. Have their own small abattoir, though I've never seen it.'

'You said it was a big place—and it really is.'

'A lot of people are employed here from local towns. They always need more help than they can readily get, though. Especially in the busy season.'

'When's that?'

'Now.'

They reached a heavily signposted gate and turned, drove to a storefront with outdoor shelves lined with produce. 'Let's go find someone.'

The shop was full of fruit and vegetables, and a large fridge and freezer of meat ran along the back wall. Off to the side, a barrel of a woman with a shock of red frizzy hair stood tending shelves of preserves. She stopped when the women entered, her ready smile dropping in surprise when she spotted them. A tall, solidly built man in work clothes and a green cap was standing close by with his back to them. Otherwise there was no one else in the shop.

'Hi, Brenda,' Jules said brightly.

The woman pulled herself together and the smile returned, warmer than the first. 'Jules! You're back! And you've brought a ... friend?'

'I have. This is Indy.'

The man turned. For a brief moment his gaze was sharp and probing. Then she was left to wonder if she'd imagined it when he mumbled something to Brenda and walked out.

Brenda returned her attention to Jules and nodded slowly. 'And is Indy looking for work?'

'No. She's working for us. Logan sent her out here to keep me company while I did a pick-up.'

'It's all ready for you. And it's great to see you back.' But the woman's curious eyes were back on Indy. 'Hello there.'

'Hi.'

'How are you finding things out at Calico Mountain?'

'I'm enjoying it, thanks.'

She smiled in response, then said to Jules, 'Let's get you loaded up.'

Jules and Indy walked outside and climbed back into the truck, manoeuvred it through the gate Brenda unlocked, then reversed up to a set of double doors at the front of a large green shed. Mason appeared from inside as Brenda came around from the gate, his face closing into a sneer when he spotted Indy. 'What do you want?'

She supposed, as he was a Cartwright, she shouldn't have been surprised to find him there. 'Mel was right,' Indy said pleasantly, 'you really are lots of pretty colours.'

'Where's Jim?' Brenda asked him before he could reply.

'Dunno. Was round a minute ago.'

'You best load this up then. Those couple of crates there, and some more in the cool room.' Without comment he got to work. Because Brenda was again watching her, Indy looked for something to say. 'I'm sorry, I didn't realise you're Mason's mum.'

'Yep. And don't go feeling too uncomfortable about it. He wanted the horse, we got it for him, then he carried on like a princess cause his pride got hurt. I reckon his ears were sorer than his nose once Jim had finished lecturing him about it. How's the mare going?'

'Really great. She's a lovely horse.'

'It was good of Logan to pay us back what we paid for her. Probably would have had to take less otherwise—try and offload her ourselves. We're not really horse people.'

'All done,' Mason muttered.

'Good to see you, Jules,' Brenda said. 'And nice to meet you, Indy.'

'Say hello to Jim for me,' Jules replied with a hand on the truck door.

'You can say hello to him yourself.' An older man with a slight stoop came into view and Jules left the truck to give him a kiss on his weathered cheek.

'Jules!' A little girl of no more than three raced out from behind him to cling to her leg.

'Hi, sweetie,' Jules returned, ruffling the little girl's dark hair.

'Can you come and play with me and Kyle?'

'One day soon, gorgeous girl. But today I need to get back to work.'

When they'd said goodbye and were on the road, Indy had to say, 'Brenda was lovely considering what happened to Mason.'

'She's embarrassed by his behaviour. And grateful to Logan.'

'I see. So ... who's the child?'

'Oh, Bindi? Yeah that's just Mel's kid.'

'As in the Mel that works for Logan?'

'Yep. Jim and Bren have three kids—Kyle, Mel and Mason. Mel's husband was a farrier, but he also did some work for the Cartwrights, which is how she met him. Just after she got pregnant, there was an accident and Matty died. Anyway, Bren minds Bindi while Mel's at work.'

Explains the opium supply. 'And Kyle is the one I saw the night after the campdraft.'

'That's him. We went to school together and I catch up with him and the others whenever I come down.' She sighed. 'Mel used to be really nice, but the thing with Matty screwed her up. We were all great friends growing up. The Cartwrights were like extended family. Logan's parents met in much the same way Mel and Matty did, when Richard started working for Jim.'

'Did you know them?'

'No. Mum and I arrived a couple of years after they left.'

'Left?'

'Mm. That's one for Logan to tell.'

'Oh, okay.' She let it go but had to ask, 'So how come Mel works for Logan? Wouldn't it be easier for her to work at Hilltop Farm?'

'She and Jim butt heads. These days, Mel and just about everyone butt heads. Logan's the only one who'll put up with her. Besides, for a long time the place was run down and not making much money. So, they added the poppy-growing element a few years back to try and make the place viable. According to Jim, it was the best thing they could have done. The farm hasn't looked back. They make a better living now than they ever did before.'

The phone rang and Connor's name came up on the car display screen. 'What's he want?' she grumbled. 'You talk to him.'

'Me?' Indy muttered. She was still putting all the pieces together in her head, but answered. 'Hello?'

Silence, then, 'Is that you, Indy?'

'Yes.'

'Are you with Jules? I need to speak to her.'

'You're on speaker,' Jules snapped. 'What?'

'I'm doing the accounts and I've just found some unusual charges to the kitchen. Have you been making any large purchases from new suppliers?'

'Yes. I have. The kitchen is out of date and needs new equipment. Mum's been slaving away with the old things for too long. It makes her job more difficult than it needs to be. Problem?'

'No.' Indy could hear the weariness in his voice. 'I just needed to check the charges were legit. It wasn't a personal attack.'

He was cut off when Jules pressed the button on the steering wheel.

Indy was going to comment when she saw the sheen of tears in Jules's eyes and changed her mind. 'Are you okay?'

'Yep. I'm hungry. Let's call in at the pub for lunch.'

'Sounds good.'

The pub wasn't busy, and Marge was out quickly to see them. 'Hi, Jules—oh and … Indy. How's it going?'

'Hi, Marge,' Indy greeted her. 'That's a good memory you've got.'

'Not so hard to remember a new face around here. What are you ladies after?'

'Hamburger and chips,' Jules said.

'Make that two, thanks,' Indy echoed.

'I'm just going to the ladies,' Jules told Indy. 'Go grab us a table.' Then to Marge, 'Oh and can I get a pub squash, too?'

'No worries. Indy?'

'Sounds great.'

Marge put in the food order and prepared the drinks. 'Where are you two off to?'

'We're on our way back. Jules took me on a supply run to Hilltop Farm.'

'Nice out there, isn't it? Did you meet Brenda?'

'Yes, she seems lovely.'

'She is. Don't think bad of her because Mason played up. She and Jim are good people. Looking for workers, too. Something to think about if Calico Mountain doesn't work out. How is the new job going?'

'Great, mostly.'

'What are you doing out there?'

'Working at the stables.'

Marge's gaze sharpened. 'With Logan, then. You be careful. That's who those girls that went missing were working for.'

Indy lowered her voice and arranged her face into worry. 'Do you really think Logan is behind it all?'

'All I know is, Latisha and Logan were pretty good mates, and we know how that turned out.' Marge gave an exaggerated shudder. 'So were Gretchen and Logan. That's why Warren's so beside himself. He was never the best father and he's a drunken loudmouth, but she just up and vanished like Latisha in almost exactly the same circumstances. Then it happened again with Caroline, after she and Logan started going around together. There's a pattern there if you ask me. Warren's worried sick. Just doesn't know a good way to deal with it.'

'Caroline and Logan were more than just friends?'

'So were he and Gretch if you believe the stories. Hard to know.'

'Someone told me they thought Gretchen might have just taken off.'

'It's possible.' Marge frowned. 'But she hung around all the way through her mother's illness, helped nurse her right up to her death, then disappeared right before the funeral. Wouldn't have thought Gretch would do that.'

'Sounds a bit strange. Thanks for the warning.'

Marge handed Indy the drinks. 'Look, you're a nice young thing. I meant what I said last time. If you get worried, come and see me. I'll have a word in Jim's ear about a job out there. Just don't mention that offer to the Athertons, if you don't mind. I don't want to go putting them offside.'

'Understood and appreciated.' She took the drinks. 'Thanks— we'll be over by the window.'

'I'll bring the food out shortly.'

Jules reappeared and followed Indy to the table. 'What were you talking to Marge about?'

'Just bits and pieces.'

'Like Logan and missing women?' At Indy's silence Jules chuckled. 'Marge has got a heart of gold but she likes her gossip.'

Indy sipped her drink and wondered if Jules would still feel that way if she'd heard the conversation. 'She's worried, like everyone else appears to be around here. She seems quite friendly with Warren.'

'She feels sorry for him.' A wicked grin spread across her face, 'Speaking of *friendly*, Logan said he sent you off with me because of the dramas with Mel.'

'I can't help but wonder why she's kept on.'

'She's good with the horses—knows how to run the place when Logan's not there. He can't afford to give her the boot.'

Interest caught, Indy put down her drink. 'Is he often not there?'

'Part of Logan's business involves running training clinics and entering competitions. Training horses and riders brings in more revenue than tourist trail rides and when he wins at comps it helps him sell horses and bring in more clients. He usually takes off several times a year, but he's missed a lot recently because of the staff shortage.'

Mel had said something similar. Could he come and go so often and keep women alive? Indy wondered. 'From what Tess was saying, I thought there might be more to the Mel thing than that.'

Jules nodded thoughtfully. 'She's had a bit of a rough time of it over the years. But if Latisha was still around he might have been tempted to let her go. Latisha was just as good with the horses and a whole lot better with people.'

'I know you haven't been around much, but did you know Latisha very well?'

'Not really. I remember it was Christmas and she gave Logan a mouthful. She said something about the best present she could give herself would be to head up to the mainland and find another job.'

'Because of Mel?' Indy asked.

'I don't know. Maybe. It seemed like Logan had sorted it out with Latisha. They were quite friendly again by the end of the day. And then she was gone.'

'I think Mel might have an undiagnosed anxiety disorder.'

Jules laughed. 'You're trying to make excuses for the fact she's a bitch?'

'Having anxiety doesn't make you a bitch—that's just personality. But she has other signs.'

'Like what?'

Indy backed off at Jules's sharp look and sudden serious interest. 'She's just nervy, that's all.'

'She's nervy whenever there's another female around Logan.'

'Here you go, ladies,' Marge said, plopping two overflowing large plates on the table.

'Thanks, Marge,' Jules said.

Indy bit into her burger with happiness. 'The cook is a genius.'

'Hey, watch it,' Jules teased. 'You haven't said anything like that about my cooking yet.'

'You haven't made me a hamburger yet.'

'A hamburger?' Jules echoed in disgust. 'You have to try the fine dining menu.'

'Does it have hot chips on it? I think fine dining's a bit wasted on me.'

'I'll work on changing your mind—and your palate.'

Indy just grinned and chewed on a chip. 'Good luck with that.'

As they drove back to Calico Mountain, Indy thought about everything she'd learned about the Cartwrights, about Mel. 'Does Mel live out at Hilltop?'

'Yeah, in one of the little cottages. Why?'

'No particular reason. It's just this place: everyone seems to be connected in one way or another. It's interesting.'

'That's small towns for you. Hey, that's Tess and Rosalie.' She pointed a little farther down the road.

'Looks like they've broken down,' Indy said.

'Hmm.' Jules pulled over just ahead of them and she and Indy climbed out. 'What's happened?' Jules asked.

Tess pulled a face and kicked the car. 'It's broken.'

Indy grinned at Tess. 'Broken how?'

Tess just looked confused. 'As in it won't go.'

She couldn't help the *Are you kidding?* look. 'Have you noticed it playing up before today?'

'It's been losing some power on the hills with the horse float on, and occasionally when the engine's idling it turns itself off. But it's never refused to start before.'

Indy moved to the driver's door and climbed in. Turning the key, she listened carefully.

'What are you doing?' Jules asked.

'Shhh,' she instructed. She nodded to herself, flicked the bonnet lever and climbed out. 'Do you have a rag anywhere?' she asked Tess.

'Maybe. There's a toolbox in the back.'

'You don't know what's in it?' Indy asked.

'Why would I? I've never opened the damn thing. It just sits in the back taking up space because Connor said as it came with the car I should keep it. I'll look.' Tess walked around and pulled out a long narrow metal container. She dropped it on the ground with a heavy thud and fiddled with the catch until the lid swung back. 'Will this do?' she asked, holding up a polishing cloth.

'It'll never do what it's meant to again, but yeah, thanks.' She focused on the job at hand. 'Got a wrench in that box?'

'This?'

She glanced up, nodded, took it.

'What is it?' Rosalie asked, intrigued.

'It could be a few things. I'm just cleaning off the battery terminals, they're filthy. We'll reconnect them and try again.' She continued to work, then lifted her head. 'Tess, try to start it for me?' she called, frowning then giving a nod when it didn't fire. 'Okay, turn off. We'll try a jump start.'

She climbed into the truck and manoeuvred it to Tess's car. Connecting the cables, she gave the nod to Tess, but again the car refused to start.

'What now?'

'Let me check a few more things,' Indy said. She looked in Tess's toolkit, and raised her eyebrows. 'This is seriously impressive.'

'Wasted on me, then. The guy I bought it off went off-road a lot.'

Indy got to work, and when she'd run through the list of possibilities, she nodded to herself. 'I'm guessing it's the fuel pump.'

'Guessing?' Tess asked warily.

Indy flashed her a quick grin. 'Reasonably certain?' She opened the back door and leant inside. Shoving down hard on the seat, she released it from the tracks and lifted it out of the car. 'Pass me that red screwdriver?'

Tess did as requested, and the women watched in fascination as Indy unscrewed the access cover and unplugged some wiring.

'What's that?' Jules asked.

'The sender unit for the fuel pump,' Indy muttered absently.

Jules's look was pure confusion. 'The *what*?'

Indy continued to pull apart the car until she had the pump in hand. 'Got an auto-parts store around here anywhere?'

'Back towards Hobart,' Rosalie said.

Indy grimaced. 'We'll tow you home.'

'Tow it?' Tess asked sceptically.

Indy's brow rose. 'No?' She walked back around to the toolbox, pulled out a perfectly good tow cable. 'You've got everything we need in here and we're just going ten minutes down the road. Logan's truck will do it.'

'Are you sure? How do you know this stuff?' Tess asked.

She shrugged. 'A family of mechanics,' she said in a tone that didn't invite further questions. She wiped her hands on the rag, tossed it in the car. 'Let's get hooked up.'

'We'll take it over to Logan's place and dump it there until it's fixed,' Rosalie decided. 'Then Tess can take Logan's car. He never goes anywhere in it.'

'Okay,' Indy said. Then to Tess, 'You're in charge of brakes and steering. Flick on the hazard lights, I'll pull, we'll go slow. Any worries, hit the horn.'

'I can do that,' Tess said, still sounding a little unsure.

When they reached Calico Mountain, Indy continued on along the road she knew took them to Logan's house. She was curious— and this was a good excuse to get to see his place up close. She wondered if she could get a good look around—possibly inside.

They pulled up on a circular driveway which contained a garden complete with a stone fountain. The house was old and pretty. Wide verandahs with curling vines that crept along the guttering, wrapped around the bottom storey. The second storey was similar, its verandah overlooking what Indy knew would be a stunning view of the countryside and mountains beyond. There was a stable block at the side of the house, and further on she could just make out a set of cattle yards, a building she assumed was a machinery shed and a few horse yards and paddocks.

'This was the original manager's residence,' Jules told Indy. 'Logan used to live here with his parents. When he grew up he moved back in.'

A gleaming horse truck sat in the drive, and Logan emerged from it with a broom when the cars crunched on the gravel. In the rear-vision mirror Indy saw Tess send him a wave. 'Car broke down. Can I leave it here and borrow yours?'

'It's all yours,' he called back.

As Indy climbed out of the truck, Logan ambled the rest of the way across and sent her a taunting grin. 'Miss me already?'

'With every beat of my heart.' She stepped past him, began to disconnect the car from the truck.

Hands on his hips, he watched her. 'You've done that before.'

'Not exactly rocket science,' she replied dryly.

'What's wrong with the car?'

'Fuel pump—I think. It's in the back.'

'You pulled it out?' he asked sceptically.

She rolled up the tow strap and put it back in the car. 'It can't stay there broken.'

His brow was furrowed. 'How—'

'I might take Rosie back with me and unload the truck,' Jules interrupted. 'We've got cold stuff in there.'

'No worries,' Logan said, then with one last thoughtful look at Indy he said, 'Why don't you ladies go inside and grab a cold drink while I put some petrol in my car?'

'Sounds good,' Tess said. 'Indy?'

Indy followed Tess onto the verandah and through the front door into a lounge room, dominated by a large television. Beyond it she saw an enormous kitchen and family room. Floorboards were scattered with thick rugs, walls decorated with paintings and framed photographs. The furniture was old and comfortable, the kitchen surprisingly modern. Beyond the family room the verandah spread out to encompass a generous-sized pool that seamlessly flowed out into a garden. Indy instantly fell in love with the place.

Tess pulled a tall glass jug from the fridge and poured juice into three glasses. When she handed one to her, Indy smiled and looked around. 'This is a lovely place.'

'Yeah, it's no millionaire's residence or anything, but it has character.'

And Indy really wanted to get a good look at it. 'Is there a bathroom?'

'Yeah, just down the hall. I'll take these onto the back deck. Come out when you're done.'

She walked down the hall and around the corner, spotted the bathroom—and the stairs. She silently bounded up, looked around.

Another living area complete with a small library and a large window to let in the view, a couple of spare bedrooms, Logan's room with a small ensuite. She did a quick exploration of each, and when she heard the screen slam, she abandoned the last spare room to hurry down the stairs. She rounded the corner and nearly slammed into Logan.

'You find what you were looking for?'

'What?'

'The bathroom.'

'Oh right. Yes. Thanks.'

'Tess is out back.' He led her out onto the deck and took a long drink from the glass Tess handed him.

'Did Dad drop the mail over?' Tess asked.

'Yeah, he left it on the table.'

'Do you not lock your house?' Indy asked.

'Someone would have to be pretty damn keen to come all the way out to Calico Mountain, past the guesthouse, past the bunk-house and down a dirt track to pinch something of mine. Besides, I'd forever be losing the key and locking myself out.'

She supposed he had a point. And allowing people to wander in and out of his house whenever they felt like it put paid to any notion he brought kidnapped women here—even temporarily.

Logan stretched out on a chair and linked his arms behind his head. 'Okay. I've got to ask,' he said. 'How do you know how to pull out a fuel pump?'

'Family of mechanics,' Tess told him.

'Mm hm.' Indy took Logan's lead and sat down, swallowed another sip of her drink. And decided to stay as close to the truth as possible without giving away too many details. Besides, it tied in with her cover story. 'We had a garage in the States. My grandparents ran it and my mum helped out. I used to help my grandfather restore old cars.'

'Is your dad a mechanic too?' Tess asked.

'He was. He died when Mum was pregnant with me. Which is why she packed up herself and my big sister and moved all the way to Colorado to stay with his parents. She didn't have any close family left over here.'

'Over here?' Logan asked.

'Um ... yeah, actually.' She decided to steer the conversation in another direction. 'So, is it safe to go back to the stables?' she joked.

Logan nodded. 'I'm sorting out a list of jobs, so when you go back tomorrow, you'll see your responsibilities outlined on the wall.'

'Trying to piss off Mel?' Tess asked.

'Occupational hazard,' Indy muttered.

'I wanted to warn you too,' Logan said. 'I'm taking Rex over to the guesthouse stables. He needs some serious work and I'll have more time for him over there.'

'Who is Rex?' she asked.

'Rex is my stallion. The one I rode at the campdraft. I was on him when I ran into you out on the trail the other day.' He sent her a look that suggested he was still suspicious.

She smiled innocently. 'Oh, he's gorgeous. I love the—wait, I suppose there's a special term for that gold and white colouring?'

'Palomino,' he chuckled. 'I'll put him in the main stables but you don't handle him, understand?'

'Why not?'

'He's not always ... polite.'

'Polite?'

'Rex doesn't like anyone but Logan,' Tess said. 'And no one likes Rex but Logan.'

'Plenty of people like him,' Logan argued with a smirk, 'from a distance. He was booked out for stud services this year,' he added.

Tess just snorted.

'So you're obviously not breeding him for his personality,' Indy deduced.

'Cow.'

Her jaw dropped in offence. 'I beg your pardon?'

Logan's smile increased. 'Cow *sense*. He really is sensational at working cattle.'

'Or he'd be dead.' Tess put her glass in the sink and took Indy's. 'You ready to head back? Maybe we can order this part for the car before the place closes.'

CHAPTER

12

Logan pulled up at the stables and took the whiteboard of responsibilities out of the ute. He'd spent a decent chunk of the night before working it out. It was a pain in the arse, but he understood why Indy had asked for one, and he had to agree it was probably necessary. Unfortunately.

'Hi.'

He shut the door and looked behind him, saw an unfamiliar woman waiting to speak to him. 'Hi. Can I help you?'

'I'm Gina. I've just started working here. I was taking a look around.'

He smiled. 'Nice to meet you.'

'You're Logan, right?' Gina smiled back and twisted a lock of her hair around her finger.

'That's me.'

'It's so pretty down here. I think I'd like to learn to ride while I'm working here.'

And he'd like to get in and start the day. 'We'll have to make sure we book you in then. I don't have the computer open yet. Pop down again later if that suits.' With another smile he headed to the office.

'Is Indy here?' she called out.

He stopped and turned around. 'If not, she won't be far away. Did you check the stables?'

'Ah … yeah. I didn't go in. Someone's in there crying so I didn't think I should.'

His face creased into a frown. 'Crying? Thanks.'

He left her there and walked in, found Mel. When she looked up, her face was red, her eyes swollen.

'Hey. What's up?' he asked. He leant the whiteboard against the wall.

Fresh tears ran down her cheeks. 'Logan, I'm sorry.' She got to her feet and wrapped her arms around him. 'I didn't mean to cause a scene yesterday.'

Though he wished to hell she hadn't and was still feeling less than friendly, he gave her a quick squeeze and moved her to a chair and sat opposite, elbows on his knees, fingers linked. 'You want to tell me about it?'

'Everything just gets on top of me sometimes, you know.'

'You've had her doing a lot of your own work. When I'm not here, I trust you to run things properly and responsibly.'

'I do! I just—there's just something about her.' She sniffed, dug out a tissue. 'Can't we just get someone else?'

'You didn't like Caroline, either, or some of the others,' he reminded her.

'I know. They come in here and they walk around like they own the place and they don't know—they don't know what I've had to deal with. I envy them, but they make me so mad. I'm sorry. I don't know what I'd do without this job. I just don't know what I'd do.'

He covered her hand with his. 'You do have a job here, so you don't need to worry about that. But I need you to try to get along with Indy, okay?'

'Okay.' She swiped at her eyes.

'I've brought a board with me that outlines what duties I expect you both to do each day.' When her head shot up he quickly continued. 'I know you more than have a handle on it, but I think it will help Indy if she can tick off a list, just for the time being.' He'd phrased it that way to make it sound like his idea, but from the look on Mel's face she wasn't buying it. The last thing he wanted to do was increase the animosity between them. 'What do you think?' And damn it—he was pandering to her. It grated on him but he kept his smile in place.

'I guess if it's there in black and white she can't accuse me of making it unfair.'

'Then everything's good. Settled?'

'Yeah.' She sighed heavily and got to her feet, hugged him again. 'Thanks, Logan.'

Indy paused in the breezeway. The corner of the office was visible—just enough to see Mel in Logan's arms. Turning on her heel, she hurried back the way she'd come. What was that about? Mel had looked upset. About what? Their altercation? Was something else going on? She refused to acknowledge the little punch in the gut it had caused her.

That's enough. That's seriously more than enough, she chided herself.

If there was anything between Logan and Mel, why were they hiding it? She went through some scenarios in her mind, but none rang true. She just couldn't make herself believe they were romantically involved; she was better at reading people than that.

All that was immediately clear was that Logan wasn't the only one with secrets. Something had happened to Mel—something that no one was keen to talk about and it was taking a toll on her life. The mood swings, the drugs, the tears. She had a gut feeling that whatever had happened to Matt, there were unresolved issues or circumstances that were impacting on her in ways that weren't allowing the hurt to heal. If she could figure out what they were, she'd know what Mel held over Logan—why he kept her on and let her get away with so much. She couldn't be sure it would have anything to do with the investigation, but it might go a long way to shedding some more light on what made Logan tick. First chance she had, she'd check if Ben had any more history on Mel than Mark had.

She saw them step out into the breezeway and head for the yards, so she went into the office, where she found a new whiteboard mounted on the wall at the entrance to the breezeway. It had the day's jobs, who was responsible for doing what. She was grateful; it looked like Logan had put some thought into the roster. Mel and she weren't likely to cross paths too often throughout the day.

'Happy with that?' Logan was in the doorway, watching her.

'It's great—thanks.'

'One of the new girls was down here just before. I think she was looking for you.'

'New girl?'

'Gina?' he said uncertainly.

'Oh—right, yep. I met her and Carly the day they arrived. They seem nice.'

'She asked after you.'

'Don't know why. Maybe she was just getting her bearings.' Indy picked up the wheelbarrow and got started on the stables while Logan worked Rex, then when Mel came back from the trail ride, she took care of the horses. Mel said nothing, left her right alone.

'You're missing breakfast,' Logan told her as she mixed feeds.

'I just want to get these done and grab another bale of hay for the nets, then I'll be there.'

'No worries.' He vanished from her line of sight and she went back to finishing the feeds. She'd barely filled another bucket when Mel stormed in, and from the way she glanced around before beginning, Indy knew she was about to lose it.

'You bitch!' she hissed. 'You think you're so fucking clever!'

Indy calmly continued working. 'Okay.'

'You're just a scheming whore!'

Was there any point arguing? 'You got me. Scheming. Whore. All the way.'

'You cried to Logan so he'd feel sorry for you. Now you've got him wrapped around your little finger!'

'I did? And he is? Great. Thanks for letting me know.'

'If you think you can just walk in and—'

Indy cut her off. 'And?'

'It's not like you mean anything to him!'

'I'm crushed. Seriously. You're good at this.' She dropped another scoop of chaff in the bucket.

'Are you listening to me?' In a fit of temper, Mel kicked over the feed bucket Indy was filling. 'I've worked hard to get where I am. I'm not going to let you threaten that.'

Indy looked from the feed bucket to Mel and sighed. 'If your job security's in jeopardy, that's on you.'

'That's not what I mean and you know it!' Mel growled. 'You're not one of us, and you never will be. Logan's mine!'

She calmly salvaged what she could of the feed, put it back in the bucket, and shrugged carelessly. 'Okay. Logan's yours. You might want to tell him about that little opium addiction of yours though. I'm not sure he'd approve.'

Mel's whole body jerked, her eyes went round then turned to tiny slits. 'You don't belong here,' she repeated squeezing the scissors she'd just picked up like a weapon. 'And you don't know what you're talking about. Just leave!' Mel stalked out.

Interesting, Indy thought. Had that comment been a loosely veiled threat?

She almost jumped out of her skin when Logan dropped the hay she'd needed from the loft and jumped lightly down after it. 'Indy, I don't know what to say. I'm sorry—I didn't realise she was that bad.'

Indy blew out a long breath and considered that as she stared into the space Mel had just vacated. 'To be fair, she's not usually that psychotic.' Then her gaze swung back to Logan. 'I did mention you interfering would only make it worse.'

'From what you just said, I'm not sure it could be much worse. You want to tell me about the opium comment?

'I, ah … I thought I smelled it a couple of times when she was here alone.'

'Are you sure?'

'Yeah, I am.'

'How do you know what it smells like?'

Shit … She went for a casual shrug. 'I had friends in high school. I think people usually smoke it for pain relief or anxiety or something. I'm surprised she hasn't confided in you about it.'

'Why would she?' he demanded.

She considered her words carefully. 'You two seem … pretty … close.' He stared hard at her, silently waiting several seconds for her to explain. And the pressure of that stare weighed on her until she cracked. 'Well, you did earlier.'

'Earlier …' Logan frowned thoughtfully. 'She was crying. I wanted to broach the subject of getting you both on a roster without her feeling like it was a slap. I obviously failed.'

'Why not?' she asked.

'Why not what?'

'Mel was crying, but she came at me, not the other way around,' she pointed out. 'You told me after the first round that if she said anything like that again, there'd be consequences. So what are the consequences going to be, another hug? I don't need you to fight my battles, but I'm curious. If you're not close, and her behaviour is so erratic and unacceptable, why do you go to such great lengths to keep her happy?'

His face closed up. 'I'm not playing favourites, Indy. Don't get upset.'

She wasn't going to admit to that. 'Upset? Why would I be upset? I'm just trying to understand, because it doesn't make sense.'

'It does. I'd just rather not talk about it.'

'Oh, well. That's okay. I'll just stay out of her way in case she decides to launch another full-scale attack and fall into your arms crying again.' Her voice was even, but the sarcasm was evident.

'Now you sound jealous. Which is ridiculous. There's—'

Her eyes bulged at the insult, and instant fury—because he was a little too close to the mark—shot through her. 'Ridiculous doesn't even begin to cover it!' She needed to get out of the stables and breathe. She stepped around him and started down the breezeway.

'Indy, would you—'

'Nope. I'm going up to breakfast.' And when he took a step in her direction, 'Don't follow me, Logan.'

She shoved his comment aside as she strode towards the guesthouse. If she thought about it too long she'd do an about-face and drop him. It had never occurred to her that Logan and Mel were romantically involved but she needed to know what tied them together.

Something must have happened. Something that made Logan feel guilty and made Mel anxious and in need of drugs to keep it under control. Whatever it was, it can't have been good. Indy's march slowed to a regular walk and her mind calmed as she thought about the possibilities. She went up the front steps and pushed through the door. It occurred to her that Mel was always getting worked up and fiddling with that locket of hers. She knew it held a picture of a man on one side and Mel's daughter on the other because she'd looked over Mel's shoulder one day. Jules had said Matty died in an accident. Could Logan have had something to do with it?

She hit the ladies room first, washed her hands and threw some water over her face. dragged the band roughly from her hair to tidy it up. Maybe with a bit of pushing, Tess or Jules might tell her what had happened. The only other way to find out would be to befriend Mel. Ha! The woman had just threatened her with a pair of scissors.

Not particularly hungry but hoping to catch Tess or Jules having breakfast, Indy walked into the dining room. She made herself a coffee and put together a small plate of fruit.

'Indy! Hi.'

Who? She followed the voice to one of the far tables and saw Gina seated by herself.

She sent her a smile and Gina waved her over. 'Sit over here. Carly's off hiking or something, and I can't find Kaicey. She said she'd meet up with me here.'

'Sure,' Indy said, because she couldn't see Tess or Jules. 'Logan said you were at the stables earlier.'

'I went for a huge walk this morning. Woke up early—unfamiliar place, you know. And of course …'

'Of course, what?'

Gina's eyes widened. 'It's not easy to sleep once you hear the rumours. Are they true?'

She really didn't need this today. 'Which ones?'

'About the missing girls—about the guy that runs the stables.'

Indy shrugged. 'I'm not much on rumours—or gossip.'

'You work down there don't you, at the stables? I heard about what you did. You're the one that had that run-in with Mason Cartwright.'

'You know about that?'

Gina leant in, spoke quietly. 'I heard it from Kaicey. Good on you, I say. Can't help but feel for the guy though.'

Indy frowned. 'Oh, why's that?'

'He only got the horse to impress that poor woman that's gone missing—Caroline? He had a thing for her but apparently she liked Logan better.'

'I can't imagine why,' Indy said dryly.

'I know, right? So anyway, he went out and bought himself a campdrafter to impress her. When she took off he lost interest but his father put his foot down, said he'd paid for the damn thing—and the entries—so like it or not he was doing the run. It doesn't sound like it was the horse's fault. More like Mason's heart wasn't in it—he was upset about Caroline and when he came off he took it out on the horse. But you know that part because you punched him, right?'

'Wrong. He tripped over me when I tried to take the horse off him and ploughed into a tree.'

'Oh, well, I guess these things get exaggerated.'

Kaicey joined them. 'Morning.'

Gina swallowed a mouthful of her cereal. 'I was just telling Indy about Mason and Caroline.'

'There was no Mason and Caroline.' Kaicey rolled her eyes. 'She was all over Logan like a rash last I saw her—talking about some trail ride he was taking her on. She had high hopes, that's all.'

'Does he often take workers out on trail rides?' Indy asked.

'Yeah of course—usually so they get to know the route for the guided rides. But Caroline just wanted to spend time with him.'

'And what happened?' Gina whispered. 'Did she not come back?'

'According to Logan they never went out.' Kaicey blew on her coffee and took a cautious sip. 'She just packed up her stuff and took off.'

'Why would she do that if she was after Logan?' Indy asked.

'Not sure of the full story. Thing is, no one saw her again to know if they went out there or not, then they found her clothes in the stables. Looked like something bad had happened to her. Police questioned Logan about it. A lot.'

Gina's gaze travelled over Indy's left shoulder and her eyes widened. 'There he is,' she whispered.

Indy kept her eyes averted as Logan walked past them towards the buffet table.

'I met him this morning on my walk. He's super-hot.'

'Super-hot?' Indy couldn't help the bland stare.

'Mm. Have you heard him talking?'

She hadn't done much more than play with her fruit. Now she felt even less like it than she had before. 'Frequently. Why?'

'It's so deep and sexy. And the way he looks at you—I could just stare into those eyes all day.' She lowered her voice even further. 'Except, they think he did it—right? Took those girls. So I guess he's probably like one of those Hollywood bad guys.'

And ... that's enough. The woman was the immature airhead Jules had pinned on the first day. 'Excuse me.' Indy took her coffee, dumped her breakfast, and walked back towards the stables.

Thankfully it seemed she had the place to herself. Logan had no private lessons planned so other than when he ducked in and out to gear up horses, she wouldn't see much of him. And Mel was rostered off for the rest of the morning, which she thought should mean a few hours of peace. She made the most of it, getting through what needed to be done, then she pulled Aurora out of the paddock for a good groom.

Mel turned up just before lunch as Indy was finishing up. She was looking more than a little upset and apologetic and stood close by, waited for Indy to finish doing up Aurora's rug and acknowledge her. Logan, Indy noted, hovered in the breezeway entrance.

A small part of her considered making Mel wait, but her temper had cooled since breakfast, so she dropped her brush into the container and looked up. 'Is something wrong?'

'I shouldn't have opened my mouth. I …' Mel glanced over her shoulder at Logan before returning her gaze to Indy, 'won't say anything like that again.'

The words weren't quite verbatim, Indy supposed, but they were damn close to Logan's. 'Okay.'

Mel nodded and walked out without another word.

Logan remained where he was. 'How are you going?'

'Fine.' She untied Aurora and led her out the opposite doorway.

Logan sighed and dragged his fingers through his hair. Hell, they were storming off in all directions. Indy had a reason. It wasn't fair Mel got away with carrying on like that. But what was he going to do about her? If it wasn't for him, she'd be managing her own place with a husband, and Bindi would likely have a brother or sister by now. He took that debt seriously, and the idea she was smoking opium to help with her emotional issues made him feel even worse.

He hadn't felt like pouring all that out to Indy, not when she'd confronted him earlier, but she'd dug her damn toes in and started on the interrogation. The woman could shoot questions like bullets; just as fast and just as lethal. And he shouldn't have thrown in the jealous comment. It was a stupid, albeit desperate attempt to move her off topic. And mission accomplished, she'd well and truly taken the bait. Her outraged face flashed into his mind and he pressed his lips together against the smile. He'd guessed that temper of hers would be challenging. It was really the only thing to smile about, because now he had to fix things. He ran his fingers over his scalp and gripped the hair at the back of his head. *Hell.* And he should probably do it sooner rather than later. His watch told him it was nearly one o'clock. He supposed lunch time would be as good a time as any.

When he went up to find her she was in the staffroom. Alone in the corner, she was checking something on her phone and picking at one of those incredibly healthy salads she liked so much. He took a deep breath, blew it out. Approached her. 'Indy.'

Glancing up, she grimaced, returned her attention to her plate.

'I was looking for you,' he began tentatively.

'And here I am.'

No, she wasn't going to make this easy. He put his plate on the table, sat opposite.

She stopped picking at her food and raised her brow as she looked up. 'Please, join me.'

In spite of the sarcasm, he gave her his best smile. 'I knew you'd get around to asking. You're not still cross are you?'

'I'm not sure. The jealousy is just so overwhelming.'

The dry tone drew a chuckle out of him, and even when she shot him a withering look he couldn't pull it all the way back. 'Seems like I'm destined to be forever apologising to you.'

'That depends. Am I still working with Mel?'

'She said she was sorry,' he reminded her.

Her hand hit the table with a thud. 'Oh please, "I shouldn't have opened my mouth"? That's not an apology, that's a ... fitting title for her memoir. As for the rest, did you write her cue cards? She said pretty much word for word ... What?'

Logan's grin was huge. 'Sounds like if she's not careful, you'll be leading with that at her funeral.'

'You think anyone would show?' She frowned again, but this time she seemed less annoyed, more concerned. 'Logan, something's really not right with her.'

'She's been through some pretty tough stuff in the last few years. I'm trying to make sure you don't cross paths too much. Can you tolerate her, please? I can't afford to lose her.'

She shrugged and dropped her attention back to her lunch. 'I'll do what I can.'

'Hey.' He got her eyes back on his. 'I don't want to lose you, either.' He thought her expression might have softened marginally and considered that a small victory.

'I'm not going anywhere—yet.'

'Good, because when I saw you sitting in here by yourself I thought you might have been contemplating leaving.'

'I was hiding.'

'Hiding? From Mel?'

'Give me a break! I was hiding from the airhead. Gina.'

He frowned, but his eyes gleamed. 'That seems a bit harsh.'

'She's quite up on the gossip for someone who's been here five minutes—and she's seriously impressed with you. After the conversation at breakfast, I just didn't have it in me to sit with her again.'

'Because she was impressed by me?'

'Smirk a little more. I believe her words were "like one of those Hollywood bad guys", said with just the right amount of breathlessness.'

He laughed, even though the jibe hit home. 'Bad guy, huh? I seem to be getting that a lot lately.'

'She knows all about it.'

'That's how it happens in a small town. You don't need to be around long to catch up on gossip. You should know that—you certainly got your fair share of it right off the bat.'

'It doesn't bother you?'

The way Indy was watching him, he wouldn't be surprised if she could read his mind. 'Should I let it? We've got two more starting next week on trial and they'll be saying the same thing.'

'Two more?'

'A kitchenhand and another cleaner. Free Tess up a bit more.'

'That'll be good. She's working long hours. She was cleaning rooms again until late last night.'

'Hopefully this new one will be okay.'

'And not get scared off,' Indy added.

He considered her. 'You haven't been.'

'No, but I'm not sure it sounds as though Gina's going to stick.'

'If she goes, she goes,' he said. After a thoughtful pause, he added, 'As long as she goes somewhere people can locate her.'

'Unlike Caroline.'

'Unlike Caroline,' he echoed.

She hesitated for effect, played with her fork. 'Did the police really find her clothes in the tack room with blood and dirt on them?'

'Yeah. The detective looking for Caroline did.'

Her brow creased thoughtfully. 'What do you think happened?'

'I don't know.' He sat back in his chair and stared past her, to the mountains. 'I took Rex out early because he needed the work. I couldn't use him for the ride with Caroline because the mare she always rode was in season. I came back and realised she hadn't shown for work. The horses that needed to come in were still out. I couldn't get her on the phone and because I was behind without the help I didn't get a chance to go looking for her until after lunch. It looked for all the world like she'd packed up and left.' He wondered why he was telling her all this, but now he'd started, he wanted to just get it out. 'The thing is, that's how the others had disappeared.

No word, nothing left behind. I had this ... feeling, you know? So I got everyone out looking for her and when she was still missing at the end of the day, I called the detective that looked into Mandy and Latisha and Gretchen's cases.'

'You called him yourself?'

He wondered at the surprise, but nodded. 'Of course I did. Anyway, Detective Robinson turned up, looked around, came out of the stables with the bag of clothes and dragged me in for questioning.'

'That must have been horrible. I heard something about her dad being someone important. That he's stirring up a lot of trouble for you.'

'You hear a lot.'

She forced herself not to squirm under that suspicious assessment. 'I think it was Rosalie who said it. When I first got here. I ... pay attention.'

He sat back and nodded, eyes warmer. 'I've kind of figured that out about you. So yeah, Caroline's father is some senator or other. Don't know how important he actually is. I met him once for all of about five minutes while Caroline was here.'

He had no idea why her eyes sharpened at that—or had he imagined it? 'Nice that he came to visit. Sounds like a dedicated father.'

Logan shrugged. 'He had business down here apparently. I remember Caroline saying he had a special interest in agriculture and was working on getting some initiative between a couple of state governments off the ground. He was around not too long before she went missing.'

'It must have been even worse when Gretchen went missing. I heard there was something between you.'

'Between Gretch and me? Not romantically. We were friends, sure. Her old man was always giving her trouble and when she felt like rebelling she'd come out to Calico Mountain to see me or Tess. In the end, Warren didn't want us associating because he was worried that the stories she was telling us would get out.'

'Stories?'

He really wasn't sure whether to be amused by her curiosity or concerned by it. 'Just what he got up to when he was drunk. Murph used to go round a bit, calm things down.' He shook his head. 'So who do I attribute that little rumour to? Is that one of the ones the new girl picked up?'

She smiled briefly and her gaze hit the roof. 'No, her juicy piece of gossip was about Caroline. How she had eyes for you and liked the horses—which is why Mason bought Aurora.'

'Mason always wanted anything he thought I had my eye on. Even if I didn't. We've had a few little run-ins over his behaviour.'

'That night he was beating up Aurora—he backed off pretty quick when you turned up.'

'He was in the wrong and he knew it.'

She picked up a carrot stick and snapped off the end. 'Would you really have hit him with a stick?'

'No, of course not.' He couldn't help the grin. 'I've got two perfectly good fists and he would have copped one of them, if for no other reason than to sit him on his backside to calm down.'

'So you're a boy-beating, woman-abducting smart arse, then.' She grinned.

He knew she was joking, but damn, it still stung. He had to fight to keep the scowl off his face. He was trying to make things right between them, not dump a tirade about his personal feelings on her. 'Are you sure that covers it?'

'Hmm, not really,' Indy said contemplatively. 'I've been warned more than once I'm taking my life in my hands working with you.'

She knew just where to strike, damn it. And though her tone was mild, there was something behind her eyes that suggested she was genuinely probing. Was that what all the questions were about— she still hadn't made up her mind about him? He stopped eating and stared, kept his gaze steady, though he was hanging on the answer. 'Do you think I'm a murderer, Indy?'

She took her time answering. 'I don't know, Logan. Are you?'

Disappointment and resignation hit him in the gut. But what did he expect? 'You don't know. And yet you're still here.'

'I can handle you,' she promised him.

Surprise overcame his annoyance and he pushed just a bit further. 'Can you? Because it's crossed my mind more than once to find out.' The comment could have been a threat, but if the look on her face was anything to go by, the heat in his stare got his message across. 'Come on, eat,' he said with a smile. 'We need to get those horses in.'

It might have crossed his mind more than once to find out if she could handle him, but he didn't seem to be in much of a hurry. Issuing a challenge like that to the sort of person she was hunting down should have garnered some sort of reaction, brought something to a head. Instead he'd just rather calmly admitted he was attracted to her, then let her off the hook by changing the topic and giving her time to process.

If anything, it had backfired on her, because the reaction had all been hers. Detective or not, she was still human. She hadn't been able to speak; to think of a single thing to say. Since then a week had passed and she hadn't had to. He'd been nothing more than his usual friendly—if not flirty—boss.

She thought about that as she brushed Aurora. The mare's coat was gleaming from the attention, and she'd fallen in love with the horse who'd been beaten but was still so gentle. She was even nickering to Indy when she saw her coming and following her around like a puppy when she was cleaning out the yards.

'She's looking better every day,' Logan said as he walked Rex into the breezeway and grabbed a brush.

Indy smiled when Rex sent Aurora a very manly nicker. 'She's enjoying the attention.'

'Rex certainly likes what he sees.' Logan chuckled at the stallion's interest. 'I think he'd like to give her some attention, too.'

Indy rolled her eyes and went back to grooming, but covertly watched Logan work, acknowledged that charge that seemed to taint the air whenever he was around. She was struggling; finding it more and more difficult to see him as her perp and because of that, the feelings she knew she absolutely should not acknowledge were seeping through the cracks in her armour. It was unprofessional, it was unacceptable. She wouldn't allow them to interfere with her case.

'Did Tess tell you about the Christmas party?' he asked, looking up to catch her watching him.

'Jules did,' Indy said, bending down to pick up Aurora's hoof to clean. 'She said she's stuck with the traditional roasts—sounds like she's cooking every animal in creation, plus she's doing seafood and salads and some fancy new canapés.'

'You wait till you taste Nat's plum pudding.'

'It's not formal sit-down though, right?'

'No, it's just serve yourself from the buffet. We tried sit-down for a few years, but with all the guests it was too big a deal and took too many staff. Still pretty good though. You're coming, aren't you?'

'I guess so.' She put down the hoof, and straightened. 'I don't have anywhere else I need to be.'

'We don't usually cover the costs of international calls made by staff, but we do at Christmas—within reason—if you want to call family.'

Indy bent down to put her brush away. 'That won't be necessary.'

He stopped to look at her. 'You don't speak to them?'

'I don't have any.' She scooped up the grooming kit and took it into the tack room. When she turned around he was in the doorway.

'You didn't mention that during the conversation at my place. What happened to your mum and grandparents?'

'Nothing I like to talk about.'

He considered her before nodding slowly. 'We're in the same boat there. I'm sorry.'

'Why?'

He shrugged, smiled gently. 'Because I know what it's like.'

She took a deep breath and plastered a smile on her face. 'It's history.' Then she stepped around him and out into the space of the breezeway. 'I'll put Aurora away. Do you want me to start on the feeds?'

'Yeah, that'd be great. I'm taking Rex out for a ride. He needs a good run.'

She made up the feeds, walked back into the breezeway and noticed Logan with the saddlebags.

'What's up?' he asked when he noticed her watching him.

'He really is a stunning horse.' She stepped forward, gave his neck a stroke, felt the silky smoothness of his coat. 'You're handsome, aren't you?'

'Careful.'

She nodded and stepped back, then decided it couldn't hurt to ask, 'What's in the containers?'

'Which ones?' he asked. She noted she had his full attention.

'The ones you pack in the saddlebags.'

He shrugged. 'This and that. I'll be gone for a while. Head off when you're done.'

'I will,' she told his back. Off he went again with his mysterious containers to a location he didn't want her to know he was going to. How could she be feeling the way she was about a man with potentially deadly secrets? Indy walked out into the fresh air and stared at the sky. He couldn't be the man she was after; her gut would tell her. Wouldn't it?

Or was it the danger that intensified the attraction?

CHAPTER
13

Indy was still debating the question of danger and attraction a couple of days later. Logan had taken the morning ride out, so she got on with her jobs. Mel had barely spoken a word to her since the so-called apology, and with Logan's new jobs list, she didn't have to. Because she was ahead of schedule, she took Aurora out and gave her some extra attention. She was just starting to look for Logan when Mel came in.

'You're wasting too much time on that horse—there are other things that need doing.'

'I've done everything I'm responsible for before breakfast. I'm grooming Rory on my own time.'

'I told Logan there wasn't enough on that list. If there was, you'd still be busy.'

Gina hesitantly entered the breezeway. 'Hi, Indy.' She looked from Indy to Mel and back. 'Is this a bad time?'

'Gina. What are you doing down here?' Indy asked.

'Looking for Logan. He said I could drop down here and organise a riding lesson.'

'He's not here at the moment.'

'Where is he?'

'He's taken a ride out. What do you want?' Mel asked.

At least it's not just me, Indy thought.

'Will he be long?'

'After the ride gets back he's checking fences,' Mel said. 'He's putting that new lot of cows and calves out. Wants to make sure there's no holes for them to escape through. He won't have time for you today.'

'That's okay. It must be lovely to ride out there every day. Does he often go alone?'

'There's not enough of us to turn it into a party,' Mel snapped. 'Some people work around here. Why aren't you?'

'It's my day off. I just thought I'd … I'll leave you to it then— come back later.'

Indy watched her walk away. Gina was not only up on the gossip but was asking a lot of the same questions Indy had looked for answers to. That made her suspicious. Was she really as immature and silly as she made out? Her character wasn't ringing true.

'You gonna stare at her all day or get that stable done?' Mel demanded.

'I'm not sure what to make of her,' Indy said almost to herself.

Mel huffed. 'She asks some pretty strange questions. I suppose she could just be after Logan. Everyone else is.' Her gaze swung to Indy.

'I was under the impression you thought of him as yours.'

'I was just having a go at you because I don't like you.'

'Okay. That's bullshit.' She rounded Aurora and, hands on hips, faced Mel head-on. 'You clearly said "Logan's mine". You try to scare off every worker Logan hires. If it's not because he might fall for one of them, then why are you so hard to get along with?'

Mel shrank back. 'I don't do that,' she said defensively.

'You're renowned for it.'

Mel went white. 'That's not true!'

Indy realised she'd hit some mark, but she had no idea what it was. Why would Mel care whether or not Indy thought she was scaring off staff? Was she embarrassed? She looked more scared than embarrassed. And Indy needed to get to the bottom of it. She softened her tone. 'You're always stressed out, you often look like you've been crying, you're smoking opium … Mel, you need to talk to someone. What's going on?'

Mel's face closed up. 'I think you should spend less time talking and more working.'

'So, I'm working,' she said. But she kept pushing. 'And I'm not quitting because you feel like being antisocial. I saw your little girl the other day. She's a real cutie.'

Mel's eyes flashed. 'What were you doing near Bindi?'

Indy's brow rose at the sharp tone. 'I went out to Hilltop Farm with Jules to get some supplies. Why?'

'Just wondering. I thought you might have been changing jobs.'

Why would Mel assume she'd head up there for a new job? 'Thought or wished? You can't really want to be another person down.'

'We coped just fine before you arrived.'

She changed tack. 'Yeah. You've been here for ages, right? You must have seen a lot of other people come and go.'

'I'm the only one Logan keeps on year to year, so I see people like you come and go all the time. You'll be going even faster if you don't get your work done.'

'Don't you ever worry ... that you might disappear next?' she asked, picking up Aurora's rug.

'No. But maybe you should.'

The comment had Indy's head whipping back around in time to see the hesitation on Mel's face. 'I mean because you're the outsider.'

'What else would you mean?' Indy asked the rhetorical question but she wasn't so sure. The comment had been more than a threat. There was knowledge behind it.

'Right.'

One more try, she decided. 'Mel ... I know something's wrong. If you ever decide you need to talk to someone, I'll listen.'

Mel twisted her hands in front of her while she frowned at the ground. 'Why?'

'Because you need a friend.' And because she now had a strong suspicion Mel held some of the pieces of the puzzle.

'Friends don't blab to bosses about drugs.'

She softened her expression. 'I didn't know he was there, any more than you did. And here he comes,' she added, spotting movement outside. 'Remember what I said.'

Finding ways to be pleasant to Mel actually helped the day go by. It wasn't easy, but she didn't intend to give up. At least not until she knew for sure that whatever was bothering Mel didn't have anything to do with her case. She said a cheerful goodbye to her when Mel left, and decided when she didn't get a snarl in response that she might be making headway. 'Logan, I'm heading off too.'

'No worries. See you tomorrow.'

It was a perfect afternoon so she wasn't in any hurry, which is probably why she noticed it—something small and dark in the long grass. Curious, she checked for cattle, though she knew they'd all been turned out, and climbed through the fence. She approached cautiously and discovered the tight little black ball was a calf. Eyes closed, it wasn't moving but she could see the little wet nostrils working to move air in and out.

'Hey.' Crouching, she tentatively touched it and the eyes opened. It made a pathetic little noise then closed them again. She looked around, wary of a hidden mother suddenly bounding out of nowhere to attack, but the paddock was empty. Another little noise, another sad little look and Indy's heart melted. 'Okay, sweetheart. I'll just ... get someone who can actually help.'

Because she wasn't too far away, she called out. 'Logan?'

He appeared at the front of the breezeway. 'What's up?'

'I found a calf.'

'What? Must be sick.' He jogged over and squatted beside it. 'He's tiny. Damn. I was sure they'd all calved a week ago.'

'He's so sweet. Look at those big eyes. Should we bring the mother back?'

'They've gone up onto the mountain. If she was interested she should be bellowing for him. For some reason she's left him behind. That size, he could be a twin and she's headed off with the strong one.'

Indy bent down next to Logan. 'You think he's sick?'

'Could be. He's certainly weak.' Logan lifted the calf onto its unsteady legs, but it crumpled back onto the ground.

'Maybe we can give him some milk.'

'It's not milk he needs, it's colostrum. I doubt very much he's more than a few hours old, so he probably didn't get any.'

'Then we do need to find his mum.'

'Indy, I can't bring the entire herd back in. They're miles away by now, and there's no guarantees the mother would take to him.'

'So what, he just dies?'

He sighed. 'Raising a calf is labour intensive and there's a big chance with the start he's had, he won't make it. Even if by some miracle he did, you'd get attached to him and him to you and that's no good.'

'Why not?'

'Because he's a little bull, and little bulls become steers. And steers get eaten.'

She stroked the tiny face. 'Surely it wouldn't hurt to keep one.'

He put a hand on her shoulder and spoke kindly. 'How long are you planning to stay around? Bulls don't make good pets. It could end up hurting you—probably accidentally, but you'll still be just as hurt—or dead.'

'But you just said he'd become a steer.'

'And what am I going to do with a useless steer?' he reasoned.

'He could be ... I don't know. Wouldn't the city people that come out here like a nice quiet steer to pat? The kids would love it. You've got the perfect little paddock between the guesthouse and the stables.'

'That's our isolation paddock—for new or sick stock.'

'You could paint the shelter and make it a real tourist attraction,' she enthused. 'Add a goat or a sheep ... a few chickens.'

The look on his face was one of genuine horror. 'Whoa. We've gone from a useless steer to a useless steer, a goat, a sheep and a few chickens ... How about a Shetland pony—maybe an alpaca, too?'

She grinned. 'How about that?'

He laughed and shook his head. 'Indy, I've got enough to do. Besides, they can't all live in the one paddock, there'd have to be new yards and more shelters and waterlines dug and special fences to stop kids crawling under said animal's legs and all sorts of stuff. Expensive, time-consuming stuff.' His face sobered. 'I know it's sad, but spending all that time, money and effort trying to save him just to kill him for meat a little further down the track—is that really fair?'

'We can't just leave him here.'

'I wouldn't do that.' He lifted the calf up and positioned it in his arms. 'It's getting late. Why don't you head off? I'll take care of it.'

'What if I put him on one of the quads and went out to find the herd—maybe ...' But his face was telling her another story.

'He can't even stand.'

'I'll buy him from you. Try and save him myself.'

'Okay that's enough, Indy.' His eyes darkened. 'Leave it with me.'

Her stomach twisted. She stroked the calf's head sadly. 'Sorry mate. I tried.'

'Indy ...'

It tore at her heart to walk away. But she'd seen something on Logan's face she wanted to believe in. He'd been cuddling the calf, not simply holding it. She wasn't convinced the baby was going to get a bullet.

Though the alarm didn't sound—it was her day off—Indy still woke at five-thirty. She considered rolling over and going back to sleep for another hour. She had every intention of getting out onto the trails again early, to go back to the spot she'd seen Logan and find out just exactly what it was he was doing out there. But not quite this early. Besides, the most pressing thing on her mind was the scene with Logan and the calf, so she dressed quickly, torn between wanting to go to the stables—just in case the calf was still alive—or not going. In case it wasn't.

She wasn't surprised to find herself heading for the stables. She was a practical person by nature but anything helpless was a weakness. A soft-eyed baby calf was no different. She had to know.

There didn't seem to be anyone around when she got there, and Logan should have been. She checked the office, the feed room, the tack room ... Then she thought she might have heard a soft snore. 'Interesting ...'

Logan was propped against the wall in one of the stables, sound asleep. The calf was curled up at his side. 'Logan?'

He opened his eyes and blinked, rubbed a hand over his face. 'Morning.'

'What are you doing?'

He checked his watch. 'Damn. Lucky there wasn't a ride on this morning.' The calf lifted his head and made a cute little bleat. 'Well, what do you know—he's still going. I wasn't sure he'd get through the night.'

'I thought you were going to shoot him.'

Logan got up, stretched, grimaced and rubbed his neck. 'I was looking at those big eyes you pointed out—kept seeing that sad face of yours in my head. So I made a call to Jerry down the road. He's got dairy cows and usually has some colostrum in the freezer. He dropped it over for me and we tubed his first dose, then this little one decided he was strong enough to suck the bottle for a bit more. I'm betting he's hungry again.'

'You slept here?'

His grin was lopsided. 'Not on purpose.'

'But you did.' She smiled, folded her arms. 'And all that talk of bulls and steers and meat?'

'We'll just need to find someone wanting a lawnmower I guess. We'll worry about that if he lives. That's still a very big if.'

Indy went in and stroked the calf's cheek. 'He's so sweet. So soft.'

'But he's far from out of the woods. And from now on he's your responsibility.' Logan patted her on the back. 'You're mum. I've got enough to do.'

'I don't know what to do.'

'He can stay in here for the time being. He's going to need a bottle morning and night, fresh water and hay and pellets and the stable's going to have to stay clean. I'll show you how to make up the bottles.'

Indy's heart melted. 'Logan.'

'Yeah?'

'Thanks.'

He stared at her for one long moment. 'You're just lucky you're so damn gorgeous.' Then he was striding down the breezeway. 'The both of you. Come on. He's hungry.'

So damn gorgeous? She shook her head and let it pass. She needed to find out how to take care of this baby.

He showed her how to mix the milk powder and handed her the bottle. 'Best to get him on his feet, hold the bottle up so he's in the position he'd take if he was drinking from his mother.' She followed him into the stables, watched as he gently got the calf up and coaxed it to take the bottle. 'Here now, you take it.'

She took hold of the bottle, smiled as the calf took long thirsty slurps.

'He's drinking.'

'The first week is the diciest. If he survives that, you're doing well.'

'He'll survive. I'll make sure of it.'

'Okay, he's just about done. Don't let him gulp too much air, ease the bottle away. That's it.'

She gave the calf another pat, and watched him take a few wobbly steps before resettling in the straw. She smiled, then turned that smile on Logan. He looked like a proud father. How could this man be her perp? In what reality could he kidnap and kill women?

The familiar sound of Logan's phone snapped her out of it. He tapped his pockets and frowned. Looked up.

'It must have fallen out when I was getting the straw out of the loft last night.'

She followed the sound to the far end of the breezeway. 'It's up here.'

Rather than walk down the other end of the stables to the ladder, he simply moved beside her and held his hands together in a boost gesture.

She looked at him sceptically. 'You want me to—'

'If it stops ringing I may never find it.'

'Oh … why not?' She put a foot in his linked hands and propelled herself up. A quick scrabble around in the hay and she found it as it stopped ringing. 'Here.'

She handed it down but instead of checking it, he put it back in his pocket and held out his hands. 'Sit on the edge and drop—I'll catch you.'

'I can go the other way.'

She'd turned around to do that when she heard a strange noise. A *chicken* noise. The ridiculous sound forced a laugh out of her, because Logan was making it. 'Fine,' she said.

She sat on her butt and dangled her legs over. It really wasn't that high. 'Just get out of the way—I can get down on my own.'

But when she sprang, he caught her around the waist. Her hands went to his shoulders for balance as he held her just above the floor. 'I've heard that before. Maybe I just want to see if I can handle you, too.'

He hadn't forgotten. She had a feeling he could hold her suspended there all day and not break a sweat. And the look on his face was enough to have her swallowing nervously. 'Hands off, Atherton.'

'Or what?' he asked quietly. 'You talk the talk, Indy. But …'

Was he testing her? She could hurt him. She knew how to get out of his hold. But that solution was probably overkill. And she wasn't a cop, she was stablehand. And stablehands didn't generally take people out. Besides, right at that moment, with her face inches from his, his hands securely on her hips and his eyes searching hers, she didn't feel much like a cop at all. She didn't feel particularly strong, either. She felt … attracted. And when his gaze dropped to her lips all thoughts of undercover operations flew out the window.

'You really are gorgeous.'

Oh hell, I'm in trouble. 'Logan …'

'Yeah?'

'Logan, I wanted to talk to you about—oh.' Mel abruptly stopped talking.

He set Indy gently back on her feet before he looked around. 'Wanted to talk to me about?' he prompted.

Mel glared at Indy, and Indy was left with the impression that any headway they'd made had just been dashed to pieces. 'I wanted to run through a couple of things with you.'

'No worries.'

Indy released a long, slow breath. That was … intense. What was she doing? She'd said she could handle him, but they both knew damn well that she couldn't. She would get her head back in the right space. She would handle it. She had to. It wouldn't hurt to let him think he had the upper hand though. Because, God help her, if this incredible man did turn out to be a serial killer, she'd need all the tactics she could find up her sleeve to come out of this in one piece.

Indy sat down to dinner and yawned widely. She'd gone out on the trails, scoured every inch of space around the spot she'd seen Logan and hadn't found a thing. It didn't make any sense.

Tess dropped into the chair opposite. 'So, I hear you're a mother. How's it feel?'

'Good. He's very cute.'

'So Logan said.'

'He thinks I'm nuts for trying to save him.'

'It can be pretty heartbreaking when they don't make it. But when they do it's great. We've raised a heap of calves.'

'It's the bull thing Logan's not a fan of.'

Tess smiled and nodded. 'That's because Logan's a grown-up these days. Tries to be rational. When he was a kid he rescued everything—came home with a nest of baby mice once.'

'Really?'

'Yep. And he might hassle you a bit but I can tell you right now he'd rather do just about anything than put a bullet in a baby animal. You were his excuse not to.' She grinned. 'Convenient.'

'Hi, girls.' Rosalie sat down with a bowl of pasta. 'How are you, Indy?'

'Indy's a mum,' Tess told Rosalie. 'She found an abandoned calf yesterday. Logan's letting her raise it in the stables.'

Rosalie's face lit up. 'How's she going?'

'It's a he,' Indy said.

The smile turned to surprise. 'What are you planning on doing with it?'

'I suggested keeping it for visiting kids to play with, but that turned into a full-on baby animal farm so Logan said if it survives he'd try and find it a home as a lawnmower.'

'I've always wanted to do that,' Rosalie said a little wistfully. 'I thought it would be nice for tourists to be able to get up close to farm animals that were quiet enough to pet and feed. But we're always so busy and it just never eventuated.'

'You never told me that,' Tess said to her mother.

Rosalie laughed. 'If I'd have said a word you'd have had the place filled with animals before Murphy and I could blink. Logan would have brought home even more strays.'

'Now you tell me. You know, Tony Harper down the road has a bunch of new lambs.'

'I'm going to get into trouble,' Indy told her.

'I doubt it,' Tess replied. 'To hear Logan talk you walk on water.'

Indy choked on her coffee. 'Right.'

'Don't tease, Tess,' Rosalie said. 'But if this baby of yours lives, Indy, it might be the perfect opportunity to bring up the idea of a few pet farm animals for the younger guests.'

'I'm *really* going to get in trouble,' Indy complained.

Back in her room, Indy pulled her laptop out of its bag. She frowned. It was warm. Very warm. She pressed her hand to the underside to check—yes, as though someone had been using it. She flipped it open and the password screen came up. Even if someone had managed to get into her room and pull it out, no one could have got into her computer. And even if they miraculously did, she didn't have anything incriminating stored on it.

So what was she so nervous about?

She was nervous about the why. *Why* would someone break into her room and attempt to get into her laptop? There was no reason to do that unless they thought she was up to something. Unless the same thing had happened to the other victims. Was the perp scoping out a better picture of their lives, learning as much as he could about them before choosing them? And … did that mean she was about to become the next one? And then it occurred to her: if someone had been tampering with the computer just now, it couldn't be Logan—or Ned. Mick had turned up as she was leaving to say they were both stuck out in the paddock fixing a fence by the ute's headlights.

She snatched up her phone and headed outside to call Ben.

He answered on the first ring. 'How's it going?'

'Looking less and less likely that it's Logan.'

'You're sure?'

She told him about the calf, about the conversation with Rosalie and Tess. 'Ben, guys that grow up rescuing baby animals and spend sleepless nights looking after an orphaned calf don't exactly fit the profile of the person we're looking for. He's not some kind of deranged psychopath. And that's what it would take, Ben, to keep women chained up for months or years on end, even if you weren't killing them. You know that as well as I do.'

'Didn't you say he was doing something secretive in the bushland behind the property?'

'Yeah, but I've been out there, scoured the place. I just don't think that's it. How is your investigation into everyone else out here going?'

'We've cleared through a tonne of backlog, found some pretty sloppy detective work. I've been on and off the phone over missing files and incomplete reports enough times to put Mark well offside. We're also chasing up leads that weren't followed through to my satisfaction, looking into each of the missing women's histories as thoroughly as it should have been done the first time. It's slowing us down. Why?'

'Because someone out here—other than Logan—is up to something. My phone made its way out of my room the other day and I'm pretty sure someone attempted to get into my laptop earlier. I'm wondering if I'm being stalked. I doubt they could get in and find anything, but on the slight chance they're some sort of super-hacker,

I'm going to send you the occasional bogus email to throw them off the track. And my phone is going everywhere with me from now on, only charging when I'm here with it. So if I need to send you anything, it'll come through that.'

'Sounds fine. Are you absolutely sure it wasn't Logan? Because those records you sent us—some of them weren't entered when they should have been. Some were adjusted weeks later.'

'So he's not good with record keeping. He's not exactly an office type, either.'

'I have analysts working on retrieving the original records. He may have been covering his tracks by changing data.'

'And he's not the only one with access to the computer system,' she said in Logan's defence.

There was a pause, then, 'Do you really believe he's not guilty or do you not want to believe it?'

'What's that supposed to mean?' she demanded, instantly offended.

'It means excuses are jumping out of your mouth before you've even had time to process them. That's not like you.'

Damn it—it didn't help that he was right. 'You wanted my opinion, this is the one I've formed. By the way, did you know that Senator Melville visited Caroline twice just prior to her disappearance? He's been back and forth from Tassie working on something with a state government department.'

'I don't think Senator Melville is abducting women, Indy. But I'll chase up the details, find out why he didn't mention it. Thanks.'

'Okay.'

'In the meantime be careful. Don't drop your guard with Logan.'

'Of course I won't,' she said with an edge of frustration. She didn't need to be told how to do her job. 'Also, can you look into a woman by the name of Gina Rosetti, twenty-five, from Melbourne?'

'I can do that. Why?'

'I don't think she is who she says she is.'

'Got it. Stay safe—keep in touch.'

She finished the call and slipped her phone in her pocket. She didn't like to admit it but Ben had a point. She'd gone into defence mode over Logan. And that wasn't like her. Just because he'd saved a calf—possibly to manipulate her—didn't mean he was innocent. But Tess and Rosalie had unwittingly vouched for his character at dinner, and she just couldn't make herself believe he was capable of turning off that caring, empathetic side of himself to abuse or kill women. Besides, someone other than Logan was looking into her life, and Mel had caught her interest. Not because she believed they had a female perp on their hands, but because Mel knew more than she was saying.

CHAPTER
14

Indy had no idea when the Christmas party was due to start. Quickly she showered off the day's grime, pulled on jeans and the only half-decent top she'd brought with her. She shrugged at her appearance in the mirror. It would have to do.

Tess and Jules weren't around when she stepped into the guesthouse and the guests who were already down were far better dressed than she was. She decided to head upstairs to find Tess. If necessary, she'd have to borrow something.

She knocked on Tess's door and was suddenly in the midst of chaos. 'Hi. Glad you could make it,' Tess said. 'I'm watching Jules in full swing. It's always an education.'

Hair and makeup done, Tess sat cross-legged on a big bed wearing a fluffy pink dressing gown. Clothes, shoes and jewellery were scattered everywhere.

Jules swept a dress in front of her and stood at Tess's full-length mirror. 'I've got it down to two,' she told Indy. 'The red silk.' She put it against her and studied her reflection. 'Or the midnight blue crepe.' She grabbed it from the bed and repeated the process. 'Tess is being unhelpful. What do you think? And what are you going to wear?'

'I don't actually have anything.'

Jules aimed her a thoughtful look and after a dramatic pause she sighed. 'Right. You wear the blue.' She tossed it at her. 'It'll suit your eyes. I'll wear red.'

Indy eyed the length of the dress with concern. 'Will it fit?'

'Why not? I'm shorter but we're similar weight. The worst it'll do is show off a bit of thigh. I bought it in Sydney. It wasn't cheap.'

'There's only a couple of chances a year to get dressed up around here,' Tess told Indy. 'And Jules is usually here for them. We're ordered to make the most of it. I even wear heels.' She looked at the pretty, strappy shoes critically. 'My feet are already hurting at the thought of actually walking around in them.'

'Don't be painful, Tess,' Jules sighed.

Indy put the dress against her to assess her appearance in the mirror. Definitely short, but hell—she had the legs to pull it off. 'Unfortunately, if I'm going to wear this dress I'm going to have to borrow some heels, too. I can't wear these flats.'

'You won't fit into Jules's,' Tess said. 'But I do own one other pair of gold ones that should suit.' She rifled around in her wardrobe and pulled them out. 'I won't lie, they're not comfortable. I fall over in them.'

'You fall over in all of them,' Jules shot at her with a grin.

Indy slid them on and did a practice walk. 'They're okay. Thanks.'

'You say that now,' Tess warned, then turned to Jules. 'Jules, not that you care,' she told her when she slipped into her dress, 'but Connor's eyes are going to fall out of his head.'

'Of course I care.' She tossed her hair and swung her hips as she made for the door. 'I could lie and be nonchalant about it, but I won't. Hurry up and get ready.'

They walked into the crowded room and were immediately swept up into a sea of people. Indy scanned the room and her eyes met Logan's. He smiled slowly, then looked her up and down in a way that had her pulse leaping. She paused for a moment, the slightest hesitation while mentally preparing herself for the evening ahead. In order to stay in character that night, she was going to have an interesting balancing act on her hands. She heard Jules chuckle a moment before she was shoved in the back. 'Keep walking.'

'Hmmm,' Tess added, throwing Indy a wicked look. 'I have to say if I know Logan at all, resistance is futile.'

'Ladies.' Logan turned his full attention on Indy.

'Ladies,' Connor echoed, appearing next to Logan and handing him a beer.

'Hi,' Tess greeted.

'You know the masses aren't quite *that* dressed up,' Connor commented.

'We aren't the masses,' Jules replied, coolly. 'Excuse us.'

Logan's gaze followed Indy as the women moved across the room. It wasn't that he hadn't appreciated her body before, but in that blue figure-hugging creation there was a lot more on display. And those legs in heels just went on forever.

'She's quite a package,' Connor commented casually.

'I like her spirit,' he said.

Connor chuckled. 'I figured it was her "spirit" you were interested in.'

Logan grinned and shrugged. 'It wouldn't hurt you to be a bit nicer to her.'

'I'm still not convinced she is who she says she is. How many women who know nothing about horses would take on a stranger in the dark, come off on the better side of a fight and—'

'You're suspicious because she can handle herself? She's a woman travelling alone. I can't imagine it hurts to have some skills.'

'You must have noticed she asks a lot of questions, and she's glued herself to Tess and Jules,' Connor rationalised.

'They like her. They're friends. *I* like her. And I thought we'd agreed we weren't having this conversation again.'

Connor sighed. 'Righto.'

'I'm going to catch up with her before anyone else does.'

Indy's back was to him as he approached, which was good, because it gave him time to drag his eyes off her legs. 'Indy.'

As she stepped back she slipped a little and his hand automatically shot out to steady her. 'Careful.'

'I'm not used to these shoes,' she told him, adjusting one.

'They're new?'

'They're Tess's.'

'I bet she can't stand up in them either.' Now that he had a hand on her, he really didn't want to let go, so he skimmed his hand down her arm, caught her fingers as he stepped back and allowed his gaze to roam over her from head to toe. 'You look … I know I should say lovely but hell, Indy, are you trying to handle me or kill me?'

'The dress isn't about you, Logan.'

'Kill me now.' He loved the way her face lit up when she was amused. He wanted to touch her. The temptation was making his palm itch. He knew she generally reacted like a viper, but she seemed more mellow tonight. Perhaps it was worth a shot. He ran an experimental finger along her cheekbone, watched her eyes darken and the humour become uncertainty. 'Can you dance in those stilts?'

Her, 'What? Why?' was followed by two quick steps away and a snatch of her fingers.

'Hmm. I was wondering how long it would take for you to get all skittish. For a second there, you forgot.'

Her eyes burned at that. 'Call me skittish again and see what happens.'

He chewed on his grin as he took a chance and moved back in, tipping up her chin so he could study her thoughtfully. She was daring him with her eyes, but she was wary. Did she still believe he could be a murderer? 'Let's get a drink.'

'I'm not a big drinker.'

'Then we'll make it a small one.'

He guided her to the bar, where they found Rosalie and Murphy. He watched Indy relax as she sipped on a chardonnay, as they discussed her calf and—hell—Rosalie's idea for more pet animals. It wasn't that he was completely opposed to the idea of it. He just knew who it would fall to, to make the yards and take care of the 'pets'. And he didn't need any extra work.

'Tess was saying the Harpers have some dummy lambs available,' Rosalie told Logan.

'And they can keep them. Indy's got her hands full with the calf, she doesn't need more babies to feed. Besides, calves are twice a day feeders, newborn lambs are every four hours or so.'

Indy winced. 'I do like my sleep,' she admitted.

'Well I'd enjoy it,' Rosalie decided. 'It wouldn't be the first batch I've reared. They bond to you like puppies—follow you everywhere. They're so sweet.'

'All you need is a paddock, right?' Logan said.

'With a little house for them—not straight away.'

Logan laughed. 'You see what you've started?' he asked Indy.

The look she sent Rosalie suggested they'd already discussed Indy getting the blame. Then she turned big blue innocent eyes on him. 'What else was it you suggested—a Shetland pony and an alpaca?'

'They weren't suggestions!' he quickly got in before Rosalie could open her mouth. But he knew he was toast. The idea had taken hold. And when Rosalie got hold of an idea, there was no letting it go. He caught Indy watching him and returned her smirk. 'You'll pay for this. Let's get out of here.'

'We can't leave.'

'We have to. Rosie's about to remember she's always wanted piglets.'

'Really?' Indy asked over the laughter. 'We could liberate some of those cute black and white ones Hilltop Farm breed for bacon.'

'I'm not sure how the Cartwrights would feel about that.'

Suddenly distracted, Indy looked past him. 'What are they doing?'

He followed her gaze to the far end of the room where guests were milling around flicking through large albums. 'Photo albums. They go back fifty years and cover bits and pieces of whatever year it was. Rosalie pulls them out every year along with the newest one she's put together. There'll be a group photo tonight at some stage for the next one.'

'You should go take a look, Indy,' Rosalie suggested.

'I'd like to.' She took her drink, Logan followed, and she sat down in front of one to flick through photos of people, places, livestock. The pictures were old and black-and-white. The place had changed, considerably. When a couple nearby closed another book Indy opened it, paged through a much more recent year. When she came to a photo of a girl and horse she looked over her shoulder at Logan for clarification. 'That horse looks just like Aurora.'

Logan studied the picture. 'Close. That's old Captain. He died a couple of years ago. He was a good old boy.'

'Who's the girl?'

'Mandy.'

'The Mandy that went missing—someone thought they saw her, right?'

'Thought they did. Out near where that photo was taken, actually. That's the Bloodtree River trail.'

'Bloodtree River trail?'

'Got its name because it follows an area of the Tyenna River that a few hundred native Bloodwood trees were planted into with the idea of timber harvesting and essential oils production. Problem was, they don't grow well down here and the enterprise was abandoned. The odd tree survived—there's one of them, behind Mandy. And yeah, a local woman reckons she had Mandy turn up on her doorstep one day just to disappear again. You're really up on the gossip.'

She smiled sheepishly. 'Like you said—hard to be here and not hear it.'

His gaze returned to the photo. 'She was one of those people that got along with everyone, always smiling. Kind. Generous. I'd like to hope she's all right, somewhere, somehow.'

'Must have been hard on the family to hear she'd shown up only to lose her again.'

He frowned as he thought back. 'She only had her mum, but she died around the same time she was spotted—didn't even hear about the sighting.'

'What happened?'

The quick sharpening of her tone didn't escape his attention. 'Not sure—some kind of accident. Why?'

'Oh it's just …' She smiled a little, shrugged it off. *No big deal*, the gesture said. But her eyes were still thoughtful. So he waited. 'Latisha's parents died in an accident just before she was found, too. Didn't they?'

Very well informed, he thought. And as far as he knew, that wasn't public knowledge around here. 'A fire, I think.'

'What a horrible coincidence.' She closed the book and got to her feet. 'Looks like everyone's moving into the buffet room.'

'Looks like.'

They followed the crowd and Indy stared in disbelief. 'Is the rest of the western world coming to eat here tonight?'

'Just be prepared to eat many, many somethings created from leftovers for the foreseeable future.'

It would have been tempting to eat too much, if Indy could have concentrated on the delicious food. But Logan was keeping a thoughtful eye on her. Had she said too much by mentioning the similarities between Mandy and Latisha? She tried light conversation, only to come off sounding nervous, so she decided she may as well play on it, but it didn't dissuade him from watching her, it just added a touch of heat to his expression. It was what she wanted, but damn it, after the way he'd been touching her earlier, it did make her nervous.

She focused on keeping her expression relaxed, on keeping her breathing regular—the tight dress didn't help—and on swallowing small bites of the sumptuous meal in front of her while she speculated as to whether he would make some sort of move that might tell her what she needed to know so she could end this ruse.

Tess and Connor joined them and conversation became easier, the energy less intense. And still, she needed to collect her thoughts. As soon as she finished her meal, she got to her feet,

'Where are you going?' Tess asked.

'Walking. I ate too much.'

Tess sighed deeply and wiggled in her seat. 'Me too. But yum. I think I'll wash it down with another glass of chardonnay. Indy?'

'No—thanks.'

'I've got a better idea,' Logan said. 'Excuse us.'

He led her back through to the main room, where music was playing and couples were dancing. 'Where are we going?'

'You wanted to work off some of that food. Dance with me.'

Dance with him? That would be a really, really bad idea. So she stepped back, attempted a casual smile. 'I don't—'

He caught her hands, pulled her back towards him. 'Why is your instant reaction always to go backwards?' His voice was low and intimate, his expression held amusement, but was gentle, warm, his hands just insistent enough as he rested them on her waist. His thumbs gently caressed her sides, the contact scorching, as the heat, the tingle, radiated everywhere.

She should have stepped back, averted her gaze, said something smart. She couldn't think. When her breath quietly shuddered out his eyes narrowed, darkened, and his gaze dropped to her slightly parted lips. His eyes were so intense; his lips so invitingly close. She wondered what it would be like to have them pressed against hers, to feel those hands at her waist move and mould—she pulled her thoughts back with a start. That was the last thing she wanted.

'Logan—'

'Shhh. We're dancing, not talking.'

'But you're—'

'Ugly?' he asked in her ear.

She almost tripped. 'Are you *joking*?' she finally managed.

'Not at all,' he replied lightly. 'You don't really want to be here, so what is it? Too fat, too skinny?'

She stared at his chest, thought about his perfect physique, and choked on a laugh. 'Oh yeah, that's definitely it.'

He grinned. 'Boring?'

This time she reluctantly laughed. 'Never that.'

'Just not your type then?'

She tried to think of any woman whose type he wouldn't fit. Couldn't. 'It's not you, okay? It's me.'

'Original. You're going to have to do better than that.' His breath whispered across her cheek as he spoke, causing another shiver. Feeling the response, his fingers tightened on her waist. 'Much better than that,' he murmured.

'No, I don't.' Flustered, she planted her feet. 'It doesn't matter how damn attractive you are. It has nothing to do with that.'

'How damn attractive I am?' he asked, enjoying himself.

'It doesn't matter,' she said again, 'because I don't want to be attracted to you, or anyone else.'

'So you are.'

'What?'

'Attracted.'

'I ... That's not the point.'

He laughed, and colour rushed to her cheeks. 'Then what is the point?'

'The point is I'm not going to do anything about it.'

He twirled the end of her hair around his fingers, studying the locks, and the moment drew out. His eyes were dark when they lifted to hers. 'I'm not going to make that same promise.'

'I need you to.'

'Hey Logan—over here!' Mick called out.

Indy took advantage of the distraction to quickly step back. 'You should go see what he wants. I might get some air—take that walk after all.'

He studied her silently, a question in his eyes before finally, he nodded. 'Okay.'

The moon was full and bright, illuminating her path as she wandered towards her room. She needed the air all right, her stomach was in so many knots she had no chance of untying them all. But now what? She headed automatically for the stables, and went to check on the little calf. He was curled up asleep, so she tiptoed out again, careful not to wake him, and began walking aimlessly through the gardens.

Though she could hear the enjoyment radiating from the guesthouse, the noise seemed distant in comparison to the gentler sounds of the night and her own footsteps crunching quietly on the gravel. She interrupted a grazing rabbit and it scampered out of her way, diving into the safety of the thick azalea bushes that lined this part of the drive.

There was something magical about the place, despite the horror of the circumstances that had brought her here. She'd fallen in love with it, and though she wanted the case solved, the women found, she'd miss Calico Mountain when it was time to leave.

Caught up in her thoughts, she didn't immediately notice the second set of footsteps, but they gradually interrupted her peace and she turned her head to see who else was wandering.

Somewhere behind her; not alarmingly close, not visible. Besides, they'd stopped. Someone walking in the garden, a guest taking advantage of the near-perfect night?

She continued to stroll, to take her time.

A few more metres along and the footsteps returned. *Crunch, crunch, crunch.* Heavy, purposeful. A faint prickle of apprehension bothered the back of her neck. She turned more quickly. Still she saw no one. The trees were thicker here, the shadows too dark. 'Hello?'

The only answer was the annoyed shriek of a nightjar.

She pressed on, picking up her pace. The footsteps resumed, matching her stride, then increased their tempo. Her walk became a jog. She rounded the bend that would soon bring the guesthouse back into view, and the road into moonlight. Another gust of cool wind whipped up, and shadows shifted and danced as the trees above her swayed. What had moments before been magical was now sinister.

In her haste she narrowly avoided ploughing into a young couple holding hands, enjoying the night. 'Sorry.' But her tone was relief. The couple passed by, moved on. This time when she listened for the footsteps, there was only silence.

Instead of going back to her room she jogged up the steps and back into the guesthouse. She needed to know who had been behind her. She saw Connor almost immediately, Murphy, Bob … Most of the guests were still hanging around. Who was missing? Logan. Mick, Ned …

The doors opened behind her and she turned quickly. Ned came in, smiled in his usual fashion. 'Hi Indy.'

'Where have you been?' she demanded.

His expression blank, he shrugged. 'Round.'

'Did you just follow me back from the stables?'

'What?'

'Did you just follow me back from the stables?' she repeated more insistently.

'Nah. Came from the other way—havin' a beer with Mick at the bunkhouse. You right?'

'Yeah,' she said, letting it go. 'Yeah, I'm fine.'

'You wanna dance?'

'No—I'm tired. Goodnight.' She walked back out, turned once to have one last check through the large windows to see if she could find Logan. Ned was still standing where she'd left him, watching her. Something cold crawled over her back, and she walked back to her room cautiously—listening, not at all sure she believed him.

CHAPTER

15

The dream starring Logan Atherton probably shouldn't have surprised her. Not after the rollercoaster ride between the fear of him figuring out she wasn't who she said she was versus the tornado pull of attraction—screw it, lust—she'd felt in his arms at the party. But the sweaty waking part wasn't any less uncomfortable because she could explain it away. She rolled over, groaned unhappily into her pillow, because it was a little too vivid to immediately shake off.

'Merry Christmas, Indy,' she mumbled. She walked into the shower and let the spray hit her face. There were no rides this morning but the horses needed to be fed and she did have to face Logan—therefore all images of what had happened had to be well and truly wiped from her mind. She wondered if he really did look as good naked as he had in her dream, decided he probably did, then chastised herself for letting her mind wander back. Again.

She dressed and tossed her things in her room, headed out and almost crashed into Ned entering the house with a large canvas bag. He was dirty, dishevelled.

'Ah … Morning, Indy. You're up and about early.'

'Are you keeping tabs?' she asked suspiciously. 'Where have you been?'

'Just had a few things to take care of. See you round.'

A few things to take care of? It looked like he'd gone bush for a month. And for once he wasn't hanging round trying to charm her. Where had he gone after she'd run into him the night before? And why did he need such a big bag?

She checked out the staff car. It was cold. Ned hadn't been anywhere that required driving. So perhaps he'd gone out into the mountains.

She needed to get a move on if she was going to feed the calf on time so she hurried to the stables. Logan emerged from the breezeway as she reached them—every bit as hot and sweaty as in her dream.

He pulled off his shirt and that tall, hard wall of tanned muscle strode towards her, pausing short at the tap to throw water over his head and rinse off his shirt. Ned forgotten, a sound she didn't even realise she'd made escaped her lips as every cell in her body stirred back up to its earlier boiling point. She couldn't have looked away if her life had depended on it.

Logan glanced up, straightened. 'You right, Indy?'

'What?'

His look was puzzled as he straightened. He shook out his shirt. 'I asked you a question.'

He had? She hadn't heard it over the light-headed buzzing in her ears. 'God. *Why?*' she asked the universe weakly.

'Why? Because I was looking for an answer.'

'I wasn't talking to you.'

'Seems like a strange time to be talking to God.'

'From where you're standing, maybe.' Her legs were actually weak. 'I have to go.'

'What? Where? You just got here ...'

'The calf will be hungry,' she called over her shoulder.

'His formula is in the shed behind you.'

'Right, yes.' She turned back around and charged in.

'Whoa. Hold up.' He got between her and the feed room. 'What are you cranky about?'

'Nothing. Why are you ...?' She waved a hand at that expanse of chest. 'It's not hot. I'm still wearing a jumper.'

'You can take it off if you want,' he replied cheekily. Then his gaze narrowed in on her face. She felt flushed—hoped she wasn't. Did his mouth move up just a fraction at the corners? 'Rex ruined the mesh partition in his stable and it came away from the frame. I was just welding it back together, got some sparks on my shirt. They were burning some small but uncomfortable holes in me.'

She saw the tiny red marks spreading across his chest and softened. 'Are you all right?'

'Of course I am.' Definite amusement now. 'Are you?'

She stepped round him and began mixing the milk formula in the bottle. 'Yeah. Don't you have some family-only Christmas morning planned?'

'In an hour or so. The animals come first.'

'I can feed them.'

'Are you trying to get rid of me?' His arm blocked the doorway to stop her in her tracks. 'First, let's talk about last night.'

Primed for fight or flight, she waited, the knot in her stomach pure tension. Was this about the questions she'd asked regarding the missing women? Or about the whole embarrassing discussion on attraction? The constant uncertainty of not knowing what he was going to do next, or why, was impacting her more than any case she'd ever worked on. 'What's to talk about?'

His lifted his hand and ran a finger lightly down her throat to hover over the spot where she knew her pulse was pounding. When her breath hitched his eyes returned knowingly to hers and his hand left her throat to cup her cheek, his thumb grazing over her lips. 'Why are we not doing anything about this?'

She had no answer. Every nerve was on fire. She closed her eyes, made herself breathe in and out, and somehow, stepped back. 'I just can't.'

Neither of them moved for several seconds. 'Is that your final answer?'

'Yes, I'm sorry,' she said, quickly diving past.

'Indy?'

'Yes?'

He stepped back into her space. 'Okay.' He slowly bent his head, kissed her cheek. 'Merry Christmas.'

'You too.' She walked away, realised she hadn't finished making up the bottle and needed to go back in. But he was heading in the opposite direction. Equally relieved and frustrated, she got on with it.

Merry Christmas. Ha. So maybe she'd been a bit obvious in her admiration of his shirtless physique. She was a cop, she was a professional. But she was still female. And maybe she was really, really relieved he hadn't bailed her up in there to murder her because she was digging into the disappearances. Not only because she'd walked away in one piece, but because if she was going to be defensive about him, it would be nice to also be right. Especially under the circumstances. Good grief, the man had her in knots on top of knots. But she'd said no, and it looked like he'd accepted that. Anything else was out of the question.

When she walked back into the bunkhouse, Gina was on the lounge in the common room with a cup of tea and her laptop open on Facebook. Ben had looked her up, told Indy everything Gina already had. Her story had checked out. It bugged Indy that her radar was off. Was it because of Logan?

Of course it was. 'Happy Christmas, Gina.'

Gina closed the lid on her computer—a little too quickly for Indy's liking—and smiled. 'Hi. You too. I didn't expect to see any-one around at this time of day.'

'It's breakfast.'

'Is it? I've got the day off, only just got up.'

'What are you up to?'

'Catching up with friends and family—you know.'

So why did she sound like she'd been caught out? 'Right. See you later.'

As soon as she was in her room, Indy opened her own laptop and logged in to Facebook. A search at the top had Gina's page coming up. It wouldn't hurt to look after all. Just to see …

It hit her straight away that the cover picture was different to the one she'd spotted over Gina's shoulder. That one had been a flower collage. This one looked like it had been taken on some cruise or other. And the woman in the picture wasn't Gina. Close— there was a resemblance. She clicked on Gina's photos, and a quick scroll revealed a picture of Facebook Gina standing next to Calico Mountain Gina. Confused, Indy went back to Gina's friends list and found what she was looking for. Gina didn't work here, her sister April did. And April was an investigative reporter. Indy closed her laptop with a satisfied smile.

'Gotcha.'

Logan wasn't sure what was holding Indy back, but it damn sure wasn't a lack of attraction. He wasn't conceited, but he knew when a woman was interested. Lately, every time they'd been within several feet of each other he'd felt the temperature go up. Could it be something to do with her family? Her past? Was there someone somewhere else he didn't know about? Or was he being obtuse? Was it possible she still believed he could be a murderer? They knew each other so much better now—did she still not trust him?

He wanted to ask, but he wasn't sure she'd tell him. Besides, she'd said no. He'd told her he was good with that—what else could he say? So that was that. Indy's secrets were Indy's. Until she decided to share them, he'd just have to keep his curiosity—and his feelings—to himself. He chewed on a chocolate biscuit and tried to concentrate on what he was doing. Then Indy's voice had him looking up from the schedule he was working on.

'You want to get out of this stable, don't you? Come on then.' Logan heard the calf trot out behind her, then saw them, the calf clinging to her side as they went past the office doorway and out into the sunshine.

'That's a nice sight,' he said, coming out of the office with the biscuit in hand. 'He's doing well.'

'I thought he'd like to stretch his legs.'

'The sun and exercise will do him good.' The calf sniffed at Logan, then at Logan's hand. 'Sorry, mate, calves don't eat Montes.'

But the calf managed to slobber on it, and with a nudge from a little nose, the biscuit slipped from his grasp.

'He really wants it,' Indy said, fascinated as he pushed at it with his nose.

'Nah, it's just something different to play with.'

Indy picked up the mangled mess and screwed her nose up. 'It can't be good for you.' She tossed it into the long grass and flicked the remains from her fingers. Looking back in his direction, she asked. 'Did you have a nice Christmas with your family yesterday?'

'Yeah. You could have come up for drinks. Tess said she invited you.'

'I'm not big on Christmas.'

His smile faded into sympathy as he remembered what she'd said about her family. 'Fair enough. Thanks for taking care of the horses.'

'No worries.' Then to the calf standing on her toes, 'Listen buddy, two inches of personal space isn't too much to ask, is it?' She tried to step around him, almost tripped over him. 'You, my Monte boy, have to go back in your stable.' The calf lifted his head, blinked those big long eyelashes at her and bleated.

Logan couldn't help but laugh. He was so damn cute. Especially with biscuit crumbs on his nose. 'He wants you all to himself,' he commented.

'Well that can't happen right now,' Indy said, still smiling at the calf.

Logan lifted the calf easily off his feet. 'I know how you feel, mate. Let's go.' And with a cheeky wink at Indy, he strode down the breezeway.

Tess appeared at the other end, her face splitting into a wide smile as she spotted him carrying the calf. 'Oh, he's so cute! Where are you taking him?'

'Jail.' Logan walked into the stable and put him down. 'He stole my biscuit.'

Tess went in and extended her hand for the calf to sniff. 'Nice to meet you.' She smiled at Indy. 'Does he have a name?'

'Monte,' Indy said. 'The biscuit thief can be sentenced to that for life.'

'Not bad,' he decided. Then to Tess, 'What are you up to?'

'I just came down to tell Indy that the part finally came for my car. Apparently Christmas got in the way of quick deliveries.'

'No worries,' Indy said. 'I'll take care of it this afternoon.'

'Great, thanks.'

'Do it after breakfast if you like,' he said to Indy, then he asked Tess, 'Does that suit?'

'Sooner the better. Then you can have yours back.'

'I'll meet you over there,' Indy promised.

When Tess left, Logan's attention returned to the calf. He really did need to be out more. The stable was only meant to have been a short-term solution.

'Everything all right?' Indy asked.

'Yeah. It's more than time he had his own yard. If you need me I'll be back in the office for a while. I've got a few things to work out.'

Indy got everything done in time for breakfast, then headed up to the guesthouse. She was hoping to run into Gina—or more correctly, April.

There was no sign of her in the dining room, but a quick check of the staffroom revealed she was having her breakfast in the spot she usually did when she and Kaicey wanted to gossip. Indy guessed she must be expecting Kaicey to join her, so she knew she'd have to work fast.

'Hi, Indy.'

'April.'

It took a moment to register, then April turned her gaze slowly in Indy's direction. 'Who?'

'Let's not play that game. I know who you are. Very shortly, the Athertons will know, too.' But throwing April at Connor Atherton wasn't the plan. There was a shuttle heading for town this morning. She intended on making sure April got safely on it.

April closed her eyes and shook her head. When she opened them, all traces of the giggly swooning girl were gone. 'How do you know?'

'I searched on Facebook—got your sister.'

April swore under her breath. 'Damn it.' She considered Indy carefully. 'Is there any way I can persuade you to keep quiet? This is going to be a big story. A huge break for someone at my stage of career. I could involve you in it. Pay you something.'

'Pass.'

'You're not worried you're next? How could you work here legitimately knowing what's happening to those women?'

'I have no idea what's happening to those women. And I'm guessing you don't either. I do have some idea of how a confrontation with Connor Atherton is likely to go though, so I suggest you get on the shuttle into town this morning and stay far away.'

April's eyes narrowed. 'You're very loyal. Unless you're hiding something, too.'

'Oh go on, please—threaten me. I'll just head up to Connor's office now and—'

'Okay—okay. You know, I was actually going to run a fair story on them.'

'By sneaking around behind their backs.' Indy pushed back her own guilt—didn't quite call herself a hypocrite. She was here to save lives, not create an interesting story based on unwarranted allegations.

'They won't do interviews,' April protested.

'Neither will I. You'd better pack, the shuttle's leaving in about ten minutes.'

April got to her feet. 'I guess I should thank you for giving me time to get out of here. Out of interest—why are you?'

'I think it's better all round.'

'Because you're not really sure something bad won't happen to me if I don't get clear, right?' April pushed.

Indy's tone dropped to icy. 'Don't put words in my mouth.'

'Oh, I won't misquote you. I'll just make sure I play up the insinuation. Last chance, Indy. I stay, they get a fair write-up. I'll make sure you're compensated.'

Indy turned to leave. 'Goodbye, April.'

'You think I'll run?' She raised her voice at Indy's retreating figure. 'With my tail between my legs like some scared puppy?'

'Run from what?' Jules asked from the doorway. Tess and Nat were behind her.

'If I can't get my story this way, I'll get it the old-fashioned way!' April blurted.

'Story?' Tess stepped around Jules, radiating anger. Nat backed out and Indy turned around.

'This was my big break—and you've ruined it!' she snapped at Indy. Then she glared at Tess. 'I have to go back with something. It can be my own observations and trust me when I say right now they're quite colourful—or you can give me a proper interview. Your choice.'

'You write one single inflammatory line and—'

'One? I've been here long enough to have plenty of them! The gossip flying around this place is gold. You may as well close your doors right now. The whole country's going to know what's going on here.' She strode out.

Tess dropped into a chair. 'Shit.'

'What happened?' Jules asked Indy.

'I walked in on her while she was on Facebook. Her name is April. She's an investigative reporter. Gina is her sister.'

'For someone who obviously thinks she's clever, that was a pretty stupid thing to do.'

'What are we going to do?' Tess wondered.

'There's not much we can do,' Jules admitted.

'We'll see about that.' Connor stood in the doorway. Indy decided Nat must have gone off to get him. 'Where is she?'

'Packing, I suspect.' When Connor turned on his heel, Indy called out, 'Don't give her a reason to be nasty. She's angry because she's been caught out, but no one's treated her badly. She can't say that. Just let her go.'

'You think I'm just going to let her walk out?'

'Indy's right,' Jules said. 'You go over there all pissed off and you're giving her ammunition and a better story.'

Connor moved his gaze to Indy. 'I want to know everything about her. Tell me what happened.'

'There's not much to tell. She just came across as a bit fake, then I saw her checking her Facebook and the account wasn't Gina's. I double-checked and figured it out. When I confronted her she offered me money to keep quiet and give her information. I refused, so she was pissed enough to cause a scene.'

'I bet she was,' he said through grated teeth. 'Let me see that page. I'm going to have our lawyer contact the people she works for, hope he can threaten them with enough legal stuff to shelve any story she might think she has.'

Indy followed Connor's stare to the window where people were climbing on the shuttle. April stood at the end of the line, staring back with an expression as dark as Connor's.

'She packed pretty quick,' Jules noticed.

'Not as big and brave as she wants us to think,' Tess decided. 'You ready, Indy?'

'To fix your car—right. Yep.'

Logan got off the phone from making the timber delivery order and looked over his design once more. It would look good there, and be close enough to the guesthouse for visitors with little family members to walk to. Indy had picked the perfect spot—though he was going to have to find another place for a new isolation paddock. He picked up the drawing to show her, get her thoughts. Then he remembered she'd been going to help Tess after breakfast.

He really needed to get his mind off Indy.

A flyer for the New Year's campdraft caught his eye. He liked the idea of it. A few competitors had put it together to try it out—a good excuse for a campout and a bit of fun on New Year's. And he had a few clients going he wouldn't mind catching up with. But he hadn't put an entry in. If he'd known Indy would pick everything up so fast he might have entered. Rex hadn't been out enough lately and could do with the run. Between Calico Mountain being short-staffed and everything else he had on, he'd had trouble getting away. But it didn't matter. He looked out towards the mountains. He couldn't afford to be gone more than a night or two at a time anyway. Not until they were safely picked up. Ned would go out there, feed them if Logan asked. But he liked his piss-up on New Year's. He wasn't sure he should mess with that.

'Logan?'

'Out the back,' he called to Connor.

Connor came around the back of the stables. 'You busy?'

'Always. What's up?'

'We may have a problem. Is Mel around?'

'Yeah. She's cleaning gear.' He led the way into the stables and paused in the tack room doorway. 'Got a minute?'

'Sure.' Mel put down the cloth and came out.

'I just found out we've had an investigative journalist working for us.'

Logan's heart somersaulted at Connor's dark look. Not Indy, surely? 'Who was it?'

'Gina Rosetti. Except, her real name is April Rosetti.'

The sigh of relief was very real. 'How'd you find out?'

'Indy figured it out.'

'Indy did?' Mel asked with interest.

'Yeah. Long story. I need to know if she's been poking around down here, asking questions.'

'She's been down here, but I haven't had much of a conversation with her,' Logan said.

'She was here the other day, asking questions,' Mel told Connor. 'She wanted to know how often Logan took off on the trails and why. Indy and I didn't really tell her anything.'

Logan swore under his breath. 'I've had just about enough of this.' He only hoped she hadn't followed him and seen anything. He figured he'd know if she had. 'Where is she now?'

'On the shuttle. It's headed north today so I'd say she'll probably stay at Hamilton and get the bus to Hobart tomorrow.'

'You let her go?'

'I didn't want to. But I know who she works for and I'm on it.'

'Have you told Murph?'

'Nat, Tess and Jules were there when Gina and Indy had their confrontation. Nat came and got me, so I'm guessing between them someone's told Mum and Dad by now.'

'Confrontation?' He grinned at Connor as he said it.

'The girls will fill you in. I have to make a phone call.'

'Let me know how it goes.'

'I'm glad you came along when this conked out on me,' Tess said a few minutes later as Indy got to work.

'You can thank Mel for that. She gave me a mouthful about Logan so he sent me off with Jules while he talked to her.'

'If you haven't figured it out, all she's interested in is being Mrs Logan Atherton.'

'That's what Jules said.' Indy wiped her brow and decided to dig. 'Though Mel denied it. It's kind of sad—if she's interested in Logan and he doesn't feel the same. I've been trying to get along with her but she still doesn't like me much.'

Tess smirked. 'Logan's been pretty much oblivious—or he says he is. I think he does a bit of side-stepping. Then you two show some interest in each other, you move straight to the top of her hate list. You're a threat.'

She paused, looked over her shoulder and saw Tess watching her expectantly. 'I'm not interested in Logan.'

Tess's mouth opened in disgust. 'You're not interested in Logan? You have two eyes and from the hints I've seen, a reasonable amount of taste. And he's pretty close to the image of every woman's fantasy. Why not?'

'No, I'm not, yes to the other three and ...' She went for the easy answer. 'Because it's not the right time in my life for me to get involved with anyone.'

'Who said anything about becoming involved? I'm sure he wouldn't mind being used.' She wiggled her eyebrows and smiled mischievously.

'Hell, Tess. You know, I don't *have* to spend my time fixing your car.'

'All right,' Tess muttered, 'It's just that you two seem so ...' At Indy's raised eyebrows Tess grinned. 'Fine, we can talk about boring things.'

'What happened between Jules and Connor?' Indy asked to shift the focus away from her.

Tess sighed and shrugged. 'Jules and Connor and Logan and I all grew up together. We were "the Calico Mountain kids" at school. It was all good. Great even. Then we all went our separate ways for a while. Connor went to Melbourne to study business and Jules went to Sydney. For a few years we only ran into each other on holidays and special occasions. Then Connor came back so Dad could retire and Jules flew home to see everyone and guess what? Suddenly they decided they couldn't live without each other. Jules turned down a position in a top restaurant in Sydney to work here and they were getting married. Together within two weeks of Jules getting back for Christmas, engaged two months after that and completely over between them before the year was out. And do you think either of them will tell anyone why? But he's still in love with her.'

'Yeah, I thought so.'

'And I know he's feeling pretty bad about the way he treated you—especially when you first arrived.'

'As it turns out he was right—about someone coming in to do the story.

'So what do you think is really going on?'

'The more of these women I get to know, and the more that comes out about what's been happening around here for years, the more I'm convinced that whoever killed Latisha is doing this to more women. Sometimes in town I just look at these people I've known all my life and wonder, is it you? Or you? Could it be him, or him, or him? But I can't make myself believe any one of them could be responsible for something like that. So I don't know who.'

'And you've never believed Logan could do something like that,' Indy said, just to gauge Tess's reaction.

It was defensive, almost angry. 'Logan wouldn't hurt a fly. He's the kindest, most generous person with the biggest heart. The accusations hurt him more than he lets on. I hope April doesn't make things worse. He doesn't deserve it.' She took a deep breath and released it, smiled a little self-consciously. 'Well, I guess I needed to get that off my chest.'

Indy smiled sympathetically. 'It can't be easy for any of you. Hopefully the police will sort it out soon.'

'You'll be careful, won't you? It seems as though you can handle yourself.'

'I can. I'll be fine.' She walked around the bonnet and turned on Tess's car. It roared to life. 'And so is your car.'

'Thanks, Indy.'

'No problem. You can pay me back by giving me a lift back to the guesthouse. It's a long walk and I'm starving.'

She had lunch with Tess, and when she walked back to the stables, saw that the horse truck was parked out the front and Logan was loading equipment onto it.

'You going somewhere?' she asked casually.

'Yeah. New Year's Eve campdraft. First time it's being held and Rex needs the run. I haven't gone to as many comps as I should have recently.'

'Oh. I didn't realise.'

He closed the tack box. 'Bit of a last-minute decision. I'm heading off a day early to catch up with some clients.' He walked back down the truck ramp and into the stables. 'Now that you have your list of responsibilities, you should be right with Mel, but any dramas, just let Connor know.'

As if. 'I'm sure I can handle it.'

'You get Tess's car going?'

'Of course I did.'

He grinned. 'You're an incredible woman, Indy.'

She sent him a level stare. 'You need your car fixed?'

This time he laughed. 'No. But how are you on tractors and quads?'

'I can probably handle them, why?'

'Because we have a lot of machinery and it's good to know there's someone around here that can handle more than the basics.'

'No problem.'

'When I get back, we'll talk more about it.'

'Okay.'

'I have a delivery coming tomorrow—some timber. Dave will turn up here, so can you show him where the isolation paddock is and have him heap it there?'

'No worries. Why?'

'Because I have a project to get started on. I need my stable back.'

'Will it be just the one little project?' she inquired lightly.

'I think that question will answer itself when you go check on your calf.'

Puzzled, Indy walked into the breezeway and stuck her head over the door. Two tiny white lambs lay curled up beside Monte, sound asleep. She heard Logan's footsteps behind her. 'Rosie's new project. She thought Monte would like the company so she put them in with him. You don't mind, do you?'

'No, of course not. They're adorable.'

'Rosie's feeding them, you don't have to worry.'

'I don't mind helping.'

'Thought you might say that.' He moved away and took Rex's halter from its hook, slipped into the stable to catch him. Rex walked around in a circle, tossed his head, snorted. 'Yeah, yeah. You're a show-off. Let's go, mate.'

Rex put his head into the halter and Logan secured it, then caught her watching them. 'All good?'

'Yeah. Good luck.'

'Thanks.' He walked the horse out and stopped, turned. 'See you in a couple of days.'

Indy gave Monte one more pat and took the bottle, stepping over hungry lambs as she attempted to get to the door. The lambs were making so much noise she didn't hear Rosalie, almost ran into her. 'Sorry! Hi. Your babies are ravenous. I was worried I was going to lose fingers.'

Rosalie smiled at them affectionately as Indy squeezed through the door. 'They're constantly starving. Good sign that they're healthy.'

'You should show me how to mix their formula up—I can feed them when I feed Monte.'

'No need,' Rosalie said, surprised. 'You've got your hands full.'

Indy shrugged, looked hopeful. 'I've never fed a baby lamb.'

After a slight hesitation, Rosalie smiled again and nodded. 'I'll show you what to do.'

They sat on an overturned feed bucket each and got to work. 'You know, you really don't need to help,' Rosalie said as two frantic little tails beat in time with the sucking of bottles.

'Yeah, it's tough,' she laughed as one sneezed milk froth at her. 'But I figure they should be used to at least one other person feeding them in case you can't make it occasionally.'

'Your boy's jealous.'

Monte was butting at Indy's elbow. 'He thinks he's getting an extra feed.'

Footsteps had them both looking up. Mel appeared. 'We've got sheep now?' She glared at Indy. 'You just don't know when to quit, do you?'

'They're mine,' Rosalie said.

'Oh, well. I guess that's okay then.' She moved off and Indy heard her go into the office.

'Personality of a brick, that one,' Rosalie muttered, then inspected the bottle. 'All done cutie.' Indy's lamb finished hers and Rosalie took both bottles to wash up. 'Thanks for that, Indy.'

'No problem. You said you're feeding every four hours, right? Do you want me to do the six and six feeds? That's when Monte gets his bottles. I'd be happy to give you a break. I'm here anyway.'

'You're a lovely person, Indy. I'd appreciate that. They won't need this many feeds for too long.' Rosalie placed a hand on her shoulder. 'Logan says you're a real asset around the stables. If you decide you'd like to stay on past the end of the season, I'm sure we could use you.'

'Thanks,' Indy said. 'That's good to know.'

'Let's get these bottles washed up and think about getting ready for dinner.'

If she'd like to stay on ... The comment had her considering whether or not she needed to still be here at all. She'd talked to everyone, learnt as much as she could, and she'd thrown everything she could at Logan and been unable to catch him out. But there was still the issue of someone actively prying into her life, and something wasn't right with Mel. As keen as she was to get on with helping Ben with the main investigation, she really needed to put together those last two pieces of the puzzle before moving on.

As she walked out with Rosalie she noticed a shadow move behind her. Mel, watching them leave? Or … making sure they were leaving? Indy walked a few more steps along the drive with Rosalie then made a show of checking her pockets. 'I think I left my phone in the stables. I'd better go check. I'll catch up with you later.'

Quietly, she went around the back of the stables. Mel was in the office so she slipped into the tack room next door.

'Yeah, I told her. Nup, not a clue. Do you really need to … I know, I know. But it's not right. Why not just use her, like the others? Logan … fine.'

The rattle of a phone hitting the desk was followed by silence for several moments. Eventually Mel swore violently. Something crashed. A click, a brief flash of light, a sigh. Then the sweet smell of opium filled the stables. Indy crept away.

What wasn't right? And use who for what? Had Mel been talking about Logan? Or to him? A sick feeling churned in her gut. Could she have been wrong about Logan? Because it sounded like he and Mel were in this, whatever this was, together.

Mel was waiting for Indy the next morning with an impatient attitude and a sour expression. Indy was glad to see the back of her when the ride went out. She hadn't gotten much sleep the night before, tossing and turning, her thoughts full of the case, the doubts creeping in about whether she'd allowed her own feelings to compromise her objectivity. It didn't matter that she couldn't see how, because something was going on, and she'd missed it this long. The thoughts continued to swirl around in her mind while she got all her work completed, just in time because the ride was early coming in.

'You'll have to unsaddle the horses and get them fed by yourself,' Mel said as she dismounted and handed Indy her horse. 'I'm going out to Logan's to take care of the ones over there and after breakfast I'm taking out the quad bikes because Carly's busy.'

'Fine,' Indy said pleasantly enough. She tied Brodie up and took another horse off a smiling guest, worked her way down the line.

'And you're going to have to get the yards cleaned out,' Mel told her as she waved off the last guest.

Not so fine. She undid a girth, lifted the saddle onto the fence and shook out the saddlecloth, flicked it over the saddle. 'Is something wrong?'

'Oh yeah, that's right. Quite the, ah … *detective*, aren't we?'

Indy froze, her breath backing up in her lungs. 'What did you say?'

For just the briefest moment there was cunning as well as triumph in Mel's expression, then she shrugged. 'Just get on with it.'

Indy's first thought was that she'd found her computer hacker. But was Mel really capable of breaking into her electrical devices and retrieving permanently deleted files? She knew it wasn't wise to make a big deal out of it, but she had to know if she was compromised. 'I asked you what you meant!'

'You figured out who April was. What else would I mean?' Mel returned, with wide-eyed condescension. It left her still unsure if Mel was lying or not.

'I don't know, Mel,' Indy said, covering up her concern with anger. 'How your mind works is honestly a complete mystery to me.'

'Don't forget the yards,' Mel called out as she walked away.

No, damn it, enough was enough. She turned and walked back. 'You know, Logan left a list of tasks for each of us—and he already allocated you less because of the extra bits and pieces you had on. Don't push it.'

Mel's glare was cutting. 'I could say the same thing. You can run to Logan and cry on his shoulder all you like. At the end of the day, I'm the permanent worker, I'm the one he trusts to run the place when he's not here. You're just someone he's happy to play with until you piss off and the next one comes along. He's not going to fire *me* to keep *you*. Just remember that.'

An idea came to her. 'Actually, just yesterday Rosalie offered me something more permanent. We might end up being stuck with each other longer than you'd planned.' She sent Mel a beaming smile. 'Ready to be friends?'

'What *is* it with you?' Mel grated. 'You're so fucking cheerful all the time.'

'I'm trying to be happy for both of us.'

'Don't wear yourself out. You've got extra work to do.' Mel turned on her heel and stalked off.

She almost laughed, but as much as she didn't want to admit it, Mel had a point. For whatever reason Logan kept Mel on, he'd done so through thick and thin. She should have asked Tess about it before this. Perhaps she'd have a chance tonight. She knew there was some sort of cocktail party happening in the guesthouse for New Year's Eve. Tess would be there, but so would everyone else. And Mel's detective comment had made her nervous. It was likely just Mel being Mel. She hadn't looked too impressed about Rosalie's offer. But she'd file the information away until she figured out what the phone call had been about.

Just in case.

Indy decided to find Tess straight after work, make sure she was early enough to catch her before the party. So as soon as the last job was done and Monte and the lambs were fed, she raced back to change into clean clothes.

How was she going to broach the subject casually? Should she ask straight out or get around to it? She pulled the keycard from her pocket to open her door. There was a scrambling sound from inside, a crash. Someone was in her room.

She fumbled with the card and pushed through, scanned for a threat. Nothing. The window was wide open. The screen was broken. She strode across the room, looked out. Nothing. She raced outside and around the bunkhouse but there was no one in sight. With a frustrated growl she went back to her room. Someone had sat on her bed; she could see the imprint on her doona. She reached for her laptop. It was warm again.

'Great.' But when she opened it, the password screen flashed up as usual. Whoever it was had either figured out how to get into it, or hadn't given up trying. She hoped they'd read the bogus email.

'Everything okay, Indy?' Mick stood in the doorway, looked around. 'Saw you running round like you'd lost someone. What happened to your window?'

'Ah ...'

He walked in, looked out onto the verandah where the screen still lay broken and frowned. 'Looks like someone went through it.'

'It's been loose for a while. I think I just leant on it a bit too heavily when I opened the window. I ran out there to try and put it back in but it's broken.'

'Yep, gonna need another one all right.' He was looking at her like he wasn't quite buying her story but he changed the topic. 'Gonna go get ready for tonight. I'll see ya over there.'

'Sure. Thanks.'

She spent some time composing another email to Ben, one that would throw any would-be hacker right off the track. She hadn't planned on saying anything about the incident to Connor, but she didn't have any faith that Mick wouldn't—he leaked like a sieve. Once Connor found out, it would only look suspicious if she hadn't told him herself.

She hurried over to the guesthouse, jogged up the stairs just as Connor appeared at the top of them. He was wearing black pants and a collared shirt, already dressed for the party.

'I need to speak to you.'

His brow shot up at her tone. 'What's up?'

'Someone was in my room when I went back this afternoon. They broke the screen getting out when they heard me coming.'

His face was grim. 'First your phone and now this?'

'Look, it's not a big deal—there's nothing much to steal, but I don't like it. And I'll need a new screen.' She went to move past him and his hand curled around her arm. 'Okay stop. Wait.'

'Why?'

'Because we need to sort this out. If you actually interrupted someone in your room, that's serious. Any ideas who it might be?'

Her eyes narrowed coolly. 'It occurred to me it might have been you—still believing I'm not who I say I am.'

'Indy, I'll let that go because I probably asked for it. I'll even apologise for my behaviour when you first arrived. I was worried about Dad, but that's no excuse. However, I wouldn't lower myself to breaking into your room. If I really believed you weren't legit, to hell with the family repercussions, I'd fire you.'

She took a deep breath, released it. 'In a funny kind of way that's reassuring.'

'And while I'm looking into it, I'll get the screen fixed, add an extra lock to your door, one that only you have the key to.'

'In which case, I'll be happy to leave it at that.' And what an enormous turnaround, she thought suspiciously. 'Thanks.'

'One more thing. I appreciate you bailing up that reporter. Given the circumstances it might have been tempting to keep it to yourself.'

'Not at all. There are members of your family I consider friends.'

He studied her silently for several seconds before nodding. 'I'll see to that lock first thing. You should go downstairs. Everyone's beginning to gather and you'll miss all the good food.'

'Right.'

But she wasn't in the mood for socialising, and she wanted to go over her laptop, see if she could work out whether or not someone was getting into it, so she went back to her room.

'Hey Indy, how's it going?' Mick asked from the verandah as she climbed the steps. 'Want a beer?'

'No, thanks. I'm not much of a drinker.'

'There's other stuff in there. Grab a cold one and come out for a while.'

Torn between tiredness and the opportunity to grill the men, she found herself complying. But she soon discovered it was incredibly difficult to steer the conversation away from motorbikes and a particularly well-endowed woman at the guesthouse. Eventually she gave up. 'I think I might call it a night.'

'You're not staying up for New Year's?' Mick asked.

'What for, fireworks or something?'

He took another long drink from his beer. 'Nah—they scare the livestock so we don't do it.'

'Then goodnight.'

'You spend a lot of time in your room,' Ned said.

'I'm not used to the work yet. I'm tired.'

'Kaicey said she can hear you tapping away on your laptop late some nights. Thin walls,' he told her.

'I'm a bit of a Facebook addict,' she lied. She saw headlights coming from the direction of Logan's place. She was too far away to make out the car—probably Mel checking the horses. 'Night.'

'Night,' Mick said.

'If you change your mind, we'll be out here for a while,' Ned added.

It was almost midnight when someone knocked on her door. She found Kaicey standing there. 'Tess is looking for you. I said I was coming back to change so I'd make sure you weren't hiding in here.'

'I'm not hiding. I'm sleeping. Is something wrong?'

'Nope. We're just going down to the river for a dip.'

'A swim? The water will be freezing.'

Kaicey grinned and shrugged. 'It's kind of a New Year's tradition around here—the midnight dunk. So, you coming?'

Swimming? In the middle of the night in a cold river? She felt like a bit of an old woman but shook her head. 'I think I'll pass.'

Kaicey leant on the doorframe and smiled sympathetically. 'You're upset about Logan and April, right? Must admit it looked like maybe you two were getting pretty cosy.'

Perhaps her mind was still fuzzy from being asleep. 'Logan and April?'

'I ran into April earlier—thought you must have too. She apologised for not telling me the truth. I'm still pretty pissed at her though. I'm surprised Logan's not.'

Indy shook her head and tried to think through her still sleep-addled brain. 'Wait ... April's here? She came to the guesthouse and now she's with Logan?'

'She's definitely at Logan's by now. She reckons he kind of ... invited her for their own little New Year's celebration. At least, that's her story.'

'Logan's not even home.'

'You sure?' At her blank look Kaicey waved a dismissive hand in the air. 'She's probably full of shit again. Just forget it and come for a swim. Have a drink for New Year's.'

'I might come down—you go ahead.'

'Okey dokey.'

Indy closed the door and leant against it. April was here to see Logan? Logan was at a campdraft, wasn't he? What the hell was going on?

One way to find out. She got changed—into jeans and a dark T-shirt—and grabbed a torch, then went out onto the verandah where Mick was still drinking with some of the other men.

'Changed your mind?' he asked.

'Kaicey wanted me to go swimming.'

'The midnight dunk? You might want to get a couple of shots of something warm inta ya beforehand.'

'I'll take that into consideration.'

'Maybe I'll join ya,' Ned said, getting to his feet.

Shit, now what? She watched him stand, sway, drop back into his seat. He laughed at himself. 'Or maybe I'll just stay right here.'

Breathing a sigh of relief, she jogged down the steps and out of sight before he decided to change his mind.

She didn't need the torch—the moonlight was enough to go by. It was almost too bright for comfort as she didn't want to be spotted on the walk over.

Logan's house shone with the reflection of the moon. There was no car in the drive, and the horse truck wasn't there. Had April lied and come out here to poke around quietly? Perhaps she decided New Year's would be the best time—while everyone was at the guest-house. Had she gone there first to make sure Logan wasn't at home? Risky. If Connor had spotted her all hell would have broken loose.

Indy let herself inside Logan's unlocked house. She still couldn't quite understand leaving everything open. She slipped into the hallway, kept to the shadows. Listened carefully as she checked every room. When she found no one, she moved silently upstairs.

The house was empty. Because she was there, she took the opportunity to have a better look around his house, but found nothing of interest. Had April already been here? The next day she intended on finding out.

Indy ambled slowly towards the stables. The scattering of stars still visible when she woke up had faded with the dawn. She was late, but there was no ride planned for the morning. All she needed to do was feed the horses and take a few rugs off. And of course, there was Monte and the lambs to look after. Then, at a slightly less ridiculous hour of the morning, she planned on grilling Kaicey over the previous night's apparent mysterious visit from April.

The best Indy could come up with was that April had been snooping again and been caught out, came up with a lame excuse. Stupid. Logan was miles away. She rolled her shoulders, dropped her head to one side, then the other as she worked the kinks loose, and stopped in her tracks. Logan's horse truck was parked outside the stables.

Her mind started to race. Logan was not miles away. He was here. Somewhere. If April had been telling the truth, they could have met here. But why? She wasn't buying the romantic rendezvous story. He'd be more likely to want to murder her.

Oh, shit. She hadn't meant that literally. But …

Yeah, I told her. Nup, not a clue. Do you really need to … I know, I know. But it's not right. Why not just use her, like the others? Logan … fine.

Had Logan done something to April?

She hurried into the stables to find him, found Mel sitting at the computer. 'Where's Logan?'

Mel jolted, spun. 'Mind your own business.'

Then she noticed her colour and dread built in her stomach. 'What's wrong?'

Mel's hand went to her forehead. 'Nothing. Nothing's wrong. Just leave it!'

'Mel—'

'Please, Indy!'

'Okay ... Just tell me where Logan is.'

'I don't know. Riding. Somewhere.'

She left Mel alone and stared out over the mountains, while a mix of nerves and dread danced in her stomach. She'd checked and checked. Damn it, there was nowhere for anyone to be kept out there. But if the conversation she'd overheard was suggesting what she thought it was, April wasn't being kept. And what did that mean for Caroline?

She pressed a hand to her stomach. Told herself she had no way of knowing whether Logan had done anything wrong. She could be completely off track. She breathed in, held the air in her tight lungs, released it slowly.

Ben. She'd text Ben, get him to check on April.

She sent the text, and with thoughts racing she mixed up the bottles. She wanted to bail up Mel and demand answers, but to do that she'd have to blow her cover. If she was wrong, if this turned out to be something else, that would be a disaster. Ben would chase this up. If there were questions to be asked, Ben would alert Mark. She didn't like it but she had to wait this out.

And she hoped she was wrong. She really wanted to be wrong.

She fed the lambs, who didn't drink much or take very long, while Monte headbutted and paced impatiently around her. 'Almost, mate. Hold on.' If April had convinced Logan to talk to her, she must have discovered something pretty important. And it sounded like Mel had set up the meeting. What the hell had they done?

She turned it over in her head while she fed the horses. And when Logan ambled in from the trail on Brodie, she kept her distance and tried to gauge his mood. He seemed happy enough, relaxed. Mel appeared, her face still grim, and Logan dismounted, put a hand on her shoulder and said something, had her nodding and smiling back up at him. Fighting back a sick uneasiness, she took the buckets back to the feed room.

'Morning.' Logan walked past with his saddle.

'Morning,' she replied with as much normality as she could muster. 'You're back.'

'Change of plans.'

'Again?'

'Yeah. All good?'

She smiled briefly. 'All good.' But was it? Or when it came to Logan Atherton, had she made a terrible mistake?

CHAPTER
17

The police four-wheel drive cruised slowly along the drive and drew to a hesitant stop outside the stables. Indy watched Mark peer out from behind the windscreen, and seeing her cleaning a nearby yard, he climbed from the car. 'Afternoon.'

She placed the wheelbarrow down, her stomach knotting at the tension behind the casual greeting. 'Hi.'

'Is Logan here?'

'He's in the round yard, working a horse.'

'Anyone else around?'

'No. Is this about April?'

Mark folded his arms, angled his body away as though not particularly interested in Indy, while his eyes stayed alert. 'She was at the pub last night—told Marge that Logan had promised her his side of the story in return for leaving them alone. She left, didn't come back. Her bed hasn't been slept in. Ben said you think she was here?'

Logan emerged from the round yard, a frown on his face as he spotted them. 'Yeah, but the reason for that seems to be differing between recounts,' she mumbled. 'Talk to Kaicey—front desk.' She walked across to take Logan's horse. 'That policeman is asking questions about April. Wanted to know if I'd seen her here last night.'

His gaze narrowed in sharply on hers. 'Last night? Did you?'

'No.'

He handed her the gelding. 'Hose him down for me would you?'

'Sure.'

The men disappeared into the office and she tied the horse in the wash bay and turned on the hose. April told Marge she was meeting Logan. Why? Had she wanted to make sure someone knew where she was going? And she'd run into Kaicey. Why would she come to the guesthouse to see Kaicey before meeting Logan if she'd already arranged the meeting? More insurance? Surely if she was that nervous she wouldn't head out there in the middle of the night. She walked out into the paddock and called Ben.

'Mark's here.'

'I know. What else have you got?'

'I'm fairly certain Melanie Cartwright is involved in the abductions of these women,' Indy told Ben.

'A woman?'

'I caught her on the phone late on Sunday night. She was talking to someone at about 9 pm. I think there's a chance she was organising April's disappearance.'

'Organising it ... You think we have more than one perp?'

Indy told him about the phone call. 'I think the women may be being used for something other than one man's perverted enjoyment. This is not what we thought it was. I'm hoping it means Caroline and the missing women might still be alive somewhere.'

'And there's possibly more. We looked into some other missing persons cases—ones that Mark had dismissed. We think they could be related.'

'How many?'

'Karen Sawyer, went missing in 1998, Laurel Wright in 2008, and Mary Goldman in 2012. They didn't work for Logan, but the circumstances under which they went missing were strikingly similar.'

'Ben, if that's the case, Logan can't be responsible. He was hardly going to be abducting women at twelve years of age.'

'We just agreed this could be bigger than we thought. He might not have been, then, but who knows what he's involved in now?'

She had to concede he had a point. 'Another thing. Mel was smoking opium—I think we'll find that has something to do with her family managing a property by the name of Hilltop Farm. They grow poppies for a pharmaceutical company. I don't know of any connection there, but it's worth looking into.'

'Hilltop Farm was one of the properties Mark searched, but we'll take a more detailed look at it. I'll get that underway and check Mel's phone records to verify if she was talking to, or about, Atherton. I'll be in touch.'

Indy slipped the phone in her pocket and stared out over the paddock. She'd been convinced Logan had nothing to do with the abductions. She reminded herself of all the reasons she'd decided he couldn't be behind it. She reminded herself of them again, then went to find him.

He was sorting through the timber delivery. Working on the yards he hadn't wanted or needed—so she could save a calf he hadn't wanted or needed. So Rosalie could have a little dream for the place come true. And she'd just got off the phone discussing the possibility he was involved in tag-team abductions.

'Hi—you busy?' Logan asked.

And she wasn't ready to talk to him yet. 'Um, yeah. I was just going to finish cleaning the yards…'

'Leave that and come and help me.'

'What do you want me to do?'

'Have a look at this, tell me what you think.'

It was a plan for a series of yards with an avenue through the middle. Areas were marked out for trees, shelters and water systems. The largest yard—paddock really—was at the back and encompassed the small dam already there.

'I think it looks great.' She tried to infuse some enthusiasm into her voice. 'That's a lot of yards.'

'Only eight—nine if you include the big one at the back. It doesn't hurt to be able to rotate the animals through them. Rest the yards occasionally.'

'So what other animals are you getting?'

'We'll just see what becomes available. I'd rather take on animals that pop up needing homes than go out and buy a bunch to begin with. And I might have a lead on another calf—bit older. He's a local kid's high-school project.'

'Kids get baby animals as projects out here?'

'They're given one to raise, to feed up and halter train. Then they compete at shows before they're supposed to—' he made a sweeping gesture across his throat with his finger, 'for the carcass competition. But the kids sometimes get attached. This one's willing to fail class before eating his pet.'

'That's awful!'

'It's just a grade, Indy.'

She pulled a face. 'I mean that they expect the kids to do that!'

'Welcome to the country.'

'I thought I liked the country,' she muttered, then, 'Monte will like the company.'

'If a few soft-hearted kids get wind of this he'll have plenty of company. He's already got the sheep. Rosie said you've been helping.'

'I enjoy it.'

'You're doing a great job with the horses, you've started this whole baby animal farm and you fixed Tess's car. You'd better be careful—you're in danger of making yourself indispensable around here.'

She would have liked nothing more at that moment than to smile back with some witty comment or other, to enjoy the look he was sending in her direction. But she couldn't. She couldn't take her mind off the possibilities.

'Logan ... what did the policeman say?'

Logan's smile dropped, and it wasn't until it did that she recognised how tightly he'd been holding it up. 'He can't find April. She said she was meeting me last night.'

She searched his face for signs he was lying. Saw tension and concern. 'Was she?'

He lifted his hands, dropped them. 'I hadn't arranged anything.'

'Kaicey told me she ran into her last night. April told her you'd invited her.'

'That's why the detective wanted to talk to Kaicey? I wouldn't have that woman on the place if you paid me. For what purpose?'

'Ah ... a little New Year's celebration.'

He laughed harshly, then read her face, frowned. 'You're not kidding. I didn't organise anything—anywhere.' He scraped a hand through his hair and Indy saw confusion, anger. 'What the hell is going on?' He stared into the distance. 'The detective asked if I'd seen her, organised anything, wanted to know where I was last night. A few other things but he never mentioned she was here. And she talked to Kaicey? It's almost as though ... I need to go find Kaicey.'

Almost as though? Indy watched him walk away. Almost as though someone wanted it to look like him? She found herself wanting to believe that a little too much.

Logan went straight to the guesthouse and found Kaicey behind the front desk. She eyed him nervously when he approached.

'Hi, Kaicey.'

'Logan. I hope I didn't say anything I shouldn't have,' she blurted out in a rush. 'I'm sorry if I did. I didn't know what to say.'

'You haven't done anything wrong. But the thing is, I never saw April.'

'I'm sure you didn't. Honest.' Her look said otherwise and when he scowled she took a step away from him, only making it worse.

'So, I was hoping you could tell me when and where you saw her, what she said to you.'

'I was helping with the New Year's party but I went back to the guesthouse to grab a jumper, around ten I think. April was walking past the bunkhouse on the way to your place. She said she'd been told on the phone to sneak in so she didn't upset your family.'

'If she wasn't driving, how did she get out here?'

'I don't know. I asked her what was going on and she said she'd been invited. She made some comment about enjoying New Year's and having a chat about everything and told me not to tell anyone she was here. She didn't want Connor crashing in and ruining her night.'

'Was that it?'

'Yeah, I had to get back to help Murph, and I didn't really like her much after what she did, so I just left it at that.'

'Okay, thanks.'

'I did tell Indy—when I came to get her for the midnight dunk. She looked a bit pissed off and said she'd come down, but when she didn't, Tess came to drag her out, only she wasn't in her room, no one could find her. I'm glad she turned up safe this morning. I guess she passed on to the detective what I told her about April.'

She was rambling, nervous. He'd thought Kaicey knew him better. 'It's fine. Thanks.'

This was getting out of control. He went to the kitchen and grabbed a couple of containers, threw some leftovers into them, sealed the lids and took them down to the stables. Indy was in the feed room so he hurried past and stashed them in the fridge. He'd been out early that morning, because Ned hadn't gone out the night before, so she'd be right until tomorrow. But he needed to ride. To get out on the trails and go as fast as possible and let off some steam. He pulled Rex from his stable. 'Let's go, mate.'

Indy appeared in the breezeway. 'Taking Rex for a ride?'

She was so damn gorgeous standing there with her untidy ponytail and her concerned expression. She had no idea how much he wanted to grab hold of her and kiss her senseless. But she'd said no. So he'd damn well keep his hands to himself. 'Yeah. Look, Kaicey said you were pissed when she told you I was entertaining April. I didn't.'

'So you said,' she replied slowly.

'Kaicey also said you disappeared after she talked to you.'

'I ... went for a walk. I was annoyed.'

'You were annoyed with me but you didn't tell anyone about April?'

'I was annoyed at the situation because it didn't make sense. If you must know I walked to your place in case she was sneaking around without your knowledge, because I couldn't put it past her to lie. The idea of some romantic evening was a bit too hard to believe.'

'I'm glad someone thinks so. Kaicey was so busy worrying I was about to murder her, she couldn't get her apologies out fast enough.'

'I'm sure she doesn't really believe it,' Indy said gently. 'The situation's just got her rattled.'

He nodded, but it was at the ground. 'I'm not so sure. I'll see you later.' He led Rex outside and mounted, turned his horse for the mountains.

Logan still wasn't back that evening when Indy let herself into Monte's stable with three bottles. The lambs charged, as eager as ever for their next feed, and she allowed them to start even as she immediately began to worry. Monte was over in the corner, and he hadn't scrambled up for dinner.

'Hi, baby. Hungry?' Monte lifted his head and bleated a small greeting, but he didn't get up. 'What's wrong, little man?' She impatiently let the lambs finish before walking over to crouch down beside him. His breathing wasn't normal. When she offered him the bottle he ignored it. He was sitting in a mess. 'Okay, okay, hold on.'

Because the lambs were still chasing her hoping for more, she scooped them up, one under each arm and took them into the next stable, and left them there while she dug out her phone. Logan should be back by now. Where was he? She called his phone, could have cried with relief when he answered. 'Something's wrong with Monte. He won't drink, he has diarrhoea, he's so sick. He was fine this morning and now he's not. What do I—'

'Indy, take a breath. I'm coming.' Logan's calm voice had her taking that breath, and she sat, stroked Monte's head and tried to quell the anxiety. She wasn't prone to panic, but this little guy had her scared. He was her baby. She was responsible for him. She loved the damn calf. 'Don't you die on me. Logan will know what to do. He'll be here in a minute, just a minute.'

Logan arrived a few moments later in the ute. 'Sorry—got caught up,' he explained as he came in.

'Where's Rex?'

'My place. Let's take a look.'

Ignoring the mess, Logan lifted him gently to a clean area of the stable and put him on his feet. Monte lay back down with a pathetic sigh. Logan checked his gums, squeezed together some skin on his neck, watched it slowly return to normal. 'His colour's pale and he's dehydrated. I'm betting he's got a temp.' He left them and returned a moment later with a thermometer. 'Not great.' He sat back on his haunches and studied the calf. 'Looks like he's picked up an infection. It happens, Indy. Not your fault. You said he won't take the bottle?'

'No. I tried twice.'

Logan squeezed her shoulder. 'He feels crook. No one wants to eat when they're sick. I'll tube him some electrolytes to get his hydration back up and start him on some antibiotics. I'm pretty sure I've got some Scourban on hand that will do him some good.'

'Can I help?'

'You sure can. Let's get set up.'

She watched Logan work, followed instructions, and learned how to give Monte an injection.

'Will he be okay?'

'Let's just see how he responds in the next few hours.' He stood up and she followed suit. She felt as sick as the calf, and grateful to Logan for dropping everything to come back. 'Be positive, okay? I left Rex at my place. I need to go wash him off, bring him back. Will you be all right?'

'Yeah. Thanks. Really.'

Logan had left the antibiotic container in the stable so she returned it to the fridge. Two more of the containers he often took in his saddlebag when he went out alone onto the trails sat on the bottom shelf. Curious, she slipped one out and opened it. It was food. Leftovers, by the look of it. Steak, pasta, some vegetables. But Logan always ate with everyone else. Why was he taking food up onto the trails?

She'd told herself she didn't believe he was a murderer, and she couldn't find any trace of a structure where women could be kept—not anywhere near the place Logan had taken that container the day she'd found him in the bush. There had to be an explanation other than the one that kept pushing itself forward: that he was taking food out there for April. Because he'd been taking those damn containers out since she got there, and April had only just gone missing. And there wasn't enough food in there for him to have multiple women out there, no matter how emaciated … was there?

It niggled at the back of her mind for the rest of the night, and as she walked back and forth from the stables, kept Monte's fluids up with electrolytes as best she could, she played around with scenarios in her head. But though she caught snatches of sleep in between treks, by morning she was exhausted, and no closer to figuring it out.

She stretched tiredly, her arms and back sore from moving Monte constantly to keep him as clean and dry as possible. He was curled up sleeping again, and though his temperature had come down a tiny bit, he didn't seem any brighter.

She heard Logan come in, the footsteps pausing in the doorway. 'How is he?'

'The same. I came in every couple of hours and syringed him some electrolytes like you said.'

'Give him time. Looks like you could do with some sleep. Go catch some. I'll tube him again, give him his antibiotics.'

'Thanks.'

She did sleep, just another couple of hours, then got some breakfast, and felt better when she went back down to the stables.

Logan was saddling up Rex. 'Monte had a bit more fight in him,' he told her. 'Didn't like being tubed. That's a good thing.'

She yawned and looked over the stable door, where Monte was sleeping again. 'I hope so. You're heading out early again today.'

'Heading out?' he asked.

'Up on the trails.'

'Why do you say that?'

'Saddlebags.'

He frowned, glanced from her to the saddlebags and back. He shook his head. 'Actually Sherlock, I'm going out to the far paddock. I haven't checked up on the cows we let out with the calves for a few days. I'll see you later.'

'Okay.' As soon as he moved off Indy raced into the office, opened the fridge. One of the containers was missing, so she guessed he'd taken it with him. She looked for Logan again and saw him disappearing into the trees. When he was just out of sight, she followed on foot.

She kept far enough behind that she just caught sight of him veering off the same area of the track he had the last time. That was definitely the place, then. No question. And she damn well knew there was nothing there. Nothing. She wasn't going to risk following him in any further, so she hurried back, made sure she'd caught up on what needed to be done before Logan returned a couple of hours later. When he dismounted and led Rex back into the breezeway, she put down the wheelbarrow and followed him into the stables. 'Hi, where've you been?' she asked casually.

'Out to the far paddock. I told you, I wanted to check on that last group of cows and calves.'

She had to force her face to remain impassive. He lied. If there was a reasonable explanation for him taking meals out into the bush, why would he lie about it?

'And ... how are they?'

'Fat.' He grinned at her and she attempted to give one back, but didn't quite pull it off. 'Is something wrong?'

'Took a while.'

His eyes narrowed. 'Then I rode out to my place to finish up a couple of jobs there, remembered I had some tax-related work Rosalie wanted done, so I got that sorted. I have a lot of the paperwork there. Problem?'

'Sorry, just worried about Monte,' she said in excuse.

His expression instantly softened. 'Let's go see if he's interested in having a drink yet.'

'I just tried, and he's not.' *Why* was he lying? 'I'll try again in an hour or so. I have things to do.'

Logan unsaddled Rex and led him to the wash bay to hose off. 'Stand up, mate. Good boy.' He looked out at the yards where Indy had the rake and wheelbarrow, cleaning up. He felt that tug of attraction, shook it off. Even when he was annoyed with her he wanted her. She picked up the heavy wheelbarrow as though it weighed nothing and powered over to the heap to empty it. There was nothing lazy about her movements, even at the end of a long day, but just then she was attacking the job with more energy than she had a right to after the night he knew she'd had.

She was onto him. She'd been beginning to trust him but she was suspicious, and she'd figured out he was taking meals out on his rides. She must be wondering where all the food was going—or to whom. Her gaze had been on the saddlebags again as he'd led Rex out of the stables earlier, and he'd almost been able to hear her mind working. Then he'd copped the inquisition when he'd returned. Damn it.

He finished hosing down Rex and turned off the hose, started scraping the water from his coat. He should just take her—before she made anyone else suspicious, before his secret was out. She'd followed him in once already: it was only a matter of time before she found them. But if anyone saw them going out there together, there'd be more questions. He couldn't afford to slip up for that. He led Rex back to his stable and thought about how to make it work. Before long, he'd be out of chances.

Why would he lie? The question kept bouncing around in Indy's head. This constant toing and froing between guilt and innocence was more upsetting than it should be. Her emotions were playing into it too much. Could she really not see him being responsible, or did she just not want to?

The police had been all over the place that morning. Robinson had men searching the property and bushland, while he was questioning everyone at Calico Mountain over what they knew. All Indy knew was that he wouldn't find April there, and she told Mark that when, for appearance's sake, he pulled her out of work to talk to her, just like he had everyone else.

He just gave her a short, sharp lecture on the value of following correct police procedure. As a detective, the man was a moron. By the end of it she was tempted to give him one back on the value of owning a brain.

'Come on, Monte, just a little sip?' He had a jaw like a vice when he didn't want to open his mouth but she got the teat in. Milk dribbled off his tongue. He took a swallow, a half-hearted slurp, then a couple more. Then he pulled his mouth away and dropped his head again. Hope surged through her. It wasn't much, but it was something. 'Good boy. How about I come back in a couple of hours, we'll try again, huh?'

Ben hadn't gotten back to her—what was with that? Surely he had an answer on the phone call Mel had made by now. If she hadn't heard by dinnertime, she'd call him herself.

The lambs were impatiently waiting for their own feeds in the next stable and made a racket when they heard her leaving Monte's. 'Sorry guys, Rosalie's in town and Tess is bringing down your new bucket of formula. You'll just have to wait.'

She left them making unimpressed noises to wash out Monte's wasted bottle. As she walked to the feed room, Rex lifted his head over his stable and leant against the door; there was a bang as he pawed at it. 'You want to get out, don't you?' The deep gold of his coat shone like glass. 'You're such a handsome boy.' He shook his head and his white cloud of mane floated around him. She couldn't resist reaching out to smooth it back.

Rex snorted, and shying back from her hand, hit his head on the rim of his feed bin, knocking it off the door and sending it crashing down to the floor of the stable. A quick look showed her it had fallen upside down; the metal hangers now pointed up dangerously between his front legs.

'Oh damn.' Quietly, she slid the catch on the stable door to retrieve the feedbin. 'Okay buddy, I'm just gonna get this out of your way. Don't want you catching your leg on—'

She was wrenched backwards by a rough arm around her stomach. She let out a small squeal, dropping the feedbin and sending

Rex sideways in a frightened jump as she was none-too-gently shoved out of the stable and the door secured.

'What did you think you were doing?' Logan's tone was deceptively mild as he turned his attention back to her, but his eyes gleamed dangerously.

'He knocked his feed bin down. I was picking it up. Why?'

'I told you not to handle him!'

'I wasn't handling him—well, I did give him a pat, and he knocked off his feed bin so I …' Realising she was stuttering she stopped, pulled herself back together. 'What's wrong with you?'

'What's wrong with me?' A muscle worked in his jaw, and it appeared he was fighting some sort of internal battle for control. 'What's wrong with *me*?' he repeated. The tone was sharp. It stung, and in her opinion was unwarranted. She didn't need this, not with where her head was.

'This is stupid. He could have hurt himself!'

'He could have hurt you!' He raked a hand through his hair. 'I told you not to go near him.'

'I was doing my job!'

'That's not your job. And if you want to keep it,' he threatened, 'you'd better learn to follow instructions.'

'Fine.' She turned on her heel but he simply spun her back around. 'Don't walk away from me, Indy.'

'Then don't talk at me like I'm an idiot! I was being careful!'

He stared at her silently for several seconds. When he spoke, his voice was too damn controlled for the murder in his eyes. 'Do you have any intention of seeing sense?'

'Do you have any intention of *showing* any?' she countered.

He shook his head in disbelief. 'Take a walk, cool down.'

It only incensed her more. 'I don't need to take a damn walk! I'm not the lunatic losing the plot because I picked up a stupid feed bin.'

'Fine.' He bit out. 'You should still take that walk.'

She should have left it there, but the anger and frustration over Logan's lie boiled to the surface, added to her temper. 'You know what? You're right,' she snapped. 'I can't go back to work. Might need to clean a stable—I could find myself in mortal danger.'

Logan swore under his breath. 'You provocative little—'

'Yes?' she got out from between her teeth.

He opened his mouth, closed it, seemed to rethink what he was going to say. 'Just go somewhere—anywhere—and do your job, Indy.'

'Take your job, and shove it,' she told his retreating back.

'Right. That's it.' He turned and scooped her up into his arms in one easy movement.

'What the hell do you think you're doing?' she demanded, struggling against his impossibly strong grip.

'Are you going to calm down?'

She couldn't. And as they emerged from the stables she caught sight of Jules and Tess running down the drive, obviously alerted by the noise she was making. Tess was carrying a new bucket of lamb milk replacement. Indy barely flicked them a glance, because Logan was headed for a horse trough. 'You wouldn't!' she yelled in his ear. 'Listen, arsehole, I—'

'That's just nasty. Apologise.'

'Not a chance in hell! You're just lucky I haven't knocked your front teeth out!' She shoved at his chest. 'Put me down!'

'Okay.' He let go, and she was unceremoniously dumped in two feet of freezing water.

The jolt to her system from the cold had her gasping. 'How dare you!' She got out, her teeth already starting to chatter. Logan casually walked away.

Too furious to be humiliated, she got to her feet, climbed inelegantly from the trough and, shivering, headed up the driveway to change. Almost comically the two women—trying to look sympathetic but failing miserably—parted to allow her through and she spared each of them a glare as she passed. 'Traitors,' she accused.

'We've been there, sister,' Jules got out on a strangled laugh.

'See you at lunch?' Tess called out nicely.

Dripping wet and freezing cold, she squelched back to the bunkhouse and grabbed a towel, headed for the shower. She'd only gone in to pick up a damn feed bin. What was his problem?

Behind the anger, she suspected she'd given him a fright, but that didn't give him the right to 'cool her down' because he seemed to think she was irrationally angry. The tightness in her chest and the need to punch something didn't *feel* irrational. No, she told herself, it was completely justified. But he didn't know her blow-up wasn't caused entirely by the scene over the feed bin. He didn't know she'd really wanted to demand he tell her the truth about where he was going with containers of food. He didn't know she was three parts in love with him and wanted—needed—him to be innocent.

As the anger drained into hurt, she leant her forehead against the wall of the shower and let the hot water cascade over her back, took some deep breaths. She should leave. She wasn't running a proper investigation. She was no longer capable of it.

Half an hour later, back under control, she went to the guesthouse to get herself something to eat. Tess and Connor were already there and though she didn't particularly feel like company, she couldn't see any way around sitting with them without seeming rude.

'Hi,' Tess said with a smile. 'I was just telling Connor about your ah ... spur of the moment swim.'

'Yeah, it's hysterical.' Connor was studying her carefully so she worked up a smile.

'I'm led to believe I'm not the first.'

'No, you're not,' he replied. 'But he shouldn't have done it.'

'Logan hates losing his temper,' Tess said, still smiling. 'He's traditionally only ever resorted to the horse trough when Jules or I would keep at him and at him. Quickest way to end an argument.'

'Interesting tradition,' Indy mumbled.

'But you work for us, you're not family,' Connor pointed out. 'I hope you're not thinking of taking this any further?'

'Indy wouldn't do that,' Tess brushed off. 'Logan just got freaked out because Indy went into Rex's stable.'

'That bloody horse,' Connor said through grated teeth. 'It should have been put down.'

Tess's expression softened. 'Mel begged Logan not to. You know that.'

'He's dangerous. That's all there is to it.'

Puzzled, Indy opened her mouth to ask what they were talking about but Tess got in first. 'Did Logan tell you why he got home so stupidly early on Monday morning?'

'Wait—what?'

Both sets of eyes turned on her before she realised she'd blurted it out. 'Sorry, it's just that I thought Logan got home on Sunday night.'

'No. He rocked up at four-thirty on Monday bloody morning because some idiot had allocated Rex a stall next to an in-season mare. He reckons he listened to the squealing and the kicking half the night then around two in the morning Rex got a front leg over the stable door and Logan had to pull the door apart to get him off. After that he decided to just put him on the truck and bring him home. So I got a phone call at four asking nicely if I'd start the coffee because Jules refused to answer her phone.'

'And you saw him drive in?'

Tess sent her a strange look but nodded. 'Yes, I did. Why?'

'I, um, could have sworn I'd heard the truck the night before, that's all. Must have been dreaming.'

Tess shrugged. 'It wasn't Logan.'

'But that cop came around asking about April going missing—'

'Logan sorted that—didn't he tell you? It's a couple of hours drive from there to here. And I know when he came in the next morning. It's the first time he's had any sort of alibi for anyone that's taken off.'

Relief, stronger than she could have imagined, washed through her. But how much stock was Mark likely to put in Tess as an alibi? 'Has anyone heard from her yet?'

'She lied about coming back to see Logan and now she's disappeared. I don't trust her not to be pulling a stunt,' Connor said.

A stunt? Indy highly doubted it. Whatever had happened to April, Mel had arranged it. When Ben got back to her, she'd suggest it was time to bring Mel in, formally question her. The thought improved her mood as she went back down to the stables. She was supposed to saddle up Gypsy for a riding lesson, she remembered, but when she got there, Logan was already doing it. Because she wasn't quite ready to forgive him yet, she decided to go into the tack room to wash the horse rugs.

His eyes slid over her as she breezed past. 'Good, you're back.'

'If you talk to me yet,' she said calmly, 'I will break something you need. Like your arm, possibly your neck.'

'You think you could?' he asked from the tack-room doorway. 'A nose is one thing but—' She lifted her brow and had him biting back a smirk. 'Okay, and I apologise. But while you're not talking to me would you mind having a go at servicing a quad bike? It's died on me. I think it's time we stop wasting your talents.'

'Aren't you worried I'll remove the brakes?' she murmured as she emptied a chaff bag of dirty cotton rugs onto the floor.

'That'd be stupid. If I'm out of action, you're back to working with Mel.'

She almost laughed. Didn't want to. 'I'll look at the damn quad.' She would have walked past, but he put himself in front of her.

'Don't take off—again.' He lifted his hands truce-style and spoke calmly. 'What's wrong?'

That damn *tone* of his. 'What's wrong? Seriously? Logan, you put me in a horse trough.'

She didn't at all appreciate his grin. But then the back of his fingers skimmed her cheek and his eyes softened. 'It was that or kiss you.'

And on a whole other level—*Oh God*. Under that gaze, that touch, her body was melting, but her tone was weary resignation. 'And you chose the horse trough?'

'Mood you were in, it seemed safer.' His expression warmed. 'Besides, you said you didn't want me to kiss you.'

Her gaze hit the roof. 'Yeah but … Just a kiss or a freezing cold horse trough?'

'Indy—' His mouth was on hers before she registered he'd dragged her in. His kiss was hot and hungry, and demanded everything. A tremor convulsed through her body and ran right to her toes. The fingers digging into her hips were hard, unyielding, as was the body she was pressed against. The sensations battering her consciousness were overwhelming. Her head spun, her body lique-fied, the strength in her knees just evaporated. As every thought in her head simply disintegrated, she held on, and kissed him back.

Gradually the kiss moved from hot and hungry to unhurried, gentle, and as she drifted on it, she was released. She had to fumble to keep on her feet. 'It should never be just a kiss,' Logan mur-mured. 'If it is you're not doing it right.'

Trembling, breath uneven, she stared at him, wanted nothing more than to throw herself back into those arms. She thought she'd seen every expression he owned, but the one he was wearing as he gazed down at her was something else. How could those eyes contain such calm gentleness and desperate heat at the same time?

Voices, one deep and one bright and childish, floated in. The one-thirty riding lesson had arrived. Logan traced a finger down her cheek. 'We'll talk about this after.'

Indy watched him walk out to greet the guests. How did that just happen? And why, for heaven's sake *why* had that just happened? She opened the washing machine and shoved the first of the rugs in, added some powder. *Because*, she admitted, dropping the lid down with shaking hands and pressing enough buttons to make it go, she'd pretty much goaded him into it. And it wasn't just a mix of stretched nerves and hormones making her stupid—oh, no. That would be easy. She'd had to go and fall in love with him.

This rollercoaster ride of 'is he or isn't he' had to stop. She knew, damn it, she *knew* he couldn't be doing those things to those women. But the anomalies just kept slapping her in the face with doubts. If he'd just tell her what he was hiding once and for all …

She let that stew in her mind until his riding lesson was over, then missed him again when another lot of clients arrived to watch him work their horse. They left, but Logan continued to work with the horse until her patience disintegrated.

So she let herself in, walked right into the middle of the arena. 'Where did you go yesterday?'

He came to her and halted the gelding. 'I told you.'

'Yes, I know. You saddled your horse, loaded your saddlebags with leftovers and tax receipts and worked on the books somewhere out in the back paddock. Except you didn't. Where were you?'

'Were you spying on me … again?' he asked, voice mild but gaze sharp.

Damn it—he knew about that? 'Maybe I was! What are you going to do about it—make me disappear?' As soon as the words were out of her mouth she regretted them. From the look on his face, she may as well have slapped him. 'Logan, I—'

'Is this because of April?' he cut in as his gaze narrowed dangerously. 'If you think I've got her stashed out there somewhere you're pretty damn brave confronting me like this.' The anger left his eyes and the hurt seeped in. 'I thought you knew me better than that.'

'So did I—I do! But I can't keep hoping you're the person I want you to be while you're keeping secrets. Don't you get it?' When he didn't immediately answer, she shook her head in defeat. 'I'll see you later.'

'I'm so sick of this bullshit!' And he sounded it. For the first time she could remember, Logan really sounded as though he'd had enough.

It shouldn't have surprised her that he cornered her against the fence like a damn cow before she could reach the gate. He jumped from the horse and took her arm in a tight grip. 'What are you doing?' she asked, pulling at his hold.

'Proving a point.' He dragged her across to the stables and into the office, shut the door hard. She flinched again at the slap of his hands against the wall, felt her heart rate kick up as adrenaline flooded her system.

'And you're still not fighting back,' he said, finally angry. 'I've picked you up, dropped you in a horse trough, kissed you senseless, dragged you across a yard and cornered you in the office—slammed my hands against the wall three inches from your face. If you really thought I could murder a woman in cold blood, how come you haven't fought back?'

He was right. He was completely right. While she kept questioning him on a professional level, deep down, she wasn't afraid he would hurt her. Hadn't been for a long time. 'I don't think you could murder anyone,' she admitted. 'I'm sorry.'

'Okay then,' he said in a much more reasonable tone. 'While we're being honest, tell me you didn't want me to kiss you.'

'I didn't want—'

'No. Look at me.' He waited until she did as he demanded, and when she did, his gaze moved over her face and his voice softened. 'Now tell me.'

It was hard to say anything when he was so close, his breath whispering across her face, his eyes so intently on hers. So she closed hers, swallowed hard against the inexplicable temptation to lean forward an inch or two and feel those lips on hers again. 'Why won't you just tell me what you're being so secretive about?'

He dropped his hands and stepped back, suddenly weary. 'Because I want you to trust me. I want someone to think I could have a secret and not be a deranged serial killer. Is that so unbelievable?'

He opened the door and walked away.

She was almost at the bunkhouse when she heard the guys on the verandah. Logan had disappeared, he'd just gone. So she'd finished her work and fed the babies, hearing his words over and over in her head until she felt sick with guilt.

The guys were singing some silly song. She didn't feel like walking into that so she veered off, walked away. When she found herself close to the machinery shed, Logan's mention of the quad bike reverberated in her mind. It would feel good to pull apart a machine, put it back together. Get some grease on her hands again. And she needed something to do to avoid thinking too much about the question bouncing around in her mind: what the hell was she going to do about these feelings she had for Logan?

She slipped into the shed and flicked on the light switch. As the overheads flickered to life they exposed around a dozen quad bikes, almost as many motorbikes, four Gators, three tractors and several pieces of general farm equipment. On the wall were plenty of tools and toolboxes, and shelves of crates hinted at more. She spotted the semi-dismantled quad, got to work.

She was mumbling to herself about the state of the machine when she heard someone come in. *Logan*. Sitting on the ground surrounded by tools and quad parts, she felt at a distinct disadvantage when he stood above her.

'You know how to put all those bits back in the proper places?'

Even just the sound of his voice, the fact that she knew his eyes were on her, elevated her pulse. 'Air filters are there for a reason. They don't work when they're full of mud.'

'Makes sense.'

'It's a wonder the whole thing hasn't fallen apart. I've adjusted the wheel nut settings and tightened the bolting system under the bracket here. You got any decent spray silicon?'

He walked a short distance away, came back and dropped a can in her lap. 'Anything else?'

'Probably. Every moment is a new discovery.'

She worked for several minutes before he spoke again. 'I have some free time tomorrow. I still haven't taken you out to Mt Field, so we could do that, but I think it's well past time you got up on a horse, so maybe we should do that first.'

Indy wiped her hands on a rag, and picked up a container of oil. Then she dared glance at him. His gaze was searching and uncertain. He looked, in that moment, so far removed from the image she'd been holding in her mind that she just melted. 'Sounds good.'

Some of the tension in him seemed to ease. He nodded and headed for the door, paused. 'Last person to bend down next to

Rex in a confined space was Mel's husband, Matty. He went in to trim his feet. We found him dead in the stables the next day. Rex gave him a fractured skull.'

Before she could say anything, he was gone.

'Well, shit,' she muttered; Tess and Connor's words now made sense. She turned the key on the quad. It roared to life and purred smoothly. Satisfied, she turned it off. *Maybe I should stick to machines.*

CHAPTER
19

She was thinking about Matty the next morning at breakfast when Tess came and sat with her. 'Logan told me what happened to Mel's husband, Matt.'

'That's one big reason why Mel still works here.'

'I'm surprised he didn't put the horse down.'

'Mel begged him not to—said Matty wouldn't have wanted that, and it's true. He was an awesome guy. We don't know what happened but Rex has been a bit funny about anyone but Logan handling him since that night. He's never attacked anyone before or after, so I reckon it must have just been a horrible accident. But you would have scared the hell out of Logan going in there like that.'

'I get that now. Wish he'd told me in the first place.' Indy's phone alerted her to a message. Ben. 'Sorry. I have to make a call—see you later.'

As soon as she was clear she called Ben back.

'Mel's phone call was to Kyle Cartwright,' he told her. 'Location is consistent with him being at Hilltop Farm at the time.'

The relief was sharp and fast. 'And Logan has alibis for the night of April's disappearance.'

'So Mark said. But he's not convinced. He's following up anyway. Planning another search of Logan's property.'

'Why? He's just done that.'

'To be honest I'm not entirely sure. I think it has something to do with the senator jumping up and down.'

'Since when do senators run investigations? Why is he even being kept up to date with this, anyway?'

'He's a squeaky wheel with a lot of influence.'

'Did you get that email I sent you on Mandy—about the mother's accident?'

'Yeah. I checked it out. It was a car accident. Brakes failed.'

'Don't you think that's a bit strange? Latisha's family die in a fire, Mandy's mother in a car accident, both around the same time the women were discovered?'

'Hard to say with only the two cases. It's most likely just unfortunate. I'll do a bit more digging.'

'Okay. I've—got to go. Mel's coming in.' She ended the call and slipped the phone in her pocket as Mel breezed in. 'Indy.'

'Hi, Mel.'

'Logan said to tell you he's working Aurora if you want to watch.'

'Thanks.' And what was with the cheerful attitude? Could have something to do with the scent of opium coming off her, Indy decided. Logan was riding in the round yard, so she climbed onto the fence and sat, watching as she waited. He was so quiet, so steady, had Aurora acting on tiny cues. Perhaps that was what made him so good at reading people—that perception of the tiniest flicker of an eye, the slightest change of posture. His touch and guidance seemed to soothe and inspire the horse and encourage it to try harder. The language between them was fascinating, each taking their lead from the other, before attempting another tiny step forward. He worked with her for a few more minutes, before his eyes flicked past her and he pulled the horse up.

Mel came in leading Ollie, one of the gentle old school horses, and took Aurora from Logan. She glanced at Indy, gave her a slight nod, then walked off again. 'I think we're making progress,' Indy mumbled to herself.

Logan reached up, took her by the waist and lifted her down to the ground.

'What are you doing?' Forced to tip her head back to meet his eyes, she squinted against the sun. His hands lingered on her sides, his thumbs caressing her hips.

'Ready?'

'Ready for what?' she asked, suspiciously.

One hand moved to her hair, tugged gently. 'To ride.'

'Logan …'

'Yeah?' he asked, tracing the outline of her cheekbone. She couldn't think. The impact of that simple touch scattered her pulse. When she stepped back he captured her hand. He lifted it to his mouth and kissed it, his lips feather-light. 'You want me to say I'm sorry I kissed you. I'm not.'

It was disconcerting the way he could melt her so easily. She took her hand back. 'Not yet perhaps …'

He really didn't hide his grin very successfully. 'You getting on?'

She stepped around him and stood by the patiently waiting gelding.

In that quiet, reassuring voice of his, he told her what to do. She wasn't the least bit nervous about getting on, but she figured if she had been, he'd have been the one to talk her up. He held the stirrup while she slid her foot in. 'That's it. Now up you go.'

As she swung herself up, his hand slid up her thigh and guided her into the saddle. That touch of that hand had her sitting a little faster and harder than was absolutely necessary. 'Okay, back straight.' His hand moved to the small of her back, massaged. 'You're all tense. Relax your shoulders.' He moved his other hand up and down her arm. 'You're okay.'

'Perfectly okay. Hands off.'

'In a minute.' While he explained what she had to do, those strong, gentle hands seemed to be all over her, adjusting her legs, her hips, her shoulders. And they knew what they were doing. Her whole body was tingling from his touch and she was sure he was damn well doing it on purpose. Finally his hands rested over hers, showing her the correct way to hold the reins.

'You're trembling.'

'I'm resisting the urge to deck you. It's taking some effort.'

With a knowing smile that told her he didn't believe it, he stepped back. 'Head up, looking forwards. Good, now just gently squeeze your legs against his sides. When he moves off, relax the pressure.'

She did as she was told, and after a few minutes was getting bored. 'Can we go a bit faster?'

'Yeah, but it's going to get bumpy. If you start to lose your balance, just sit down and put some pressure on the reins.'

It was bumpy, and after a few more minutes she was getting sore. 'You know, I had hopes of this being a hell of a lot more comfortable.'

'You just have to get the hang of rising trot.'

'Isn't there another gear? I want to do the other one—a canter.'

'So squeeze him up again.'

The horse lunged forwards into a rocking motion. She struggled with her balance, but got used to it. 'Oh, yeah. Why didn't we do this in the first place?' She was starting to see the appeal. She laughed, took a chance and squeezed the horse even faster.

'Slow down! You can't go flat out in the round yard.'

'Why not?' Then she lost her balance, spent the next few awkward moments trying to regain her seat. The horse dropped back to a walk and she repositioned herself. 'Okay, let's try that again.'

He laughed. 'Let's just concentrate on balance and control. Slow down, learn to put him where you want him. Once you can do that, I'll take you out for a good run.'

'So what do I have to do?'

He instructed, while Indy listened. She could have listened to that quiet, deep voice all day. All too soon the lesson was over.

'We do that a few more times, you'll be mustering cattle and taking rides out in no time,' Logan said.

'That'd be nice.' She jumped off, walked a few steps. 'Ow.'

Logan stopped Ollie. 'What's wrong?'

'Just a few complaining muscles. My legs want to move like I've still got a horse underneath me. I suppose that's why all the cowboys in the old movies are bow-legged.'

'Don't worry, you'll still be hot.'

'With bow legs?'

Flustered, she had her hand on the girth to take off the saddle when he turned her around. 'Are we okay?'

She sighed. 'You kissed me to prove a point.'

He took her hands to stop her fiddling with the saddle. 'No. I did it because having to prove a point gave me an opportunity.' He released her hands and his finger slid down her throat, lightly traced the line of her collarbone. 'I'd been looking for one since I first laid eyes on you.'

'And I told you, I'm not looking for anything other than a job and a place to stay.'

'I know,' he replied quietly. Her hair slipped slowly through his fingers, and he slid the locks behind her ear. 'But that's not stopping either of us wanting this. And just so we're clear, there's no ulterior motive here.'

She could have stepped back. He came in slowly, gave her plenty of time, plenty of opportunity. His lips were warm, unhurried, gentle but insistent. Her body trembled once as the tension inside her dissolved. She didn't think. Didn't process. She ignored the thin thread of guilt—wouldn't believe this kiss was anything but right. Her mind was a blur. Everything was flooding sensations and swirling emotions, so she let the rest go and floated on it.

When, eventually, he shifted back to look at her she took a deep breath. She pressed her eyes closed, shook her head. 'You touch me and think you'll make me change my mind?'

'Change it? I'll make you lose it.'

She was pretty sure he already had. 'Would you stop? I can't think.'

'Then what aren't you sure about?' His thumbs slowly caressed her jaw as he considered her. It wasn't helping. 'Come on, I need to show you something.'

'What?'

'You'll see.' He walked to the back of the stables and called out, 'Mel? Can you take care of Ollie? Indy and I will be back shortly.' Then he sent Indy one long, penetrating stare she didn't quite understand and went into the office, to the fridge, pulled out one of those containers. 'Hop in the ute.'

For just a moment her feet dug in. 'Where are we going?'

'You know where we're going.'

He was taking her out there. To show her ... what? Or who? *That's ridiculous*, she berated herself. Did she still believe it? If there was any doubt left, any at all, this was madness.

Logan waited patiently by the ute. 'You coming?'

She studied his expression much as he was studying hers. Then she got in the ute and closed the door.

'I appreciate the fact you didn't run for your life assuming I'm luring you to your death.'

'It occurred to me. But even if you were, I'd see what I wanted to see, then take you out first. I said I could handle you.'

'Except when I kiss you.' He smiled, started the ute and headed out towards the trails and because she had nothing to say, she remained quiet. They were almost at the spot she'd seen him disappear into on a couple of occasions before he said anything else. 'You have to keep this to yourself.'

'Keep what to myself?'

'All of it. No one can know about them, not yet.'

'Them? Are you trying to see if you can make me run for my life?'

He pulled up and turned off the engine. 'Too late.' His arm shot out and a hand at the back of her neck pulled her towards him for a short, hard kiss. 'You're mine now.'

'That's not funny,' she said, but a smile escaped.

They climbed out and he started off the track. She followed him along the creek, past where she'd stopped the first time, on down what looked like an animal trail, until he stopped at a large hole in the bank.

'Is that a wombat hole?'

'Was. You're going to need to be quiet. Sit over there.'

She sat where directed and watched Logan approach the opening, whistle quietly. 'Up until four years ago, Murph always used to have a cattle dog or two trotting around after him wherever he went,' Logan told her quietly. 'He had a bitch—a favourite. I can't tell you how much he loved that dog. He had her put in pup to a neighbour's dog. It was a gorgeous thing with a show record and it was brilliant on stock. But there were complications with whelping.' He whistled again. 'Murph lost her and all but one of the pups. He was heartbroken. He hand-raised the remaining pup. I helped him. It's not easy raising a lone puppy, but she did well. He called her Brandy.' An orange face appeared tentatively at the opening to the hole. 'This is Brandy. Hi, girl.' He opened the container and hand-fed her a piece of meat. She gulped it down, her whole body wagging nervously as she scented Indy. She ducked back inside, then reappeared for more food, her eyes on Indy the whole time.

'What happened to her?' Indy asked. 'Why is she here?'

'When she was about five months old Murph took her out with him to check some cattle in the back paddock. A cow had gone and got a leg stuck in a fence and Murph got distracted getting it free. He heard a commotion, couldn't see Brandy so he took off up the hill. She'd wandered a fair way off, right out to the edge of the trees. A pack of wild dogs had come through—were attacking her. Murph tried to get over there and chase them off, but Brandy had already disappeared into the scrub to get away from them. She must have run a long way and got lost, because Murph spent hours— days—out there looking for her. When he couldn't find her he was devastated. He never got another dog.' Logan gave Brandy a rub on the back.

'And you found her. She's thin.'

'She's got pups in this hole. She was too timid to come near me for the first couple of weeks. I've been bribing her with food and she's getting better. She was skin and bone when I first saw her.'

'Why don't you tell Murphy?'

'I didn't tell him at first because she was in an appalling state and I honestly didn't know if I could catch her. If he'd seen her like she was only to have her run off it would have broken his heart all over again. So I decided it'd be better to get some condition on her, gain her trust. She's going on three now and hasn't seen a human since she was five months old, but she remembers people, because as you can see she's coming round pretty quick.'

'And she won't let you take her home yet?'

'She likes me, but I'm not going to push that trust to the limit by crawling down that hole after her puppies.' He gave her what was left in the container. 'They're getting adventurous though. A couple came to the edge of the hole to suss me out the day you came out here wondering what I was up to. So I've been spending some extra time out here with them the last few days, just playing with them and letting them climb all over me.'

'If you knew I was here, why didn't you say something?'

'Thought you might have.'

Brandy stretched out and sniffed at Indy's foot, quickly retreated. 'I wasn't sure I was supposed to be here. Hi, girl.' Indy extended a hand and Brandy sniffed it, wagged her tail once, then ducked back in the hole.

'You weren't. But it doesn't matter.'

'When are you going to tell Murphy?'

'When I have Brandy and her pups safely back home. Oh look— there you go.'

A puppy appeared, then another. One red and cream like its mother, the other black and grey. 'They're so small and cute. Are there only two?'

'Yeah. Because of the condition she was in, I'd say she was lucky to raise two.'

'Has there been any sign of daddy?'

'Not when I've been around, but that's not unusual. Wild dogs are good at keeping their distance from humans. I just hope he hasn't already knocked her up again.' Brandy herded the pups back into the hole. 'Right. She's had enough of us. Let's go.'

She got to her feet and dusted herself off. 'Thanks for showing me.'

His hand cupped her jaw, his thumb smoothing over her cheek. 'Thanks for trusting me.'

Guilt crashed through her. 'I didn't—in the beginning.'

'The beginning doesn't matter.'

But it did matter. *I'm breaking all the rules. When you find out who I am you'll hate me.* 'Logan ... You're not the only one with secrets. You don't really know me.'

'What do I need to know? This?' He pulled her in, covered her mouth with a slow, sizzling kiss that left her defenceless. Absorbed in the feel of him, the scent, the taste, she shuddered lightly as he slid his hands over her soft curves and drew her closer. She heard the murmur of pleasure in her own throat as he deepened the kiss, and it drew out until, eventually, he released her mouth to speak. 'I know what an incredible person you are. I know I look forward to seeing you every day, know how being around you makes me feel. I know how you look at me, how you respond when I touch you. I know that much, don't I?'

She closed her eyes on a deep breath. 'Yes,' she admitted, because there was no point lying. And it wasn't fair. 'You know that much. We should get back.'

Logan's gaze stayed on her a moment longer before he reluctantly checked his watch. 'Yeah. We'll go finish up at the stables, head back to my place. Jules told you she wants to try out her new canapés on us?'

'I'd forgotten about that.'

'There's plenty of time. Indy?'

'Yes?'

'I can be patient. But not too patient.' He winked, sent her that contagious smirk over his shoulder as he started back towards the ute. It made her smile. Perhaps there was a slim chance for them, when all this was over. When she could tell him who she was … if he didn't decide to hate her forever, if he really meant what he said, then maybe, just maybe she could take a chance on whatever this was. Because she had no choice but to admit to herself, she'd never felt anything like it.

CHAPTER
20

'She's a natural on a horse,' Logan told everyone as they sat on his back deck sipping white wine and eating morsels of Jules's canapé experiments that tasted like heaven. 'Fearless.'

'Are you sure you don't want another glass, Indy?'

'No thanks. If I'm a natural,' Indy complained, shifting in her chair uncomfortably, 'why does everything hurt?'

'You'll get used to it,' Jules replied. 'You want another prawn?'

'No, thanks. They're delicious but … no. Logan said he'll take me out into one of the paddocks so I can go faster.'

'When you're in control,' he reminded her with a grin. 'Right now, who knows where you'd end up.'

'I stopped.'

'In the round yard. We'll try one of the turnout yards tomorrow.'

'Not big enough.'

Connor laughed and saluted her with his beer.

'Quad's running like a dream,' Logan mentioned.

'The poor thing is loyal, I'll give it that. Not even a dog would've put up with that sort of mistreatment.'

'What was wrong with it?' Connor asked.

'What wasn't? You need to look after your machines.'

'No,' Logan said, planting a kiss on her temple and getting to his feet. 'You need to. You can play with the horses some of the time, but when machinery needs maintenance—you're it. Work out a schedule and I'll work it into your hours.'

'Sounds like a plan,' Connor agreed, brow raised at Logan's casual gesture.

'And less Mel,' Tess added. 'Where are you going, Logan?'

'Feed-up. I've still got mine to do.' He sent Indy a warm look as he passed. 'I'll see you later.'

'I think I'll come with you,' Connor said.

'Good idea,' Jules muttered. She hadn't had much to say since he'd invited himself over. That changed as soon as the men were out of earshot.

'Well?' Jules demanded.

'Well?'

'You, Logan …'

Indy lifted her brow. 'Me, Logan … what?'

Tess's eyes widened in impatience. 'You know *what*.'

Indy shrugged. 'There's nothing to say.'

Tess took a sip of her wine and rolled her eyes. 'Honey, I've known the guy my whole life. Try again. Make it believable.'

'It's nothing.'

Tess waved her wine glass dismissively. 'Of course it's not. Logan goes around kissing random people he's not interested in all the time.'

'It's a wonder he gets anything else done,' Jules added in agreement.

Indy pulled a face. 'It's nothing. I mean, even if it was something—'

'Which it's clearly not,' Tess teased.

'There's still not anything to discuss.'

'We don't want a discussion, we want details,' Jules said. 'Logan hasn't been interested in anyone for ages.'

'That's true,' Tess said. 'Women have been chasing him for years but he hasn't gone out with many of them. One of them even— Jules, who was that one that wrote him a song?'

Jules frowned in thought. 'That was ages ago—before I left for Sydney. Who was that ...'

Tess clicked her fingers. 'Laurel. She got listed as a missing person but she really took off because she made a fool of herself over Logan. Not because some serial killer came and dragged her away in the night.'

'That's right!' Jules agreed. 'She told everyone she was going to convince him to marry her and sang him a song at the pub after her shift. It didn't exactly go down as planned. Poor thing. That was really embarrassing for her. Logan was nice about it though.'

'Mel wasn't.'

'Did Laurel work here too?' Indy asked.

'No, but Mel worked with her at the pub for a couple of years after the Maydena Nature Cottages closed.'

And that was just too big a coincidence. 'Mel worked at both those places?'

'Sure—for a good few years before starting here. Marge is her aunt,' Tess told her. 'Why?'

'Marge is a Cartwright too? There seem to be a lot of them around.'

'Marge and Jim are stepsiblings.'

Which explained why Marge was so sure she could get her work out at Hilltop Farm, Indy supposed.

'Why the interest?' Jules asked.

'Just curious.' She got to her feet and stretched her sore limbs. 'Thanks for this. I need to go coax Monte into drinking a bit more milk.'

'How's he going?'

'He's still on the antibiotics. Not drinking enough yet, but he's brighter and I'm getting some down him. The scouring has eased up so he's not as dehydrated.'

'She sounds like she's been doing this all her life,' Jules told Tess.

'She might be, if Logan sets his mind to it,' Tess said with a teasing smile for Indy.

If only things were that simple. She went back to her room and looked up everything Ben had sent her on the missing girls. She knew from the employment records that Mel had begun working for the Athertons in 2013. Tess had said she'd worked at the pub for a good couple of years before that, which would put her at the Maydena Nature Cottages before 2011.

She compared the dates and work locations of the missing women against Mel's history. Mandy's file, Gretchen's, Latisha's—they all matched. As did many of the other possible victims.

This should have been picked up by the police, but Mark's quick dismissal of the other missing women had obviously let it go overlooked. Indy sat back and stared at the screen. Mel had known and worked with every single one of these women in several different locations, right before they disappeared. If there'd been any doubt, this sealed it. Whatever was happening to those women, Mel had the answers.

She picked up her phone, noticed Ben had left a couple of messages to call him back. She went to her usual spot and called him, got straight to the point. 'I need to talk to you about Melanie Cartwright.'

'You're going to tell me she worked with all our missing women. We know. And there's something else. I think you should consider withdrawing from this case.'

'*What?*'

'Those extra records you sent me showed up some more details—details Mark hadn't put together.'

'You're kidding,' she replied, voice dripping with sarcasm, then she asked more seriously, 'What could they possibly show up that could have me removed from this case?'

'You know Latisha's parents and younger brother died in a house fire shortly after she was discovered.'

'Yeah, and?'

'Mandy's only relative, her mother, died in a car accident two days after she was spotted.'

'I know. So?'

'So the fire was deliberately lit and the car was sabotaged. Both cases remain open. My guess is whenever anyone attempts to escape from whatever this is, their families are murdered.'

'It's a form of control. And that sort of organisation suggests we're dealing with something bigger than we thought.'

'And thanks to you, we're on top of this, Mel is our lead, and so that puts the Cartwrights in the frame. We can push forward officially with an investigation into the Cartwrights. You don't need to stay there.'

'Of course I do. We're finally getting somewhere.'

'Family crimes hit you the hardest, you told me that yourself. When we crack this open, there could well be more to deal with. I don't think you want to do this one.'

'I'll deal with it. My cover is established and I'm gathering intel all the time—you wouldn't even have this information without me being here. It's stupid to pull me out now. I need to throw more time and effort at Mel. She's worked with every missing girl just prior to their disappearances. Not Logan—Mel. And you know I caught her discussing April's abduction on the phone the night before April went missing. Give me more time. I can crack her. I know I can.'

There was a sigh. 'It's your decision. Good luck with Melanie.'

She stared up at the sky. Killing families. It turned her stomach. She couldn't help but see her pop, her sister, her mum, her gran. All the hurt, all the grief. Years of upset, of no home, no family. Just police and investigations and hopelessness.

And Mel was involved. Mel, who was always depressed or agitated or just plain pissed off, who smoked away the anxiety. Or tried to. What was her role in all this, and how was she being manipulated? Because Indy had no doubt she was being manipulated. By Kyle Cartwright. But who was he working for? She didn't know nearly enough about him. Except that he was a friend of Jules's ...

She framed some casual questions in her mind and walked out, considering ways to bring up the subject of Kyle with Jules. Carly was just letting herself out of her room, with her things, and some very red eyes.

'Hi, Carly. Where are you going? What's wrong?'

'I'm leaving. Apparently because I turned up with April, I'm guilty too. I only met up with her waiting for the shuttle bus out here, but we sent our résumés in at the same time and turned up together so—'

'And Connor had a go at you?'

'Well, no, but he asked questions at the time, and then a policeman came and spoke to me, and I know what they're thinking.'

'So you're fired.'

'Not exactly. No one knows I'm going. There's another place around here that I can get a job, but I'm not supposed to let the Athertons know because it'll cause friction. Please don't say anything.'

I meant what I said. If you get worried, come and see me ... Just don't mention that offer to the Athertons, if you don't mind. I don't want to go putting them offside. 'Would that offer have come from Marge Cartwright?'

'Um, I'm not supposed to say.'

'That's okay, she made me the same offer.' And Indy's mind was racing. Was Marge offering all the workers out here a job at Hilltop Farm—asking them not to tell the Athertons about it? If so, why would Marge think the Athertons wouldn't find out? It was a small town. There'd have to be a chance Tess or Rosalie or one of the others would run into whatever staff the Cartwrights pinched.

Unless they never left the farm.

Were these girls leaving Calico Mountain under their own steam, secretly going from one job to another, not telling anyone because Marge asked them not to—and never coming back? If that's what was happening, why? What could Marge's brother need these women for? Hilltop Farm wasn't a large enough venture to warrant hiring hitmen to murder families.

'Indy?'

'Sorry? Oh, listen, do me a favour? Don't leave yet. Give it a few days.'

'Why? You're not going to get there first and take the job are you? Because I don't—'

'No. I promise. It's just that I know Connor didn't mean to make you feel uncomfortable. And ... there's something happening in the next couple of weeks that you really need to stick around for.'

'What?'

She had no clue what to say, but she had a feeling convincing Carly to stay could save the girl's life. 'I can only say it will be worth your while.'

'A couple of weeks? I suppose—'

'Good. Go unpack.' Then, because Carly still seemed unsure, Indy put a hand on her arm and squeezed. 'Trust me. This is the right thing to do.'

Indy went to the guesthouse and signed out the staff car.

Indy pulled up across the road from the pub, sat for a moment, mentally preparing herself to question Marge. But how best to approach it? Perhaps she should pretend she was looking to move on, curious about that other job Marge had suggested.

She had a hand on the door handle when she saw him. Marc D'Angelo was walking out of Marge's pub not ten metres away. She froze, then ducked down as though collecting something from the floor of the car as he passed by. She straightened, and watched him stroll down the road to a green van. She got the plates, called Ben. Voicemail. What was D'Angelo doing in Hamilton—coming out of Marge's pub?

She waited a bit longer, then when Ben again didn't answer, she went into the pub. Marge smiled warmly when she saw her. 'Hi, Indy, what can I do for you?'

'Hi, Marge.' She ordered some food she didn't want and took a drink to one of the window tables. She had to know if D'Angelo came back, but she didn't need him to see her. She tried Ben again, but still couldn't get him. She needed him to run those plates—see whose car he was driving. Was this where his illegal shipments were coming from? Tasmania was the largest producer of opium poppies in the country, and most of her intel on him was linked to heroin—a drug derived from opium.

Mel was a Cartwright, Marge was a Cartwright. The Cartwrights produced poppies. Mel had access to opium. D'Angelo was visiting Marge's pub. Yes, it was possible that last part was coincidence— there were plenty of other farms he could be out this way to visit.

But it was all falling too conveniently into place. Especially if the women weren't going missing from Calico Mountain, but from Hilltop Farm.

'Here you go, love.' Marge placed her food in front of her. 'Is everything all right?'

'Sorry?'

'You look a bit preoccupied.'

'Yeah, sort of.' Indy sighed and chose her words carefully. 'I'm just considering some possibilities.'

Marge's gaze sharpened. 'You're not planning on leaving town are you?'

'No, well—I don't think so. Just a bit tired. Needed to get out of there for a few hours, have a think about things.'

'Good. If you decide otherwise, talk to me before leaving, okay?' Marge left Indy to her lunch and went back to the bar to serve someone else.

So the job offer was still open. Once she figured out what was going on with D'Angelo, she'd chase that up. Her phone rang, making her jump. Tess. She let it go to voicemail. If the Cartwrights were her link between illegal drug importation and D'Angelo, were the missing women becoming mules?

She kept her phone out, waiting for Ben to call her back, and noticed Tess had left a message. She put the phone to her ear and played it back.

'Indy, where are you? We need you at the stables. The cops are here searching Logan's place and dragging the dam. He's stuck out there with some detective and Mel's gone AWOL. Call me when you get the message.'

How was that possible? She'd only been gone a couple of hours. The phone rang again: Ben. She answered with a 'Hold on.'

She left the pub, got into the car.

'Is everything okay?' Ben asked.

'I don't even know where to start. Yes, I do. I just got a call from Tess Atherton saying Mark's out at Calico Mountain.'

'Then you'll know they've already found two bodies in his dam.'

It stunned her almost speechless. 'Oh my God.'

'Where are you?'

'In Hamilton, about half an hour away. He didn't do this, Ben.'

'Indy, we have physical remains. You need to consider whether you jumped to that conclusion too fast. And why. Sometimes if you don't want to see it—'

'I believed you!' she cut in with a snap. 'When it looked like Mia was responsible for those deaths related to the Hunters Ridge murders I took your side. I never wavered because I trusted your judgement. Logan didn't do this!'

There was a moment of silence as her words were processed. 'He means something to you.'

'Probably more than he should. And I couldn't be in love with a serial killer, Ben. I nearly had myself believing it once, when all the evidence ... but this is not Logan. It's all connected. The missing girls, D'Angelo, Hilltop Farm—'

'D'Angelo? Indy, what are you talking about?'

She went through what she'd seen, what she'd figured out. He listened and when she was finished, said, 'If the girls are being taken for D'Angelo's drug operation, then why are two of them in Logan's dam?'

'I don't know. But I need to go and make sure Mark doesn't make any stupid decisions. We're so close.'

'I'll call him. Indy—'

'Jules does a pick-up from Hilltop Farm every second Tuesday and when I was out there the shed was packed with crates going elsewhere. If I'm right and D'Angelo is sourcing from Hilltop Farm, the shipment has to be going through D'Angelo's warehouse so they can remove any drugs before sending the crates on. All you have to do is be there when the next shipment is getting into Sydney.'

'I'll alert the Drug Squad, give them enough time to get the paperwork in place for a raid.'

'D'Angelo is here. Let me see what else I can find out from this end. I'll concentrate on Hilltop Farm. I won't do anything stupid, Ben. I promise.' She ended the call, tossed the phone on the passenger seat and started the car. She performed a U-turn, put her foot down.

She called Mark as she wound her way out to Calico Mountain. 'What are you doing?'

'My job.'

'Ben said you found bodies?'

'Wrapped up and weighted. One is April, the other is older and the bones are clean. From what I've seen I'm going to say it's been down there a long time. But we won't know that for sure until they're properly examined.'

'I'm on my way back. How did you know to drag the dam?'

'Senator Melville wanted to know why we hadn't already done it—because Latisha was in the water when she was found. I didn't have a good answer so I ordered it. I have another call coming through. I'll speak to you when you arrive.'

'Not officially you won't,' she warned, worried he'd inadvertently give something away. 'I'm still in. See you soon.'

The report she was going to have to write on Mark's conduct was not going to bode well for any future promotions. *April*. Hell. Had she been targeted because Indy had caught her out? It was an uncomfortable possibility. Because the other women were being kept alive. What had April gotten close enough to that she was so quickly eliminated? The other remains were skeletal, but that didn't really give her any definitive answer on how long they'd been there. Though water could speed up decomposition, the temperatures down there could also retard it. Until the skeleton had been tested in the lab, she couldn't know if the remains had been down there five years or fifty.

She drove straight to Logan's and parked behind several police vehicles. Logan was talking to Mark, others were busily doing their jobs or standing around talking. Logan looked shaken; his stance rigid, his face tight and pale. Not sure what to do she looked around for any more of the Athertons. Behind her a car skidded to a halt. Warren Bailey leapt from his car and charged. Without thinking, Indy got in his way. 'Stop there, Warren.'

'That bastard's killed my daughter and—'

'It's not your daughter.'

'What?'

'That's not your daughter Warren, you need to leave. Let the police do their work.'

'It's not Gretchen?'

'No. I promise you, it isn't.' She had no idea if the second body was Gretchen's, but by the looks of things Warren didn't know there were two. She wasn't bringing it up.

'Well, whoever it is—I hope he gets what's coming to him now.' His gaze moved past her and he raised his voice to a shout. 'They've got you this time! You're getting locked up! Where's my daughter?'

An officer came to put him back in his car and Indy stepped back. Her eyes turned to Logan and his were on her, gaze narrow. Then his attention was drawn back to the detective. 'Excuse me miss, you can't be here, either.'

'Yeah—sorry.' She got back into her car and began back down the drive. They'd take Logan in for questioning, and the circumstantial evidence was building. But they wouldn't find anything concrete. Someone had murdered April because she was a reporter and that person had wanted to dump the blame on Logan. Kyle? But who was the other body?

She found Tess at the stables. Red-eyed, she was filling hay nets. 'Tess. Are you okay?'

'Indy,' she said with a relieved sigh. 'Thanks for coming back.' She dragged her fingers through her hair, swiped them across her eyes. 'They've found two bodies in the dam. They're going to blame Logan. Everyone's going to blame him.'

'The more evidence they find, the more likely they are to find the real perpetrator. This could clear him.'

'You think so?'

'I certainly hope so. I've got this. Why don't you go spend some time with your family?'

Tess shook her head. 'Sitting around waiting would be worse. I need to keep busy. Besides, we couldn't find Mel and the horses needed doing. Then she finally rang an hour ago to say she had a headache and couldn't work today.'

'Yeah, right.' Mel was sure to have a headache if she knew as much about this as Indy thought she did.

'Huh?'

'Nothing. Just—what a day for a headache.'

'That's what I thought, but I can't force her to show up.'

'Right. Tell me what you're up to. I'll feed Monte and give you a hand.'

CHAPTER
21

Indy turned up at the guesthouse for dinner, more from a need to find out what was going on than out of hunger. When no one she wanted to find was there, she considered heading into the kitchen to look for Jules. She'd taken two steps in that direction when her phone alerted her she had a text message from Tess. *Logan's back from questioning. Come to his place.*

Indy sent back an *okay* and hurried to the machinery shed. The staff car had disappeared so she jumped on a quad. Her phone rang. Ben. Damn, she wanted to hurry but she couldn't ignore this. 'Hey.'

'I've had people watching the airport and the ferry. D'Angelo was spotted driving onto the *Spirit of Tasmania* about two hours ago.'

'Did you look into Hilltop Farm?'

'Yeah, and got a copy of their most recent delivery sheets.

'As you suspected, while Hilltop Farm sends multiple shipments of produce to merchants in Sydney each month, they're all unloaded and distributed through that warehouse. A raid is being organised for the arrival of the next shipment.'

'If the police charge in there and D'Angelo has a chance to warn the Cartwrights, what do you think will happen?'

'They'll destroy any evidence … possibly by killing anyone who can talk.'

'If we can coordinate a simultaneous raid from this end, I think we'll have a much better chance of pulling this off with minimal loss. If the Cartwrights do have these missing women under their control, I'd hate for anything to happen to them now that we're so close to finding them. And Ben, there's a couple of things I'd like you to check out for me.'

'Fire away.'

She quickly ran through her concerns and got off the phone. She needed to see Logan.

Tess let her into Logan's house and led her through to the lounge room. Rosalie and Murphy were on the lounge; Logan was leaning against the fireplace, smiled tiredly when he saw her. 'Hey.'

'How did it go?'

'As expected.' He released a long breath and took a sip of something amber in a small glass. 'They haven't got an ID on the second one yet.'

Rosalie pushed to her feet; upset, she wrung her hands. 'It's her. I know it's her.'

'Who?' Logan asked.

Rosalie just stared at her husband. It was Murphy that shook his head. 'I don't want it to be, but I never believed Evelyn would leave—any more than you did.'

'My mother?' Logan asked in surprise. 'Why would my mother be in the dam?'

The couple exchanged glances. 'Let's just wait and see.'

'You can't make a statement like that and let it go! Why do you think it's my mother?' he demanded.

Rosalie walked to a chest of drawers and pulled out a framed photo. She stared at it for a moment then hugged it to her chest, closed her eyes against tears. 'He was a bastard.'

'Not always, Rosie.' Murphy stared at Logan as though trying to formulate the words. 'It was the accident—then the drugs.'

'You're right. But that doesn't change the fact he could have done this.'

'Hold on—back up. What accident? What drugs?' Logan asked.

Murphy sat and sighed heavily. 'We've never really talked about your father, Logan. We should have. It was just easier not to, I suppose. And you never asked.'

'I'm asking now.'

Murphy looked at Rosalie, and at her nod, continued, 'I was going round with your mother when Richard drifted into town. He picked up work right away, looking after the livestock for the Cartwrights. He was a larger-than-life type, a bit of a charmer, always finding fun, and Evie—well, he set his sights on her right from the outset.'

'Really?' Logan cut in. 'You and my mother were a thing before you and Rosie?'

'I didn't know Rosie back then. Your mother had come down to fill a teaching position at the local school. Rosie was in Melbourne with her family.

'Richard swept Evie right out from underneath me. We'd been going together for about six months. Oh, he wasn't nasty about it. The fact is, Evie and I were better friends than we ever were anything else. I didn't really know what it could be like until Rosie walked into my life a year after that and knocked me for six.' He smiled at his wife with real warmth.

'And then?'

'It was only a few months into the marriage when the accident happened,' Murphy continued. 'A feral bull had gotten in with some cows. Nasty big bugger. He should have shot the damn thing, but instead he saddled up one of the horses and he and Evie managed to cut it from the herd. He got off his horse to mend the fence and the bull charged—went right through him.'

'We didn't think he was going to survive it,' Rosalie said. 'When he did, he was always in pain. He used to pinch the poppies and smoke. It was the only thing he reckoned helped. It didn't seem to be such a big deal back then.'

'It wasn't,' Murphy said, 'but he didn't stop at some pain relief. It wasn't just his body that was broken. He'd been so fit and strong and capable. Then he wasn't. That accident crippled him emotionally too. He went from the occasional smoke to snorting heroin. Wouldn't say where he got it and Evie couldn't stop him using it. He'd go into these rages occasionally. They scared Evie, and she was too ashamed to go home, so she packed up and came and stayed with me for a while. That's when Rosie came down to visit. But he turned up all apologetic and promised to get off the drugs, so she went back to him. A few weeks later she was pregnant with you, and he tried—I think he really tried to get clean. But it got the better of him. The pain of the accident gradually eased but the withdrawal was too difficult.'

'Evie used to say he wouldn't so much as shoot a rabbit before the accident,' Rosalie said. 'By the time I got down there he could shoot just about anything with the blankest, blackest stare I've ever seen. When you were born, he idolised you, but he didn't stop with the drugs, so Evie never knew what to expect. She was on tenter-hooks the whole time but she stayed.'

'And then they disappeared,' Logan concluded.

Rosalie nodded. 'One day Evie turned up at the door with you and said they needed a day or two—just to themselves. Would we mind you. That was that. But she would never have left you, Logan,' she said in a pained voice. 'She loved you more than anything.'

Indy sat quietly and took it all in. So Rosalie and Murphy were blaming an opiate addiction for Logan's father's violent behaviour. But that wasn't how heroin worked. The drug rarely led to violence, anger or aggression; in fact, it was more likely to inhibit it. It gave users a euphoric rush followed by drowsiness. Withdrawal could lead to desperate, violent behaviour though. Perhaps that was the problem.

'So you think he killed her and took off?'

'We don't know that,' Murphy reminded them.

'I'm sorry, Logan,' Tess suddenly piped up. 'But I hope it is her.'

He turned sharply. 'What did you say?'

'Because you can't have killed anyone when you were three years old. No one can accuse you of that. And if Mum says she wouldn't have left you, I'm inclined to believe her. At least this way you'll have some closure.'

'If my father killed my mother, I won't have closure until he's found and he pays for it.' He sat down. 'I remember bits. Not much, just some images really. And her voice. She used to sing. I know on the day she left she had tears in her eyes.' He looked at Rosalie. 'She was upset that day.' Rosie nodded and he continued. 'I remember that and I've held onto it. To believing that, for whatever reason, she was upset that she had to leave me.'

'She was upset because Richard was giving her a hard time. But she was coming back.' Rosalie put the photo she'd been cradling down on the coffee table and Indy stared in disbelief. *What the hell?*

She knew that face. In the picture he was younger; fewer lines marred his features. But she knew that face. She got to her feet abruptly, startling everyone.

'Indy, what's wrong?' Logan looked from Indy to the photograph and back again.

She tore her eyes off the image with difficulty. 'I'm sorry. I—this is a family discussion. I should …' Her eyes went back to the picture of their own accord. It was the guy in the baseball cap at Hilltop Farm. She'd only caught a partial glimpse but she was sure of it. 'I should go.'

'I think we've all had enough,' Murphy agreed. 'Come on, Rosie, it's been a hell of a day. Tess, I'll run you back too.'

They all filed outside and Indy headed for the quad, her mind still racing.

'Hold up a minute,' Logan said.

She waited, watched the others drive off. 'Why?'

'What's wrong?'

The look on his face wiped everything else from her mind. 'Logan, I'm sorry. This must be so difficult.'

'Would you come back in for a bit? I don't feel much like sitting in there alone thinking about it all.' He took her hand and led her inside. For a while he didn't say anything, then when they were back in the lounge room he asked, 'What was that about?'

'I just thought I should give you all some privacy.'

'No. You saw a picture of my father and freaked out. So …?'

She should have done better, but it had just been such a shock. She couldn't tell him she'd seen his father at Hilltop Farm. She needed to figure this out first. 'They looked so happy in the photo. To think he could have turned on her and killed her—taken a mother away from a little boy. It's evil. Drugs or no drugs. I'm sorry, I just couldn't deal with it.'

Accepting that, he held onto her for a moment. 'I don't want her to be dead, but if she is, if they've found her … I'm going to find him.'

'It's not fair. You've got enough to deal with without this. Not now.'

He drew her back just far enough to look at her. 'They haven't got anything on me, Indy. They won't get anything on me. I haven't done anything.'

'I know.' She pressed her lips to his. It was a seal of sympathy, of support, but he met it, held on. He needed her. And right then, she needed him too. So she pushed down the guilt and gave all she could, moaned in protest when he dragged his mouth from hers. There was a question in his eyes.

'Stay.'

'Try making me leave.' She slid her hands into his hair, and fused her lips to his, felt the thrill of his arms closing around her, wanting her. Clothes fell away, bodies meshed, a fast, hungry meeting of lips and hands, a tangle of limbs that had them tumbling onto the thick softness of the floor rug.

Don't think, she told herself. *He needs me, I need him. Simple.* Then his mouth closed over her breast and even that thought disintegrated. Those hands, those big, gentle hands were driving her up, up. *More.* Did she think it or say it? And then he gave it, sent her over the edge. She sprung up over him, took him in. The rhythm was fast, elemental, his eyes hypnotic, hot. She arched back with the pleasure of it, gasping, her body slickening as the tempo increased. And then she was under him again, his mouth locked on hers as he drove her back up with him, until he absorbed the sound of her cry in his own throat and shuddered, held on, fell with her.

CHAPTER
22

'How could Atheron's long-lost father be in town and no one knows about it?'

Phone pressed to her ear, Indy dropped her head back to stare at the sky, realising how ridiculous it sounded. 'I don't know. It doesn't make sense—but it has to, somehow. I just don't have all the pieces in place yet.'

'And,' Ben continued, 'why would he hide from them?'

'Because he killed Logan's mother? Because he's wrapped up in something dodgy with the Cartwrights? I didn't say anything to Logan.'

'Indy, there might be nothing to this but pure coincidence, but I find it a bit strange that you've walked into something involving D'Angelo down there, right at the time you were beginning to breathe down his neck up here. I think we should bring you back while we figure this out.'

'I agree. But if I leave now, they'll know something's up,' she reasoned. 'We'd be risking the entire operation. How long is it going to take you to set up the raids?'

'Another week. We missed the last one reorganising ourselves for the simultaneous raids on the warehouse and Hilltop Farm.'

'Then let me lay low and stick it out.'

'Indy—'

'It's just a few more days. They haven't hurt me, Ben. Between the phone and the computer hacking, I'm guessing someone—probably Mel—is using me to keep tabs on what we know. I'll send you an email. Something frustrated and off-course. This is working. We need to see it through.'

'I'm coming to Tasmania. I'll set up with my team in Hobart. On the way down I'll decide whether you really need to be there until Friday.'

'I will need to be here. Talk soon.'

She knew he was doing it to protect her. She knew he looked at her as family. She loved him for that. But she wasn't leaving. She'd come down here to find out if she could get Logan on all this. Now she knew better. Now she was going to finish it for him.

She smiled to herself, hummed a little as she had a quick shower. Logan had kissed her awake, then gone down ahead of her to start the day, told her to take her time. But Monte would be hungry, and there were things to do.

Monte drank a full bottle. He was still a little lethargic, but his eyes were bright and his personality was mostly back. 'Don't you ever scare me like that again, understand?'

'Mummy, babies!'

Startled, she looked up to see Bindi in the doorway. Mel wasn't far behind. 'Good morning, Mel. Hi, sweetie.'

'Indy. I had to bring Bindi with me. She's gonna be quiet—sit in the office and watch movies. Bren couldn't watch her today, she had something on.'

'She should have a play with Monte and the lambs. They'd like the company.' Then to Bindi, 'Want a pat?'

Bindi's eyes lit up and she looked at Mel. Mel shrugged. 'Sure, whatever.'

Indy smiled when the little girl laughed delightedly. 'Look Mummy! The lambs are following me!'

It was the first time Indy had seen Mel's eyes soften. 'That's great baby—good job.'

Indy got up and washed the bottles out. When she returned, Bindi was stroking the calf. 'She's so sweet. You have a lovely daughter, Mel.'

'Thank you. Indy, why do you insist on being nice to me?'

She smiled and spoke carefully. 'I know that, for whatever reason, you're unhappy. And I imagine it must be horrible not to be able to talk to anyone about why.' Bindi squealed and laughed as Monte licked her. 'You'd do just about anything to keep her safe, wouldn't you? No one could blame you for that.'

It was just guesswork, but shutters went over Mel's wide-eyed stare before she turned her gaze, and her entire body, away. 'Come on, Bindi, Mummy has work to do. I'll set you up with *Paw Patrol* in the office.' As Mel herded her daughter out of the stable and down the breezeway, she paused in the office doorway.

Indy would have pushed further but Logan arrived back with the guests from the morning ride, so she left Mel to think about what she'd said and went out to help unsaddle the horses.

'Good ride?'

'Couldn't get back fast enough.' He pulled her hard against him, and she felt the barely controlled desperation just below the surface of that long, unhurried kiss. Then on another deep breath, he stepped back. 'Unfortunately ...' He took a long look at her, groaned. 'Very unfortunately, I have to prepare for a riding lesson.'

She smiled and pressed one more quick kiss—a promise—on his mouth. 'There's always later.'

'Count on it.'

She was counting on it. And as it got closer to the end of the day and Logan's looks got hotter and hotter, she found herself wondering if she'd survive until after the animals were fed. She pulled down the stable bedding, had begun sweeping out the breezeway when Mel's voice caught her attention.

'Baby, no! Don't move—help! Don't move, baby!'

Indy dropped the broom and ran outside. Mel was climbing through the fence to the paddock, Bindi was already on the other side of it. She couldn't see at first what was wrong so she jogged over and froze when she noticed the tiger snake, head lifted, staring down the little girl, mere inches away.

'Don't move, baby!'

'Mummy, I'm scared.'

'Don't move, don't move, please don't move.' It wasn't much more than a breathless whisper. It wasn't working. Bindi took a small step, the snake's head lifted higher, its tail flicked.

Indy approached carefully. 'Hey, can you be a statue, Bindi?'

The little girl sniffed, nodded.

'Good. Look at your mummy and we'll count how many seconds you can be a statue. If you can keep still until I say stop, you get a prize.'

Bindi sniffed again. 'Okay.' When she shifted again the snake coiled, its head waving.

It was the most terrifying moment Indy had experienced since becoming a cop—and there'd been some bad ones. She moved slowly. 'Mummy's going to start counting. Off you go Mummy. Slowly.'

Mel's voice wobbled as she began. 'One ... two ...'

Indy crept closer and the snake's head turned towards her, attention caught. 'You're doing really well Bindi, just stay really still.' As she continued to creep closer the snake's body fluidly adjusted its coil to more fully face her. Now what? She was hoping it would move off. Why the hell wasn't it moving away? Bindi wasn't going to stand still forever. Everything inside her screamed at her to launch herself at the child and drag her back, but could she risk it?

'Mummy I need to move.' Bindi jiggled and the snake whipped back around. A loud *crack* had it throwing itself into a frenzied, gyrating mess. Indy dived at Bindi and shoved her aside, getting a way too up-close-and-personal view of the frantic snake in the throes of death.

'It could still strike,' Logan said steadily from somewhere behind her. 'Move out of the way.'

'You shot it!' Mel screeched, clinging to her daughter. 'What if you'd hit Bindi?'

'I didn't,' he replied. 'But if I hadn't shot it, we'd be rushing one or both of these two to a hospital. Indy would probably have had a good chance, Bindi might not have been so lucky.'

'Oh, God. Oh, God. I'm sorry, Logan. I just got such a fright. Thank you.'

'You should be thanking, Indy. Once you're done, I'm going to give her a lecture.'

Mel's gaze turned to Indy. 'Thank you. I don't know why you did that. But thank you.'

'Welcome.'

'Take her home,' Logan suggested. 'You've both had a bad scare. I'll finish up.'

'Thanks.'

Indy dusted herself off, keeping an eye on the still moving snake. 'Are you sure it's dead?'

'See the enormous hole in it?'

'Yeah but—'

'It's dead. I wouldn't let anything suffer.'

'Lucky you happened to have a shotgun on hand,' she thought out loud.

'Yeah, it was,' he said without explanation, then dragged her over and held her tightly.

'I thought I was getting a lecture, not a hug.'

'I'm not sure if walking up to a five-foot-long tiger snake saying "here, bite me instead" was brave or just plain stupid.'

'She's only a baby, Logan. You said yourself it could have been fatal.'

He sighed and she felt his nod. 'I have the shotgun in a locked box bolted to the floor in the back cupboard in the office. I have to have one around in case I need it for livestock. The bullets are kept separately. It took me a moment to get everything together but I was coming right behind you.'

They were interrupted by a police car appearing. It crawled to a stop by the fence and Mark climbed out. 'Afternoon.' He spotted the gun dangling from Logan's hand and frowned. 'Everything all right here?'

'Fine,' Indy said. 'Snake problem.'

'You know there's a fine for—'

'It was that or a dead three-year-old,' Indy cut in.

'Right, anyway, I guess I can let that go, under the circumstances.'

Logan stepped up and put a hand on Indy's shoulder. 'What do you mean?'

'I have the results through of the second body found in the dam. I'm sorry, Logan. The body was your mother's.'

Indy had never seen Logan with less colour. 'Perhaps we should move this conversation elsewhere. Logan, you need to sit down.'

Logan shook his head but then nodded. 'Rosie needs to know. And Murph. We should tell them.'

'I'm right here.' Rosalie appeared from the stables carrying the lambs' bottles. 'It's her?'

'Yeah.'

'Damn bloody Bull. You find him!' she said to Mark. 'He did this!'

'Wait—what?' Indy snapped. 'You said Bull.'

'I meant Richard. Everyone just nicknamed him Bull after the bull attacked him and he got so damn mean.'

She stared hard at Mark. Yeah, he'd got that too. 'I'm going to need a photo, Mrs Atherton.'

'I'll get it. You can give me a ride back to the house.'

'I'll feed the lambs, Rosalie,' Indy offered and took the bottles. Her hands shook just a little bit. It was him all right. Logan's father was D'Angelo's hitman. She'd come here to investigate Logan for doing horrible things—and he'd been innocent. And now he had to face all this. She watched Rosalie and Mark climb into the police car and drive away, didn't realise tears had welled in her eyes until Logan looked at her and she saw his expression.

'Don't,' he said gently. 'It'll be the end of me. Come here.'

'I'm so sorry, Logan.' Here he was hearing that sort of news and he was comforting her. And she was going to hurt him too. Because she was who she was and she couldn't change that.

'It was a long time ago. I'm okay, I'm fine, stop that.'

She nodded against his chest and pulled herself together. 'I need to feed these lambs.' She looked over Logan's shoulder at the sound of another car approaching. She recognised Warren. The car screeched in, slammed to a stop much as it had the day before.

Warren seemed to have some trouble opening the door, then he fell out, got up awkwardly, charged at Logan. 'You bastard!'

Logan ducked one awkward, heavily thrown punch, used Warren's own weight to send him sprawling to the ground on the next.

'Cut it out, Warren.'

'And you!' he spat at Indy. 'You lying little bitch!'

In the time it took her to blink in surprise, Logan was between them. 'That's enough.'

'That's my daughter they found, isn't it? There were two! Rot in hell you murdering bastard!' Warren got his feet back under him, came again. 'The cops won't do anything about it, I will!'

Indy saw the flash of the blade. Logan didn't. She lunged around Logan, side-tackled Warren and had him crashing to the ground. His arm arced up. Indy heard a vicious curse from Logan as she blocked the blade, then Warren was thrown across the drive. A long way across the drive. He skidded in the gravel, took a bit longer this time to find his feet. Logan's chest was heaving from the effort and still Indy wondered *how*?

'Are you okay?' Logan asked, frantically checking her over. 'What were you thinking?'

'I didn't think you saw the knife.'

'I didn't but Indy, I can—don't you move!' he finished for Warren. 'Or I swear bringing that knife will be the last mistake you ever make.'

'There were two girls down there but they won't say who the other one was. It's Gretch, isn't it? At least have the decency to tell me, let me bury my little girl.' He sat on the side of the drive and fell apart.

Logan took a step towards him and Indy held him up with a hand on his arm. 'Don't. He's still armed.' But the look on Logan's face was almost as devastated as Warren's, and he shrugged her off.

'It's all right.' If Indy had still been under any doubts as to Logan's innocence, that look alone would have quelled them. He didn't just have empathy for animals. He felt deeply for a man that a moment before had tried to kill him. And she loved him for it. Logan sat beside Warren. 'It wasn't Gretch. The other woman they found was my mother.'

Warren stopped sobbing to stare. 'Evie? Evie was murdered?'

'Looks like it.'

Hurried footsteps on the drive had them all looking up. Connor was jogging. 'What happened?' He eyed Warren, then Logan. 'Do I need to get the detective down here?'

'Nup.' Logan patted Warren on the shoulder. 'But Warren needs a lift back.'

'I'll have Ned run him home,' Connor said, still suspicious. 'He can organise to collect his car when he's sober.'

Warren got off the ground with effort and stumbled down the road with Connor.

As far as Indy was concerned, this sealed it. This needed to be over. 'You should go talk to Rosalie and Murphy, make sure the detective gets what he needs.'

Logan nodded. 'Thanks.'

She waited until he was out of sight before picking up her phone. 'Ben, Logan's father is Bull.'

'Seriously? Are you absolutely certain?'

'I am. And I think there's a chance Senator Melville is on D'Angelo's payroll.'

There was a long pause. 'Go on.'

'To cultivate poppies in Tasmania, you need a contract with a licensed processing company as well as a grower's licence from the Poppy Advisory and Control Board. Logan told me in passing that Caroline's father had come to visit Caroline on more than one occasion when he was down here on business. He didn't know what specifically for, only that Caroline had mentioned her dad had a special interest in primary industries. I can't prove it, but I'm speculating that Melville has somehow manipulated the system to allow the Cartwrights to evade compliance regulations. It's the only way I can think of that they could be growing enough on top of their quotas to make blackmarket sales to the mainland a viable venture.'

'You think D'Angelo is holding Caroline to ensure Melville does as he's told—that someone else took her from the stables that morning?'

'It's crossed my mind. I believe D'Angelo set this up so I'd come down and investigate Logan, right? Because women have been disappearing after working for him. But if we go with the theory Marge is recruiting women for Hilltop Farm and Marge keeps offering to help me—'

Ben cursed. 'Of course. She wants you to disappear too. What better way to pin the disappearances of the other girls on Logan than have you down here investigating, only to go missing the same way they did? D'Angelo gets you out of the way and the heat for the missing girls is kept off Hilltop Farm in one hit.'

'I need to get back out to Hilltop Farm, get a good look around. Right now this is all just supposition. We don't have any actual evidence. And they're not going to be keeping those women out the back of the shop. They're probably off the property somewhere close enough for convenience but far enough away for safety. We need to know where they are. Otherwise they might be moved or murdered once D'Angelo's warehouse and Hilltop Farm are raided. I just want to go in, look around.'

'That's exactly where they want you. If you think I'm going to sign off on something so reckless—'

'It's not reckless! I'll be careful.' When Ben didn't speak she pressed harder. 'I just had a father of a missing girl attempt to stab Logan to death. This situation's out of control.'

'Would you listen to what you're saying? You want me to risk allowing members of a drug cartel abduct you and hold you against your will for who knows what reason, God only knows where. That's if they don't kill you immediately. It's not happening.'

'Ben—'

'No. This is why you shouldn't be down there. You're not being objective, not thinking clearly. You said yourself we can't risk the investigation. The people that are responsible will be locked up in just a few days' time if you can just keep it together. Can you keep it together, Indy?'

'Fine. I'll stay put. But keep me in the loop.'

'I will.'

Indy looked up and saw Logan.

Logan had started walking towards the guesthouse, realised Rosie would have taken the detective to her house for the picture, and come back to take the ute. He hadn't heard much, but his stomach was doing a slow roll.

She must have heard him because she turned. He saw shock first, then guilt as the colour drained from her face. 'I have to go.' She ended the call and faced him, smiled, but it wasn't convincing. 'Hi.'

'You want to tell me what that's all about?'

He could almost see her mind racing, scrambling for something to say as she didn't quite meet his gaze. Surely she wouldn't bother trying to lie to him, not now. 'You were listening in,' she finally accused, but the words lacked any real punch. 'You tell me.'

Fair enough. 'I heard you mention Warren's attack, that you're rather unhappily prepared to stay put. I'm thinking maybe I should have turned up a bit sooner. Just tell me you're not a reporter!'

Her eyes flashed angrily back at him from a face that was still too devoid of colour. 'I'm *not* a reporter! I told you that.'

'Then what the hell are you?' He heard his voice rise, worked on controlling it. 'You told me I didn't know you. But I thought I did. I thought whoever it was you were, you were honest and you cared about me. That's what mattered.' He huffed out a self-depreciating laugh and shook his head. 'I'm an idiot.'

Her expression softened. 'You are an idiot if you think I don't care about you. Of course I do.' She reached out. He shook her off.

'But have you been honest?' Her hesitation was enough. It sent his temper into overdrive. 'Well?'

She closed her eyes and drew her brows together in a pained expression, opened them slowly. She was calmer, like she'd made some decision that was inevitably going to cost her, like she was steeling herself for it. And the resignation he read in her eyes terrified him. 'I haven't told you everything. I'm not a reporter, I'm a detective sent down here to investigate Caroline Melville's disappearance.'

A *detective*? She couldn't be. But after several seconds of silently staring at her, allowing that to sink in, he realised it did make sense. It made a lot of sense. And it hurt like hell. 'To investigate me, you mean. So who were you reporting to? Ben? I suppose you've decided that because my father was a murderer, the apple doesn't fall too far from the tree. Is that what you couldn't wait to tell *Ben*?'

Temper tinged her cheeks as she shook her head and glared. 'Don't be stupid.'

'I don't think I am being stupid. You still want to come out and feed Brandy? There's a little cabin just down the trail a bit further along from that spot. Want to see it?'

'Why?'

'Gretchen did. She was always asking me to take her trail riding. She loved the horses. I took her out there. I took Latisha out there too.'

He saw something in her eyes, but it wasn't suspicion or fear like he'd expected. It was anger. 'So what?'

'So let's go out there, let's go look at that cabin together.'

He was circling her slowly and she was backing up. It hurt. And the hurt made him angry.

'What are you doing?' she demanded.

'I thought you didn't believe I'm a monster?'

'No—it's not that.'

'Okay then, let's go.' He dropped a hand onto her shoulder and she twisted, ducked, stepped out. 'Interesting. What else have you got?' He stepped in again. Quickly. Again she evaded. 'You're still not fighting back, Indy.'

'Of course not! What do you *want*?'

'I want the truth! You think a murderer might have fallen in love with you?'

He watched the colour leach from her face for the second time as she shook her head. 'Someone like that wouldn't fall in love—it's unlikely he'd be capable of it.'

'Then it's not me.'

He heard the air rush from her lungs as his words and the accompanying look he sent her sank in. He'd never seen her look more helpless. And suddenly tired and over it, he walked away. 'Leave.'

'Don't ask me to go.' It wasn't much more than a whisper.

He turned, furious. 'You lied to me. Befriended me. Slept with me. What was last night, Indy—research?'

Her gaze dropped to the ground then lifted, eyes desolate. 'I had to lie. I didn't mean to fall in love with you. Logan, wait.' Her voice cracked on the words and nearly tore him in half. 'Please. I'll explain.'

He almost caved. But his own pain, her betrayal, was too fresh, the anger was too much. 'Goodbye, Indy.' He turned just once, when he was almost out of sight. She'd slid down the wall, a tight ball with her arms shielding her face, hands clutching her hair. He wanted to go back, but what could make this better? Nothing. So he walked away.

Indy sat where she was until she had herself under control and began to think one step at a time. She had to leave. But she couldn't leave without seeing Monte, giving him one last bottle. She had to feed the lambs anyway. So she sat and fed the babies, gave Monte a cuddle. 'Goodbye, little buddy. You'll be fine.'

'You're leaving?' Mel asked from the doorway.

'I'm ...' she swallowed hard, took a deep, controlling breath. Now that Mel knew, she'd be bound to tell the Cartwrights. 'Yes.'

'But ... you can't just pack up and leave. We need you around here.'

She wanted to tell her to drop the act, cut the bullshit, but the raid depended on her keeping quiet. And the colour had drained from Mel's face. 'Mel, you've been trying to get rid of me since I arrived. I'm leaving. You should be happy.'

She watched a range of emotions flicker over Mel's face as she twisted the locket around and around. Eventually she nodded—a jerk of the head. 'You're right.'

Could she get her to talk? 'I thought I might head out to Hilltop Farm. Apparently there's always ... work going there. You'd know, wouldn't you?'

'I can't ... don't ... know what you're talking about.'

'Then I guess that's what I'll do. Will you look after Monte for me?'

Mel looked hesitant. 'As if I don't have enough to do. Especially now.'

She got to her feet and approached the door, stopped in front of Mel. 'Please.'

Mel sighed and pursed her lips, but she looked down at the calf curling up with the lambs and her expression softened. 'Yeah sure. Whatever.' She walked a few steps away, turned around. Her face was tortured. 'Don't do it.'

'Do what?'

Mel visibly struggled for something to say. 'Indy, you don't want to … work for anyone else round here. It won't end well. I think you know that. Take the staff car and get out of here. I'll get it later.'

'Is there something you want to tell me, Mel? Because now's your chance.'

'I'm telling you to go home! Get away from here. A long way away from here.'

'Why?'

'Indy, I'm sorry. I can't.'

'Yes, you can. Mel, I'll make sure …' But Mel hurried away, wasn't listening.

At least Mel had tried to warn her. She considered doing exactly what Mel suggested. But then what? What did she have to go back to? This couldn't all be for nothing. If she just disappeared the Cartwrights, D'Angelo, Bull, would get nervous. The raid could be sabotaged, the women killed. So where was she going to go?

CHAPTER
23

She was putting the last of her things in her pack when Jules appeared in the doorway. 'Indy, I—what's going on?'

'Jules. Sorry. I had a fight with Logan—I have to go.'

Jules came in and sat down, her face a picture of concern. 'What happened?'

'He doesn't think I trust him. I don't know … Maybe I don't. I need some space.'

There were a few seconds of silence while Jules considered that. 'Logan can be pretty intense—and he has just had a pretty bad shock. Why don't you give things a day or two to calm down?'

'He made himself pretty clear.'

Jules looked at her watch. 'We need to talk about this, but I have to do the supply run. Brenda's out and Mason's minding the shop for a couple of hours.' She placed a hand over Indy's. 'Come with me and we can talk.'

Indy considered that. Another look at Hilltop Farm. One more chance to see it in daylight. 'Okay, fine.'

On the way out, she gave Jules some version or other of a quickly put-together story. But her mind was elsewhere.

'Damn,' Jules said as they pulled up at the shopfront. 'The shop's not supposed to be closed yet.' Jules jumped out and keyed a code into the gates. They swung open.

'Are you allowed to do that?'

'Yeah. Occasionally if no one can be here, Brenda leaves the stuff in the shed for us. But Mum always sends Logan or Connor on those days to help get it in the truck. I wonder if I can find Mason …'

If the place was empty, even better. Indy looked around as they left the truck and headed past the shop down the private road. A cluster of packing sheds, fields of crops, a house just visible among trees on the ridge. And the road veered in all directions, heading over a rise and disappearing. 'This place is huge. Didn't you say they processed their own meat here?'

'Yeah—the abattoir is down the end of this road. It's all separately fenced off. You don't want to go down there. It's not very nice.'

She wondered if Jules realised she'd just caught herself up in a lie. On the previous trip she'd said she'd never seen it. They arrived at a large open-sided shed containing machinery, packing crates and an assortment of cars.

'Anyone around?' Jules called out. When no one answered, Jules's face creased and she pointed. 'Go look in that shed, I'll look in these.'

Indy pushed through a door, called out cautiously. No one around. Crates and pallets, tables and chairs, a small office. Nothing out of the ordinary. Around the back of the shed a handful of workers were moving though rows of vegetables, and beyond them were fields she decided could be the opium poppies. Her phone rang. Ben.

'I'm a bit busy. Is everything all right?'

'No. It's about Jules.'

Indy swung around, checked, saw no one. 'Go on.'

'She makes several trips to Tassie every year. Her phone records show a history of regular phone calls to Hilltop Farm and to Kyle Cartwright's mobile. From the texts we've procured I can also tell you they're romantically involved. When Kyle is in Sydney—which is a lot of the time—he uses her address.'

'Shit,' Indy groaned. 'I didn't want her to be involved.'

'But she is. Which means she knows who you are too.'

'That most likely explains the stolen phone and computer hacking. I thought it might have been Mel, but couldn't quite figure out how. But thinking back, Jules was always in the vicinity when things like that happened. She's probably been trying to find out if I've discovered anything.' She headed back around the front of the shed to look for Jules.

'Hey!' Indy spun around again. Mason Cartwright was framed in the doorway. There was annoyance in his features but also nervous tension. 'What are you doing here?'

'I'll keep you posted,' she muttered to Ben and ended the call. Then she plastered a smile on her face. 'Hi, Mason. How's the nose?'

'Where'd you come from?'

'I came out here with Jules. We got separated trying to find someone.'

'You're not supposed to be here.' He was fidgety, uncomfortable. If necessary, she could take him. Then another guy appeared. Bigger, older and more of a challenge. Kyle Cartwright.

'Indy.' As he spoke to her he inclined his head in a 'go away' fashion to Mason. 'Jules said she'd sent you in here.' He smiled reassuringly. 'Don't worry about Gidget. He's supposed to be keeping an eye on things. Last week he closed up early and a couple of backpackers snuck out the back here and helped themselves to the poppies. One of 'em ended up in hospital. Police gave him a lecture. He probably thought you were about to get him in trouble again. Regulations are so tight we can lose our licence if we're not careful.'

'There you are!' Jules came in, all smiles. 'Brenda just drove in. She's offered us a cuppa.'

'Sounds good,' Kyle said. 'Jump in the car, I'll give you ladies a lift up.'

Indy was getting more and more uncomfortable by the minute, but with little choice, she climbed into the back of the Landcruiser next to Jules.

'How do you like working at Calico Mountain?' Kyle asked her casually.

'It's great,' she said, then she flicked a glance at Jules. 'Generally.'

'She's had a fight with Logan,' Jules told Kyle. 'He doesn't like the fact Indy doesn't trust him.'

'With what he's been accused of doing, I don't think it's fair to hold that against you.'

'I was just telling Jules what an impressive place this is,' Indy said, changing the subject. 'Marge said I should come and take a look around. I have a feeling it would take days.'

'It's not that big,' Kyle said. 'But it does the job.' He pulled up in front of a sprawling country home and they got out. Brenda was at the front door. 'Hi, Indy, nice to see you again,' she said with a welcoming smile. 'Come in.'

They walked into a wide entryway, then through an open archway into a dark tiled kitchen overlooking a densely planted garden. 'I was going to put the kettle on, then I remembered the nice batch of lemonade I made yesterday is still in the fridge.' She pulled out two jugs of the stuff, took some glasses out of a nearby cupboard. 'I'll be glad to get my feet up for a minute, it's been a busy day. More problems in Sydney,' she said for Kyle's benefit. She drained the last of the first jug into a glass and handed it to Indy. 'Tell me what you think of this.'

'Brenda's lemonade is legendary around here,' Jules told Indy.

Indy took a sip, and the tart sweetness was cool on her tongue. 'It's very nice, thank you.'

As Brenda began on the next jug, serving the others, Kyle opened a packet of biscuits and offered Indy one.

'Oh, no. Thanks.'

'So what was the Sydney issue?' he asked Brenda.

'Staff problems. The kid that we sent in to collect on an outstanding payment—you know—the one that didn't toss himself out a window? He decided to blab to the cops for a deal.'

'And?' Kyle was watching Indy closely. So many alarm bells were ringing in her head she didn't know which one to focus on first. Couldn't focus on any. She stared down at the lemonade. Brenda had poured hers from a separate jug to the others ...

'And now Bull's been held up again. Kid's out on bail but he's hiding. Got some sense I guess. Shouldn't take too long to find him, but we're gonna have to hold on to this one,' she said with a casual wave at Indy, 'until he can get here.'

'What?' Indy tried to keep focused on the conversation. Couldn't. She needed to get to her feet, get out of there. Her limbs felt like ten-tonne weights.

'You didn't really think we were going to let you walk out of here, did you?' Jules asked. 'Not after all the effort that went into getting you here.'

Kyle wrapped his arms around Jules from behind, dropped a kiss on her head. 'It was perfect timing, bringing her here straight after she has a fight with Logan. Probably even better than originally planned.'

'He nearly had you at the Christmas party,' Jules told Indy. 'Then a couple of guests walked in and ruined it.'

'My own fault,' Kyle admitted. 'I was enjoying scaring her too much. I hope at least a few people know about Indy and Logan's fight.'

'Tess will know. She'll defend Logan but she won't lie,' Jules told him. 'I'll make sure I drop into the pub all concerned when Amy's around, she leaks like a sieve and Marge'll fuel the fire—make sure Warren's told. Mel's got the disappearance story sorted.'

'Are you sure? I don't trust my sister at present. Her behaviour's been erratic lately.'

'She knows what'll happen if she blabs,' Brenda reassured him. 'She's got Bindi to think about.'

Indy pushed to her feet. The chair toppled as she stumbled, fell over.

'What are we going to do with her until Bull gets here?' Brenda wondered as the world faded behind Indy's eyelids.

'We'll put her down with the others,' Kyle decided. 'She may as well work.'

Logan dropped the fencepost into the ground and checked the angle, looked up when he heard a horse approaching. It was Tess, on Flash. 'How did you make time for a ride?' he asked her.

'Since we have new staff. This is looking good. I didn't know you were so far into it.'

He hadn't been. But since his argument with Indy he'd needed to keep busy. Keep his mind off her, off how she'd looked when he'd told her to leave. It had kept him busy, but it hadn't kept his mind off her. 'It's got to get done. Monte needs a yard, and I've got another calf coming to keep him company.'

'Indy will be thrilled with this. It's such a pretty little space for him.'

He decided he may as well get the conversation over with. 'I'm not sure she'll even see it finished. She's leaving.'

He expected the blank look, the frown. 'Indy's leaving? No way—really? Why?'

'I told her to.'

Tess's eyes widened in disbelief. 'You *told her to*?'

'I just said that.'

'You want to tell me why?'

'It doesn't matter.'

'Of course it matters!' He picked up a fencepost, kept working. 'Okay then, tell me this,' she continued. 'Is whatever happened so unforgivable that it's worth never seeing her again?'

'I'm still trying to work that out. She's a cop.'

'Oh great, we finally had one on side and you sent her away?'

He dropped the fencepost back onto the ground in frustration. 'How can you come straight out with that? Don't you need at least a small amount of time to process? She lied to us. She came in here to investigate Caroline's disappearance and pretended to be someone she's not. She used us, Tess.'

'It stings. It does. But are you mad at who she is, or what she is? Indy's done a lot around here that goes above and beyond a police investigation. She's become one of us. And she's not faking her feelings for you. You can't believe that.'

'Then she should have told me.'

'When? When would have been the right time? Logan, talk to her. Maybe you'll still feel the same way after you've had that discussion, maybe you won't. But you can't let her go forever without knowing.'

He stared at the sky and took a deep breath. 'You're probably right.' When she just waited he frowned. 'What—now?'

'No time like the present.'

'Fine.'

He went to the bunkhouse and when she didn't answer the knock on the door, went looking in the stables. It was Monte's feed time. She wouldn't miss that. Sure enough he heard the calf slurping away on his bottle as he walked in.

But it was Mel feeding the calf and something in his stomach took a deep dive. 'Where's Indy?'

'Um … I don't know. Gone?'

'Gone?'

'Didn't she come and see you?' Mel looked surprised. 'She was organising to leave. Asked me to take care of Monte.' Monte finished the bottle and Mel gently pulled it from his mouth. Then she looked up at Logan with something a lot like guilt. He wondered why, even as she asked, 'Are you all right?'

'I didn't think she'd take off until the shuttle bus left in the morning.'

'I told her she could take the staff car to Hamilton because the shuttle's running through there tomorrow so I can pick it up. She was going to get the bus to Hobart from there. I thought I'd hitch a ride out with the shuttle tomorrow and pick it up, bring it back.' She stumbled over the explanation just a little too much. But there was no reason for her to lie. Or to look guilty.

He was on edge, decided he was probably just making her nervous over her admission. But he couldn't help but snap, because he knew Mel had wanted her gone from the beginning. 'After everything you've done, you choose today to be nice to her—to help her leave?'

'I ...' Mel's gaze dropped.

He closed his eyes and released a long slow breath. 'Sorry. This is not your fault.'

'I have been mean to her. I'm sorry too. But we'll be okay. We'll cope without her. We did before, right?'

'Yeah sure.' There was only one person to blame for Indy leaving, and it wasn't Mel. 'Thanks for looking after Monte.'

He walked outside and stared unseeingly at the mountains. Well, that was that. He wanted to be mad, wanted to wonder how she could be so quick to leave if she felt the way she'd insinuated she felt. But he'd walked away—left her on the ground in tears. And now he'd lost her.

He took out his phone and stared at it. He could call, see if she was still interested in talking. His finger hit her number. The phone went to voicemail. He hung up.

She was gone. And that was all there was to it.

Indy blinked a few times against blurry eyes. Her head was pounding and as she tried to shift position, a sharp cramp in her right calf muscle woke her all the way up with a vicious jolt. She sat up, then almost toppled from the bunkbed when her leg didn't go where she'd wanted to put it.

'You might want to slow down. You'll fall over.'

'What?' She followed the voice to her left, where a too-thin young woman with a tangle of dark hair and a wan smile sat cross-legged on the bed a foot or two across from her. Where was she? The metal walls were a rusted red, with air vents skimming the length of the top. A shipping container. The air was cool, smelled stale, the blanket underneath her itched. Four bunk beds inside. A filthy mattress and blanket on each.

She rubbed at her calf. 'Who are you?'

'I'm Gretchen.'

'Gretchen? You're alive.' Indy smiled at the woman then, cramp easing, dropped her aching head into her hands. 'I'm guessing that's about the best news I'm going to get for a while.'

Gretchen's expression was confused. 'Do I know you?'

'No. But traces of your blood and hair were found in Logan's ute when you went missing. No one was sure you'd be found alive.'

'I'd fallen off my horse but it didn't exactly kill me. I cut my leg, got my hair all muddy and tangled in my helmet. Ripped half my scalp off untangling it. But Logan would have told them that. The police don't think Logan hurt me, do they?'

She sighed heavily. Had Mark deliberately left that out to strengthen his case against Logan? If she got out of this, he was going to pay. 'Something like that. Where are we?'

'Your new home. Luxurious, isn't it? Who are you?'

'Indy.'

'Let me guess. Brenda invited you into the kitchen for a drink after offering you a job. She drugged you, and you ended up here.'

'Pretty close.' Head still in hands, she glanced up to study the cuff at her ankle. It was tight and cutting in, and four feet of heavy chain led from it. But it wasn't attached to anything. 'Where is here?'

'Not too far from the farm. Far enough away not to be seen but close enough to work in the fields during harvest.'

'Harvesting poppies?'

'And processing them. That's why we're here. This place is a prison. They use the excuse of the poppy farming to lock the place up like Fort Knox, and it's too far to get out on foot even if you could make it off the farm. Then of course, they let their dogs out at night so if you escape from the containers you'll get attacked. They take your things: your money, your passport, your phone. Everything. They need workers to process the poppies, they're growing more than they're supposed to and skimming some for private manufacturing, and they can't risk anyone leaving and dobbing them in.'

'Processing into what, heroin?'

'No, we make morphine bricks. They're hidden in false floors in shipping containers with the legit produce sent up for the Melbourne markets and collected by workers at the docks for the company that owns this place.'

'How long does it take to get to the poppy fields from here?'

'In truck, only about five minutes.'

Indy thought about that. 'Past their abattoir?'

'Yeah. We're down near the creek.'

Indy thought about what she knew of the property, decided she had a fairly good idea where they were. And a truck coming in and out meant a decent track to and from the main part of Hilltop Farm. That should mean less trouble for Ben to find them. He'd be here, but not for almost a week. She silently cursed her stupidity for slipping up. But at least she could do her best to protect the women until the raid

'I know what you're thinking, but you can't escape. If you try, they kill you. A few have gotten out—past the men and the dogs and the fences, but the terrain is so rough, so difficult. And this damn heavy chain slows you down and catches on everything … That's why we have them.' She tilted her chin at the wall. 'They get caught. They always get caught.' Indy turned and looked behind her. Stuck to the wall were horrific photos of mostly-starved women hanging from trees, along with news stories on dead families. 'Those pics and articles are deterrents—to stop us bolting. It's not only our lives on the line. They tell us the girls should be an example to the rest of us. A big production is made out of it. This is what will happen if we catch you trying to escape. If we don't catch you here, we'll follow you home. Then we'll kill you anyway. We'll kill your whole family.'

That explained Latisha's wounds. But how had she ended up in the river?

'Indy?'

She dragged her eyes from the newspaper story. 'Sorry what?'

'I said do you have any family?'

She shook her head. 'No. No, I don't.'

'My mother died before I got here, but I have a father. He was never very good at being one, but I miss him.' She stared off into space. 'I wonder if he thinks about me. Worries maybe at least a bit if I'm okay.'

'He worries about you every day.'

Gretchen's gaze flew back to Indy. 'You met my father? Is that how you knew who I was?'

She smiled gently. 'Yeah, I've met Warren. He's putting pressure on everyone he can think of to find you. He hasn't given up, Gretchen. He won't.'

Tears spilled down Gretchen's cheeks and she swiped at them. 'Oh God, I want to get out of here ...'

'And that's what we need to work on,' Indy said. 'I need to know the routines, the habits of the people holding you here, what they're going to do and when they're going to do it. There's a lot to learn and not much time to learn it.'

'What do you mean?'

'I mean one way or another, I'm going to get you out of here.' Indy's gaze flicked back once more to the pictures. These bastards were going to pay for what they'd done.

'Did you not hear what I just said?' Gretchen demanded. 'No one's ever escaped and lived.'

'That's about to change. Tell me everything you can.'

Gretchen was wary but shrugged. 'It's you and me and two other girls—Mary and Jackie—in here. There's seven other women divided between the other two containers. Mostly they smuggle in women from overseas, illegals that don't speak English. It's only occasionally they'll fill a spot with one of the backpackers coming through.

'The illegals come and go each season. Not sure where they are in between. Unless they die. I've seen a couple just drop dead. I've been told there's always plenty more.'

Indy fought back the shudder. 'And what do you do in between?'

'Whatever we're told,' Gretchen said, playing with the corner of her blanket. 'Usually working in the fields.'

'What happens to the bodies of the ones that die here?'

'Don't know. Kyle always threatens to chop 'em up and put 'em through the mincer for the dogs. Not sure if he's lying. He's a sick enough bastard to do it.'

Indy's stomach did one long roll. 'That didn't happen to Latisha. She washed up in the river. Where's everyone else?'

'Working. I got last night and this morning off to give you a run-down when you woke up.'

'Last night and this morning?'

'You've been out a while. Kyle came in and gave you a kick earlier. He thought you might have been dead. Apparently Brenda was a bit heavy-handed on the drugs because you'd beaten up Mason. I got the impression she was worried if she didn't knock you out all the way you might have put up a fight.'

A series of loud bangs had Indy jumping to her feet. 'Who's out there?'

'Three big guys with guns—intermediaries between the corporation and the Cartwrights. They're the guards that shuffle us around and watch us work. Now you're awake we'll be expected to collect opium this afternoon.'

The container door opened and a brick of a man wearing army greens and carrying a large gun stood staring at her. 'About time you woke up.'

'Who are you supposed to be, Rambo?'

The butt of his gun struck her in the jaw, sent her backwards with a painful thump. 'Get out.'

She rubbed her jaw, tested it by moving it around. 'Sure. Seeing as you asked so nicely.'

Gretchen grabbed her arm and towed her out. 'You won't last a day if you don't shut up.'

'Just getting a feel for the place,' Indy promised under her breath. She stopped by a truck and took in her surroundings. Tall white gums towered over them, thick scrub underneath gave little clue to what lay beyond the track. She could hear water, a gurgle of it, and a look to the left revealed an old rusty shed. It was long and narrow, open-fronted. Drums sat over fire pits, equipment she didn't recognise was scattered around in some sort of deliberate arrangement. Two enormous Rottweilers sat in a fenced enclosure on the edge of the workspace. Slight women with long dark hair and blank expressions shuffled around quietly, murmuring the occasional sentence or two in Mandarin as they worked.

'We help with the processing in the mornings,' Gretchen said from behind her. 'To extract the morphine, which is what they need to eventually make heroin.'

'Because the morphine base is about one-tenth the weight and volume of raw opium, it's easier to ship—and hide—and it has a long shelf life, so it can be stored for long periods of time,' Indy said.

'You know about this stuff?'

'Not enough,' Indy decided.

'We need to get in,' Gretchen told her.

The chain was dragging behind her, and clanged noisily as they climbed into the back of the small truck. Six other women were already inside. Indy recognised two as missing backpackers and scanned her memory for their names.

'Indy, this is Jackie, and Mary,' Gretchen said. 'The two we're sharing the container with.'

'Hi,' Indy said, trying not to be too distressed by the state they were in. 'Why are we doing this so late in the afternoon?'

'If we try to collect the opium too early, the sun makes it coagulate on the pod and that blocks the flow,' Gretchen told her. 'You get less opium, then you get in trouble.'

'More importantly,' Jackie added, 'the guards carry guns and knives. It's so tempting to run to the trees, but they'll catch you and Bull will kill you.'

'Thanks for the advice.' Mary was quiet, too thin. 'Are you okay?' Indy had to ask.

She smiled vacantly. 'Yeah.'

'Mary has been here the longest. It's not easy.'

As the truck engine revved to life and they bounced up the dirt track, she caught a small woman with a pretty face sending her a quick smile. Indy sent one back.

'They don't all speak English,' Gretchen whispered. 'But they understand enough. They have nowhere to go—nothing to lose—and they're rewarded if they tell tales. The one on the end, Ainie, snitches to Bruno.'

'Bruno?'

'One of the guards. They have an arrangement.'

'Oh, but … Of course they have somewhere to go,' Indy said, watching them closely to assess if they understood. 'Trafficking and slavery is more common in Australia than most people think. There are support programs set up on the mainland to help people just like them. When they get out, they'll get everything they need to resettle.'

'You're a cop, aren't you?' Gretchen guessed.

'Yep.'

Jackie's eyes rounded. 'You should shut up,' she hissed, with a telling look towards Ainie.

'They already know,' Indy said. 'That's why I'm here. I think. I was interfering with their drug smuggling, so it sounds like they're sending Bull down to kill me.'

Gretchen looked at her strangely. 'You seem to be taking it very well.'

Indy shrugged. 'I didn't say I was going to let that happen.'

The truck jerked to a stop and the back was unlocked. Rambo One pulled open the doors. 'Time to go.'

Indy jumped out behind Gretchen and looked around, saw a square stretch of poppy field bordered by thick stands of tall trees.

'Over here.' Gretchen moved over to a shed partially obscured by the truck and Indy followed her inside. 'Here.' Gretchen handed Indy a small bag. In it was a tool with three small blades bound tightly together on a wooden handle, a short-handled iron blade, and a container. 'I'll show you what to do.'

They walked back out to the field, right around to the far end of it. 'We have to work our way from the far end to the front or we end up brushing against the sticky pods on our way back.'

Indy looked at the staggering number of pods on the dead-looking plants. 'How long does this go for?'

'We've only been harvesting this section for a couple of days—and the pods produce opium five or six times so we'll be out here a few more yet.' Gretchen grabbed a pod and took out the flat-bladed tool. 'Watch. You scrape off the sap and collect it in your container, like this. You do that one.'

Indy copied Gretchen, who nodded. 'Pretty simple, right? Okay, now watch this. You need your scoring tool. The three-bladed one.

'You need to run it down the pod, on two or three sides. But you have to be careful. If you make the cut too deep, the opium will flow out too quickly and go everywhere. If you don't cut deep enough, it won't flow out fast enough and the opium will harden in the pods. Either way, that's wasted opium and you'll cop it. See that? I've cut in about a millimetre.'

Indy watched the milky sap slowly start to ooze. 'Is that it?'

'Yep. It'll keep coming slowly and coagulate on the pod overnight. In the morning, it'll have darkened up and thickened like the stuff we just collected.'

'Right.'

'You work this line, I'll head up the next.'

Indy spotted Rambos One and Two and the driver—three, still back at the shed. They were seated at a table, occupied with something. They were too far away for her to see what it was. 'You said they check your work but they seem happier sitting in the sun. I don't think they're even watching.'

'That's what Latisha thought.'

She had a go at collecting the black goop on a nearby pod, made a mess of it. 'What happened?'

'I told her not to run—begged her not to. But she did. From a couple of rows across from you, straight into those trees behind you. And they caught her. Bull arrived and made the usual production out of it.'

Indy stopped. 'Bull killed Latisha, not the guards?'

'He always does it. These guys can rough us up to keep us in line but they're not supposed to kill us.'

She remembered Latisha's wounds. 'He hung her, right?'

'Yeah. Lined us up and told her and everyone else she was going to die and then he was going after her family. It was her fault, he said with this sick grin. Then he strung her up, balanced on this old broken stool, and we worked around her all day.'

'Standing on a stool?'

'It'll stay in place while you're balanced on it, but wobble too much and it falls over.' Gretchen's voice cracked and she composed herself before continuing. 'It's not enough to hang them. He leaves them there struggling to balance until they get tired, until they give up. She pleaded for help for hours. And then she just got tired, too tired ...' Gretchen turned sharply and got to work.

Indy shuddered. The man was not just a hired killer, he was sadistic. She cut into a pod, watched the sap ooze out. Not bad. Then she saw how far in front the other workers were and decided she'd better hurry up.

Gretchen didn't talk to her again until they reached the end of the first row. 'They'll weigh what you bring back, so get as much as you can. Latisha showed me what to do when I first got here. She said she heard Kyle say he expected something like 80 milligrams per pod.'

Indy looked around. 'They can't possibly know how many pods there are in each row.'

'I suppose not, but if you come back with the lowest weight you don't eat. Oh—and if you get a plant that's producing heaps you're supposed to tag it with one of the twisties in your pouch so they can collect the seeds to use for the next crop. But they won't expect that until you get an eye for it.'

'I don't know how long that would take, but I don't intend to be here long enough.' They worked until the light was gone, then their bags were inspected and their tools returned. They were lined up like animals, while Kyle walked the line. He stopped in front of the woman who had smiled at her. And struck her to the ground.

'Not good enough!' The woman stayed down, her lip split and bleeding. Small and impossibly thin, she looked like no more than a child. Kyle dragged her back to her feet by her hair and pointed at

Indy. 'The new bitch did better than you!' He shoved her away and she shuffled over to stand at the end of the line, head down. Then his gaze caught Indy's expression and he smiled slowly, moved in front of her. 'Enjoying yourself, *Detective*?'

She just smiled that smug smile right back at him. 'Living the dream, arsehole. Looking forward to prison?' She caught a few noisily indrawn breaths, the glances. But when Kyle looked up the line, the women hushed, averted their gazes. She expected the slap, but not the intensity of it. Stars blurred her sight and blocked the light. But she stayed on her feet.

'Don't get too used to it,' she heard through the ringing in her ears. 'You'll be dead soon.' Then to the guards. 'Take them back! Don't feed this one.'

Her head felt like a runaway chainsaw had carved through it. The loud bangs and crashes of the container doors opening, the blast of cold air and the sudden infusion of light into the room was painful. There were noisy footsteps, then jarring movement in her leg as her chain was yanked on. 'Get up!'

She opened her eyes—her left one with difficulty. It was swollen, sore. Rambo Two was standing over her. 'I said get up!' The chain was yanked again and she was dragged with a thump off the bunk.

'Ow ...' She squeezed her eyes shut, opened them cautiously. Refocused. 'I'm up.' She got her legs under her and stood. Her throat was parched. 'Hey Ram—What's your name?'

Another yank had her crashing back to the floor. Her hip hit the edge of the bed on the way down; more glancing pain. And over it, anger. 'I only asked—'

'No questions!'

She took a breath, then another, and another. Even injured she might be able to take him. If she was smart about it. But she could hear the other men issuing orders close by. She didn't have a hope against all of them. She got back to her feet and stumbled past.

Outside, Gretchen's expression was sympathetic. 'You're partnered up with me. I'll take you through it. You ready?'

'Yep,' she managed, wincing as she prodded her cheek. Before this was over, she decided, Kyle was going to cop one back.

Oil drums full of boiling liquid sat on bricks with fires burning underneath them. One woman was adding a large amount of raw opium to water. Two others stood at drums, stirring, while others were pouring water through sieves.

'The wet opium gum contains a lot of water, so it has to be dried for days before we can start processing it,' Gretchen told her. 'What we're working with now was harvested last week. See what Mary's doing? The opium dissolves in the water, and anything stuck to it that we don't want—like leaves and dirt—floats, and you scoop it out. When you've got clean, liquid opium you put the lime in— that's the stuff in those white bags. It turns everything except the part you want into a sludge at the bottom of the drum. Look at this.'

She showed her another drum with a white band of substance on the top. 'That's the morphine. We have to collect that and filter it. Then it's reheated with ammonia and dissolved in hydrochloric acid. You have to be careful with that stuff or—'

'You have access to ammonia and hydrochloric acid?'

'Yep, then we add the charcoal, reheat it. Then it's filtered a few more times, and poured into those moulds over there which are dried in the sun. I'll show it to you—over here.'

Indy looked at it; a dark brown block that reminded her of primary school modelling clay. No wonder morphine bricks were said to be much easier to smuggle than opium. Thinking back to the sticky, smelly mess she'd been collecting and looking at the finished product, she could see why.

'We'd better get to work before we get into trouble.'

She learnt the process, did her best to ignore the churning in her empty stomach and the pounding headache, and managed to avoid drawing the guards' attention again. But she watched closely, and she listened, and when she could, she asked Gretchen questions. She overheard the names of all three Rambos: Matteus, Bruno and Manuel. She kept an eye on the two Rottweilers that were caged near the shipping containers, knew that if she got too close they growled or barked. She noticed Bruno and Manuel smoked, that Matteus liked to play solitaire and chew gum and seemed to be in charge. That Ainie watched her carefully, smiled a lot at Bruno.

The day dragged on. She was beginning to wonder if they'd ever get fed when a four-wheel drive appeared. Jules and Kyle got out. Kyle sent her a threatening scowl and went to talk to the men, while Jules took a plastic container from the boot and brought it over to one of the tables in the shed.

'Hey Indy. Come over here.'

Indy left the filtering and approached Jules. 'I was wondering when you'd show up.'

'Make yourself a sandwich.' Jules put a loaf of bread on the table, a container of half-empty peanut butter, Vegemite, some plastic knives.

'You know, you need these women. It wouldn't hurt to feed them properly.'

'We used to, and they always felt good enough to try and escape. And then we'd have to kill them. Better to be hungry, don't you think?'

Pride came a poor second to hunger so she dug out some Vegemite and added it to a couple of slices of bread. The other women got a nod from Jules and descended on the food, so Indy stepped away, sat on the ground. 'How long have you been involved in all this?'

'Do you know how long I chased Connor? I grew up in that family's shadow. The cook's kid that got to hang with the Athertons. How lucky. Yeah. Right. Mum put her heart and soul into that place and I worked my butt off every spare moment helping them with whatever came up. Why shouldn't I have had a share in the place? But I was never quite good enough for Connor, nope. Not until I took off and came back with stories of how I'd made something of myself. Suddenly he took notice. But I knew the gloss would wear off, there's only so long you can play a role, right?' She laughed, 'You'd know all about that. So I got pregnant—he's so damn honourable he was always going to marry me. But even that didn't work out, did it?'

'What happened to the baby?'

She screwed up her face and shook her head rapidly. 'It doesn't matter. Why do you care?'

'I'm trying to work you out.'

Jules huffed out a laugh. 'Give me an out, you mean. Explain my behaviour? How could Jules be involved in all this?'

'Oh, no. I know how you're involved—through Kyle. I just wanted the why.'

'You knew about Kyle and me?' she asked with raised eyebrows. 'How?'

'The trip out to Hilltop Farm. We ran into Bindi. You seemed pretty familiar with a three-year-old when you've supposedly only been in town a couple of brief times since her birth. She wanted you and Kyle to play with her so I looked into him too. Kyle takes lots of trips to and from Sydney. His listed postal address is your flat in Paddington.'

'Clever. Thing is, Kyle was always there for me. Before I left to study, we hooked up. When I worked in Sydney he'd come visit. I was making nothing, the pay was a joke. So he gave me a side job in the business.'

'Dealing drugs?'

'Deliveries at first. Even let me take a bit on the side when things got a bit much, you know?'

'And you got hooked?'

'It's only opium. Never had any need for heroin. It was working okay, but then Kyle and I had a bit of an argument, you know how it is, so when I went home to visit and Connor was interested, I was over the moon. I'd always wanted him. Least I thought I had. Didn't work out, no problem. Kyle didn't just give me my job back, we got back together and he gave me more responsibility, introduced me to all this. I've never been fucking happier. So I really don't feel bad about Logan, or anyone at Calico Mountain. I don't feel particularly bad about setting you up, either, because you came down here to screw all this up.'

'So why am I still alive?'

'Because Bull isn't here yet. This was meticulously planned from the outset. You were on this missing persons case in the first place because it was orchestrated that way. You have no idea how powerful D'Angelo is. Who his friends are.'

'Senator Melville?'

'Senator Melville does what he's told. If he didn't get you down here, his daughter really would have been in trouble. I'll bet he was a mess when he met with you. A lot rode on that conversation.' Jules's eyes narrowed thoughtfully. 'What else have you figured out?'

'I know Bull is Logan's father. That he killed Evelyn and went on somehow to become D'Angelo's hitman.'

Jules looked genuinely surprised at that. 'How the fuck did you figure that out?'

'Logan's father was nicknamed Bull after the accident. Both disappeared, Evelyn was found in the dam. I already know from the Sydney investigation that Bull is alive and killing for D'Angelo. It doesn't take a genius to put it together. Why'd you kill April?'

'She was at Calico Mountain snooping. And a body in Logan's dam was just another nail in his coffin.'

She swallowed back the flash of anger. 'And that doesn't bother you—pinning all these disappearances and murders on Logan?'

'I've got nothing against Logan. Unfortunately, Latisha washed up, so there was always going to be an investigation into the Athertons because that's where the Cartwrights have sourced a few girls over the years. Best to keep the finger pointed in that direction, right?'

She didn't enlighten her otherwise. 'How can you be so sure I haven't already told the cops what I've figured out?'

Jules's look was smug. 'Because I've been reading your emails. This is not some backwater operation going on here, Indy. If we can hack into the government databases to manipulate poppy production estimates, we can get into your laptop.'

'I thought Senator Melville took care of that for you.'

Jules sent Indy a small smile. 'Not everything can be done via computer. He … irons out the kinks. And he's well paid for it.'

'Of course he is.' She got to her feet and dusted herself off. It was a pointless exercise, she was filthy.

'You shouldn't have worked D'Angelo's case, Indy. You were getting too close to too many of his contacts. He couldn't risk just offing you back in Sydney—it was bound to bring even more heat down on his operation. So he came up with a way to kill two birds. D'Angelo owns Senator Melville, so he had him send Caroline to Calico Mountain—'

'Jules, let's go,' Kyle called out, heading for the car.

'Right behind you.' Then she turned her attention back to Indy. 'Anyway, I'm sure you can figure it out. You came down to investigate Logan, disappeared from Calico Mountain like the other girls. This way Bull gets to kill you and you just look like another Logan Atherton victim. I'm sorry, Indy. I really liked you.' Then at Indy's shake of the head. 'Why so sad?'

'I'm picturing what it's going to do to your mum when she finds out who you really are.'

'Even *if* she does, you'll be dead by then. It's not something you need to worry about.'

Indy watched the car bump back up the track and scowled. 'Don't count on it.'

CHAPTER
25

Logan walked into the pub with Jules and found a table. Amy appeared. 'Hi, you two. What can I get ya?'

'Couple of coffees, thanks Amy.'

'How's Indy doing out there? Haven't seen her around for a while.'

Logan's head snapped up. 'You didn't see her a couple of days ago?'

'Nope.' Amy shook her head and her brow creased in thought. 'It's been a couple of weeks, I'd say.'

'But she was supposed to call in—drop the staff car keys off with Marge.'

'First I've heard about it.' She turned back to the bar. 'Hey, Marge!'

'What?' Marge came out wiping her hands on a tea towel. 'Oh hi, Jules, Logan.'

'Did Indy turn up a couple of days ago with some car keys?' Amy asked.

'Indy, why?' A look passed fleetingly between Marge and Jules. 'Was she supposed to?'

Jules shook her head.

Logan frowned at the pair. What was going on? 'Are you absolutely sure?'

'Is something wrong?' Marge asked.

'I'm sure everything's fine,' Jules said.

So why was his stomach beginning to churn? 'Mel said Indy was taking the staff car out here and was going to give you the keys. Mel was going to pick it up the following morning—yesterday.'

Marge's head shook slowly. 'I was here from open to close.' Then her eyes widened. 'She hasn't gone missing, has she?'

'Oh, no,' Amy murmured, chewing a fingernail.

Jules pulled her phone from her bag. 'She just doesn't want to talk to Logan.' He waited while she dialled and after a moment she hung up. 'It's going to voicemail. She's barred us all.'

'I'll get your coffees,' Amy offered.

'Do you remember seeing the staff car here?' Logan pushed Marge. 'The little red one?'

'I know the car—and I don't remember seeing it. Wasn't looking for it though, so can't say for sure.'

'She might have got the shuttle in instead,' Jules said calmly. 'We'll ask Bob.'

'You ask Bob.' He dug out his phone and tried Indy himself. 'Indy, it's Logan. I know I'm the last person you want to talk to, I just—I need to know you got off all right. You don't have to call me back but can you just—please—send a quick text? Call Tess? Anything. Please.'

'Oh dear, did you two have a row?' Marge asked.

'Kind of. Thanks Marge.' He got to his feet and Jules followed his lead.

'What about your coffees?' Marg asked.

'Thanks anyway. We've got to go.'

He climbed back in the truck with Jules and headed back to Calico Mountain.

'She's probably just got a lift in with someone else, that's all,' Jules said as he sped towards home.

'It's possible,' he said.

'And either not charged her phone on her mad dash out of there or just doesn't want to talk to anyone.'

'Also possible.'

'But you don't sound convinced.'

'Jules, every time a woman disappears from Calico Mountain I'm the last one to see them alive. Until I hear from Indy, I'm going to worry. I need to talk to Mel.'

'But you told Indy to go, didn't you?'

'Yeah.'

'So this is different.'

'I hope to God you're right.'

Back at home, he found the staff car parked where it was supposed to be, kept going until he reached the stables. 'Mel!'

She appeared with a rake in her hands. 'Hi—what's wrong?'

'When did you pick the staff car up?'

'I didn't have to,' she said. 'Indy never took it.'

His hand made a fist in his hair. 'You said she was driving it back to Hamilton and you were going to pick it up.'

'Yes, but she never took it. I thought she must have gotten a lift in with someone else.'

'You never saw her drive out?'

'No. I told her if she wanted to take it, I'd collect it. She thanked me and left. But I didn't actually see her drive away. All I know is, she said she was going to go see you and that was the last I saw of her.'

'Of course it was.' It was happening again. And there was nothing he could do about it. He checked his phone for the twentieth time since leaving Hamilton. Tried Indy again. Nothing. When he looked up, Mel had gotten back to work.

He went to reception, asked Kaicey. No, she hadn't seen her for a couple of days. He took the key to her room, all but sprinted over there. The room was clean—and vacant. All Indy's belongings were gone. It should have reassured him she was safely on her way wherever she was going. But it didn't. Because all the women that had gone missing had also taken their things. He raked a hand through his hair and checked his phone again. 'Damn it, Indy, call me!'

Where would she have gone? He realised he didn't know a thing about her life other than that she was a cop, could pull apart an engine and had no family. How had that happened? Because she'd shut him down, he realised, and she'd done it so smoothly he hadn't really paid attention. Tess might have found something out. A clue to something. He found her in Connor's office going over some paperwork.

'Hi, Logan—what?' Tess's smile died on her lips as she looked him over.

'Do you know where Indy went?'

'Went? No. I didn't see her before she left. It's a bit late to be worrying about it now, she could be anywhere.'

'That's what worries me.'

'Honestly Logan, you told her to go. Now you want an itinerary? Indy was a friend. I'm still annoyed with you about that.'

'What's the urgency?' Connor asked.

'She was supposed to take the staff car to Hamilton, leave the keys with Marge and get on the bus to Hobart. Mel was going to get the shuttle bus out the next day to bring it back. She never took the car. Marge never saw it—or Indy. Mel said the car never left here.'

'And yet she's gone.' Tess's face lost some of its colour. 'No one's seen her for two days?'

'Her room is cleaned out. Her phone's going straight to voicemail.'

Connor pushed to his feet. 'Let's not panic yet. She's probably just gone off with someone else and doesn't want to talk to you.'

'I did this. If anything has happened to her ... I don't even know who to call. I don't know anything about her.'

'You know she's with the police. What if we ask Mark?' Tess suggested.

'What did you say?' Connor asked sharply.

Logan dropped to a seat and put his head in his hands. 'I found out she was here to investigate Caroline's disappearance. That's why I told her to go.'

'She was here undercover. Damn. I knew there was something about her!' Connor said. 'Stuff this. No one's taken her. She's just gone. Let her go.'

'Being a cop doesn't give you magical powers,' Tess argued. 'She didn't float out of here.'

'She probably got a police car to pick her up. I can't imagine they're allowed to hang around once they've been sprung.' There was a pause while Connor looked from Tess to Logan, then back with a sigh. 'But ... it wouldn't hurt to check. There was a contact for a next of kin on her résumé,' Connor said and moved to the filing cabinet to pull it out.

'She said she didn't have a family,' Logan said.

'She wouldn't exactly have been honest with her personal information, would she? And this could be part of that lie. Let's see.' He opened it up. 'I have an address in Colorado, a next of kin … strangely enough with a Sydney address. A Patricia Langdon. I have an emergency contact number here for her.'

'Let's have it.'

As Connor called it out, Logan dialled the number. Breathed a sigh of relief when it rang, only to get an answering service. He left a message. It was all he could do.

The phone rang almost immediately. Logan picked it up.

'This is Ben, a friend of Indy's. You called?' The tone was clipped and professional.

Ben? The guy she'd been talking to on the phone. He'd have to know where she was. If anyone did. And what was he supposed to say? 'Yeah … hi, this is Logan Atherton. I'm guessing you know who I am.'

There was silence for several seconds, then, 'How can I help you?'

'Like I said in the message, I'm hoping to contact Indy.'

'She left?'

'Two days ago. I tried to contact her but can't get her. I'd appreciate it if when you do, you could get her to call me.'

'Do you know where she was headed?'

The guy sounded as on edge as Logan felt. 'To Hobart, I thought. But up via Hamilton so one of our other staff could pick up a car she was going to leave there the next day. It's possible she got a lift into town with someone and we haven't figured out who yet but … I'm concerned.'

'I'm on my way.'

'We're at Cal—'

'I know where you are. Keep looking.'

Logan ended the call and stared into space.

'And?' Tess asked impatiently.

'He's a cop. He knows what's been going on down here and he's worried enough to be on his way. Maybe her boss or something, I don't know.'

'When did he say he'd be here?' Tess asked.

'He didn't. And he asked us to keep looking. We need to ask everyone on the place if they know anything.'

'Then let's do that,' Tess agreed. 'It'll make me feel like I'm being useful.'

Three cars appeared before nightfall. Logan watched a tall, perfectly postured man with an air of authority about him step out of the first car and knew that had to be the man he'd spoken to on the phone. He walked across the drive to meet him. 'Ben Bowden?'

'Correct.'

'Logan Atherton.' He shook hands, tolerated the man's quick appraisal. 'Please come inside.'

'Anything?' Ben asked.

'Nothing. You're welcome to search my place—it's been picked over several times already but Indy wasn't missing then so you may as well go again.'

'That won't be necessary. But some of my men will be interviewing your staff. That all right with you?'

'Of course.'

Ben looked at Tess. 'Tess Atherton?'

'Yes.'

'Would you be kind enough to take my men around and introduce them to your staff? I'd personally like a word with Melanie Cartwright and Julie Miller, if you could send Julie first?'

'I'll go find her.'

'A private word?' Ben asked Logan when Tess left. 'How many other people know who Indy is?'

'Just me, Tess and, since today, Connor. I overheard her talking to you on the phone and told her to leave. She was gone that afternoon.'

Ben studied him closely. 'So you find out April's a reporter and she's dead within twenty-four hours. Then you find out Indy's a cop and she disappears within the same timeframe.'

The question made sense, but Logan wasn't in the mood. 'If you want to make an accusation, come right out and say it.'

Ben considered that, considered Logan, before answering. 'Indy's smart, and she's got a whole lot more of this figured out than you realise. She's gone into bat for you and I'm inclined to believe the argument she's presented. But I'll also tell you this.' Ben's whole face darkened. 'I'll get to the bottom of it. I always do. And if I find out you have anything to do with any of this—most especially anything to do with Indy's disappearance—I'll *crucify* you. So if there's anything—anything at all—you want to say, you'd better hurry up and confess it while you have witnesses close enough to keep you in one piece.'

If nothing else, the man obviously cared for Indy. Logan figured that was a good thing under the circumstances. 'Got it.'

'Last chance.'

Logan dragged his hand through his hair. 'Can we just get on with finding Indy? If I find out someone has taken her, I'll be the one doing the crucifying.'

Ben didn't look convinced. 'When all this comes out in the open—that might be a little harder to do than you think.'

'Why's that?'

'Let me worry about that.'

Tess knocked on the door. 'Jules has already left for the evening. Nat's doing dinner.'

'Is Melanie Cartwright here?'

'Yeah. She'll still be around,' Logan said. 'I'll go get her.'

He walked into the stables, gave Rex a pat as he went to walk past—and did a double take. Mel was sitting cross-legged, elbows on knees, head in her hands, dangerously close to Rex's back legs.

'Mel ... get off the floor,' he said very slowly.

Mel lifted a tear-stained face and sniffed, shook her head and swiped her fingers across her eyes. 'He's not going to hurt me.'

'Is smoking that shit you're on making you suicidal? Move—slowly, let's go.'

She laughed harshly. Rex snorted, shifted his legs. 'I can't do this anymore.'

He haltered Rex, turned the stallion's hind legs away from Mel. 'What can't you do?'

She got to her feet and stroked Rex's neck. 'Rex didn't kill Matty. He didn't even kick him. They did it. They did it to punish him and teach me a lesson.'

Logan wasn't sure he heard right. 'What? Who's they?'

She shook her head as fresh tears fell in a stream down her flushed cheeks. 'You're the only one who's always been nice to me and you love her and I've done this.'

Dread settled heavily in the pit of his stomach. 'What have you done?'

'Do you know who she is? Did she tell you? Did the police?'

'You knew?'

She nodded. 'I didn't want you to get hurt. I always push them towards Hilltop—I have to—but I liked her, I didn't want to. It makes it harder. Especially because I know what he wants to do to her. She saved Bindi, she saved my daughter's life. But I have to protect Bindi too. That's the only way I could do it. But I tried to warn her. I tried.'

He didn't mean to tighten his grip on her arm so hard, released it when she flinched. 'You're not making sense. You need to talk to Ben—the detective. We're going to Connor's office. Let's go.'

She dug her heels in and shook her head frantically. 'They'll kill Bindi.'

'No one's going to hurt Bindi.'

'They will. I have to get her. I have to get her off Kyle.'

They were outside the guesthouse, Mel still begging to be allowed to go when Connor appeared. 'What the hell is wrong now?' he asked from the steps.

'She knows what's happened to Indy,' Logan said.

'And you didn't tell us?' Connor demanded.

'I didn't want to be involved. I never wanted to be involved.' Mel slid down to the step and sat, crying quietly.

'Involved in what?' Connor asked.

She sniffed, turned her tear-stained face up to the men. 'My "job" is to recruit workers for Hilltop Farm. To bully out-of-towners out of Calico Mountain so Marge can pat them on the back and whisper in their ears about how Hilltop is a better place to work. "There, there," she says, "it's horrible out there—Mel's mean, and you have to watch that Logan—he's a serial killer. You come work for us—just don't tell anyone. We're scared of the Athertons, too." She even tells them how to do it—to make arrangements with Logan for the day so he's not suspicious they're leaving, so they can get out unnoticed. She promises them more money and an easier job and once they're in they aren't coming back. That's it. They work there till they're dead.'

'And that's where Indy is now?' Logan asked.

'Sort of. They keep them right down the back. Near the creek.'

'For what purpose?' Connor asked.

'To process poppies into morphine base. My family are running the business as a front for an illicit drug operation.'

'You've got to be kidding. If you didn't want to be involved, why are you still doing this?' Logan asked, shattered.

Mel sniffed again, loudly, and swiped at her eyes. 'When I married Matt and got pregnant he wanted us to go away—start our own place up somewhere. Dad was ropeable and refused to let us leave. I said if he didn't, I'd tell the cops about the women. They smashed Matt over the head with a tyre jack and tossed him in Rex's stable.

It was like some sort of sick dream he couldn't escape from. 'Who?' Logan demanded. 'Who is "they"? Jim?'

She shook her head. 'Kyle and ... your father.'

The shock hit him like an electric current. 'My father?'

'He made it look like an accident. Bull's good at that.'

'And they've got Indy?' Logan turned on his heel and took several steps away. This couldn't be true. His father had killed his mother and Matty, and now he had Indy? 'You knew my father was alive and killing people and you came to work every day like nothing was wrong?' Logan exploded.

'Do you think I wanted to die? I have Bindi to worry about. They own me! I did what I could. I made sure Latisha was found. She was in a shallow grave in the soft ground near the river. I dug her up and rolled her in. It was horrible! And I called the hotline to tell the police there were more women out there. I tried to help. But they can't know I'm talking to you. You can't let them know.'

'How did she get there?' Connor asked.

'Indy said she was leaving, so I told Jules—I had to! Jules took her out there. I made up the stuff about Indy taking the car, about her coming to see you before she left.'

'So it would look like I was the last person to see her,' Logan growled.

'Wait,' Connor interrupted. 'What do you mean by, you had to tell Jules?'

'She came back to be eyes and ears here once Indy turned up, but she works for the family. She's with Kyle.'

'I don't believe that!' Connor snapped.

'What are you all doing out here?' Ben said, appearing in the doorway.

'Mel has something to say,' Logan said in a tone that brooked no argument.

Mel buried her face in her hands. 'I liked some of the girls—liked Indy. She was kind to me—even when I was a cow. She wanted to help. She doesn't deserve to die.'

'You said they take the women as workers,' Logan said as his stomach lurched. 'Why would they kill her?'

'She's a cop. Because she caused them so much trouble.'

Logan didn't know what they were talking about, didn't care. 'Tell me how to get her out!'

'They're on the farm, down the back. You can't get to them. And once Jules tells them I'm talking to you, they'll all be dead. They'll just kill them.'

'You need to calm yourself down,' Ben told her. 'And you need to come inside and start from the beginning. If we're going to save Indy and the rest of those women, you're going to have to help us.'

CHAPTER
26

Indy poured a batch of morphine base into the moulds and wiped a filthy arm across her damp brow. It was hot work, and the insects were relentless. She scratched at a bite as she walked back to collect another bucket. The night before had been freezing in the shipping container. Now she wanted nothing more than a cool shower. She couldn't imagine living like this for years on end. Not that there was any chance of that happening.

Bull was coming soon, but she could only guess when, and Ben wouldn't be raiding Hilltop Farm for another few days. Even if Ben arrived before Bull, the risk that the guards were under instruction to eliminate the women in that instance would be too high to chance. She put down her empty bucket and as she swatted another mosquito, scanned the camp.

Something was wrong with Jackie. She'd been fidgety and distracted all morning, hadn't eaten the night before. Indy was about to risk approaching her to find out what the problem was when the truck rattled down the track. It was time to harvest opium. The guards stirred, left their card game to get to their feet. 'Let's go!' Bruno shouted.

Indy climbed in the truck behind Gretchen. 'I'm worried about Jackie,' Indy said quietly.

'She's not very stable,' Gretchen said, eyeing her friend sadly as the thin woman stumbled towards the truck. 'She's tried to kill herself a couple of times. She has … episodes.'

'Hey!' The sharp shout came from Matteus. 'Stupid bitch!'

Jackie was running into the cover of the undergrowth, struggling to hold the chain and move quickly at the same time.

'No …' Gretchen whispered. 'That's suicide.'

'Looks like we've got a chase on, boys!' Matteus called out with sick excitement. 'Let the dogs out!'

Bruno loped over to the cage and unlocked it. The two Rottweilers bounded out. At Matteus's whistle and hand signal, they shot out into the scrub.

'The men aren't going after her,' Indy said, jumping from the truck, primed to fight.

'They don't need to. The dogs will hold her. Indy, get back in here!'

'Will they kill her?'

'No—no, they'll wait for Bull. *Please* Indy. Get back in the truck!'

There was a scream, agonised wailing, then Bruno and Manuel pushed their way into the scrub. Matteus's smile slid over Indy as they dragged Jackie back. 'Looks like a double execution coming up. Haven't had one of those before.' He spat his gum on the ground and sneered. 'Chain her up, get this lot to work.'

Everyone did as they were told, the atmosphere heavier than usual. Indy worked, but her mind was elsewhere. She had to get these women out. As an idea formed in her mind, she played with it, tightened it, looked for flaws. It was risky—there was no safe way out of this. But it just might work.

When they returned from the fields, Indy noticed Jackie was chained to their container, the life already gone from her stare. It was enough to know what was coming. Would she have the energy to run? She scanned a spot on the darkening ground, and spotting what she was looking for, she bent down to tie her shoe and picked up the gum Matteus had discarded earlier. She'd need it.

'Get inside!' Matteus ordered.

Indy indicated with a hand to Jackie. 'She's going to freeze out here.'

'Dogs'll keep her warm.' He sniggered to the other men.

'At least let me get a blanket for her.' Indy went in and grabbed it. When she tried to get out again, Matteus blocked her.

'You want to be out here with her?'

Indy met his stare and held it. 'No. I want her inside with us.' When Matteus's hand landed on his gun, Indy's pulse jumped but she raised her brow. 'Oh, I know you want to. But the thing is, I know Bull a little better than you might think. And I know what he'll do if he gets down here with his grand plans for me and I'm in no fit state to appreciate them.' She caught the quick flicker of hesitation behind his gaze and took advantage. 'It'd be better all round if you just gave her the pathetic excuse of a blanket, wouldn't it?'

He snatched it from her hands and threw it at Jackie. Then he got in her face. 'I could cut fingers and toes off you and you'd still be in a fit enough state to scream when Bull does what he's got planned. You take me on again, I'll start collecting souvenirs. Got it?' He shoved her hard, backwards into the container. 'Don't forget that, bitch.'

She took a few deep breaths and pulled herself together. Gretchen and Mary filed in and a plastic bag was tossed on the floor. Indy opened it. A loaf of bread, some reject apples from the farm. Manuel chained them to their beds and shut the container door. In the dark, at least she couldn't see the state of the food. 'Well ladies, dig in.'

She ate her share, tossed and turned on the scratchy mattress and tried not to smell the staleness of the space. She couldn't sleep. There was a cold down in this gully that leached through the air vents and seeped relentlessly into her bones. Her filthy blanket smelled like urine and didn't hold any heat. At least there were three of them in there to generate some. There should have been four. She wondered what state they'd find Jackie in when the sun came up. Matteus couldn't be intending to leave her there too long. Bull couldn't be far away.

Running through her plan in her head helped pass the time that should have been spent sleeping. As soon as first light shone through the cracks in the vents, Indy was ready to get started.

'Hey Gretch. Wake up.'

Gretchen moaned and rolled into a sitting position, squinted. 'It's barely light, Indy, the days are long enough.'

'What's going on?' Mary wanted to know.

'I need a bobby pin,' Indy told Gretchen.

'Are you kidding? I'm down to two. It's not like they're going to buy me more and my hair is too frizzy around my face without them.'

'When we get out of here, I'll buy you a truckload,' Indy promised. 'Please?'

Mary gasped. 'Get out of here? Are you insane, did you not see what happened to Jackie?'

'And she's still out there—waiting to die. I can't do nothing.'

'Indy, I've told you what they do to runaways.' But Gretchen passed her the bobby pin.

Indy began shaping it, putting the wire in the lock and bending it one way, then the other. Satisfied at the result, she slipped the makeshift key back in the lock, jiggled it around and freed her ankle.

'You—that took you five seconds,' Mary said.

'I'll get you all out, handle the guards while you escape.'

'But the shipping container's padlocked from the outside,' Gretchen reminded them.

'That's a bit beyond me,' Indy agreed. 'I just wanted to make sure I could still take care of a cuff lock—for Jackie's sake.'

'You're going to free Jackie and handle three armed men and two Rottweilers while the rest of us run for our lives?' Gretchen asked sceptically.

'What have I got to lose? Bull is coming for me. I either get out or I wait here to die. And I'm not leaving you behind.'

'If you tell Ainie about this she'll run straight to Bruno.'

'Leave her to me. Here's what I need you to tell the other girls.'

'Mate, I'm not really sure this is one of your better ideas.' Connor lashed at some thick undergrowth with his machete, and headed off somewhere to his left. 'The police have a plan, right?'

'I'd say so. But I'd feel a lot better if we knew what it was. The hostages will be the first to die once they know the police are on to them. That can't be allowed to happen.'

'Where the hell did you get these machetes from, anyway?'

'Army supply.'

'When?'

'When I was looking for new trails to push through last year. I wanted to get the tourists to that waterfall I was telling you about and I needed to know what the terrain was like.'

'A damn sight better than this, I imagine.'

He was right. Logan looked around, though he couldn't see much further than his nose. The bush was so dense. He looked at his map again, decided he probably had a bit of an idea where they were. 'If we can get up the hill a bit it might thin out.'

'Back part of Hilltop Farm borders the old Bloodwood plantation, doesn't it?'

'Yeah. You got something?'

'Wet feet. On the map a creek ran out of Hilltop, through that area. Come over here.'

Logan pushed through some branches and spotted Connor. He was following a trickle of water. 'I don't think this qualifies as a creek.'

'But I reckon that's an old Bloodwood.' He studied the stunted, rough-barked tree that seemed so out of place and supposed it could be. A few minutes later, he discovered Connor was right. 'Okay, now I know where we are.'

'We were lost?' Connor asked with a look over his shoulder.

'Not exactly.' Then when Connor's eyes widened, 'Not really … Okay, a little bit.'

Connor laughed out a sigh. 'Next question. Even if we do get through, what do you think you're going to do?'

'I just need to take a look,' Logan said. 'I won't do anything unless it's absolutely life and death, okay?'

'Assuming she's still alive.'

'Of course she's still alive!' He dragged in a breath and continued more reasonably. 'But as far as she's aware, no one even knows where she is. I don't want her doing something stupid thinking she's not going to be rescued. Shit.' He broke through some dense foliage and came to a stop at a wall of rock.

'Pretty little waterfall,' Connor commented, looking at the trickle of water pelting from it.

'That's unscalable,' Logan said needlessly. 'We need to cross over here, see what it's like up the other side a bit.' He held his breath as he negotiated a fallen tree over a steep drop into the shallow, rocky water below, swore when his foot slid off some rotten wood and nearly unbalanced him. 'Watch that green branch.'

On the other side, Connor shook his head. 'I'm not sure this looks any easier.'

'There's got to be a way round.'

They found one, but it cost them some time. 'This would be a lot easier if I wasn't carrying a shotgun,' Connor complained, resettling it on his shoulder.

'If we ever find this place, I think you'll be happy to have made the effort to bring it.'

'You want some water?' Connor offered.

'Yeah, thanks.' He stopped briefly and accepted the bottle. 'Can't be too much further.'

'I'm sorry she's a cop. I know you had feelings for her.'

Logan grinned. 'I can still have feelings for her. She's a cop, not a mass murderer.'

'I just meant the whole lying to you part.'

'Not many other ways to do something undercover is there?'

'You've changed your tune.'

'It's amazing how fast clarity hits when the woman you're in love with goes and puts her life in danger.' He put the lid back on the bottle and tossed it back. 'And, I have to say, thanks for doing this. I know she's not your favourite person.'

'Actually, I like her. More important, you love her. Enough said.'

Logan nodded. 'You want me to take the bag again for a while?'

'Nah. Let's go.'

They struggled through mud and clinging vines and dense foliage for another half hour before Logan spun and lifted a finger to his lips. They listened, heard two men talking, a laugh. Creeping closer, they got into a better position. Then they saw them. The canopy of trees was just as thick, but the undergrowth was cleared. Three rusting shipping containers, an open-sided tin shed. Three men were sitting around a camp table, smoking. All had radios and guns strapped to their belts. Three ... no, four women were at the front of the shed, working around large barrels, another was chained like a dog to the far shipping container.

'It's like a scene from a horror movie or something,' Connor whispered. 'Look at the state those women are in.' Another woman came out of the shed carrying buckets. 'That's Gretchen!' Connor hissed.

Logan hadn't even recognised her. 'I don't know the others. I can't see Indy or Caroline.'

'Could be in the back—wait—there.'

Indy came out of the shed with a plastic cup and moved towards the chained woman.

'Oi! What are you doing?' One of the guards got up and wandered towards her.

'Giving Jackie a drink.'

The guard knocked the cup from Indy's hand. 'Leave her alone and get back to work.'

Logan tensed as Indy stood, jaw clenched, staring at the cup. She picked it up and went back into the shed. A moment later she was back with the cup.

The guard, who'd just resumed his card game, got back to his feet with an expression of disbelief. 'What the fuck did I say!'

'If she dies before Bull gets here, do you think he'll be happy?' Indy snapped back. 'She's hypothermic and dehydrated. She was already weak to begin with. Think about it!'

'Let her have the fucking water,' another guard called out. 'And she can have the bitch's dinner too, she won't be getting any.'

The one near Indy laughed. 'How stupid are you?'

'Around you lot I feel quite bright, really.'

Logan saw the guard's fist curl and shook his head. 'I wish she would just shut up.'

But the guard returned his attention to the other men while Indy squatted in front of the chained woman. There was a short discussion and the woman curled up into a ball. Indy checked over her shoulder and placed a hand on the woman's ankle.

'What is she doing?' Connor whispered.

'Other than trying to get herself killed? Can't tell,' Logan said. Then Indy stood, slipped something into her pocket and walked away. The chained woman slid her ankle under her as she changed position in the dirt.

'Don't do it,' Connor whispered to Logan.

'Do what?'

'You're coiled like a snake.'

'We can take them—there's only three.'

'With radios and guns. And the dogs. Don't forget the dogs.'

'If we take them by surprise and shoot them they won't have a chance to use the radios or guns or dogs.'

'Man, you can't kill a mosquito without an attack of the guilts. Can you hear yourself?'

'I can if it means saving Indy.'

Connor sighed. 'This is stupid. Where are the police?'

'I should take a couple of photos of this place—send them to Ben so he knows it's down here.'

'You won't be able to send anything. You're not going to get reception down here in this jungle.'

The guard that had yelled at Indy pulled out his smokes and walked the line of women, checking on their work. Indy had gone back into the shed.

Connor shifted position to get a better look. 'What are you doing?' he asked Logan.

'Loading my gun. This is not going to be an easy wait.'

Indy went into the back of the shed to where Gretchen was waiting with three of the weaker Asian women. 'Did you do it?'

Gretchen rolled a spare barrel aside and showed her the hole they'd made in the dirt under the shed wall. It wasn't huge, but neither were the women. 'Are you really sure about this?' Gretchen asked.

'I'm sure.' She turned her attention to the other three and smiled reassuringly. 'Don't stop, just keep following the creek until you reach the river. I'll take care of the dogs, but if somehow they get out, get up a tree and wait for me. I *will* handle the guards, and I *will* find you. Understand?' One nodded, the other two looked uncertain. The first spoke to them quietly and quickly in Mandarin and they nodded rapidly.

Indy studied Gretchen's face. 'You ready?'

Gretchen took a deep breath. 'Okay.'

'Wait until Ainie and Bruno are out of the way. Then I'll see you out the front.' Indy took a couple of steadying breaths then walked out into the sunshine. She made eye contact with Ainie. She'd said she was in, but in case she wasn't, Indy had given her misleading information on what the other women were up to and where they were going. She would have felt a whole lot better had she had enough time to know everyone here before trying to pull this off. But Ainie smiled at Indy, then as planned, wandered towards the men and caught Bruno's eye.

Bruno smiled and got to his feet. Dropped his cards on the table. 'Back in a minute.'

As soon as the shipping container door swung closed, Gretchen approached the guards. 'Excuse me,' she began nervously. 'I want to know if I can swap containers? Mary's stealing all the dinner. I'm starving.'

'Am not!' Mary yelled out from her station.

'Yes you are! You took all the fruit last night.'

'Shut the fuck up!' Matteus said.

Diversion in place, Indy slipped into Ainie's shipping container. Bruno had his back to her, his hands all over Ainie on the bottom bunk. Indy carefully dragged the blanket back that was screwed up on the end of the opposite bunk. As she'd hoped, it revealed a football-sized rock.

'Hey,' she said.

Bruno let go of Ainie and spun around to sit up. Indy slammed the rock down on his head. There was a sickening thud. He slumped off the bunk and onto the floor.

Ainie stared wide-eyed at Bruno's prone figure and the gash the rock had left on his head. 'Ainie,' Indy said, swallowing back her own revulsion and getting her attention. 'You ready to get out of here?'

'Is he—'

'Nah, he'll live. Look here, at me. Good. As soon as you hear Mary scream, go out, get Jackie, keep going.' Indy bent down and took Bruno's gun, before looking Ainie in the eyes again. 'Ready?'

Ainie took a deep breath and straightened her clothes. 'I thought about telling. But I didn't. I hope we can trust you.'

Indy hoped so too. She peeked out of the container. The guards weren't watching so she slipped back out, gun shoved into the small of her back. She waved at Mary.

Mary muttered something Indy didn't catch, but Gretchen's 'You bitch!' was loud and clear. Mary screamed and suddenly, they were fighting.

'Hey—that's enough!' Matteus ordered. Gretchen dived on Mary, Mary got a fistful of hair. Indy grimaced. They were acting, but they were doing a super job of it. The men's attention was once again caught, so Indy gave the nod to the remaining women who were watching her carefully. They went into the shed. Ainie slipped away with Jackie. Heart in her throat, Indy hurried towards the dog pen, pulled the chewing gum from her pocket and jammed it in the lock, used a small piece of stick to wedge it up into the key space as far as possible, then broke the stick off inside it.

One dog leapt at her and snarled; the other growled, stayed back. Before she drew attention to herself, Indy prayed the job would be enough and hurried back to where she was supposed to be. She needn't have worried—the men were standing back, enjoying the show. She needed to get the two women out of the way. The men had positioned themselves behind them and she wouldn't be able to get two clear shots off without risking one or both of them. 'Hey!' she called out. 'Gretchen! Don't we have enough to deal with? Mary, get off her!' The women separated, made a show of giving each other one last shove.

Gunshots echoed in the distance. Indy's head whipped around towards the sound as Matteus and Manuel pulled out their guns. A radio started up and Matteus pulled it from his belt as Manuel grabbed Gretchen and put his gun to her head.

'It's cops!' Matteus announced. 'We need to pack this shit up.'

'Bullshit. We need to grab a girl each as leverage and take off.'

'Fine, but we deal with the rest first. Get your gun off her head and get them inside.' Matteus looked around. 'Fuck! Where are they?'

'Already in here!' Indy improvised. 'They were scared by the gunshots.' Was it Ben? She had to hope so. But the raid wasn't due for days. Had he somehow figured out she was here?

'Get in with 'em!' Matteus ordered, giving Mary a shove. Indy wanted to go for her gun, but there was one trained on her not four feet away. 'Move it!' Damn it—she'd just needed five more minutes. Five more minutes and she would have had this sorted.

Gretchen and Mary were watching Indy nervously. She knew what they were thinking. This was about to go very bad. She went for a reassuring smile, and scrambled for a solution.

'We need to do something,' Logan said.

'The cops are on their way.'

'Indy'll be dead by then.' Logan lined up his rifle and fired a shot at the far end of the shed. The sound of the bullet hitting the metal had the guards spinning and ducking.

As he repositioned, he saw Indy pull a gun from her back. 'What the hell …'

'Gretchen, Mary—get out of here!' Indy yelled. The two women scrambled around behind the shed and out of sight.

The guards recovered and turned their weapons on Indy. 'Let the dogs out!' one ordered the other, his gaze never leaving Indy. Logan's finger shook on the trigger of his gun. Indy looked steady as a rock, her eyes trained on the remaining guard.

The guard at the gate swore. 'It won't open!'

'Then go after the others! Shoot them!' He walked slowly around Indy, gun trained on her. 'We'll take the cop with us.'

'You think?' Indy dived left and rolled. Logan jolted as a bullet exploded in the dirt too close, but she came up firing. The guard ducked behind a barrel. Another shot, this one from the guard that had tried to release the dogs. Logan lowered his gun slightly. Fired. The bullet exploded at the back of his knee and he went down with a scream. 'The bigger they are …' Logan muttered.

Three shots in quick succession rang out in their direction. The big guy was behind the barrel.

'Give it up, Matteus!' Indy called out as she cautiously walked towards the barrel. 'Toss the gun away and stand up slowly.'

'Okay! All right!' Matteus's arm extended to the side, gun in his fingers as he got slowly to his feet. The gun dangled, threatened to fall, then as he got his feet under him he snatched it back and swung it around.

Two shots. Logan wasn't sure from what gun until he saw the stains appear on Matteus's chest. The man collapsed. Indy cautiously approached and kicked his gun away, pressed two fingers to his neck. She stared at him a second longer then looked around. Logan thought she was probably wondering where her back-up was, then she got up, moved towards the one still clutching his damaged leg. 'You're under arrest,' she began.

The third guard stumbled from the container. Blood dripped down one side of his face and a nasty-looking knife was clutched in his hand. Logan pushed through the foliage and charged. 'Don't do it!'

Her gun still on Manuel, Indy's head whipped around. 'Logan ... Connor ... what?'

The guard dropped the knife. Logan saw her eyes soften before sharpening. 'Was the gunfire up further from you?'

'Just the ones down here. Up there will be Ben,' Logan told her. He saw the relief.

'Thanks for playing interference. I don't suppose you'd be nice enough to go get them?'

'You won't live that long.' Kyle and Jules were standing at the top of the track. They were both puffing, but both armed. They started firing.

'Head for cover!' Indy ordered and dived into the shed, crawled behind a stack of bags of charcoal. Logan and Connor fell in behind her. Her gun was empty so she tossed it aside.

'Give me your rifle,' Indy said to Logan. Then to Connor, 'If you get a chance to shoot, shoot.'

'I can't shoot Jules!'

'That's okay, I can. You aim for Kyle.'

The look he gave her would have been comical under any other circumstance. 'Indy, don't!'

Indy set Logan's gun on the top of the stack and waited.

'I mean it, Indy. The police will be down here any second. Please.'

A bullet tore through one of the bags they were taking cover behind. 'Damn—I can't see them,' Indy whispered. 'How much ammo have you got?'

'Not much,' Logan admitted.

'We're outgunned.' She looked around. 'Cover me – the both of you.'

He shot a hand out and grabbed her arm. 'Don't be stupid! If anyone's going to kill you, it'll be me, later, stay put.'

She sent him a look that would have melted steel. 'I know how unfair it is to say this, but you need to trust me.'

He reluctantly softened his grip and she disappeared.

'You may as well come out,' Kyle called to them. 'It'll be less painful to die quickly than to be taken apart piece by piece. The cops aren't going to find you down here.'

'Jules,' Connor called out. 'This is not who you are. We need to talk.'

'Oh, we sure as hell do. Why don't you come out?' she called back.

They were getting closer, Logan could hear them, but he didn't dare lift his head to look. 'Keep her talking,' he whispered to Connor.

'Are you going to put the gun away?'

She laughed. 'Of all the things you are, you were never stupid. I'm going to enjoy doing you.'

'Why?' To Logan's mind he sounded broken.

'You killed our baby! Our child!'

'It was an accident! I was trying to stop you hurting yourself!'

'It was payback! You didn't think I should be using while I was pregnant. Too dangerous for the baby, you said. What a joke! You threw me down the stairs!'

'You fell! You wanted to get away from me and you stumbled. I couldn't catch you in time.' Connor risked a look around the bags.

'Connor, what are you—'

'Liar!' She fired several shots in rapid succession. Connor jerked, clutched at his shoulder.

Logan dragged him back. The sight of blood soaking into his shirt had him battling panic. 'How bad?'

'I don't know. I'm still breathing. Shit.'

'You need to get over this psycho,' Logan said, just for something to say. Connor was turning pasty white.

'She's your friend.'

'I have a feeling she hasn't been our friend for a very long time. Is she going to have to kill you before you believe that?'

'We need to move. Around behind that next pallet where Indy went.'

'I don't think you should.'

'Then you move.'

Logan thought about that. If he did go over there, he'd get a look at anyone who got too close to Connor. 'You stick your head out again, I'll have you committed the second I get you out of this. Got it?' Connor swallowed and nodded. 'Give me your gun. I'm sorry, in advance, but I'm gonna shoot whoever gets too close to you.'

Logan quietly slipped around behind the next lot of pallets. He got a look at Kyle, standing back a bit, scanning around them, but Jules was getting closer to the pallet Connor was leaning against. He lined her up. Hell, he couldn't do it. Could he? Where were the police? And where was Indy?

Indy squeezed out under the back of the shed, using the hole the other women had made to escape through. As quietly as she could, she made her way around to the front, paused behind the edge of the shed to take a careful look.

The gun was ripped from her hands as Kyle swung out from his spot against the inside wall of the shed. The wrench sent her stumbling backwards and she tripped on the edge of one of the bricks supporting a barrel of boiling water. She clipped the barrel, felt the burn of it as she crashed painfully to the ground, saw the end of Kyle's gun. Heart pounding, she threw herself sideways, dodged the bullet. Out of the corner of her eye she saw Logan spring out from behind a pallet of chemicals, firing at Kyle. As Kyle took cover behind another barrel, Jules stepped into view and fired back.

Kyle was on the ground, gun trained towards Logan.

No! Even as the thought of what she was doing chilled her, Indy bunched her legs together and shoved them as hard as she could against the barrel. It tipped, and one more desperate shove with her foot had it upending. Boiling water spewed out, drenching Kyle's prone figure. Kyle screamed and staggered to the creek, fell in. Indy jumped to her feet to avoid the splash back.

'You bitch!' Jules charged at Indy, firing.

'Drop it!' Ben and two other officers stood behind them, gun on Jules. 'It's over. Drop the gun.' Three cars came down the track behind him, lights flashing.

Jules looked from one gun pointed at her to the next, then dropped her gun and lifted her hands. An officer hurried in and cuffed her, while more moved towards Kyle.

Indy dropped to her knees, then to the ground in a combination of exhaustion and relief. She stared up at the sky, took several deep breaths.

'Hey.' Ben knelt and taking her arm, hoisted her up. 'You all right?'

She nodded, threw her arms around him and held on. 'Yeah.'

He returned the embrace. 'That was too close.'

'Connor's been shot and Kyle's burned—we need ambulances.'

'One's already here.'

She looked around and saw a paramedic heading towards Connor. 'You took your time, Bowden,' she said with a smile.

'Gretchen and Jackie found us, told us where to find you.'

'They were supposed to run away. The rest are following the creek.'

'We'll find them. You did good.'

'Thanks.' She spotted Logan staring at her, and smiled. But he turned and walked over to where a paramedic was treating Connor.

She went to join them. 'How is he?' she asked Logan as Connor was helped into the ambulance.

'He'll be fine. I'm going with him.'

'Okay, of course.'

'Indy—we need you over here,' Ben called out.

Indy offered Logan an apologetic smile. 'Sorry, I'll catch up with you as soon as I can.'

'No need. If the police want to talk to me, they can do it later.'

She watched him go, confused by the abrupt words. He'd come here to help her, so she'd assumed … Perhaps she shouldn't have assumed anything. He may have saved her life, but he hadn't forgiven her.

CHAPTER
27

'Indy!' Tess jumped out of the car and raced to give her a hug.

'Don't!' Indy put out an arm to stop her approach. 'I haven't had a shower for days.'

'Are you okay?' Tess asked, scanning Indy from head to toe. 'I was so worried. Connor and Logan told us what happened.'

'How's Connor?'

'Yeah, fine. He's being cleaned up and bandaged. Apparently, the bullet grazed him but didn't do any real damage.'

'I'm sorry I had to call you. Everyone's busy and there wasn't a car free to get me out of here.'

'Don't be silly. Once I knew Connor was okay, standing around the hospital was boring. Mum and Dad are there, and Logan. You need to go in?'

'Yes, please. I want to see Gretchen and the others.' She opened the car door, paused as she caught sight of Brenda through the window. Brenda caught sight of Tess and Indy, and dropped her gaze.

Tess looked miserable. 'I just can't believe it.' Her eyes welled with tears. She sniffed, huffed out a laugh. 'Sorry. I just keep doing this.'

'It's understandable,' Indy said gently.

'Is Jules in there?'

'Yes. She and the others will be transferred shortly, I'd say.'

'Did you get them all?'

'Everyone who was here.'

'Bull?' Tess asked.

'Still on the mainland as far as we know.' Indy closed her eyes and swayed just a little. 'I think I'll get in the car.'

'Of course—sorry. You should probably get checked out, too.'

'I'm fine, just tired and hungry.'

They got on the road and Indy closed her eyes. She needed a shower, some sleep—something to take the edge off. 'I haven't had a chance to ask how Logan and Connor found me.'

'To cut a very long story short, Logan discovered you hadn't left the way you were supposed to and called Ben. When Ben turned up, Mel came clean. She blurted out a lot of details to Logan and Connor before Ben could shut her up. Apparently she's been dropping hints and made sure Latisha was found, but she was worried what would happen to Bindi if she blabbed. Ben went off to organise what he was going to do, and Logan and Connor decided to find you, in case there was any trouble when the police turned up.'

'Where is Mel?'

'At the Maydena police station, I think.'

Indy knew the others were all being taken straight to Hobart. She wondered if Mel knew when Bull was due to arrive. Ben might not have had a chance to get that far with his questioning yet. 'Do you mind a quick stop-in? I want to ask her a couple of questions and make sure she's all right.'

The scowl returned to Tess's face. 'Why?'

'Tess,' Indy said quietly, 'Mel stuffed up, but she tried to fix it.'

'All right—I suppose I could call in. For you. But I don't think I can even look at Mel.'

A few minutes later Tess pulled over outside the small fibro building.

'Are you staying in the car?' Indy asked Tess.

'No. I changed my mind. I think I'll come in and glare at her.'

Indy got out and led them up the path to the front door. She pushed through—then backed quickly back out, forcing Tess out with her. 'Get back in the car.'

'Why? What's going on?'

'Tess—'

Instead of getting back, Tess stepped around her. 'Oh my God!'

The officer was sprawled on the ground, a gunshot wound to his chest. He lifted his head a centimetre off the floor. 'He's still in here!' he whispered desperately. Indy listened intently, but the building was completely silent. Eyes everywhere, she crouched beside the officer and took off her light sweater, put pressure on his chest. 'What happened?'

'Robinson came in, shot me. As soon as I was down another guy came through the door, took my weapons. They both went down to the cells. I heard another shot.'

'Robinson shot you?' *Of course!* Mark Robinson wasn't incompetent. He was on D'Angelo's payroll. 'Tess, do you have Ben's number?'

'No.'

'Give me your phone.' Indy took it and typed in a number, then handed it back to her. 'Get clear. Then tell Ben to get out here—now. With an ambulance and back-up.'

'What about you? Indy—'

'Now! Tess.'

Indy took the officer's hand and pressed it over the sweater to his wound. 'Help is coming,' she reassured him.

She crept across the small reception room, slipped behind the desk to the little hallway. She checked every room until she got to the one at the end. And came face to face with Bull. She quickly pressed herself back against the wall just outside the room.

'Oh, it's you Indy,' Bull said happily. 'What a nice surprise.'

She risked another quick look. He had a gun to Mel's head. Mel was a mess. Trembling and crying, she could barely hold herself up. On the floor, Robinson lay dead in a pool of his own blood.

'Let her go!' she called out.

'I guess I'll have to shoot her if you're going to make me come out there and find you. Why don't you come in and we'll talk about it?'

Indy took a deep breath and closed her eyes. She couldn't leave Mel; besides, if she did back away to wait for assistance, he might follow. Tess was out there somewhere. 'Okay! I'm coming in.' She held her hands palm out, slipped cautiously into the room. Bull backed up a step, his bulk behind Mel as he eyed Indy warily. 'Now you can let her go.'

'But she has to pay for what she's done,' he continued in that same, pleasant tone. 'There are rules, Indy. She talked.'

'I'd already figured it out. Nothing Mel did had anything to do with what happened today.' She glanced down at Mark, noticed his gun was still on him.

'Doesn't matter. Irony is, she wanted to help you. Now she's responsible for you coming right to me. The boss is not happy with you.'

'Boss? You mean D'Angelo?'

'You ruined his little operation down here.'

'Right, I did. You should let her go.'

His face closed into a scowl. 'Shut up. Rules are clear: you run away, you dob, you pay for it. So does your family. Why should this one get away with it?'

'Because it's me you want, right?'

'Oh, yes. I was gonna have some fun with this one.' He risked taking his eyes off Indy long enough to flick Mel a glance. 'But now you're here, you're right, she just doesn't seem that important.'

He fired, sent Mel careening back into a heap in the corner of the floor.

'No!' Indy lunged on Mark's gun and leapt back to her feet. Each had their weapon trained on the other. Mel was limp, blood seeping from the wound to her head.

'Now, now,' Bull said. 'We're talking, remember?'

'The time for that was before you shot Mel.'

'Oh, what do you care—do you have any idea how many women she's sentenced to slavery—death?'

'Because of coercion and threats. You killed her husband—her child's father.'

'Had to be done. Stroke of genius using the horse to take the blame, right?'

Mel made a noise, her body jerked. She wasn't dead. Bull frowned. 'Hmm. Losing my touch. I suppose if I take this gun off you to finish her you'll shoot me?'

'You're not quite as dumb as I thought you were. Go on, try it.'

He laughed as though he was having the time of his life. Sirens echoed somewhere still too far away. 'Well Indy, I'm going to have to go. I have something on I can't miss. I won't forget about you though.'

'You think I'm going to let you walk out of here?'

'You can chase me, of course. But Mel's dying. If you don't do something to stop all that bleeding she'll be gone before help arrives. Your decision.' He backed up, kicked open the back door, his gun levelled on her the whole time. Then he was gone. She wanted to go after him, desperately wanted to chase.

'Damn it!' Quickly she moved across the room to Mel, dropped down beside her. The wound was in and out on the right side of her head. *How are you still alive?* With shaking hands she gently applied pressure, was relieved to hear the sirens right outside. 'You're going to be all right, Mel,' she whispered with no idea whether she could hear her. 'Just hang in there.'

'She's a lucky lady,' the doctor told Indy. 'The bullet passed through a non-critical part of the brain and she arrived here still breathing and with good blood pressure. All these things are in her favour. The surgeon is removing part of her skull to allow the brain to swell without becoming compressed. If she makes it through surgery, we'll know more when she regains consciousness. Even then, we may not know for quite some time the extent of any permanent injury.'

'Thanks.'

Ben strode down the corridor towards her. 'Indy—how is she?'

'Alive, but it doesn't sound like we'll know too much more for a while.'

'You did the right thing.'

'You think?' She rubbed her tired eyes and stood up straighter. 'I had him, Ben. Right in front of me.'

'And you made a decision—the only decision you could have made and lived with.'

'Yeah but ... I didn't get him.'

'No. You just brought down a multi-million-dollar drug-running operation, freed several captives, solved the disappearances and murders of several women and incriminated a senator and a drug mogul we've been trying to bust for twenty years. That'll do for the time being.'

'You get my message about Robinson?'

'Yeah.'

'The bastard set the whole thing up. Right from the start.'

'There were some pretty large deposits sitting in his bank account. Funnily enough, the senator's got a few to explain, too.'

'Did you find Caroline?'

'Safe and well. She'd hitched a ride out with Mel, grabbed a taxi to the airport. It's possible Mark doctored the paperwork and the blood wasn't hers. We'll find out as the results come in.' He slung an arm across her shoulders and squeezed. 'Let's get you out of here.'

They walked back down the long corridor and saw Logan and Tess at the desk. 'What are they still doing here?'

'Tess wanted to wait to see you.'

Logan looked up, his features haggard. 'You're all right.'

'Yeah.' She wanted to step in, but his tone, his expression kept her feet where they were.

'Thank God!' Tess added. 'Are you okay?'

Indy nodded, closed her eyes and ran her fingers across them. When she opened them they were slightly more focused. 'I should have called, sorry. Um, it's Mel. She got shot. She's alive, but … we'll have to wait and see.'

Logan's cool expression became uncertain—she guessed he was deciding whether he wanted to see her or not.

'She's still in surgery.'

He sighed. 'Right. Not much we can do then.'

'So …' Tess said. 'What's next?'

'Hours of work for me,' Ben said. 'Indy, we'll have to follow up, but not yet. Go get some rest. You're absolutely shattered.'

'I have to help. I can't just walk away from this.'

'You can't be involved any further in this investigation. You know that.'

She did know that, and she hated that he was right. 'I get that. But I can't do anything else. This is all I can think about.'

'Understood. So, you'll write up your reports then take some time out until this is sorted.'

Her eyes narrowed in disbelief. 'You're forcing me to take leave?'

'No, you're taking leave because you know it's the right move to make. I still need to catch Bull, and you shouldn't be alone until he's caught. I'll organise for protective—'

'He said he had somewhere he needed to be,' she remembered.

'Then I'll assume he could be heading back up to the mainland. There's been an attempt on the drug dealer you arrested.'

'Brenda said Bull was going to be taking care of that.'

'And when he realises he's not going to be able to, and this has all died down, he'll be straight back after you.'

'Why would he come after Indy?' Tess asked.

'He may not,' Indy said. 'D'Angelo might decide he's too valuable to risk sending back after me. They're going to have to believe I'm going to be difficult to reach for a while.'

'And so you should be,' Ben told her.

She thought about all the time she spent in protective custody as a teenager. 'I know what you're thinking,' she told Ben, 'and you know me better than that. I'm not going to sit around under protection somewhere until he turns up again, hoping you catch him before I lose my mind. I want to stay here, at least for the time being—see how Mel goes. And I'd like to see Gretchen, and Mary and Jackie—and make sure the others have access to the support they need to get home or assistance over here. I can do that, I can get everything underway.'

'She can stay with us,' Tess said to Ben.

'You want to follow up on the women's welfare?' Ben asked Indy.

'I promised them I would.' Indy's gaze flicked nervously to Logan. He hadn't said a word. 'But I'm not sure staying out at Calico Mountain is the best idea. I don't expect your family to put me up, Tess. And if Bull does turn up, I don't want to put any of you at risk.'

If anything, Logan's expression became even more remote.

'Nonsense. Where else would you stay?' Tess looked offended. 'Ben said you need keeping an eye on, and we can do that.'

'Yes, but ...' She looked at Logan, let her sentence trail off. It was up to him. She wouldn't push. Wouldn't expect.

'You got your pack?' he asked eventually.

'It's probably still at Hilltop with the other women's belongings,' Ben said, then turned to Indy. 'I'll send it over with a couple of armed officers, have them hang around for the night while we get a better idea of Bull's movements.'

Tiredness sat at the back of her eyes; the emotional punch of the last few days threatened to flatten her. *Just for tonight*, she promised, then she'd find something else. And she realised she hadn't even asked, 'Is Connor still here?'

'Yeah. All bandaged up,' Tess said. 'I'd feel better driving Mum and Dad back with Connor. They're pretty upset. Logan can take you back in my car.'

She wished she could read what was going on behind Logan's eyes. She stared into them for several moments. Eventually she dropped her gaze, turned it on Ben. 'Thanks.'

'I'll talk to you tomorrow,' Ben promised. 'We'll get everything sorted out.'

Logan shot a quick, sideways glance at Indy as they walked out into the carpark. Her face was grim, her gaze straight ahead as they headed for Tess's car. He'd felt absolutely gutted when she'd gone into Ben's arms out at Hilltop. He'd desperately wanted to hold on to her. And he'd been a few seconds too late.

Was there anything to sort out between them? Or now that she was back to being Detective Indiana O'Meara, did she have a whole other life, other ... lover, she was ready to get back to? He wouldn't have thought it was possible for Indy to start something with him if she was involved with someone else. Not the Indy he thought he knew. But then he didn't really know her at all. Did he?

She stopped at the car and waited for him to unlock it. And out in the daylight, without the pressure of conversation and well-meaning friends and the uncertainty of whether he was ever going to see her again, he got a better look. She was completely washed out and her eyes were suspiciously damp and darkly shadowed. A reflection of the hell she'd just been through.

And all he'd been worried about was his feelings? The urge to walk around the car and wrap his arms around her was almost over-whelming. Instead he opened the car door, then changed his mind and slammed the door closed again. 'Indy, was it all ... was any of it ... was it ever just you?'

She rested an elbow on the car, dropped her forehead into the heel of her hand and closed her eyes. 'I don't know how to answer that.' Then those tired, bloodshot blue eyes opened and settled on his. 'It was always me. And I was always working.'

'Always?'

'Logan, I came here not knowing any of you and it didn't mat-ter: didn't matter what you thought, didn't matter that I lied by omission. That's my job. But then I got to know you. And to know that you're all good people that I liked and respected. But I couldn't break cover. I couldn't tell you even after we ... I knew there was a chance you'd kick me out—I wouldn't have blamed you. And I couldn't take that chance. I was making progress. If it were your daughter, your sister, your family that had been taken—you'd want to know. You'd need answers. I needed to get those answers.'

Logan thought about that. *Liked and respected? After we* ... She couldn't even say it. She had given him an answer but it wasn't an answer. Not to what mattered. So he sighed. 'Fair enough.' And got in the car.

He didn't speak again, and Indy didn't seem to have anything else to say, so they travelled back in silence. When he dropped her back at the bunkhouse she climbed out. Hesitated before closing the door. 'I'm sorry.'

'For what part?'

The question seemed to surprise her. 'For not being able to be honest with you. And I'm grateful, that even though I lied to you, you still did what you did today. Thank you.'

He supposed they both needed time to think things over. And she was worn out, so though he wanted to push, he didn't. 'Have you eaten anything?'

'Yeah, I had a sub at the hospital café.'

'Get some rest then.' He drove away slowly, watched in the rear-vision mirror as her gaze dropped to the ground. Head down, she just stood there, was still standing there when he rounded the bend that put her out of sight. Was she regretting coming back? They'd have to talk. Later. But would there be a later? She had a life, a career, elsewhere. If she was going back to that, what was the point?

CHAPTER
28

Indy dragged herself up the steps to the bunkhouse and let herself into her room. She still had no clothes so she walked out again, over to the guesthouse, borrowed a towel and a guest robe and some of the pretty little toiletries stocked for the guests, and brought them back. By the time she'd showered, dropped her ruined clothes into the washing machine in case her others didn't show up, and fallen on the bed, she was already three parts asleep.

She woke early. Her head felt like a heavy lump of concrete and every muscle ached. She was cold—she hadn't even gotten into bed. She considered crawling in, resting longer, but her internal alarm had gone off and she knew there'd be no more sleep. Besides, Monte would be wanting his breakfast. She dragged herself up. Yawned and tentatively stretched. Grimaced. She'd have another shower. Make it hot, and … Her pack was sitting against the wall near her door. Someone had brought it in while she was sleeping.

Well, at least she had clothes. She hadn't taken her others out of the machine before falling asleep the night before. Now she could throw them away.

Logan was already at the stables when she got there, dropping hay from the loft. 'Morning,' she said tentatively.

He jumped down. 'What are you doing?' That remote look was back again.

'Feeding Monte and the lambs.'

He lifted a bale and took it into the feed room, came back for another. 'You don't need to worry—I've got the new girl doing it.'

Ouch. 'New girl?'

'Larissa. She started just after you disappeared.'

'Okay, but I want to do it myself.'

'You're not employed by Calico Mountain anymore.'

She frowned, hurt. 'Logan, I don't expect to be paid for feeding Monte.'

'Lucky.'

And her temper started to fray. 'Can I please just give the babies their breakfast?'

He picked up the last bale of hay and put it with the others. 'You need to rest, recover, remember?'

She followed him into the feed room to argue, but there was a feminine 'Logan?' and he slipped past her back into the breezeway. 'Morning Larissa. Let's get these horses ready.'

'You bet. Has Rosalie been down yet?'

'Not yet, and we've got an extra for the ride, think you can go bring in Gypsy?'

'Sure.'

Battling tears, Indy called herself an idiot for feeling hurt, and—damn Logan and his 'rest and recover'—mixed the bottles.

The babies, at least, were happy to see her. Monte came over noisily, rubbed his head on her, sniffed around for his bottle while the lambs drank. 'Sorry buddy. Almost done here ...'

She stroked him as he drank his milk, smiled into the big dark eyes that were so concentrated on his task. 'Missed you, little man.' She heard the clip-clop of hooves as a horse was led in, smiled as friendly a smile as she could muster at the figure that appeared at the door. 'Hi.'

'Hi, who are you?'

Indy studied the girl that looked no more than sixteen or seventeen—the pigtails didn't help. She probably thought they looked cute. 'Larissa, right?'

'Yes.'

'Larissa, I'm Indy. Nice to meet you. I used to work here.' She hoped the girl would go away. She wasn't in the mood for small talk.

'Oh, right. Nice to meet you too, but did Logan give you permission to feed Monte?'

'Not exactly,' Indy said truthfully, 'but—'

'Then you shouldn't be in there.'

She clenched her teeth and breathed in and out. 'It's fine,' Indy said.

'No, it's not! You need to stop.' Larissa came into the stable. 'Monte's my calf to look after.'

The comment tipped the scales on her already fragile temper. 'Larissa, other than for the last few days while I was busily attempting to liberate slaves from a high-stakes drug operation, I've been feeding this calf his entire short life. I found him in the paddock, taught him to drink from the bottle and named him myself.' Her voice took on a very definite threat. 'Due to those less-than-comfortable

few days, I'm feeling a little out of sorts, and right now I'm prepared
to fight to the death to give *my* calf his breakfast.'

Suddenly much less sure of herself, Larissa studied Indy with
a mix of suspicion and apprehension. 'You need to give me that
bottle or I'm telling—'

'You should also probably know,' Indy cut in just to seal it, 'that
while I was on my little adventure, I successfully took out a couple
of really big, really mean men. I smashed one over the head with a
block of granite and shot another one dead with a real gun. So, you
need to ask yourself, are you sure you want to argue about this?'

Larissa backed away. 'Logan? Logan! There's some weird woman
in the stable feeding Monte. I think she just threatened to kill me.'

There were footsteps, a loud sigh from somewhere in the breezeway. 'I'll deal with Indy. You take the horses out. Tie them in the
yard ready for the guests.'

'Okay.'

Logan appeared at the stable door. 'So what form of execution
did you have in mind for the petrified nineteen-year-old?'

'Nineteen, huh? The pigtails threw me.' Monte finished his bottle and she gave him a cuddle. 'Regardless, she did as she was told.
There was no need for violence.' She wasn't sure if she saw a smirk
but she did notice the way he rubbed his fingers up and down his
forehead. 'Headache?' she asked innocently.

'I need to keep staff, Indy. I don't have enough help right now
as it is.'

'So I'll help.' She closed the distance between them and when he
opened the stable door, stepped out past him.

He shook his head with a 'whatever', and walked into the tack room.

What did she expect? Logan had every right to be mad. But
she couldn't stay and keep taking these slaps. She'd just physically
threatened a teenager and was ready to lose it with Logan.

Rosalie walked in. 'Morning!'

Indy sucked in a breath and swore silently, pulled herself together as best she could. 'Hi, Rosalie.' Waiting for the next slap, she gave Rosalie a chance to have her say.

'You've done the babies? Wonderful. It's good of you to help. I bet you missed little Monte.'

'Take your life in your hands trying to keep her away,' Logan muttered as he walked back past them.

Indy's gaze followed him out before dropping. She forced a smile onto her face before looking back up. 'I'll get out of your way.'

Rosalie held her up by placing a hand on her arm. 'He was very worried about you when you went missing.'

'I have the impression he wishes I'd stayed missing. But thanks.' Indy washed out the bottles, and was surprised to see Rosalie still waiting when she finished.

'It was a shock to find out who you are, to find out about all of it—to lose Jules and Mel, to find out people we trusted could betray us so badly. We're all a bit at sixes and sevens, probably will be until we've all got our heads around it. But I want to thank you for everything you did.'

'You're thanking me when I thought you'd be angry.'

'You risked your life to rescue those girls, saved Connor's. And you gave Logan the benefit of the doubt when everyone else had him guilty. You're welcome to stay here as long as you need a place to be. You don't need to worry about Murph or me holding a grudge. Tess said you're following up with those poor women.'

'Thank you. But I don't think I should—'

'Have you seen Monte's new yard?' Rosalie cut in. 'With everything going on, Logan hasn't had a chance to introduce him to it yet.'

'Huh? Oh, yes, I walked past the new yards. They're really coming along.'

'Well, the old shelter is now a proper lock-up stable so we'll leave these three together for the time being and they'll be all snuggly and warm as toast. We should take them over there.'

Indy blinked in surprise. 'Now?'

'Why not?'

'Ah ...' She looked over her shoulder and noticed Logan saddling horses. 'Sure. Okay.'

Quite a few guests were heading towards the stables for the morning ride. They stopped to meet and pat the calf and two little lambs bouncing around behind Indy and Rosalie as they made their way up the drive towards their new home, and the trip took longer than expected.

'You see how popular this is?' Rosalie said with satisfaction. 'They're crowd-stoppers.'

When they finally reached the gate, Indy led them through. The pretty post-and-rail fenced yard was reinforced to stop animals getting out and children getting in, and the lovely old twisted jacaranda tree, which Indy had often admired, shaded a corner by the impressive new stable. Monte sniffed around, not moving too far from Indy's legs, so she sat on the thick grass and encouraged him to investigate. Rosalie sat beside her, sighed happily as the lambs crawled all over her. 'How lovely is this? Logan's done a wonderful job.'

'He has. And I don't think he minded quite as much as he made out.'

Rosalie tipped her head to look at Indy. 'You're the reason for it. You know that, don't you?'

Indy swallowed back a fresh surge of hurt. 'Because I found Monte.'

'No. Because there's not a thing in this world he wouldn't do for you. He loves you.'

The words weren't easy to hear, because she knew she'd ruined it. She dropped her head. 'He might have,' she said, staring at the grass, 'but not anymore.'

'He's just hurt,' Rosalie said gently. 'He's hurt that his father could do that to his mother—to those girls and their families. He's hurt that Mel and Jules have been lying to him, allowing him to take the blame. He's hurt that you were put in danger because of it. But he got over you being a police officer the second he found out you were in danger. All he wanted to do was get out there and get you back safely. You should know, he's never really taken to anyone before this. There's never been a you before.'

Indy's brow furrowed as she tried to make sense of that. 'I don't understand.'

Rosalie stared at the sky, still changing colours with the sunrise. 'I was worried for him, in my heart, because I thought it might have had something to do with him being abandoned as a child. He was such a sad little boy for so long. I think that's where the love of animals came from. He couldn't stand for anything to be lost or alone. If it needed someone to care for it, Logan was it.'

The image squeezed at her heart. 'It must have been very difficult for everyone.'

'I couldn't fix it for him. He stood at the door every day for so long, waiting for them to come back. It was heartbreaking. And I couldn't even offer him any hope, because I knew, deep down, Bull had killed her.' Rosalie stroked one of the lambs when it hopped into her lap. 'And this beautiful, kind little boy grew up into a man I'm proud to have had a hand in raising. But he never quite settled. And then in you walked. And I thought, *maybe. Just maybe.*' Rosalie's hand covered Indy's and squeezed. 'I know I shouldn't interfere, but if you love him, don't be too quick to give up on him. Okay? Don't leave just yet. Let him get his head around it all.' She patted Indy's hand and got to her feet. 'Oh, and I'm cooking a big roast dinner at my place tonight. After everything that's gone on, I want my family to myself for an evening. You'll come.'

'But I'm not family.'

Rosalie brushed herself off and sent Indy a friendly yet authoritative look. 'I'll expect you around seven.'

Because Larissa was at the stables and Indy didn't really need to be, she drove to Hobart to check on the case and the women. But everything was under control. She was able to speak to Ainie, who was going home to Malaysia; some of the others were staying. She went to the hospital—Mel was stable but not awake, and Gretchen had already been discharged, as had Mary. Jackie was happy to see her but her family were there and Indy didn't want to stay and intrude.

The police officer that had been shot, Senior Constable Jarred Denham, was recovering. He was a nice guy and full of thanks, so she spent some time talking to him, but after a while, feeling as unnecessary at the hospital as she had at Calico Mountain, she went back to Calico Mountain to work on her reports.

After two hours of writing reports, she was stir crazy. She wanted to do something physical, but wasn't sure what to do except go back to the stables—where she wasn't exactly welcome. She thought about what Rosalie had said and wondered whether it was better to stay out of Logan's way, or in it.

'Stuff it.' She went back to the stables, pulled Aurora out of the paddock and brought her in to groom. Larissa walked out of the feed room when she heard the horse come in, hesitated in the doorway when she saw Indy leading her.

'Um … right.'

'Larissa wait,' Indy called when the girl all but ran in the other direction. She tied Aurora and walked around her. 'I'm sorry about earlier. I really wasn't feeling myself.'

'That's okay,' Larissa replied slowly. 'Logan kind of explained a bit to me. And I shouldn't have snapped about Monte. It's just that Logan drilled into me hard how important that calf is and how I have to get everything exactly right. I think he really loves him. So I was worried.'

Indy's heart squeezed, warmed that Logan had gone to those lengths to make sure Monte was okay. 'I appreciate you being so careful. I love the little guy too.'

'It's those big eyes, right?' Larissa said, suddenly more relaxed. Then with a curious stare, 'Are you hanging around? I've heard so many bits and pieces about what's been going on. What you said this morning ... can you tell me what happened?'

'Sure, why not?' Indy breezed through some of the general details while she groomed Aurora. Larissa was a nice kid, talkative, and between the light conversation and the familiar work, Indy was soon feeling more relaxed than she had in days.

She was just about finished when Logan walked into the breeze-way leading Rex.

'I thought you'd left,' he said.

'I went to check on the case.'

He walked Rex into his stable and undid the halter, gave him a pat. 'Fair enough.' He closed the stable. 'All done, Larissa?'

'Yeah, I was just talking to Indy.'

'You're friends now? You can head off. Thanks for today.'

'No worries.' Then to Indy, 'Maybe we can ... Will you be at dinner?'

Indy remembered Rosalie's invitation. 'Ah, probably not tonight.' She glanced at Logan. 'I'll see how it goes.'

'See you tomorrow then.' Larissa gave Indy a smile and a wave and walked out.

'Looks like you've got a fan,' Logan commented.

'She's nice.'

He nodded at his boots. 'Rosie said she invited you to dinner.'

'But … you'd prefer I didn't come. Right?'

He scowled. 'Indy, do whatever you like.'

When he turned to walk away she dumped the brush she'd been using on Aurora into the tack box with a bang. 'When you risked your life to come and get me, you told me the only person who was going to kill me was going to be you. So what are you doing, making it as slow and painful as possible?'

His head dropped back before he turned to face her. 'My mother turned up dead, my father is apparently some sort of psychotic murdering bastard for hire, one of my closest friends is in custody for supporting a woman-stealing international drug operation and trying to kill my best friend … and the woman I thought I was in love with turns out to be an undercover cop sent in to investigate me. Yeah, I came to get you, of course I did! But you're not the only one having a difficult week, Indy. Maybe I'm not ready to talk about it yet.'

'Fine. *Maybe*, I'll just get out of your way then.' She scooped up the grooming kit to return it to the tack room. When she went to walk out, he blocked her exit.

'I'm gathering that smart mouth wasn't part of your cover.'

She noticed he was looking her in the eye for a change, so she resisted the urge to snap back and answered truthfully. 'I was supposed to be meek and mild.'

The laugh broke from Logan's lips so fast he almost choked on it. 'Guess whoever issued that order doesn't know you very well.'

'It was Ben, and he knows me better than anyone.'

His gaze snapped back to hers. 'Yeah, Ben. And he's … what exactly?'

She frowned at the sharpness of his voice. 'My friend.'

'I thought you two might have been a couple.'

She stared at him in disbelief. 'What? How could I have—'

'How could you have … what?' His gaze went from sharp to very, very intense.

'So … we're ready to discuss this now?'

She felt his energy pull back. 'You're leaving soon, going back to whatever life you led to be whoever you really are.' His tone was once again cool. 'What's the point?'

Indy fed the lambs and Monte in their new enclosure and hurried back to the stables to wash the bottles out. She wasn't particularly looking forward to dinner at Rosalie and Murphy's. She was emotionally on edge and sitting near Logan at the table and eating, trying to pretend everything was all right, when it wasn't, wasn't going to be easy.

Two boys aged about nine and twelve were in the breezeway when she walked in. They'd been talking rapidly but stopped when they saw her. Rex's door was open. An uneasy feeling washed over her. 'Boys?'

'Uh-oh,' one said and glanced at the other one.

'We didn't mean it!' the older one said. 'We just wanted to pat him.'

Shit. 'Where did he go?'

The smaller one pointed out the back. 'He stopped by the paddock with those horses in it and he was acting up real bad. We tried to shoo him away from the fence and he ran off up the track.'

She wasn't surprised Rex had stopped at the mare paddock; she just wished he'd stayed there. On the trail he could go for miles. She grabbed his halter and lead rope then dug out her phone and pressed Logan's number, handed it to the boys. 'Tell Logan Rex is loose and Indy has gone to find him on the south trail. Will you do that?'

'Yes.'

'Okay.' The older one put his ear to the phone as Indy jogged towards the trail. It was nearly dark but she hoped Rex hadn't strayed too far from the other horses. He wasn't near the mares, so she kept going, and the further she went, the darker it got and the less convinced she was she was going to find him. Where was he? And why hadn't Logan turned up?

She stopped near an old gum tree, unsure whether to keep going or turn back. No, she wasn't leaving Rex out. What if he was in trouble? He could get lost up here in the dark. Or hurt. This horse meant too much to Logan to be careless with. Logan had drilled Larissa hard over Monte's welfare. He'd made sure he was all right. The least she could do was get his favourite horse home in one piece.

The sounds of dogs barking had her turning her head to listen. Wild dogs? It sounded close. Then she heard a squeal. Rex. 'Okay, okay …' She picked up a fallen branch and headed after the noise. If dogs had Rex bailed up, he must be injured. Would wild dogs attack a person? Logan had said they avoided people. She veered off onto a smaller track, then pushed through some scrub that had already been partially bulldozed by what must have been Rex. She grimaced as a branch scratched her face and paused to listen when the dogs suddenly stopped barking. The silence was absolute. Then a fresh commotion broke out to her left. A large black dog stood about ten feet away, hyper alert and barking madly. Another one came up behind it, joined the noise.

'Get lost!' Heart in her throat, she threw a rock into the scrub and waved the branch. The dogs scattered, disappeared.

Another noise, trampling, sent her in a bit further and she saw Rex. 'Hi, mate,' she crooned quietly.

Rex angled himself around to face her, then snorted when she approached. 'Okay mate, I need your best behaviour. What's wrong?' She kept talking as she approached, tried to see. It wasn't until she got close that she realised his back legs were completely tangled in the boundary fence.

She laid a hand on him cautiously, jolted at another sharp snort. 'Well you're not getting yourself out of that, are you?' She wasn't sure who was eyeing who with the most distrust but she dropped the branch and slipped the halter on.

She tried to detach his rug from the barbed wire. It was stuck in too many places, got caught in more as she tried to free it. Rex stumbled on the spot, alarmed by her fiddling, but too trapped to get anywhere. He was damaging his legs the more he tried to free himself. 'Right, this is not going to work.' She undid the chest strap, got a hand behind his rump and got the leg straps undone. 'I'm just going to slide this … off.' She did, and laid it over the fence, leaving it caught. 'Now your legs,' she soothed. 'And just so we're clear, when you do get a foot free, don't go sending it anywhere near my head or I'm not helping you. Got it?' She ran a hand along his side and down towards his back leg. 'Okay. Here we go.'

Abrasions and a couple of nastier lacerations marred his hind legs, and a small amount of swelling bulged against the tight wire. She held the very end of the lead rope between her knees and worked with both hands. She picked up his hoof, manipulated the wire around his leg with difficulty and wished for bolt cutters. 'Sorry mate, take it easy …' She got the first one free, placed the heavy hoof down, then walked around the other side, repeated the process. It was so damn tight on this leg she had to back him up into the fence, try again. And it was getting harder to see. The wire dug into her fingers as she tried to untwist it and just when she almost had him out, Rex wrenched his hoof back, tightened it again. 'Not helping …' she muttered.

When she finally got him out of it she took a moment, rolled her shoulders and wriggled her sore fingers. It was time to go. She looked around, found the spot where she was pretty sure she'd come in from.

It wasn't until she'd been walking several minutes that she decided it hadn't taken her this long to come in off the main trail. She stopped and tried to see. Had she somehow veered off? Rex stomped an impatient leg and began to paw at the ground. Everything looked different in the dark.

Something crashed through the bushes, startling Rex. He fought the lead rope. She almost let go, and was dragged a couple of feet before she found some traction. 'Please, Rex. Be good,' she pleaded. 'I have to get you back to your dad. If you run off again ...'

Another snapping sound and more rustling bushes had horse and handler spinning around. She heard panting, a low growl. Indy's heart leapt into her throat. The dogs were back.

CHAPTER

29

Logan sat on his back verandah nursing what was left of his beer. Indy was right, they needed to talk, but he hadn't been lying when he told her he wasn't ready for the conversation. There was no point hiding from the fact that he was petrified. If he got it wrong, there'd be no going back, and he hadn't got his head around exactly what it was he intended on saying, or how. Hearing that Ben was a friend, not a lover, had gone a long way towards making him feel better—after he'd finished feeling like a low-life from the look on her face when he'd thrown the question at her—but even if she felt the way he hoped she did, could he ask her to stay? Because he wanted her to stay—no, damn it—he *needed* her to stay. And all he was doing by delaying the conversation was pushing her away.

Was it fair to ask her to walk away from her life to explore what they'd begun? Would she even want to? What would he do, if she asked him to leave his life behind? It wasn't an easy question to answer. He loved her. Would that be enough?

And he couldn't shake the other issue—the one that shouldn't matter but did. His father was a murderer. A cold-blooded killer. He was about to bury the mother he'd only known for three short years because of Bull. Could Indy look past that, ignore the blood ties?

He checked his phone. Nearly seven. He was due at Rosie's. Indy would be there. Perhaps he'd ask her back after. He couldn't write a damn speech, so he'd just have to wing it, hope he could come up with the right words.

He got up with a sigh and went inside, tidied up. The house wasn't too bad, but if he managed to convince her to come back for that talk, he wanted it tidy. By the time he got himself over to Rosie and Murph's, he was late, but Indy wasn't there. He walked into Rosie's kitchen, gave her a peck on the cheek, made a comment about how good dinner smelled. And looked around, just in case.

'She hasn't arrived yet,' Rosie said, reading his mind. 'Why don't you go out the back with Tess and Connor. Murphy's just grabbing a nice bottle of wine from the guesthouse.'

'Okay.' Tess and Connor were sitting at the outdoor table. It was decorated with the stuff Rosie only used on special occasions. He sat down next to Tess, eyed Connor's bandaged arm. Connor was sipping a glass of water and nodded in greeting, his eyes shadowed and his mouth a grim line.

'How's the arm?'

'It's been better.'

'How are you?'

Connor shrugged with his good shoulder. 'All right.'

He knew Connor would find a way to blame himself—take some of the guilt from Jules. 'That's good to hear. Because I had this idea in my head you'd somehow go deciding this was all your fault.'

'She blamed me for the accident. And the drugs—she was already so dependent on them. The addiction on top of the depression she fell into made her an easy target for Kyle. I believe what she said, that it started out simple and she just got in way over her head—'

'Oh bullshit,' Tess interrupted. 'What Jules did, Jules is responsible for! We loved her, we all did, but don't make her out to be a saint. She was always the risk taker—always in the middle of trouble. Add drugs to the equation? It was bound to end in disaster. And in hindsight, maybe the drugs explain why she could never settle at anything. She told everyone she was flitting from job to job apprenticing to get experience, but the truth was every time she got a job somewhere, she got sick of it, messed it up and moved on. She did exactly the same thing to your relationship. Got sick of it, messed it up and moved on. Add to that she always had an eye for Kyle even when she was with you—I'm sorry but it's true. I'm sure she was seeing him in Sydney. I want to slap the bitch.'

'She's your best friend,' Connor reminded her with a frown.

Tess shifted in her chair to more fully face him, her expression livid. 'Connor, I've got to hand it to you, when you love someone, you just don't give up on them. You're loyal to a fault. Jules was my best friend when we were kids, and for most of the growing-up part. She was even my friend when she came back from Sydney to work here and you two got together. You never told anyone she was having substance abuse problems or that she got pregnant, and neither did she. Maybe if one of you had, things wouldn't have turned out this way. We'll never know. But she walked back in here this time for the sole purpose of ruining Logan's life and ending Indy's, just to score points with some drug-dealing arsehole. She is not my best friend. She's a cold, twisted, deceitful bitch and I hope she gets everything that's coming to her.' She huffed, turned to Logan. 'I'm just glad Indy's okay. Where is she, anyway? I thought you might have been off with her somewhere.'

'Why?'

'Because you weren't here and neither is she.'

'I don't know where she is. Rosie said they moved Monte and the lambs over to their new home this morning. She could be over there.' But he frowned. It was dark and she knew she was supposed to be here.

'Mum said they caused quite a stir with the guests.'

'Apparently.'

'Logan,' Rosalie said from the door. 'Murphy's back with some guests. They need to see you.'

'What? Why would he bring them here?'

'Not sure but he said it's important.'

Logan pushed to his feet and hurried through the house.

'Sorry Logan,' Murphy said. 'But Mr Malloy and his sons came into the guesthouse looking for someone from the stables. When I heard the story, I thought it would save time to bring them to you.'

'Hi,' Logan greeted the man and the two boys. 'What's up?'

'I'm sorry about this ...' Mr Malloy looked at his children, frowned. 'These two have something to say to you.'

The older one kicked at the floor, was prodded by his father. 'We're sorry.'

'What are you talking about?'

'We were supposed to find you, tell you the horse was out,' the smaller of the two piped up.

'What horse?'

'The big gold-coloured one with the white mane. We just wanted to pat him.'

'Just now?' He really didn't need something else to deal with.

'No ... ages ago. He ran off up the trail behind the paddock full of horses and ... Indy? Told us to tell you. But you didn't answer your phone and we couldn't find you. Here's her phone back.'

'Rex is not back,' Murphy said. 'I checked on the way over here.'

Logan took the phone, his head starting to spin as he put it together. 'What time was that?'

'About six, I'd say,' Malloy said.

His gut lurched. Where was she?

'Thanks for letting us know,' Rosalie said when Logan remained lost in thought. 'We'll sort this out. Have a lovely evening.'

The three loaded back into their car and drove away. Logan ran a hand over his face as anxiety clawed at him. 'She can't handle Rex. She should be back. What's he done to her?'

'She probably just can't find him,' Tess said from behind him. But she was already heading for her car. 'I'll get a quad, head up the way she would have gone.'

'Or she's gotten herself lost in the dark,' Connor said. 'I'll head up, too.'

'You're injured,' Logan reminded him.

'I'll drive the ute. I can manage that one-handed.'

'Be careful,' Logan warned, and looked at Tess. 'I'll cut into the main trail from my place. If she's followed Rex far enough in, they might end up on that one.'

'Make sure everyone has their phones,' Rosalie ordered. 'And be careful. Logan, you know Indy can take good care of herself. I'm sure Rex will be fine, too.'

'I don't care if he's broken his damn neck—as long as he hasn't broken Indy's!'

'Logan,' Tess said calmly, 'We'll find her.'

He knew Tess was right to stay calm. Indy was probably fine. But his stomach was twisting with worry. 'I just got her back, Tess. I can't lose her again.'

So much for wild dogs keeping their distance. Indy was pretty sure there were at least four pacing, tracking, running around them.

She crouched down occasionally for more stones and threw them in the direction of the sounds, and as any direction was better than standing still, hurried along the trail, soothing the nervous stallion as she moved as quickly as she could on the uneven ground. Cold and tired, she desperately needed a breather but she didn't dare stop.

Rex suddenly jerked on the lead and propped, squealed and kicked out. There was a thump closely followed by the sharp cries of an injured animal. Swallowing back panic, she swung round and round again. The dogs weren't giving up. She couldn't outrun them, couldn't see them. What could she do?

She almost fell over the fallen tree that partially blocked their path as she turned around again to keep the horse moving. It scraped at her knee and nearly sent her toppling. She grimaced and rubbed it as she thought about what to do. She had no idea how much further she was from civilisation. Didn't know whether she was heading towards it or further away. What had Logan said to her the first time she'd been going to come out here ... A horse would find its way back?

She eyed Rex critically. Would he take her home? Or kill her? 'Rex, I know what I'm asking, all right?' She climbed onto the tree, hesitated. 'You just remember who made you all those feeds and kept your stable clean.' She took a deep breath and threw a leg over his back, propelled herself on. 'Please be good, please be good ...' He jogged sideways and she lost her balance, gripped his mane and accidentally grabbed on too hard with her legs. He shot forward, almost sending her over his rump before a tug on the lead turned him in a circle to a halt. Indy got herself off his neck and back into the proper position, her legs shaking. Riding bareback was a very different proposition to sitting in a comfy saddle with stirrups. 'Let's try that again.' He jogged off again and again she turned him.

A light swung past them, an engine purred. But the light was scattered through thick foliage and no clear path pointed in that direction. She called out but it had already passed. They must be looking for her. The knowledge helped calm her nerves and she tried again.

She might have missed whoever it was but the engine, the light, seemed to have discouraged the dogs. Rex quietened as they pressed on, settled into a steady walk.

She heard another engine, a quad. She was frustrated she couldn't get close enough to flag anyone down, but too scared to get off Rex in case she couldn't get back on.

The trek seemed to go forever. At one point she realised they were back on one of the main trails, but as she had no hope of getting her bearings and Rex had got them this far, she left him alone to keep going his way. The rhythmical pace of the horse was hypnotic and had it not been for the bone-deep ache of her muscles, her eyelids might have drooped closed.

Then he stopped. Indy lifted her head. They'd reached an area of cleared land and there was light in the distance. Logan's place. She realised Rex had stopped at a closed gate so she sank down over his neck and slid stiffly to the ground. She led him through the gate, through Logan's back paddock. The gratitude she felt to the horse almost had her in tears as she wearily hugged his neck. 'You did it. Thanks, mate. You're in for some spoiling.' Once in Logan's stables, she found the light and put him in a clean box. His rug was on the railing so she threw it over him then moved to the hay room, grabbed him a biscuit of lucerne. The routine was ingrained, and she wanted to make sure he was all right.

She walked to the house where a light illuminated Logan's front verandah, but when she banged at the door no one answered. She tried the knob, it turned. The door was, as usual, unlocked. She almost fell inside, the relief was so great. As soon as she found the phone, she called the guesthouse. It was late; the office would be closed but maybe there'd be an extension she could call. She didn't know Logan's mobile number by memory. But the phone was answered.

'Rosalie?'

'Indy! Where are you?'

'I found Rex, but it got dark and I got a bit lost. Rex brought me to Logan's.'

'Does Logan know?'

'No. No one's here.'

'That's because everyone's looking for you. Logan's out of his mind. I'll let him know you're okay.'

'Thanks.'

Out of his mind? That was a nice thought. She hung up and sank into a chair. Closed her eyes.

The sound of the door flying open startled her awake. Logan's frame filled it. 'You're all right. Damn it, Indy, I was terrified!'

'Logan, I'm sorry, I—'

He was already across the room and pulling her roughly into his arms. 'Why did you go after him?'

'I wanted to make sure he didn't get lost or hurt.'

He drew her back far enough to frown at her. 'He's just a horse! You're irreplaceable.'

You're irreplaceable. He'd said it, but had he meant it? She stepped back, walked a few steps away and hugged her arms around herself, missing his warmth. 'Rex was so good. There were dogs. God, the dogs. A pack of them. Give me armed men any day. But those things ...' She shuddered. 'I put Rex in one of the stables. He has a blanket on, and some hay. I gave him some lucerne.' She wasn't sure why she had to get it out, the routine of it, but it helped with the frayed nerves. 'You have to check his legs. He was caught in the fence when I found him. Hell, I forgot. He let me ride him with cut legs.'

Logan stared in disbelief. 'You untangled Rex's legs from a fence and rode him to my house bareback in the dark?'

'I didn't know where we were and the dogs wouldn't leave us alone. You'd said horses can find their way home ... Would you just go check on him?'

'Okay, I'll check. But let's check you out first.'

She lifted her hands to stop him. 'No—I'm fine. Honestly. Just check Rex.'

He studied her a moment longer before agreeing. 'Okay, put the kettle on, rest, I'll be back.'

Logan got outside and took some long, deep breaths. He'd been terrified, true, but he hadn't meant to take it out on Indy. He couldn't get his head around it. He knew Rex wasn't responsible for Matty's death, but he still wasn't the easiest to handle. Indy had freed him from a fence and ridden him home bareback with a halter, being stalked by a pack of dogs in the dark. And all just a couple of days after the other drama. He shook his head. She blew him away. He'd just wanted to hold her, but she'd pulled away.

He supposed he couldn't blame her for that.

Rex was eating his hay, shifting his weight from one back leg to the other. Logan grimaced when he saw the damage the wire had done, wasn't surprised the horse was uncomfortable. 'Hey boy. Let me fix that up.' He went into the stable and ran a hand over the horse's neck. 'I owe you, mate. I really owe you. Let's look at these legs.'

He looked after Rex, and when he came back in, Indy met him at the door and handed him a tea. 'How is he?' she asked.

'He's done a bit of a job on himself. I've cleaned up the cuts and got some cold boots on him for the swelling, given him an anti-inflammatory. I'll have to go back out there soon and take the boots off for a while.' He took her hand and led her back to the lounge. 'Sit down and tell me what happened.'

She did, and when she'd finished his stomach was in knots. 'I've never known wild dogs to be so aggressive. They must have already been stirred up from Rex being caught. Perhaps the darkness made them braver, or they were just a large, hungry pack. I'll have to coordinate with the National Parks to get rid of them.' He gently brushed the hair from her face. 'Thank you for what you did.'

'I couldn't leave him there.'

'You've had a hell of a week.'

'I'm pretty tired,' she admitted and got up. 'Could I get a lift back to the bunkhouse?'

'Don't leave.' He hadn't meant to say it out loud. Could have kicked himself when her eyes went from tired to confused, a little annoyed.

'You won't talk to me, yet you're asking me to stay?'

He stepped in slowly to gauge her reaction, and when she didn't move away, lifted a hand to her cheek. 'I'm sorry. Of course I'll talk to you. I was going to, tonight. I just haven't quite been able to figure out a way to say what I want to.'

She considered that for a moment, then dropped her gaze. Looked almost nervous. 'Before you do, I should explain to you about Ben. I know what you thought but it wasn't like that. But this isn't easy to talk about.'

He was guessing as she sat back down and wasn't making eye contact, that whatever it was probably wasn't good. So he sat and waited. 'Okay.'

'My entire family were murdered when I was seventeen. I was angry … lost. Ben … got me through a really bad time. Made sure I was okay. There's nothing romantic between us. Never has been.'

He got to his feet and paced up and back a couple of times because he didn't think he'd be able to sit still. 'Would you tell me what happened?'

Her gaze dropped away again. 'I just did.'

'Indy—'

'I don't want to talk about it!'

He caught the pain in her voice so he sat beside her and, taking a chance, wrapped his arms around her. She tensed as though about to get up, then slowly relaxed against him. They sat there like that for several minutes. He didn't push, just waited, and eventually she spoke.

'I'd been out with my friends. It was my seventeenth birthday and I'd been to the movies—had to get home because I knew my family had prepared a special dinner. Lilly had just got back from Australia and she and I were going to go do something after— just us. We hadn't really had a proper chance to catch up. Pop had bought me a car, a Mustang—I'd always wanted one to do up. That's what we did. Pop's specialty was taking old wrecks and restoring them. We were going to do the Mustang together.

'When I got home I went straight to the shed. I knew he'd be down there. I didn't know he'd be dead.' She rested her head against him. 'He'd been shot. So had Lilly. Pop in the chest, Lilly in the face.' He tightened his arms at the hitch of her breath. 'I just kind of stared. I can't remember feeling anything, I don't even remember moving but I ended up at the house. Mum and Gran were lying in all this blood on the lino floor. The decorations were all up for my party. They'd made me a Happy Birthday banner.'

Logan's forehead dropped to hers. 'Oh hell, Indy. I'm sorry.'

'I went into protective custody for a few months until they found the guy that did it. He wasn't much older than me and wanted to steal our television. He got high before he broke in and lost the plot. Ended up deciding it would be cool to kill everyone. I was seventeen-and-a-half and the police were talking foster care. I took off.

'I didn't have much money because our place owed a lot to the bank and there were so many bills after it all happened. And I hated everyone. I was so mad. I got in with a bad group of teens and started stealing, got into a bit of trouble on the street and needed to get away so I scammed enough for a plane ticket to Australia. I knew I could get dual citizenship because my parents were Australian, and I figured any place was better than where I was.'

'Then what?'

'Then I got off in Sydney and broke into a corner store for dinner. A cop happened to be there, busted me. He gave me a lecture and a meal at Macca's.' She looked up, smiled. 'That was Ben.'

'The detective?'

She nodded. 'He made sure I had what I needed to stay out of trouble.'

'And you became a cop, too.'

'The only way I could think to stop being self-destructive was to do something to help the hurt. I couldn't bring my family back but I thought that maybe if I could help someone else's ... and it did help—does. Every time I catch the bad guy it helps. Probably sounds pretty corny.'

'Not to me.'

'And now I have a chance to get the guy that started all this. I need Bull behind bars.'

'Agreed.' He gently stroked her cheek. 'You're exhausted.'

'And you still haven't told me what you were going to say.'

'Will "I love you" cover it for now?'

She smiled and his heart took a huge sigh of relief. 'It's not a bad start.'

He kissed her gently, and she returned it, built on it, and the kiss slowly became more urgent. He traced a line of kisses down her throat as he drew her to her feet. 'Please stay.'

'Okay.' She wrapped herself around him and he carried her to the bedroom.

CHAPTER
30

Indy woke up to the sun pouring through Logan's bedroom window. She smiled, stretched, because technically this was the second time she'd woken up that morning. The first time had been the most enjoyable morning wake-up she'd ever had. She turned her head to see Logan missing. After driving her insane that morning, he'd pulled her into his arms and stroked her hair until she'd gone back to sleep. Then he must have gotten up to make a start at the stables.

She got herself ready for the day and hurried to the stables to mix the bottles. The babies would be starving. She was almost there when she ran into Rosalie.

'All done,' Rosalie told her. 'I called Logan to see how you were and he mentioned you were having a bit of a sleep-in, so I came down and fed Monte, too.'

Because Rosalie's eyes were dancing, Indy chewed on a smile, not exactly embarrassed, more ... self-conscious. 'Right, thanks for that.'

Rosalie placed a hand on Indy's arm and squeezed. 'I'm glad you worked things out with Logan.'

Her smiled widened. 'Thanks, so am I. And thanks for what you told me. It made a difference.' She continued to the stables, the smile still in place, and found Logan in the office. He was on the phone—feed delivery—so she came in behind him and slipped her arms around his neck. He lifted his head from the phone, kissed her, went back to talking.

'You didn't wake me,' she said when he ended the call.

'Thought you might like a sleep-in.' He spun his chair around, dragged her onto his lap. Kissed her properly. 'Rosie fed the baby animals.'

'I know. I ran into her.'

He smiled. 'She likes you.'

'I'm a pretty likeable person.'

He ran his hands up and down her ribcage. 'I feel like I need to get to know you all over again.'

She shook her head, smiled softly. 'You know me. I could never lie to you when it came to what mattered between us.'

'I know. And no more secrets, either. There's something I need to do today. With you.'

Her smile turned wicked. 'Again?'

He chuckled low in his throat, 'And again, and again,' he said, nibbling on her throat, 'but other than that.'

'Oh yeah? What?'

They drove up to Rosalie and Murphy's place with Brandy drooling in Logan's ear, and two puppies climbing all over Indy's lap. Logan had sent Connor a message and he had Murphy out the front with Rosalie and Tess when they pulled up.

'Here we go,' he said under his breath.

Indy patted his leg. 'This is a good thing you're doing.'

'I hope so.' He got out of the car.

'What's going on—what have you got in there?' Murphy asked.

Logan coaxed Brandy out by the rope around her neck and lots of verbal encouragement. Indy allowed the pups to scamper out, trusting they wouldn't stray too far from their mother, and climbed out.

Murphy stared at Brandy, his frown deepening as recognition hit but understanding was slower to follow. 'It can't be.'

'I hope to hell it is,' Logan replied lightly.

'Brandy?' Murphy crouched and studied the dog again. 'Brandy.'

Brandy's ears went up and her tail wagged nervously. She took a few hesitant steps towards him.

'Come here, girl. Come here, Brandy.'

She slunk in, licking ferociously at his hands and face. Murphy laughed, looked up at Logan with tears in his eyes. 'How'd you find her?'

'She wasn't too far away. Had this couple of little ones with her.' The pups in question were busily demolishing Logan's boots, but stopped to bound over to their mother and sniff at Murphy.

'I don't know what to say. I just don't know what to say. Hello, girl. Oh, it's good to see you again. Didn't think I ever would.' He swiped at his eyes, took the rope from Logan. 'Thank you. Thanks. I should get her inside, feed her up. Rosie, we'll need to get some dog food. Look at these pups! They'll have to stay. Let's get them in so I can get this rope off her.' Murphy coaxed Brandy and the pups up onto the verandah and inside the house.

With tears in her eyes, Rosalie put a hand on Logan's shoulder and kissed his cheek. 'Well done.' Then she followed her husband inside.

'Guess we've got dogs again,' Connor commented.

'I like the little red one,' Tess said. 'I might go have a play.'

Logan threw an arm across Indy's shoulders. 'You want to go in?'

'Do you?'

'Maybe later. I'm thinking Murph should have some time with his dogs.'

'What?' she asked when he frowned.

'I probably should have told Ned to come over, too.'

'Why?'

'He's been going out there for me when I couldn't. He'll be pleased to see the dogs here.'

That explained a few things, Indy concluded. 'Maybe let him know.'

'I will.' He sent her a contemplative look. 'You like flowers?'

'Flowers?'

'You know what they are, right?'

She laughed. 'Sure. You just threw me with the question.'

'Jump in,' he said. 'We'll saddle up, go for a ride, I'll show you some flowers.'

It was tempting, but her legs were still sore from her ride on Rex. 'I suppose it couldn't possibly make my thigh muscles any worse. As long as it's not bareback.'

'I'll let you use a saddle. And ... as you're brave enough to ride Rex, we should get you up on Aurora.'

Her enthusiasm increased. 'Really?'

'Yeah.' He kissed her and started the ute. 'Let's go.'

They rode along a long winding trail to the mountains, climbed higher and higher. On the other side, the land beneath them was filled with colour, from palest pink to yellow, white and vivid orange, covering the ground as far as the eye could see. Logan reined in and Indy copied him, stopping beside him.

'It's beautiful.'

'I don't know why they always grow best here, but they do. How's Rory going for you?'

'Fantastic.'

'You want to go for a canter?'

Indy's eyes sparkled. 'Are you kidding? You said I couldn't.'

'I changed my mind. After you.'

'Let's go, Rory.' She pushed the horse forward, wobbled a little in the transition. Logan came up beside her, reminded her what to do. She found her balance, and the horse stretched out. Just a little faster ...

'Be careful,' Logan warned her, but his grin was enormous as he kept pace. Indy laughed. 'I love it! It's like flying!'

'Lean forward.'

She did, and the horse picked up speed again. They galloped side by side on a long, winding trail, through the flowers, towards more mountains, and when eventually they reined in, Logan jumped off his horse and dragged her down into his arms.

Breathless from the ride, buzzing from the exhilaration, she pressed her mouth against his, wrapped herself around him. When he eventually lifted his head, his expression had her heart somersaulting in her chest. 'If I'd known all you needed was a fast ride ...'

'I like fast rides,' she murmured, pulling his mouth back to hers.

They made love on a soft blanket of mossy ground, with the horses grazing lazily against a backdrop of flowers, as the sun gently warmed the earth around them. *Perfect*, Indy thought, *just perfect*. Her head tipped back and her gaze moved to the blue of the sky as Logan sent her body soaring. This was worth everything. Every hurt, every trial, had brought her here. To Logan. Her heart filled with him, and she turned into his body, held on. 'I love you.'

It was getting late when they reached the stables. They dismounted and washed down the horses. 'I'll put these two back out in the paddock while you mix up the bottles,' Logan offered.

'Thanks.' She fed Rory a peppermint and handed the lead to Logan. Got a quick kiss. Smiling, she hummed to herself as she prepared the bottles. She gave them one last shake as she stepped out into the breezeway. Once the babies were fed, they'd—

Bang! She cried out as the pain sent her into the stable wall, almost knocked her over. The bottles fell from her fingers as, in shock, she looked down, saw the blood soaking through her jeans at about mid-thigh. The wound looked like a bullet hole. Her gaze swung around, landed on the figure at the end of the breezeway. *Bull.*

Far behind him on the drive, two young girls stalled in their walk, then went running. *They'll get help,* Indy thought. *They're running for help.*

Clutching at her leg, she swallowed down the pain and tried to think.

'Sorry about that,' Bull said jovially. 'Didn't want you running off again.'

She gritted her teeth, dragged in two deep breaths, tested her leg with some weight. It was like bearing down on broken glass. Choking back a sob, she limped around to fully face him.

'I told you I'd be back. How've you been, Indy?'

She looked around for a weapon—anything. There was a hoof pick in the tack box, a broom nearby. Not much good against a gun. She backed up, mind racing. 'Give up, Indy. There's nowhere to go.'

Logan walked into the breezeway. 'Hello, *Dad.*' His voice was low and full of threat. The look in his eyes was deadly.

Bull laughed. 'Well, well. If it's not the whore's kid.' He shook his head at his private joke. 'Hello, Logan. But I'm sorry to say I was never your dad. Why do you think I killed your bitch of a mother?'

Logan's face went blank. 'What?'

'We had one argument and she went running back to Atherton. She got pregnant all right. But you're all his.'

'Murphy Atherton's my father?'

'Funny thing is, he doesn't know it. I'm not even sure your mother did. One silly doctor's appointment and I sure as hell knew. Now you do too. Won't live to tell him though.'

Logan was white, but no less aggressive. 'You have no idea how happy you've just made me. Get your gun off her. Now.'

'Back the fuck up. I'll shoot you too, you little prick.' After another glance at Indy he said, 'In a minute.' He turned his gun back on her. Instead of backing off, Logan launched himself at Bull.

Indy's breath stopped. He was unarmed, completely exposed. What was he doing?

'Shit—can't wait your fucking turn ...' Bull threw the gun around at Logan and fired. The bullet hit Logan in the stomach. Indy screamed. Logan barely flinched.

'You bastard, you think I'm going to let you kill her?'

'I don't think you're going to have a lot of say in the matter.' Bull levelled the gun again.

Ignoring the pain in her leg, Indy snatched up the hoof pick and dived on Bull, just as he got another shot off on Logan. This time the bullet hit him in the chest. Logan doubled over, straightened, kept coming. The hoof pick buried itself in the base of Bull's neck. Bull collapsed.

Logan stumbled to the floor, slouched against the stable wall, face pale and beaded with perspiration. Indy fell down beside him. 'No ... no. Why! Why did you do that? Logan!'

'He had you.'

Her whole body was shaking, while tears fell freely down her face. Her own wound forgotten she frantically assessed Logan's, pressed her hands against them. 'You're bleeding, you're bleeding. There's so much blood. God. I can't stop it. I can't—no! Not again. I can't ...'

His eyes closed, opened slowly. 'Hey.'

'What?' She kept her unsteady hands pressed over the wounds, looked up at the hoarsely spoken word.

'He's getting up. You need to stop him.'

She shot a look over her shoulder. Bull had pulled the pick from his back and was dragging himself back to his feet.

'I can't,' she sobbed. 'I can't do it.'

'Yes, you can.'

'If I let go you'll ...' She dropped her head to her chest and closed her eyes as the world spun wildly. The weakness, the pain, the fear, disabled her. She saw her sister, her pop, her mother, her grandmother. Then she opened her eyes and saw Logan. It was too much. 'I'm done. I just want to stay with you. I don't care.'

'Don't you dare give up. Of course you care.' He looked past her, then somehow he got her head in his hands and dragged her face up to his. 'He's coming. Get up. Get up, Indy, and fight back.'

A shuffle of footsteps behind her had her closing her eyes, prepared for whatever came next. 'Shall I finish him off first, Indy? Be kinder. Look at him.'

The tears wouldn't stop, blurred her vision. She pressed her lips on Logan's, her heart breaking. 'I love you.' She saw him nod—encouragement—but the life was fading from his eyes.

'Do you believe in an afterlife, Indy? Nice thought, I suppose, that in a moment you'll be heading there together.'

The pain she felt couldn't be survivable. On top of it, hate blew through her; an overwhelming, emotional force that had her face twisting into a reflection of the grief and rage that consumed her. 'Don't expect me to visit you in hell.'

She let go of the man she loved and fought, knocking the gun from its aim, sending the bullet wide. She struck again, again, again. He got some in, but they didn't register; neither did the fact that she was dragging one leg, could barely see. It didn't matter. This man was going to hurt. He was going to die.

Not even the flashing lights, the shouts, the general chaos of armed men descending on them made enough of a dent in her consciousness to slow her down. Not until Bull was on the ground, lifeless, and two hands gently pried her away, did she realise anyone else was even there. She screamed, fought to be released. She wasn't done.

'Indy. That's enough.' Ben's voice. Where had he come from?

'I want him dead!'

'I know. But you need to stop. Indy. You're hurt. Stop.'

Her breath caught in her throat, became sobs. 'Logan.'

'I'm sorry, hon.'

'No.' She tore away from Ben, dropped to Logan's side. A paramedic had his fingers at Logan's throat, was shaking his head while another ceased compressions. A police officer sat back on his heels, released the pressure to the wounds.

Indy's head swam, and her heart shattered into pieces. 'Ben.'

Ben's head swivelled towards the officer and paramedics. 'Get him on that ambulance! Don't you dare give up!'

As the darkness welled up, the fight drained out of her. She wanted to come back. Couldn't.

The beeping of a machine was annoying. It kept pulling her more and more insistently from the warm fuzzy darkness that surrounded her. One hand was a little cold, the other warmly engulfed in another's. Reluctantly, because the light hurt her head, she opened her eyes and focused in on Ben.

That was enough to bring it all back. And her heart exploded all over again. It must have shown on her face because Ben was on his feet. 'He's alive,' he said, squeezing her hand. 'Indy, he's alive.'

'Where?' Her voice sounded like a chainsaw.

'He's in surgery.'

She tried to speak, barely croaked. 'Water.'

A nurse handed her a glass with a straw. 'Just a little sip.'

She tried to sit up—what was wrong with her? 'I need to see him.'

'Go easy,' Ben told her. 'You're in recovery. The bullet in your leg didn't go through, it had to be removed surgically. You can't get up yet.'

'Logan's alive?'

She didn't like the look on Ben's face, but he nodded. 'He's lost a lot of blood and there are some serious internal injuries. He's been in surgery a long time. But I was given an update a few minutes ago to say he was still with us.'

'Did I kill Bull?'

Ben wiped the hair from her face and shook his head. 'No,' then with a small smile, 'You didn't do him a lot of good though.'

She looked around, noticed other beds, other patients. 'How did you know? Why did you all come?'

'We caught D'Angelo. He told us Bull was headed back out to Hilltop. His instructions were to burn the place to the ground. Apparently there's stuff hidden in the house we haven't found and they didn't want us to. We took three cars and an ambulance, guessing he wouldn't come quietly, but he wasn't there. Then we got a call about screaming and gunshots at Calico Mountain. It wasn't hard to figure out what was going on. I brought everyone.'

'Thank you.'

He sat back down. 'We've shut them down, Indy.'

'And now you've got Bull.'

'And now we've got Bull. You did a hell of a job.'

'So did you.' Her brow furrowed with worry. 'Logan—I thought he was dead.'

'Technically he was. And I won't lie, it's not good. But I have a feeling if anyone's stubborn enough to pull through, it'll be that guy.'

'He came in unarmed, with nothing to defend himself. He charged at Bull, took two bullets. He did that for me.'

'I know. He's a good guy.'

'I love him.'

'I got that. Want me to see if I can find anything out?'

'Please.'

But for the second time that day, she sank into unconsciousness.

CHAPTER
31

'Hey, Indy!'

Indy spotted Larissa coming towards the arena at a jog, and trotted Aurora over to the gate. 'What's happened?'

Puffing, Larissa dropped her hands to her knees to catch her breath. 'The piglets are out. I can't get 'em. They were headed towards the dam.'

'Again? Right.' She dismounted and handed the reins to Larissa. 'Take care of her, I'll go get them.'

'With pleasure. Little buggers think it's a great game running me around in circles.'

'I'm on it.' She went into the feed room and put some pellets in a bucket. In the week since they'd arrived, Ham and Bacon had escaped on at least six occasions. It was becoming routine.

She hurried down the road towards the dam behind the yards. 'Let's go boys!' She shook the bucket, rattling the contents until two very wet, muddy pigs bounced out of the long grass. They raced around her on short little legs, then took off snorting and squealing, beating her back to their feed bin. 'Let's see what you've destroyed this time … mm hm. This wire's not strong enough to stop you pushing through it.' Monte mooed at her from the next yard and came to the fence to sniff at her head as she bent over the fence. 'Hi, buddy. You were never this much trouble, were you?'

'You wanted them.'

She smiled, hearing Logan behind her. 'Because no one else did. That was the plan right? Take the ones that needed somewhere to go?'

'That was part of the plan, yeah.' He bent down beside her and used the pliers he'd brought with him to tighten the wire, then re-clipped the mesh to it. 'That should hold them … for five minutes.'

'If we're lucky,' Indy agreed. 'What was the other part of the plan?'

He turned and wedged her gently against the gate. 'I was hoping to keep you, too.'

She ran her hands up to link them around his neck. 'It seems to be working. It's been five months and I haven't left yet.'

'And you've almost used up all your leave.'

'Then I'll have to work on earning some more.'

He nodded slowly as he thought about that. 'I guess you love being a detective.'

'It has its moments. Since my family were murdered, it's the only purpose I've had.' She smiled up at him. 'That's changed.'

'Are you going back to Sydney?'

She'd been wondering about that herself. Was hoping she wouldn't have to. 'That's where I live.'

'Yeah but, I've got enough to do without looking after piglets.'

A smile stretched across her face. 'I suppose so.'

'And you started this whole farmyard thing.' He rubbed his lips over hers, nibbled at them. 'How am I supposed to fit all that in?'

'It's not going to be easy,' she mumbled against his mouth.

He lifted his head just enough to look at her. 'And if my truck breaks down?'

'The machinery around here has never been in better shape.'

He winced dramatically. 'And you know, I've got these bullet holes that are still slowing me down.'

A laugh gurgled from her throat. 'Not sure what you expected would happen when you charged unarmed at a psychopath with a loaded gun.'

He returned her smile. 'And there's also the other thing.'

'Other thing?'

He ran his fingers through her hair then took her head in his hands. 'I love you. And if I have to live in Sydney too, things are really going to get out of hand around here. The commute's going to be a killer.'

Floored, she stared. 'You'd do that? But this is your home. You'd hate it in Sydney.'

'How could I hate it if you were there?'

'Logan ...'

'You want to know why I charged at Bull unarmed? Because I saw him point that gun at you and in my head I saw him fire. And I imagined you gone. And that one, split-second thought hurt more than those bullets. It hurt more than anything.'

She closed her eyes and leant her forehead against his chin. 'And when I thought he'd killed you I wanted to die too.' She laughed a little. 'I'm not an emotional person. I don't talk like this. Since you, every second thought through my head has been a damn Hallmark quote.'

There was the beep of a horn as Murphy drove past and waved. Indy waved back. 'I like your new dad a lot better than the old one.'

Logan smiled at the passing car. 'So do I. They took it well.'

'They love you. So do I.'

His expression was suddenly serious. 'Enough to stay?'

She pursed her lips in consideration even as her eyes shone with mischief. 'What's your offer?'

'Come with me.' He took her hand and led her out of the yard.

'Where are we going?'

'The kind of offer I have in mind shouldn't be presented to you in a pig pen.' He kept going, kept towing her along, past the stables, to the back paddocks that stretched out and became bush and mountains. 'The first day you came to Calico Mountain you sat here.' He caught her by the waist and lifted her onto the fence. 'You asked me if I wanted something and I told you I wasn't sure I'd figured that out.'

'That's some memory.'

His hands lingered at her waist as he stood in front of her, head tipped back enough to keep that warm stare of his pinned on her. 'I remember it because I lied. I knew exactly what I wanted.'

Her brow lifted. 'You lied?'

'The night of the campdraft, when you took Mason's horse off him, I had an idea of what I thought I might have wanted. Then the next day, when I got a proper look at you, I had an even better idea.'

'Hmmm.' Her voice trembled with amusement. 'How shallow.'

He shrugged but smiled back. 'And then you turned up at Calico Mountain and you thought I was actually going to let you walk out?'

'Ben made me promise I'd leave if there were any doubts about my identity.'

'Yet you stayed.'

'I never was very good at taking orders.'

His gaze dropped then, and she lost sight of his face under his hat. 'I'm not going to lie and say your job doesn't worry me.' He looked back up, his expression serious. 'But I'll deal with it, if you'll let me.'

'Let you? What are you asking for?'

He took her down from the fence and put his hands on each side of her face. 'I'm asking for you. I want you to stay here. I want you to marry me. I want us to have a family. I want all of it. But I'm willing to negotiate on all of those wants. Right now, I'm just asking for you, and for whatever that brings with it.'

Love flooded through her, along with a happiness she hadn't been sure she'd ever get to feel. 'You've already got me. And I want to stay here, I want you to marry me, I want us to have a family. I want all of it, too. I don't want to give up my job, not yet, so I'll apply for a transfer. But if I marry you, if we have a family, I won't do any more undercover work, I won't put myself in those sorts of situations. I didn't have anything to lose before. I do now.'

She saw everything she was feeling reflected in his eyes as he bent to kiss her. After a moment, Aurora nudged him in the back, stepped up to put her head between them. With a sigh, he gently pushed her back. 'I think your horse is happy you're staying, too.'

'*My* horse?'

'From the moment you rescued her.'

A shout caught their attention. 'Indy! Piglets are out again!'

'And *my* piglets,' Indy groaned.

Logan threw an arm across her shoulders and pressed his lips to her temple. 'You still want the Shetland pony and the alpaca?'

ACKNOWLEDGEMENTS

There are always so many people to thank. I could write a short story on who you all are and how you've contributed. I'm so grateful to every single one of you.

Of course, a big thank you goes to my readers, especially those who asked for Indy's story.

I'd like to give a special mention to one of those readers, Meredith Gillie, a winner of a copy of my previous book who just happened (spookily) to live in the same area *Bloodtree River* was set. Thanks so much Meredith for all the inside local knowledge you helped me put into this book.

To Tangil and Fred Kinch, there are no words. Thank you for being available to answer my silly police questions and work through endless criminal scenarios, over and over and over and over ...

To my amazing friends Tea Cooper and Ann B Harrison, who take time out from writing their own bestselling books to labour through the pages of my first drafts, and for too many other reasons to list.

To Kathryn Coughran, a very special editor, author and friend who knows how to come to the rescue.

To my family, for somehow ensuring most of the general household chaos held off just long enough.

As always, thank you to the whole sensational team at Harlequin. A special thanks to the fabulous Jo Mackay for all your hard work and support, and for being so much fun to work with. Also, Annabel Blay—who can somehow make me laugh even when she's sending me more work to do (and because she's super good at author bios!).

To the truly awesome editor Alex Craig, whose input went a long way to making this book the best it could be. Thank you!

And last but far from least, to Kate Cuthbert, because I owe you, times many, and to Kate's genuinely lovely mum, Gwen, for reminding me of that xx.

Turn over for a sneak peek.

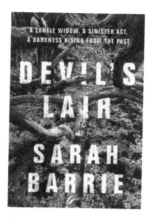

DEVIL'S
LAIR

by

SARAH
BARRIE

Available July 2019

FICTION

CHAPTER

1

Hunter Valley, New South Wales, 2017

Callie leaned against the solid warmth of her husband and sipped her coffee. From the back deck they looked over the sparkling pool to the long, neat rows of vines and the sun rising over the lush green mountains beyond their estate. Birds sang their first songs of the day in the blue gums that dotted the grounds, while the sweet scent of daphne caught on the warming breeze. Dale rested his head against hers. Callie could feel her eyelids drooping as the tranquillity seeped into her, even as the coffee slid down her throat.

'Quiet day today?' Dale murmured.

'Yeah. You?'

'Not so much.' He played with a curl of her hair, letting it slide through his fingers. 'How did I end up with such a beautiful wife?'

She lifted a hand and tucked the auburn curl back behind her ear. 'What do you want?' she said with a laugh.

He smiled against her forehead. 'Do you think you could update the prices on the wine catalogue for me? It needs to go out.'

She contemplated the request, took another sip of her coffee. 'Sure. Do you think you could bring one of those 2008 vintage merlots back after work to fix the headache it's going to give me?'

He chuckled. 'Deal. We're a pretty great team, you and I.'

'I think so.' Rosellas flocked to the grass by the property gates, catching her eye and reminding her, 'I think I want to put in another garden bed where that tumble of rocks sits near the front gate. It could look really great with the right plantings.'

'I was going to take them away with the backhoe.'

'You've been going to do that for the last five years.'

'Things keep getting in the way.'

She tipped her head back to smile at him. 'Right. So, I should plant it out.'

'You can take the girl out of landscaping, but you can't take the landscaping out of the girl.'

'I don't think that makes sense.'

'I think you're right. Go ahead. It'll look spectacular.'

'Great.'

'Paisley's back today, right?'

'Yeah. Should be. If she's managed to tear herself away from Tassie.'

'It's a nice part of the world.'

'Maybe we should find time to zip down there one of these days. You could show me where you grew up,' she suggested.

'I think we've got enough to do, don't you?' Dale asked.

As though in agreement, the office phone rang. Callie groaned, untangled herself from the warmth of her husband and walked through the pair of glass doors to the cosy kitchen, snatching the cordless off the bench. It was unlikely the call would be business at seven in the morning, but habit had her answering, 'Highgrove Estate, may I help you?'

Silence. Then a mumbled ... something. Dial tone.

'Have a nice day,' she grumbled as she replaced the handset on the charger. She picked up Dale's mail, which was stacked by the phone. He was hopeless with correspondence. Unless she put it in his hand the mountain would only continue to get higher. A black envelope amid the more businesslike white collection caught her eye and she pulled a face. That one had been sitting there for close to two weeks. She carried it out along with the rest and dropped them in front of him.

'Oh, ta. Who was on the phone?' he asked.

'Wrong number, I think.' She sat down beside him. 'What's the black one?'

A flicker of irritation flashed across his face. He shrugged, got to his feet. 'Just something from an old school friend.'

'Who is this old friend?' she pressed, because his reaction was odd.

'Not someone I want to renew ties with.' He dropped a kiss on her forehead. 'I'd better get moving.'

'Do you have to start this early today?' She caught him behind the neck before he could straighten, pressed her lips to his. 'I could make breakfast ... or ...'

'Witch,' he groaned, removing her hand before kissing her fingers. 'You know I do. And you need to look over that catalogue.'

'Hmm.' She sulked into her coffee.

'I'll make it up to you later.' He leant in and kissed her until her toes curled. 'We've got forever to look forward to lazy breakfasts.'

'Okay ... But take your mail!' She reluctantly finished her own coffee as he scooped up the letters and his cup and disappeared into the house. She heard his car start up, the engine noise fading as he headed down the drive towards their winery. She stretched, took one last appreciative look over the grounds, over what they'd achieved in just five short years. Forever, she thought, sounded just perfect.

Callie started on the catalogue right away, eating a slice of toast as she altered prices and checked her calculations. Assuming her assistant, Paisley, did get back today, she'd have her give it a final once-over before sending it out.

She scanned emails and online bookings, and paid the latest assortment of bills, then, satisfied the office work was under control, decided to reward herself with time in the garden. She snatched her cap from the stand by the door and tucked her hair up underneath, then walked out into the sunshine. After a quick trip to the gardening shed, she pointed the wheelbarrow towards the wide, winding drive lined with rose hedges. Most of the roses were finished and required deadheading. White blooms looked so lovely, but the brown mess that was replacing them did not. She worked quickly, humming to herself.

'That's quite a job you've got ahead of you,' a friendly voice remarked.

'Mrs Bates, good morning,' Callie said to the woman staying in room five. 'How are you enjoying your weekend?'

'Everything's perfect, dear. Which is why we come back every year—well that, and to restock the wine cellar,' Mrs Bates said, eyes full of fun.

'Are you sure you wouldn't like me to make you some breakfast this morning?'

'We're eating on the fly, but I'll take you up on one of your delicious omelettes tomorrow.'

'No problem.'

'The gardens always look so beautiful here. You do a remarkable job.'

'I enjoy it,' Callie said. 'Landscaping used to be my job but then I married and—' she smiled, added a little lift of her shoulders, '—plans changed.'

'Well, I just think that's wonderful. A husband to love you, a beautiful home and business, and all these incredible gardens to play with. You're living a fairy tale!'

'I pinch myself occasionally,' Callie agreed. 'How is Gerard doing?'

'Getting fat!' Mrs Bates said of her son. 'Being one of the top food critics in the country certainly doesn't help the waistline! Did you happen to catch his review of that new restaurant down the road from here?'

'Yes,' Callie said and bit down on her grin. 'It was a little rough.'

'It was abysmal,' Mrs Bates corrected. 'I told him he would have been better off coming here.'

Callie laughed. 'For bacon and eggs?'

Mrs Bates chuckled and gently touched a still fresh flower. 'I do love these roses. I have a few at home. Haven't managed to find one quite as incandescently white as this one, though.'

'These are Icebergs. Make sure I give you some cuttings before you leave.'

Mrs Bates's face lit up. 'I'll do that. Thank you. Oh, here's my ride,' she said as tyres crunched behind them. 'Never let it be said women take all the time in the shower. We're off to McWilliams to stock up on their muscat. Marvellous stuff.'

Callie sent the couple a friendly wave as they drove away. What would she and Dale be like together at that age? Still happy? In love? She hoped so.

Her gaze fell on the pile of earth and sandstone that would soon become her next garden. She planned it in her head, mapping out what would go where. Some pretty groundcovers would crawl among the cavities in the smaller sections of rock, spilling over them in vibrant splashes of colour. Brightly coloured flax could fill the deeper holes. She'd include deciduous trees: a lime green robinia, and perhaps something red—a prunus?—to go with it to provide some shade in summer. There was a perfect spot for a pond in the low corner, so she'd measure it out.

Callie had worked her way around most of the drive when she heard the hum of a car engine. She looked over her shoulder. A dusty silver Audi crept along the otherwise empty road. At the gate, the driver touched the brakes, once, twice, then drew the car to a stop. Idled.

She wasn't expecting new guests today, but she pulled off her gloves and tossed her shears on the pile of cuttings in the wheelbarrow. Smile in place, she moved around the hedge and approached the car.

'Hi, can I help you?'

The woman was too thin, dressed in casual clothes that spoke of a good fashion sense and a healthy bank balance. But even through the woman's designer sunglasses Callie could see the edgy stare in the eyes framed by untidy bottle-blonde hair. The woman's hands clutched the steering wheel, and one leg jigged up and down in a nervous staccato. 'I'm looking for—'

A quick beep from behind them made Callie look up. Paisley had pulled into the drive. She waved. Callie sent her a distracted smile and returned her attention to the woman now staring into her rear-view mirror.

'Looking for?' Callie prompted.

The woman's eyes darted back to Callie and her head shuddered from side to side in an erratic negative action. 'Doesn't matter.'

The car jerked forward. 'Hey!' Callie jumped out of harm's way, then watched the car speed off down the road. 'What the hell?'

'What was that about?' Paisley called.

'No idea. But there was something wrong with her.'

'Who?'

'The maniac driver I've never met before.' Callie sighed and shook her head, glad her toes hadn't been run over, and walked over to Paisley's Pajero. 'How was your trip?'

Her assistant's mouth twisted. 'Eventful. Got time to hear about it?'

'Yeah, I could do with a break,' Callie decided, with one last glance back at the road. 'I'll catch up with you in the office.' She followed Paisley's car through the gates, picked up the wheelbarrow and steered it down the drive. By the time she put everything away, Paisley was on the phone, so she went through the office and into the house, made some cold drinks and took them back.

'If you want coffee, I'll go get you one. I felt like something cool.'

'All good, thanks,' Paisley made a note on the computer, then took a glass, sipped, and smiled. 'Everything run smoothly while I was away?'

'Of course. I've just updated the wine catalogue. You probably should do a last check.'

'I'll do it now.'

'I think Dale was hoping you'd run straight over to the winery and help him when you arrived. He's got a lot on today.'

'Then I'll be quick with the catalogue.' She flicked through it. 'We don't have any check-ins today?'

'No. I think I might go tree shopping. I want to play around with the front area by the gate.'

'The boulders,' Paisley guessed. 'I knew you'd get to that one day.'

Callie smiled. 'Dale's all for it.'

'So he should be. You love it, and you're damn good at it. This whole place looks like a magazine cover.' The computer pinged with new email and Paisley read it.

'What is it?' Callie asked when Paisley's brow shot up.

'Next door has put another offer in writing.'

Callie pulled a face as she took a long sip of her lemon sparkling water. 'The place is not for sale. Besides, Dale hates them and would rather die than see them turn this place into a hundred-room concrete monstrosity. I'm inclined to agree.'

'It's a lot of money.'

'Hmm.'

Paisley turned the computer monitor around. 'Look at it.'

'Fine.' She looked, and choked on her water. 'Wow.'

'Yeah. Wow.'

'And no.'

Paisley nodded. 'Good. I like my job here. Had to show you, though.'

'So … Tasmania?'

Callie regretted the question when Paisley's eyes lost some of their spark.

'It was freezing, as you'd expect at this time of year, and my welcome wasn't a hell of a lot warmer. You know Dad and I haven't been in each other's company much over the last few years.'

'But he asked for your help, didn't he?' Callie asked, confused.

'No, Ned told me Dad needed my help,' Paisley said. 'They are two very different things. And he's right. Dad's having trouble managing out there. He's always been fine on his meds, but dementia's kicking in and he keeps forgetting to take them. His moods are all over the place with the bipolar and he's paranoid someone's out to get him because of the schizophrenia. He had a fall recently and whacked his head. Luckily, Ned turned up to mow the lawns. It's only going to get progressively worse. He won't be able to stay out there on his own forever.'

'They have a good relationship, don't they? Can't Ned convince him to move into care?'

Paisley leaned back in the office chair. 'Ned can't cope with the heavy stuff. He has the emotional strength of a wounded deer, and his IQ isn't exactly up there, either. You know the story.'

Callie nodded slowly, remembering Paisley's parents had taken Ned in because his mother was very young and didn't want him. 'Your mum was a psychologist, right?'

'At the asylum down there. Pretty much ran the place— and ran Dad. If they'd stayed together, everything would be a lot different.'

'Mmm.' Callie silently wondered how Eileen Waldron could have worked with the mentally ill all day then come home to a mentally ill husband and raise someone else's child with issues of his own. An amazing woman. Though she'd left, eventually. Perhaps she'd had nothing left to give.

'Anyway,' Paisley continued, 'I've organised for a community nurse to check in on Dad a couple of days a week. That should buy him some more time.'

'Well, that's something.'

'Best I can do. Dad's digging his heels in, refusing to leave, and honestly, packing up would be completely beyond him. He's a hoarder. Not as bad as some of the ones you see on the TV but he's got fifty years of stuff in piles around the place—rubbish everywhere.' She chewed on a fingernail, thinking. 'I might have to try and get down there a bit more regularly to tackle it. I'll need the money from the house to fund his care so it's going to have to be done. Otherwise no one will ever buy the place.'

'If it's as lovely as you say it is, surely someone will see past a bit of mess?'

A hint of wistfulness touched Paisley's expression. 'A huge old home on acres, right on the River Derwent. Completely buried in junk as old as it is. Tell you what,' she said brightly, 'why don't you buy it as an investment property?'

'Ha. No. Sorry.'

'It'd make a gorgeous bed and breakfast. If we clear away a foot or two of mess in the kitchen we might even find some of the original pots and pans.'

'As much fun as that sounds,' Callie replied, 'I've already got my hands full. And speaking of—you'd better look at this catalogue before Dale realises you're back.'

'Can do,' Paisley said, spinning her chair back around to the monitor. 'I've also got to go over the new artwork for it with Dale. I sent some ideas across before I left last week but I bet he hasn't looked at them.'

'I bet you're right.'

'I'll make a note.' Paisley pulled up another screen, frowned. 'I think I forgot to tell you the couple coming in tomorrow requested a bottle of bubbly and a cheese platter on arrival. They're celebrating a wedding anniversary.'

'That's okay, I'll do a supply run this afternoon. We're now officially out of that quince paste and low on the triple brie.' She glanced up. 'Uh-oh,' she teased as Dale's car stopped out the front. 'Sprung.'

Paisley groaned good-naturedly. 'I'll go through the rest at lunch.' She got to her feet. 'I'll see you—Hey, that car's back.'

'What car?' Callie followed Paisley's gaze out the window to where the silver Audi sat. 'It's that woman again! What the hell could she possibly want?'

'Dale's heading over,' Paisley said.

They both watched from the office window as Dale approached the car, leaning in the driver's window. There was some sort of conversation. Then the car slowly pulled away. Dale's expression was exasperated as he removed his cap and dragged his hand through his hair.

'That's weird,' Callie muttered, and went to the door to meet him as he came back. 'Who was that?'

'In the car? Just a lost tourist,' he said. 'Hi, Paisley. I need you at the winery.'

'To look at the artwork for the catalogue or go over my advertising proposal that you've no doubt forgotten about?' Paisley asked.

'You'll be surprised to learn,' Dale replied smugly, 'that just last night I marked up some ideas. It's all back in my Dropbox folder.'

'Surprised is an understatement. Thanks, boss. Will I go ahead and order the material?'

'Not until you've taken in the comments I made—and I've seen the new costing.' His grin was there, Callie noted, but there seemed to be an underlying tension from speaking to the woman on the drive.

'Dale, that woman you just talked to was here earlier. She looked upset when I spoke to her.'

'You spoke to her?'

She didn't expect the snap in his voice.

He turned to Paisley. 'What did she say?'

Paisley shrugged. 'Don't look at me, I didn't talk to her. Cal?'

'She was jittery and upset. I think she was looking for something but I didn't get a "lost tourist" vibe.'

'More like a lunatic vibe!' Dale took a calming breath and wrapped Callie in a hug. 'I'm sorry—I didn't mean to jump down your throat. I didn't want to worry you, but she was strange. I don't think she'll come back. But if she does show up again, call me.' He straightened and looked her in the eyes. 'Don't go near her again, okay?'

'Ah … Sure.'

With a nod, he let her go. 'You right if I pinch Paisley?'

'Go ahead. I'll need her back after lunch.'

As they left, she looked past them to the gate and the road beyond. Was the stranger likely to come back or had Dale scared her off for good?

LET'S TALK ABOUT BOOKS!

JOIN THE CONVERSATION

HARLEQUIN
AUSTRALIA

@HARLEQUINAUS

@HARLEQUINAUS

HQSTORIES

@HQSTORIES